Also by Swan Huntley

We Could Be Beautiful

The
Goddesses

Swan Huntley

A NOVEL

Doubleday

New York London Toronto Sydney Auckland

This is a work of fiction. Names, characters, places, and incidents either are
the product of the author's imagination or are used fictitiously. Any resemblance
to actual persons, living or dead, events, or locales is entirely coincidental.

Book design by Maria Carella
Jacket design by Emily Mahon
Jacket illustrations: photograph of woman by Mint Images / Gallery Stock;
tendrils by Shutterstock

Library of Congress Cataloging-in-Publication Data
Names: Huntley, Swan, author.
Title: The goddesses / Swan Huntley.
Description: First Edition. | New York : Doubleday, [2017]
Identifiers: LCCN 2016045701 (print) | LCCN 2016035886 (ebook) |
    ISBN 9780385542210 (hardcover) | ISBN 9780385542227 (ebook) |
    ISBN 9780385542982
Subjects: | GSAFD: Suspense fiction.
Classification: LCC PS3608.U5958 G63 2017 (ebook) | LCC PS3608.U5958 (print) |
    DDC 813/.6–dc23
LC record available at https://lccn.loc.gov/2016045701

MANUFACTURED IN THE UNITED STATES OF AMERICA

10 9 8 7 6 5 4 3 2 1

First Edition

FOR FLANNY, ZARA, AND FLETCHER

Each friend represents a world in us, a world possibly not born until they arrive, and it is only by this meeting that a new world is born.

—ANAÏS NIN

Earth

1

We came here to escape. Escape our mistakes, our boring selves. Escape the constant feeling of being half-asleep, escape our house— the tedious moan of that garage door, the roof we promised to fix every time it rained. Escape dry heat and coyotes and the roads we knew by heart—we knew where those would take us. In paradise there would be new roads and new routines. Different friends, a different house. A different life. In paradise we would be different.

Chuck had cheated on me with his assistant manager. That was the main reason we left. Her name was Shelly and Shelly was blond and Shelly was everywhere. Every blond woman in San Diego was Shelly until something confirmed it wasn't—wrong car, wrong walk, wrong face. The real Shelly—I never saw her again after the affair, but it was bound to happen at some point. She lived close by.

I probably never would have found out if Shelly hadn't called to confess. She just had to get this off her chest, she said; it was eating her alive. She swore it had only happened that one time. She'd quit the job right afterwards to make sure it would never happen again. She was so so so so sorry and she was crying very hard.

Chuck was sorry, too. He hadn't been thinking clearly. They'd been drinking; one thing had led to another. He actually said, "It's almost like someone else did this, not me. It's hard to explain." I said, "But it was you, Chuck. You did this. After eighteen years, this is what you did."

When the transfer opportunity for Costco Kona came up and

Chuck was elected for it, he said, "Maybe Hawaii will remind us why we love each other."

When he said that, it was hard not to imagine Hawaii in the way it's always advertised—a fit couple at sunset under a neon-pink sky— and this was very stupid. I also wondered if it could be us. Later, after the anger passed. Later, after I forgave him. Later, after I could trust him again. If any of that was possible.

The twins were stoked. That's how they said it, one right after the other. "Stoked," Jed said. "Stoked," Cam said. They'd miss their friends, but their friends could visit. They'd miss their team, but the incoming coach that year was supposed to suck anyway. Kealakehe's water polo coach had been a big wave surfer—that was rad. And they could start surfing. And when their friends came to visit, they could take their friends surfing. It was all just going to be totally sweet. "Plus, Mom," Cam said, "you love mangoes."

There were reasons other than Shelly to leave. I did love mangoes. And I'd only been to Hawaii once, when I was ten, which barely counted anymore. I'd lived in San Diego my entire almost fifty years of life, and my days had begun to feel like the same spin in the same hamster wheel. Same postman at the same time delivering the same bills. Same grocery store, same place I always parked. Same minivan under the same tree. I'd been trying to lose the same five pounds for the last thirty years. When had I become so redundant? And joyless? Was it normal that everything I did had the same tone as flossing? I don't want to do this, but I should do this. I wasn't ready to call myself depressed—my mother had been depressed and killed herself, and I was nowhere close to that—but I strongly felt I could be happier. Still, a part of me wanted to say no, wanted to hang on, wanted to clutch my little hamster claws to the familiar wheel and stay. But I knew I couldn't do that. If I said no, it would prove I had truly lost hope that life could be better than this.

"One year," Chuck said. "If things aren't going well in a year, we can always come back."

•

We rented a place up on Kaloko where the land was green and lush. Two acres with a house and a guesthouse, which people called an ohana here. With the money we'd make renting the San Diego house, it was a wash. Brad, who'd also transferred from San Diego, knew someone who knew someone who knew the owner who gave us a good deal. Brad and Marcy had been ripped off at their first place in Kona, and Brad wasn't going to let that happen to any friends of his! Especially not Chargers fans! Brad hit Chuck's arm when he said that, and Chuck chortled and looked at his poor arm as if it were bruised already. Chuck never watched football. But he didn't say that to Brad. Because he was a liar.

The house was small and lovely. Very basic—the shape of a rect-angle. The ohana was the shape of a square. Alone, just as buildings, they weren't very special, but the gorgeous backdrop made them spe-cial. The grass, how green it was, rolling softly up the hill. All these plants I'd never seen before. All these birds. The light. How it was thick and buttery yellow. How San Diego's light in comparison was hollow, washed-out, drained. How the humid air felt like a warm hug.

We drove around the island and were in awe. The sky, the sun, the ocean. It was incredible how the landscape changed so quickly— from dewy rain forest up on our mountain to sun-bleached fields of lava down by the water. The lava fields were vast and magical and strange. "This is like Mars," Cam said from the backseat. It was like another planet, but it was also this one in the most basic way. Oh, earth is formed by lava, and here it is. The two-lane highway that cut through the fields seemed equally uncomplicated. Oh, and then we built a road.

We stopped to write our name in the lava with white chunks of coral by the side of the road because we saw other people doing that. MURPHY. Jed held out his long arm to take a picture of us in front of it. The three of them in matching Hawaiian shirts and me in a tank top. Chuck had woken up early to buy these shirts at Walmart. He'd gotten me a small—as a compliment?—and of course it didn't fit. "I can go back to the store!" he'd said. I told him it was fine. "I don't need a matching shirt, Chuck. Just keep driving."

We drove and drove. The Big Island was somehow much bigger than I'd imagined. Bigger than all the other islands put together, according to Chuck, who also told us that the clouds in the distance weren't clouds but volcanic fog, which people here called vog. The volcano had been erupting since 1981. The flow was on its way to Pahoa now. Soon it would wipe out that town.

We stopped at a beach. Chuck and the boys jumped in the water. I watched them dive into the curling waves. My boys, their strong, beautiful bodies. Chuck, he needed to work out. I found broken shells in the sand and put a few in my pocket. I overheard a woman say to her friend, "Fuck it, let's move here," and I smiled to myself.

We were pink faced and giddy in the car. "Those waves were gnarly," Cam said. "We should get a surfboard," Jed said. Chuck looked more refreshed than I'd seen him in a long time. "You're right," he said, happily tapping the wheel, "we should do that."

Our first dinner at the new house was a Costco pizza, Hawaiian-style. We ate at the new table off our old IKEA plates. Chuck was excited to start work. Jed was excited to kill it at tryouts. Cam was excited they finally didn't have to share a room anymore. "Only took seventeen years," he said. Before they went to bed, Cam peered out from the doorway of his new room and said, "I'll miss you, brother."

Jed said, "Me, too." And then in unison, they shouted the same strange term: "Ass clown!"

Chuck had been sleeping on the couch since the night Shelly had called to confess, so it was unclear where he would sleep in this new house. The ohana was empty. Maybe he'd sleep in the ohana. I kept waiting for him to leave. Dinner was done, the dishes were done, the boys were in bed. But he still hadn't left, and his suitcase was still by the door. I could tell he wanted to say something and he wasn't saying it. The way he kept putting his hands in his pockets, the way he was repeating himself: "Can you believe we're here?" "I can't believe we're here." Chuck was a bad communicator. He hated conflict. He'd always been that way. I peeled an orange slowly. Somewhere during the peeling, I realized I was giving him time, I was waiting for him to speak, and this was very generous of me. Too generous. I peeled faster while he pretended to care about the texture of the wall—he was sliding his palm up and down the wall now, saying, "I never thought we would live in *Hawaii*." I couldn't be patient anymore. With half the orange still unpeeled, I said, "I'm going to bed, Chuck, good night," and walked past him.

"Wait. I—" and when I turned, he whispered, "Where do you want me to sleep tonight?" The worry in his eyes. He scratched his neck just for something to do. I felt bad for him. He looked so pathetic. Oh, sweet Chuck, you are such an idiot.

In a tone I hoped was emotionless, I whispered back, "Where do you want to sleep tonight?"

Slowly, while contorting his face to show me that yes, he understood it was a lot to ask, he pointed to the bedroom.

A long pause and then I nodded since we were speaking without words now. Chuck looked so relieved. He went to get his suitcase.

The truth was I had wanted him to ask; I'd been waiting. Also I knew our sleeping apart really bothered the boys. They'd started sneaking out at night to light illegal fireworks from Mexico the same week Shelly had called to confess, which I didn't think was a coincidence. Plus this was about trying now. Hawaii meant we had agreed to try.

That night, we slept on the farthest sides of the same bed. It was closer than we'd been in months.

2

Our cars arrived. We'd had them shipped. Chuck's champagne Honda Accord. The boys' blue Honda Accord. My gray Honda minivan. Chuck was a big fan of Hondas because they lasted forever. That was his line in defense of Hondas. "Well, they *do* last forever."

The sight of my minivan in the sunny lot should have delighted me. I had a car now; we didn't have to share the rental anymore. But when I got in and smelled that old fake pine-tree smell and felt that old bald fabric on my legs, I wondered how long "forever" meant for a car. It was already ten years old. "And also," I said to Chuck that night, "I don't need a minivan now. Our children have grown up." Chuck said once we got more settled, maybe we could explore other options. He said this carefully and with a forced optimism, his head bowed and his eyes looking up at me. This was his new submissive way of having a conversation. He was trying to please me now. He was trying to undo his mistake.

And I appreciated this. I liked the little bit of power it gave me. But since the affair, I'd also begun to resent conversations like these. Conversations that pointed out how powerless I actually was, how much I relied on Chuck. I was a housewife who had to ask her husband for a new car. The word that kept repeating itself in my mind was *weak*. Nancy, you are weak. Other women would have left him. Other women would have found a good lawyer by now. Other women had careers to fall back on. Some women had chosen not to get married at all. Some women had chosen not to be mothers. Some women were movie stars or teachers or politicians. Those women had goals.

They had direction. And meanwhile here I was, lost in an unfamiliar kitchen, searching frantically for the ice cream scooper—"I *know* I packed it!"—until Chuck opened the lucky drawer and proudly, too proudly, said, "Here!"

I almost said, I hate how I rely on you, Chuck, but I wasn't in the mood to fight. I pushed the tub of ice cream across the counter. "You scoop tonight," I said.

"Of course!" he agreed, joyfully peeling back the lid. He was happy I'd given him a tangible way to show me that he loved me.

•

Chuck had started saying "I love you" a lot, which was new. "You don't have to say it back, I just want you to know."

Sometimes I said, "Thanks," but that was awkward. Sometimes I smiled. Sometimes I thought he was being manipulative and other times I may have wanted to say it back, but didn't.

He was being his most perfect self these days. He went to work on time and came home early and he didn't drink at all. He brought me the multicolored bouquet of roses from Costco and the three-pound bag of raw almonds I'd asked him to get because I was eating healthy now. He scooped the ice cream at night and made his side of the bed in the morning and told me my hair looked pretty. These efforts were nice, but they were also small deposits into the bank account of our marriage. Chuck would need to bank a lot more small deposits to make up for the huge withdrawal of his affair.

He also started taking me on dates. One night he took me to a restaurant built on a wooden pier right over the water. Brad had told him it was fantastic. A view of the ocean, starched white tablecloths, the sound of waves crashing beneath us. We rushed to get there before sunset and made it just in time to see the last bit of orange disappear. "Did you see the green zap?" he asked me. He looked so eager.

"No, did you?"

"I think so. Maybe a small green zap."

His optimism these days was almost tiring, but it was better than the sullen way he was when he drank.

I ordered the salad with ono and Chuck ordered the lobster BLT and we didn't talk about the past. It felt like an unspoken agreement, a part of moving on.

We talked about the food. We agreed it was very good.

We talked about how Hawaii was different from San Diego. How it was America but also another country. A country where people were in a better mood. An island mood. I told Chuck how chipper the baristas were at Starbucks. They offered me samples and said "Aloha" at the end. Chuck said the people at this Costco were more laid-back. "In an island mood, like you said. I hope it doesn't mean they're lazy."

We talked about the boys. We agreed they were adjusting normally. They'd made the varsity team—no surprise to either of us. Chuck thought they had a good chance at getting scholarships as long as they kept their grades up, and he couldn't help but recite his own history here as if I didn't know it. Chuck had gotten a water polo scholarship. He wouldn't have gone to a good college like USD without that scholarship because he was a B minus student. I could have said: I know, Chuck, I met you at USD, remember? But I didn't. I just looked at him across the table and let him talk. I let the sound of the waves drown him out. I might have been studying his face again, trying to find signs that I did or didn't still love him.

I was also looking at that face thinking what I had thought so many times since it had happened: how could *you* have done this to me? *You*, Chuck, of all the husbands I could have chosen—how could *you* have done this? I had chosen Chuck because I'd thought he was a safe choice. He was the opposite of my turbulent childhood and that's what I had wanted. I wanted no violence and no neglect, and I had gotten those things. Chuck was never violent or neglectful. He was a good dad. But I also wanted fidelity. Obviously, everyone wanted that. And yes, eighteen years of marriage was a long time and people strayed, but I never expected *Chuck* to stray. I never expected him to start drinking the way he did either. When the drinking got worse, I thought, Wow, you can make every single choice in life with the intention of not repeating your past, and it repeats itself anyway.

Finally, Chuck had stopped talking. It took me a second to notice.

The waitress was standing there with a dessert menu. "Do you want anything?" Chuck asked.

I want to go back in time. Start over, make different choices. Maybe choose a different husband.

"No thanks," I said.

We gave the menus back to the waitress, and then Chuck got a look on his face like he'd just remembered something. With his head bowed lower than his new usual way, he asked, "Is it okay if Brad and Marcy come for dinner on Saturday?"

"Did you already tell them yes?"

Chuck scratched his neck. "I can tell them to come another time."

"It's fine. We need friends here." And then, in my new emotionless tone, I said, "All I have right now is you."

Chuck looked up at me. "I love you, Nancy." Several waves crashed in the pause. "You don't have to say it back. I just want you to know." Several more waves crashed. The waitress took his credit card. "The way you look at me." Another wave. "I think you still love me, too."

·

Brad and Marcy on the lanai, taking off their shoes. They looked like they belonged together. Thick necks, small eyes, sandy hair. Their doughy bodies were almost cartoonlike. He wore a too-tight polo shirt and a thick gold watch that was either very expensive or very cheap. She wore a floral tunic and was holding a pie. I wore a pink tunic and khaki shorts—my daily uniform, though the color of the tunic changed—and I'd put on a little makeup for our guests. The house wasn't messy at all, so I don't know why the first thing I did was apologize for the mess.

"Noooo," Brad said, like he was falling into a well.

Marcy made a swatting we-don't-mind motion with her hand. She handed me the pie. "Mulberry," she said. "It's fan-tas-tic."

"Drove down south to pick it up this morning," Brad said.

Marcy and I chatted in the kitchen while the boys set the table and Chuck mixed Brad a vodka drink. "Where's yours?" Brad asked Chuck. "I'm sticking with soda," Chuck said too loud. He looked at me for approval and I ignored him. I was trying to pay attention to what

Marcy was saying about her lei-making class. Maybe that was something I wanted to do. It sounded a little tedious, but no, maybe it would be fun. Maybe I'd become the type of woman who did crafts now.

"And afterwards, we can do a power walk," Marcy said. "That's what I usually do."

The shepherd's pie looked done enough. I took it out of the oven. Marcy took it upon herself to make the announcement for me. "Dinner's ready!" she called out like a siren.

We learned more about our new friends as we ate. Their daughter Elizabeth was a sophomore at UC Santa Cruz. She was "a great kid," Brad said. "Who dyes her hair such fun colors," Marcy added. Marcy, like me, had never worked after she got pregnant. "And I love it," she whispered to me loud enough for everyone to hear. Marcy had been a teacher. "Absolutely not my calling," she said. "What about you?" she asked me. I told her I'd worked at a clinic. I didn't tell her it was an abortion clinic, and I didn't tell her it was absolutely not my calling either. I'd studied sociology in college. I thought I wanted to help people, but I was wrong. The desperation of those women—I think I was scared it would rub off on me.

We talked about San Diego and how much it had changed since we were kids. The freeways! The traffic! The inferior beaches with their muddy sand and too-cold water. "And kelp vomit," Jed chimed in.

"Everything is better here." Brad looked at his wife. "And we are never leaving."

Marcy shrugged. "Kona, who knew?"

The boys cleared the plates and Marcy helped me with the pie. She had tons of people to introduce me to, she said. She knew how hard it was to start over and make new friends, and she wanted to help in any way she could. Marcy reminded me of the water polo moms back in San Diego. She was a little overbearing and a little insecure and very, very sweet.

The pie was also very sweet. It was delicious. I ate too much. We all ate too much because we finished it.

On their way out, Marcy said, "Thank you, dinner was fantastic," and she promised to be in touch soon. Brad hit Chuck's arm. "See you at work, my man!"

And the four of us stood on the lanai like a happy little family, waving at them as they drove away.

3

I unpacked. Slowly and carefully and indecisively. I hadn't moved in eighteen years. And all this furniture was new. I wasn't used to it. But that was good; we needed new. I would arrange things in a new way.

I put the mugs in the cabinets facing up instead of down. I arranged the clothes in the closets by color instead of by style. I hung a photo of the four of us above the dining room table. I took it down. In its place I hung a picture of the boys after a game. I took it down.

I went to the store for nails.

When I came back, I stepped into my new house with my shoes on because I had forgotten we were following the Hawaiian no-shoes-in-house custom.

And that was the moment.

My new house was not my new house. The same photos and the same mugs and the way I had instinctively put the mail on the counter right next to the fruit bowl. This wasn't new. I'd even saved the pie box Brad and Marcy had brought, so I could use it for the cupcakes I'd make for the team later, just like I'd been doing for years. Why were we always making friends with people who brought us pies? Brad and Marcy weren't new. They were our old friends all over again. This house was our old house all over again. This was just us, so exactly and predictably us, and this was the moment I thought, Nancy, you have two choices. Get back on the hamster wheel or reinvent yourself ASAP.

•

The 7:00 a.m. class was on a swatch of grass right near the beach. I'd read online that yoga had transformed many people's lives, and I needed a transformation. Plus, I'd been meaning to try it for years.

I arrived at 6:45 with my new purple mat and watched as people gathered. I was nervous about getting out of the car. These people were in better shape than I was. They plopped their mats in the grass with no hesitation because they knew what they were doing. Maybe I should go home and do some yoga DVDs on my own and come back later.

A knock on my window. I was so startled I spilled hot coffee all over my hand. I inhaled sharply and put the stupid coffee back in the drink holder and looked up.

First I saw what she was carrying. A yoga mat and a bulging brightly colored bag with tiny mirrors built into the pattern. Pale hands. Tattoos on her wrists. Tight red shirt with a scooping neckline. Her hair was short and black except for one shocking chunk of neon pink that cradled her face. Her face was open, inviting. Warm brown eyes and dewy skin that everyone in Hawaii seemed to have because it was so humid all the time. She smiled at me. Her teeth were perfect and white.

I rolled the window down.

"Hi there," she said, placing her hand on the car. She looked at the mat in my lap. "You here for class?"

I opened my mouth, prepared to speak, unsure of what I would say. I was still half planning to go home.

"The first day is always the worst." She chuckled. "It's like being the new kid in school, right?"

My mouth was still open and I still wasn't finding words. I definitely didn't want to acknowledge I felt like the new kid in school. I was stronger than that.

"I'm Ana," she said. She pronounced her name *On-a,* not the other way.

I cleared my throat. "Nancy."

"Welcome, Nancy," she said. "I'm glad you're here." She smiled again. "I'm going to go set up. I'll see you over there, yeah?"

Somehow, that was all I needed. "Yeah," I said. I grabbed my mat and followed her to the grass.

•

Ten minutes after seven, she hit the gong bowl, and when it was done reverberating, she said, "Good morning, yogis. We have a new student today. Everyone, this is Nancy."

The chiseled man on my right gave me a little bow. "Welcome."

"Nancy, that's Kurt," Ana said. "And this is Sara Beth and Patty." She pointed to them in the row. Sara Beth was young. Bleach-blond pixie cut and her eyebrow was pierced with a hoop. Patty was older, early sixties maybe. She had bed head and wore an oversized T-shirt with a picture of a cat on it and she was tugging at her ear. She waved at me and I waved back.

"Now," Ana said, placing her hands in her lap. "Sit up tall. Close your eyes. Imagine your head is attached to a string. Imagine the string is attached to a cloud right above you. The cloud floats up. Your head lifts from your body. Your neck is long, as long as a skyscraper. Length. Lengthen. Relax. Relax your tongue. Relax your throat. Relax all the muscles in your body. Feel as muscle slides away from bone. Feel that tectonic shift."

A pause.

"Lift your heart. Lift it higher. Lift your rib cage. Lift it higher. Imagine there's a balloon under each of your lungs. Two balloons nestled inside two cages. Fill those balloons. Expand. Expansion. Expand expand expand—now hold your breath at the top and keep holding. Hold it for as long as you can. Hold it for longer than that. Your brain will give up before your body. Always. Skyscraper neck. Unclench your jaw. Lift your heart. Lift your heart. Lift your heart, and when you absolutely have to, let it go."

I exhaled, feeling dizzy.

"Good," Ana said. "Now in, out. Hear the ocean. Breathe like the ocean."

After a few breaths, I peeked to make sure I was doing what she was doing. Her hands were on her knees. I put my hands on my knees.

Her face was relaxed. Was mine? I kept studying her. She was pretty. Full lips and high cheekbones, a good nose. Her eyes were deep-set. They made her look like a thoughtful person. Her body was curvy like mine, which was comforting—curvy women could do yoga, too. Her breasts were large, definitely larger than mine. Large and intact and proudly displayed in her plunging red tank top because she was obviously very confident. Mine were covered by the new zip-up jacket I'd bought at Foot Locker in preparation for this.

"You are at the beach. It is morning. Listen to the sounds." She paused. "Birds, waves." A car honked and she laughed. "When your mind wanders, come back. Back back back. You're not at the grocery store yet. You're not surfing yet, Kurt." She chuckled. Then she opened her eyes and reached for a book. "I'm going to quote a little Pema this morning. It's short."

She fingered her bookmark, found the page. "Here it is: The truth you believe in and cling to makes you unavailable to hear anything new." She paused. Then she said it again. Then she set the book in the grass. "We all have a story about how this day is going to go. How this *life* is going to go. Cop to your story. Let go of your story. Expect nothing." Pause. "Expectation is disappointment waiting to happen. It's bad for your heart. Broaden your chest. Lift your heart. Lift it onto a higher plane."

Her words, so unexpectedly poetic, gave me the chills. I felt moved. I felt like more was possible, which was exactly what I'd been wanting to feel. I thought of something I'd heard Oprah say once. We are most teachable during the hard times in our lives. Hard times make us open. They make us available to hear new things. I unzipped my jacket a little and inhaled the fresh salty air and thought: That's right, Nancy, you are not at the grocery store yet, and you are not trapped, and this breathable jacket you bought was a very good choice.

"Let's start with three oms," she said.

I was self-conscious at first—my om sounded too high-pitched next to Kurt's—so I deepened my voice. By the third om, I was thinking: Okay, I can do this.

We moved on to poses. I copied Kurt when I didn't know what to do. Ana walked around adjusting our bodies. In downward dog, she said, "Imagine your lungs have migrated south to the space above your pelvis. Now breathe into that southern place." She pulled my hips back and when my spine cracked she said, "Aah."

When Kurt's leg touched mine by accident, she said, "If you bump into the person next to you, don't worry about it. We're all in this thing called life together. We're all in the same boat, paddling through the same water."

She spoke in a soft and confident tone. In cat/cow, she told us to move like our bodies were scraping peanut butter from the inside of a jar. She told us to glom our hands into the mat like we were glomming them into mud. She quoted Lao-tzu and Rumi. She said wise things I agreed with. I'd probably read versions of these things before, but there on the beach with the waves and the birds and the certainty of her mesmerizing voice, every word felt more powerful. She said our thoughts would create our destinies. She said letting go was the bravest thing a person could do. She said wretchedness and generosity needed each other to survive, the same way fire needed water and water needed fire, and the earth needed the sky, and all of it—the whole thing—needed wind to keep moving, to keep breathing. She reminded us to keep breathing.

As we breathed and moved and the sun rose higher in the sky, I found myself wondering about Ana. Who was this woman with the pink in her hair and the tribal bracelet tattoos around her wrists? And had she always been so confident? That's what I really wanted to know. She carried her curves without apology. When her tank top rode up her stomach, she left it there to expose her alabaster skin. She wore no wedding ring and smelled deeply of coconut oil, and she kept telling me I was doing great. "Great, Nancy, that's beautiful, yes."

At the end she said, "Peace to all beings, no exceptions." And as she bowed forward: "And that means no exceptions."

She said we could put our ten dollars in the basket. I rolled my yoga mat up as tightly as possible and thought about how nice it was to feel so relaxed.

Getting to the basket included taking part in a small procession. Everyone had something to say to her.

"I really needed that class," Patty said. "I think Marbles is going to die any day now."

Ana hugged her. "Oh, Patty," she said, "you're suffering."

Patty frowned and looked down at the cat on her shirt. Which—oh, this wasn't a generic cat. This was Marbles. I could now see that MARBLES was literally written across the bottom.

"We all have our own journey," Ana said. She inhaled and exhaled deeply, showing Patty how to breathe. "We are born alone and we die alone. That's just how it is, Patty. There's only one way to cure your suffering."

Patty perked up. "What is it?"

Ana's hand on Patty's shoulder. "Acceptance, my friend."

Patty's whole body slumped.

"Here," Ana said, "have a few Red Vines." She held out the tub, which I knew was a Costco purchase. As Patty reached for her Red Vines, I was reminded of the boys, who used to love it when I bought these tubs—this was before they had switched to Reese's cups—and I was also reminded of my mother for some reason. Maybe the red straws she used to drink from.

Patty took a handful, and Ana kissed her cheek. "Enjoy your life, Patty. You only get one."

Next it was Sara Beth's turn. "I adore you, Ana." Sara Beth draped her skinny arms around Ana's shoulders.

Just then Kurt turned to me, extended his hand, and said, "Kurt." We shook. He flashed a perfect white smile, made whiter by his very tan skin. How did these people have such perfect teeth? Kurt was maybe fifty-five, and his skin was good-tan, not yam-tan. He had the beautiful, light-damaged eyes of a surfer. They were rugged and pristine like water you might want to swim in.

"You live here or visiting?"

"We just moved here," I said.

"I moved here from Idaho seven years ago and it's the best thing I ever did."

I didn't have anything to say about Idaho besides *potato,* so I just nodded.

"Well hey, if you're looking for a dentist, I'm a dentist."

"Thank you," I said, understanding his teeth now. "I'll keep that in mind."

When Sara Beth was done with Ana, she circled back to me and said, "Come back, okay?" She gave me a thumbs-up. Her nails were painted bright green.

What was wrong with these people? They were so friendly! Sara Beth was probably too young to be a friend-friend, but then maybe I could have young friends now. Maybe I could be open to that.

Kurt thanked Ana. "Gotta shove off," he said. "The waves are calling."

"Take some Red Vines," Ana offered.

"Not today." Kurt patted his abs. "I'm on paleo." With that smile and that body and the beach behind him, he looked like the star of an energy drink commercial.

"Don't you just love perfectionists?" Ana asked, looking at me, and I laughed awkwardly.

Kurt kissed her cheek and then turned to say good-bye. He lifted his hand as if about to wave, but then he stopped. He looked at Ana. He looked at me. He looked back at Ana. He looked back at me. He said, "You two look like sisters."

Ana and I looked at each other. "We do have a resemblance," she said, and I was flattered. Because Ana was pretty—prettier than me, I thought—and also because she just seemed so wonderful.

"Aloha, ladies." Kurt gave us the hang-loose sign and walked toward the truck with the surfboard in the back.

"Oh, Kurt!" Ana called after him. "My veneer thing!"

"Call me at the office! We'll figure it out!"

Ana rolled her eyes. "Veneers are such a pain."

I smiled with my mouth closed so she wouldn't see my yellow teeth, and I put my ten dollars in the basket. "Thank you for that class. It was really nice."

"You feel better, right?"

"So much better, it's incredible," I said breathlessly. I was still feeling electric. And I might have been a little nervous. I wanted her to like me.

"Thanks for dragging me out of the car," I said.

"You weren't hard to drag." She smiled.

In the silence that followed, Ana took my hand. Her eyes were dark and glimmering and so alive, and I thought, This is a person who is truly living. This person gets it. This person definitely knows something you don't know.

"Have we met before?" she asked. "For some reason I feel like we have."

"I don't think so."

"You never lived in Vegas, did you?"

"Vegas? No."

She chuckled. "I must be confusing you with someone else. It's hard to keep track of everyone when you get old. Every new face looks like someone from the past."

"Tell me about it."

"Well," she said, "come back next week. Your back will love you for it."

"I will."

"Here"—she held out the tub—"take a Red Vine."

I plucked one from the side.

"Only one?" Ana asked. "Don't you want more than that?"

I didn't argue, so she plucked out three more, and without hesitation I took them. A flash of understanding seemed to pass across Ana's face then—just a flash, so quick—and she blinked her big, serene eyelids, as if to mark her understanding, and I wondered what it was that she had just understood about me. And then I wondered why I felt like this woman I'd only just met somehow knew me better than I knew myself.

She winked. "Don't hold yourself back."

•

What was it about her? In the hours that followed, I kept asking. It wasn't until dark that I realized what it was.

Ana reminded me of my mother's friends: women who spoke their mind, women who were completely themselves all the time, even when it wasn't beautiful. Women who lived without apology. They were brash and brazen and full of grace all at once. Hard edges and big hearts, hearts so big that if you stood close enough, you could hear the blood pumping. Those women, like Ana, were alive, truly alive. Every moment was lived full beyond the brim; every moment overflowed. Many of my mother's friends had been drug addicts. Many had been their husband's victims. There was always a chance of police. The police could appear unannounced at any time, like rain.

That was one reason for the way they approached life with their arms outstretched and their legs spread wide and their chests cast forward, asking for their hearts to be ripped out or soothed or just heard. Asking for anything. They were ready for anything.

I remembered these women fondly. Some of them I thought of as second mothers. Most of them, like my mother, had died too young. Bad choices stacked together, stacked high, stacked against them since before they'd been born.

But the particular way they seized every second like it was about to tick by—Ana had that way about her. It was under the surface, but I could feel it from the start.

4

I started a new routine. After the boys left for school and Chuck left for work, I laid out my purple mat on the lanai and stretched. When I couldn't remember the poses from class, I found pictures online and printed them out. I reminded myself to breathe. I came to know the sounds outside and then I came to expect them: the kissing noise of geckos, the rumble of the water heater, the cars on the road, the squawking birds and the singing birds and the one bird that seemed to be laughing. The hum of crickets was constant and soothing. I did an hour every day. I always wanted to stop early but I didn't, and when the hour had passed I felt better.

I made hot oatmeal for breakfast the old-fashioned way on the stove. I had been meaning to do this for years. I added tart apple and banana slices and a few of my raw almonds from the giant bag. I googled "Healthy food that tastes good" and got inspired. I bought kale at the store and actually cooked it. I also googled the name Ana had mentioned, Pema, and found out her last name was Chödrön and she was kind of famous. I bought her book about falling apart, which I hoped was about how to put yourself back together. Again.

I bought spandex at Target and a yoga block I wasn't quite sure what to do with, but I would figure it out. I switched the boys' towels with our towels. They would have yellow now. We would have brown. We didn't have enough money to throw everything we owned away and start from zero, but I did make a few smart purchases. I bought three green pillows for the couch, a stainless-steel trash can you could open with your foot, and a new bedspread patterned with luscious magenta hibiscus flowers for Chuck and me. Chuck liked its tropical look. He also liked the new healthy food I was cooking for dinner. The boys did not. "Can we have sloppy joes tomorrow night?" Cam asked, moving his salad around his plate with disdain.

"If you want to cook them, be my guest," I said.

Chuck nodded enthusiastically at me then, as if to say: go, Team Parents!

The biggest change I made was outside. I planted a garden in our yard. My new favorite health food blogger said that if you had good weather and enough room, there was absolutely no excuse not to grow your own food. I measured a rectangular space and tilled the soil. The soil was dark and rich and there were worms. I felt outdoorsy and adventurous. I added fertilizer to the rectangle. The guy at Lowe's had told me to do that. I dug holes with my new shovel. I was having a whole fantasy in my head about sustainable living. The money we could save doing this. The quality of these vegetables. Our connection to the earth.

I added my seedlings into the holes. All the healthy things I planned to eat: lettuces and broccoli and tomatoes and bell peppers. When I was done I stepped back and felt proud of my work. I was sweaty and accomplished. The birds were chirping. The crickets were humming. The sun was low in the sky. The boys would be home from practice soon.

The Lowe's guy had told me an orange tree would take years. I didn't know if we'd be here for years, but I had bought the seed packet anyway. It was on sale. I took it out of my pocket then. Near the mailbox was a bald spot in the grass. I dug there. I thought: I am blessing this house by digging this hole. Or: I can use it as leverage later. "We can't leave, Chuck, the orange tree needs us!" I filled the hole up and tapped the earth with the back of my shovel, and then I was filled with a thought that barely seemed like my own. Hope, Nancy, this is about hope.

5

I hadn't returned Marcy's calls so one day she just showed up at the house. "I was worried you might be a lonely little Nancy up here." She held out the familiar pie in her hands. "Mulberry again. It's really the best one they have."

I thanked her and invited her in because I had to.

"Oh, I don't want to interrupt you," she said when she saw my clothes strewn all over the couch. I was going through them to see what I could give to Salvation Army.

I was polite. "No, no, it's fine. I was just getting ready to donate this stuff."

She touched the pair of khaki pants I had just decided were hideous. "Can I look through it?"

"Sure, go ahead."

I made sugar-free lemonade while Marcy picked through my unwanted clothes with such joy. "And this? You're getting rid of this? Are you sure?" She held up a San Diego Zoo shirt I had bought in the '80s. "This is probably a collector's item. You could sell it on eBay."

"It's all yours," I said.

When she was done making her pile—she'd taken almost everything I no longer wanted—she told me she was lonely. Well, she didn't say that, but that was what I heard. She said that after six months of living in Kona, she still missed San Diego. She said Brad worked longer hours here, and she told me unconvincingly that it was a good thing, maybe, because it had given her a chance to enjoy nature more.

She told me about a trail near my house people called the Pig Trail and how she had walked it alone once. She had felt afraid doing that. "Because there's no one else. It's just you in the forest. I prefer walking down Ali'i now." She said her new friends—all great people I *had* to meet—were so incredibly great but also incredibly busy. Which was why it was important to stay busy herself. Marcy talked almost the whole time and I barely said anything. As I watched her restless hands move around with every new thought, I understood that Marcy had not come here to check up on lonely little Nancy. Marcy had come here because she was a lonely little Marcy.

When she'd said enough about herself, she moved on to the topic of the volcano—"Can you believe it's going to destroy that town? I won't go anywhere near that thing." And then, after a long sigh, she said, "We should do something fun."

"Like what?" I was ready for her to leave.

"Let's get our nails done! I know a great place down near KTA."

I was about to say no, but then I remembered Sara Beth's bright green polish. And Ana—her toes and fingers had been a sparkly purple. And then I thought of myself at yoga with my ugly naked nails, and I said, "Okay, I'll follow you." This way, we could take a little break from each other in our own cars.

"Fun!" She sprang from the couch.

"Fun," I repeated, because she was waiting for me to speak.

•

The nail place was crowded, so we couldn't sit next to each other. "That's okay," Marcy said, "We're going to be spending so much time together soon anyway."

I chose a shocking red that was out of my comfort zone, and Marcy chose a responsible red. Afterwards I said no thanks to Orange Julius and thought about how it was going to be hard to avoid a person who thought coming to your house uninvited was an acceptable thing to do.

•

When I got home, Chuck and the boys were kicking a soccer ball around in the grass. It was dusk. The light was pink. The grass was green. Richly, fully, unbelievably green, and, again, I was amazed by just how beautiful it was here. I'd been living in a washed-out, dry land for so long and not even known it.

I already had my plan, of course, because I always had a plan, and I'd already imagined myself carrying it out. I would park and go inside and make dinner and do everything gingerly so as not to ruin my nails. I had already decided Chuck wouldn't notice my nails, and I had decided to use the black sesame seeds I'd bought at KTA. Salad with black sesame seeds? Brown rice with black sesame seeds?

I don't know what it was that made me stop. But for some reason, instead of getting out of the car, I sat there instead, watching my family kick this soccer ball around. They waved when they saw me and then kept kicking. They were barefoot. Their faces looked joyful. The boys are doing well here, I thought. Thank God, because I hadn't been sure how it would go. Cam, in particular—he had trouble with change.

And then, despite myself, and despite all my anger at him, my eyes wandered from the boys and fixed on Chuck. Chuck in his well-worn "hang-out shirt." Chuck's calves, which I had always liked. I was fighting myself a little. It wasn't hard to find reasons to be angry. Shelly Shelly Shelly. Everything that had led up to Shelly—every imagined interaction between them—and everything after. And then all the other reasons I was annoyed, which had nothing to do with Shelly, but which, really, were all about her. Chuck's drool on the pillow, which had never bothered me that much, was now a reason to spray my Shout with vengeance. Even the slow way he walked, which I used to think said something positive about how patient he was, had begun to piss me off. In the airport I'd wanted to kill him. Because in my head, I was thinking, You would probably walk faster with Shelly, you asshole.

But in this moment he was very hard to hate. The soccer ball was new, which meant that he'd just bought it. My husband had bought a soccer ball to kick around with our sons after school.

Even now, years into my suburban adulthood, scenes like this had the power to astound me. I had no memory of playing on lawns as a kid. And if I ever had a soccer ball, I'm sure it was stolen, and I might have been trying to sell it. Lawns during my teenage years, and after that too, and maybe also a little before, were a place to have quick sex with men who were probably in jail now. They were lawns that usually belonged to a golf course.

So yes, Chuck had failed me, but it was, compared to what it could have been, a small failure. It was also a failure that one couldn't see just by looking at him, and this was comforting: how virtuous and clean he looked there on the grass with his sweet and dapper boys. And then there was me, the responsible mom, coming home to make dinner. No one looking at this family would have thought we were anything but innocent.

6

"Good morning, yogis." She yawned. Her face was dewy and pale and glowing, and an orange scarf hung loosely over her shoulders.

"Normally, now," she said, sitting taller, "I'd ring the gong, but I don't have it with me today. I left the house in a rush. I don't have my books either." Her eyes landed right on me when she said, "We are creatures of habit," and I wondered if this meant something, which of course it didn't—we were all creatures of habit.

"Even the way you guys have organized yourselves—you're sitting in the same way you sat last time."

We looked at each other and smiled because it was true. Patty, Sara Beth, Kurt, and me had laid out our mats in the exact same order.

"Habitual momentum," she said, "dictates of our lives. It's hard to change our patterns. And it's easy to get stuck." She nodded at that thought, and looked almost a tiny bit worried for a second, gazing beyond us at the ocean. And then she yawned again. "Excuse me. I didn't sleep well last night," she said, patting her lips with her fingertips a few times before going on. "The point of yoga is not toned arms. Maybe that's a nice side effect, but it's not why we're here. We're here to open up. We're here to change. I know it sounds lofty. But I promise you, it's very real. When you come here and you stretch and you feel different afterwards, that's because you *are* different. You've created a new space for yourself. You've opened the door to a new room."

She rolled her shoulders back. "What's in that new room? Love?

Gratitude? Fearlessness? *Who* is in that new room? Your dog, your partner, the guy who works at Stop and Shop? Let's set an intention. Dedicate your practice to someone or something that feels important to you today—whomever or whatever you want in that new room."

What came to mind, and I don't know why since I rarely thought about her, was my mother. But I didn't want to dedicate the practice to my mother. Did I? Next was Chuck, which would have been fine, but it felt like a default setting—choose your husband—and not completely right for me today. The boys—that always felt right; they were my children. I settled on "family" and in my head I said, I dedicate this practice to my family, even though really I knew it was for my mother because I couldn't stop picturing her swollen face.

•

Despite being tired, Ana was present and attentive during class. We focused on hip openers, which looked easy but which were not. The hips, she told us, are where you hold your anger.

She left us in pigeon for ten long breaths. I thought I might die; it was so uncomfortable. "Deep, even breaths," she said. "Your bones are made of jade. Heavy. Jade bones. Breathe."

A never-ending pause, during which the feeling that I might die intensified.

"Feelings will come up. Think of it like you're walking through a loud party. That's your brain talking to you. You can say, 'Hi, crazy brain, how's it going today?' But you don't stay there. You pass through the party and go down to the basement. That's where we are, deep down here with all the gunk. Exhale, exhale, go deeper. Ungunk. We are ungunking now." She chuckled at herself, maybe because *ungunk* wasn't a real word. "Every time you exhale, you're going a little bit deeper into how you really feel. The feelings underneath the chatter."

She told us to imagine the energy below every living thing like a light. She told us to undulate like seaweed. She asked us to picture our bodies just as bones, just as skeletons in an X-ray. She said, "You are bones and water in movement and that's it. Don't make it complicated. It's not complicated."

As the sun rose higher in the sky, I thought about many things, both complicated and not. What would I make for dinner? If my mother were still alive, would we be speaking? What time did Target close? How many times had I googled Shelly since the affair? Fifty times? Eighty?

At the end Ana said, "Peace to all beings, no exceptions." She bowed. "And that means no exceptions."

•

We waited in line for the basket in the same order as last time. I pretended not to watch Kurt pull his shirt down over his abs, which looked like an eight-pack of those Pillsbury biscuits I was no longer eating.

I was spilling over with my post-yoga energy, which apparently included verbal spilling as well, because out of nowhere I said to Kurt, "Ana is such a good yoga teacher!"

"The amazing thing," Kurt said quietly, looking at her, "is that Ana has had a pretty rough go of it, but her take on life is still very positive." He looked somber for a second. "She's an old soul."

When everyone had left and it was just me and Ana, she said, "Sorry, I forgot the Red Vines today."

"Oh, it's fine," I said. "I'm sorry you didn't sleep last night."

She shook her head. She seemed upset. It was the first time I'd seen her be anything but completely confident.

Automatically, I was consoling. "That was a wonderful class. Thank you so much!"

"Thank *you*," she said, really meaning it. "I appreciate you saying that." She touched my arm. Her fingers were somehow cool and warm at the same time. "You're doing a fabulous job. You're showing up, really showing up. It's great, Nancy, really."

"Thank you," I said, raising my shoulders and shrinking into myself. We were saying *thank you* too many times. "Well," I went on, taking a step toward the car. But right as I was about to leave I thought, Wait. Here's a person you find interesting, Nancy, and you need friends, and you should obviously ask her if she wants to get together outside of class. The thought made me skittish. I hadn't asked a new friend on a friend date since—forever. My friends in San Diego naturally became friends because our children were friends. But this was a new chapter now. I felt like I was back in high school when I said, "I'd love to get together sometime outside of class."

"Yes," Ana said. "Why don't you stop by sometime? I live right over there." She pointed down Ali'i. "Number 75-6016. We can sit in my Jacuzzi."

"That would be lovely," I said, memorizing the number.

"How about Friday. Anytime after two?"

"Perfect."

I walked toward the car with a bounce in my step, feeling like I could take over the world. I was all stretched and open and ready for the day. New people, new chapters. Because Nancy, you have a friend date. And your marital problems are fixable. And your body doesn't feel like a log. Let's go home and throw away that secret stash of Hostess CupCakes because you don't need those anymore. And Hostess CupCakes are disgusting, by the way!

•

I went straight to Target and bought a swimsuit. I safely chose black because it was slimming, and I got out of my comfort zone a little with the deep V neckline. I was trying it on in the bathroom when Chuck got home from work.

"Nancy?" he said from the other side of the door. "Can I use the bathroom or do you want me to use the other one?"

"You—" I was about to tell him to use the other one, but then I thought I might want his opinion. I put my hand on the doorknob.

"Hello?" he said again.

And then I thought, Screw it, and opened the door.

"Wow." He looked me up and down twice, and I realized this was what I'd really wanted: for Chuck to think I was sexy again.

"You like it?" I asked, wanting more.

"I love it," he said. I could tell he wanted to touch me.

"Okay." I might have giggled. "Thanks for your feedback, Chuck."

I put my hand on his chest and gently pushed until he'd backed away from the door.

"You're beautiful," he said, right before I closed it.

In the mirror I looked elated. And relieved. Because exchanging swimsuits isn't easy, I thought. And because yes, I did look good. Not perfect, of course, but different somehow, and that was even better.

My face was flushed and glowing.

Imagine the energy below every living thing like a light, she had said.

And imagine us, me and her, going over more facts about energy in her Jacuzzi. Imagine us complimenting each other's swimsuit purchases. Imagine us sinking into warm water. Imagine us enticed. Imagine us open. Imagine us unarmed.

7

Ana lived in a pink house by the sea. A pink the color of Pepto-Bismol, with white trim. Vines grew fiercely up the walls and over some of the windows. I thought it was charming.

Right as I was about to knock, she opened the door. She was wearing a gecko-green top and red linen pants with wide parachute legs. She looked very relaxed, like maybe she'd just woken up. In a gravelly voice, she said, "I heard your car."

"Wow, you have good hearing!" I exclaimed. You're nervous, Nancy. Calm down, Nancy. It's only a friend date, Nancy.

"I was just doing a little meditation." She motioned to the yellow yoga mat on the floor behind her. On it was a blue satin pillow, and at the edge a stack of books with a gold Buddha figurine on top.

"Oh, is this a bad time? I can come back if you want," I said too fast.

We both knew I didn't mean it.

"This is a perfect time," Ana said. "Please, come in." She smiled her flawless smile. In the shadows of the house her face looked more angular. Her cheekbones were enviably pronounced. I slid off my shoes and added them to her bamboo shoe rack by the door and wondered if my cheekbones looked more pronounced in this light, too.

Her house smelled like a blend of incense and orange spray. It was very tidy and bursting with color. Tibetan prayer flags on the wall and orange curtains lining the sliding glass doors and vibrant afghans in perfect taquito rolls near the couch. Her furniture was minimal and low to the ground. It gave the illusion of spaciousness, even though the house itself was pretty small. On the coffee table was another Buddha figurine. And another in the corner. And on the bookshelf. And in the soil of a leafy plant. There were Buddhas everywhere.

"I brought you some jam," I said, and handed her the jar. I'd bought it in town from a woman named Sylvia who was obsessed with whales. She told me she'd moved to Hawaii just to be near them, and then she went on and on about their blowholes and their migration patterns and this one mother and baby she was tracking, and I stopped listening after a while because it was just too much information.

"Thank you," Ana said. She looked at the label. "Oh, Sylvia's jam." She cocked her head. "Did she tell you about her whales?"

"Yes!"

"Of course she did," she said, and I was glad I'd bought Sylvia's jam and not another jam so we could bond over knowing her.

Ana seemed to be pondering my face, which made me nervous. She was so present, much more present than I was, and obviously very intuitive, and what was she thinking? My swimsuit had shifted into a bad position under my clothes. I tried to ignore it.

"I'm just going to put my stuff away, and then let's have some tea."

"Sure, no rush," I said, trying to relax. Adding new people to your life is always a challenge, I reminded myself. The getting-to-know-you part is the worst, and after that it gets better.

While Ana rolled up her yoga mat and put the blue pillow on the shelf, I put my hand on my waist and did my best to act natural.

"I like your Buddhas," I said.

"The Chinese ones are my favorite. They're so fat and happy. Look at him." She pointed to the one on the coffee table. "He's laughing his ass off."

I picked it up so that my hands had something to do. The Buddha was heavy, cackling, and wearing a necklace.

Ana bent to pick a speck of something off the floor. Then she fluffed a pillow on her couch.

"You're very neat," I told her.

"Did you expect me to be messy?"

"No," I said. "No!" Although maybe I had expected her to be messy, or at least a little messier than this.

"You know what they say about neat people." Ana took the Buddha from me and set it down and swiveled it back and forth until she'd found the right angle. This was when I realized that all the Buddhas were facing the same way: out the window. "Neat people fear death more than messy people. It's about control."

"Right," I said. And I really meant that. It did seem right. It seemed like kind of a revelation, actually.

I followed her to the kitchen, which was right there, and looked out her sliding glass doors and said, "Your view!" She was literally right on the ocean. Which I'd known, obviously, but seeing it from here—it was stunning. And so close. After the doors was a cement deck with a small Jacuzzi perched on the edge, and right after that all you could see was the light blue ocean and the lighter blue sky.

"Sometimes it reminds me of heaven," she said, like heaven was a place she had been to.

I sat myself on a bar stool and watched her add water to the kettle, which was scratched and dented but very clean. On the counter was a basket filled with miniature soaps.

"Oh, that's for you," Ana said. "It's a welcome basket. Welcome to Hawaii. Alo-ha!"

"What?" I picked up a soap and smelled it. Lime. They were all different flavors. "This is so nice of you. Thank you."

I said "thank you" at least four more times, and then I said yes to green tea. Ana took out two packets and set them inside two small mugs that were chipped and baby blue, and then she stood there, looking sort of at me and sort of at the view, and then she traced her eyebrows with her fingers. She seemed to be making sure they were still there. "If you're wondering why my eyebrows are basically nonexistent," she said, "it's because I had breast cancer."

"Oh," I said. Her eyebrows looked completely normal to me. Losing them must have given her a complex. I put the soap in my hand back in the basket. I didn't look at her breasts. I now understood why they were so perky. Implants. And her hair—of course. Of course it was a wig. How had I thought it was real? "I'm sorry to hear that," I said. "But you're okay now?"

"I hope so." She chuckled. "I'm in remission. It's funny though, I always had a feeling I would get cancer." She set her elbows on the counter and clasped her fingers together. "I'm kind of surprised it took so long, really. Karma is a strange creature. A mysterious bitch. That's what my friend calls it. Funny, right?"

"Right." I looked at the floor to find my thoughts. Cheap linoleum but sparkling clean. "But wait. Do you think karma had something to do with your cancer?" I asked slowly.

She nodded as if to say: that's a great question. "Well, I guess I mean that in a way, I feel I deserved cancer. I know—it sounds so self-flagellating. But deeply, that's how I feel. I . . . let's just say I haven't always been an outstanding citizen. When I was younger . . . well . . ." She sighed. Then she tucked her short black hair with the neon pink shock behind her ear, and I wondered what it was like to wear a wig all the time. "The point is that moving forward, I'm going to be as good as I can be. For the rest of my life. Because karma works both ways. You do bad, you get bad. You do good, you get good. I mean, right? It's pretty simple. It's almost like a little game."

We were quiet for a few moments while Ana poured the steaming water into our mugs from a high angle like a bartender, and then it dawned on me that maybe in her mysterious younger years she'd actually been a bartender. The idea of a checkered past made her more intriguing than she already was, and so unlike the water polo moms in San Diego, whose entire past, present, and future existed safely within the same four freeway exits.

"Because the worst thing would be if the cancer came back," she went on. "Death, obviously, is the worst thing. And I'm not ready to die yet. So," she shrugged, "I'm working the universe."

I'd never heard anyone talk about karma in this way. Which—of course I hadn't. I didn't know anyone who talked about karma at all. But I thought it made sense. I mean, in theory.

"So I've been thinking about how to be more compassionate," she said. "Which is something we should all do anyway, but I'm trying to step it up. I want to do good in bigger ways. I'm not sure exactly how yet, but I have some ideas." She rubbed her hands together, and I was even more intrigued.

"So far, I've been doing small things, like opening the door for people and smiling at people, which is just common courtesy. It's not groundbreaking. I was probably doing a lot of that stuff before." She looked at the welcome basket. "But like this, for example," she said. "Would I have given you this soap before? I don't know. Maybe. But honestly, maybe not." She laughed a deeper laugh than her usual chuckle. "I'm covering all my bases."

"Thank you again," I said, absentmindedly tugging my tea bag.

"No," she said, "thank *you*. You might be saving me from death right now."

•

After tea, Ana showed me her bedroom. Clean and colorful with her bed low to the ground like everything else. A tattered hardcover book on the floor because she had no nightstand. On the windowsill were three baby succulents. "And that's my snake." She pointed to the terrarium I hadn't seen behind me. "If anyone asks, she's a lizard. Snakes aren't allowed in Hawaii." The snake was black and white and moving. "Portico gets excited when I come in here, don't you, Portico?" she cooed.

"Portico?"

"It's not a symbolic name," she said. "It's just a good word. I like the way it rolls off my tongue."

"Por-ti-co," I said phonetically.

"Exactly." She put her hands on her hips and looked at the tank. "I've thought about turning her in," she said, "since I'm being good now. But I'm not sure my god cares about the snake law."

I nodded in a way that said: Okay, uh-huh, tell me more.

And she did.

She told me that she didn't mean God like crucifix-goatee-capital-G God. But that she believed in a greater *something*, you know?

Something beyond herself. She said, "And if you didn't make the sun rise this morning, Nancy, then you believe in something greater than yourself, too."

Ana's lowercased god was nature, really. She saw her in the clouds, and yes of course it was a *her,* and she'd even given her a little nickname, which was Celia. Because Celia sounded like "ceiling," and the ultimate ceiling—"obvious!"—was the sky.

When she asked me if I believed in anything, I said I didn't know. "You can borrow Celia until you figure it out, if you want," she said. She told me she used to not know either, but cancer had changed that. She saw her life clearly now. Of course I was glad I hadn't gotten cancer, but I envied her clarity.

When Ana looked out the window, I watched her, wondering what it was that she saw so clearly. It turned out to be simple. "The Jacuzzi is calling us," she said. "I'll change and meet you out there."

•

The plastic Jacuzzi was set right on the ocean. It was like heaven. All that horizon, and the waves crashing against the rock wall, spraying me a little, just enough. I was happy she'd left me to undress alone. I lowered myself in, let my body melt into the heat. I looked at the palm trees moving in the wind and I thought: This. This is it. This is what living is like.

Ana appeared in a red suit, the same red as my nails. "How is it?" she asked.

"Divine."

"Good word," she said, enthusiastic, and it pleased me to know that I had pleased her.

She sat on the edge and put her feet in. She tipped her head back and let out a long guttural sigh and kept going until there was no more air left in her lungs. Looking up at the sky, she said, "When I'm feeling in the zone, Celia isn't just a metaphor for clouds. She's literally *in* the clouds."

I thought of the boys when they were younger, finding trains and horses in the clouds. They seemed to find whatever thing they were obsessed with at the moment.

"See that one?" Ana pointed. "It looks like a plus sign. It means I'm doing a good job at being good now." She smiled, blinked her eyes slowly. Her head was lazily slung to one side.

After a short silence, I told Ana that this was a beautiful spot. And that her house was so charming. She looked longingly at the house and said, "I wish it were mine." It turned out she was taking care of it for her friend Eunice, who lived at a nursing home now. Ana was a "permanent house sitter, basically," and this was perfect, except for the fact that Eunice was now thinking of selling, which would mess everything up.

When she was done talking, Ana looked at my face and then at my shoulders, and then she rolled her shoulders back, broadening her chest. I didn't look at her breasts. "How are you feeling right now, Nancy?"

"Great," I said. Because that's how it went, didn't it? Question: How are you feeling? Answer: Great. But something about being with Ana made this pleasantry seem wrong.

Slowly, she stood. "Will you do something for me?"

I said, "Sure"—of course I did—and then Ana told me to get ready because this was an odd request. "Just lie down however you're comfortable on the ground."

I looked at the ground, which didn't look comfortable at all. "That *is* an odd request," I said, laughing to make light of it.

I felt self-conscious getting out of the Jacuzzi. I thought my breasts were going to pop out of my suit. I also thought I might faint. I pulled the deep V up again and collapsed a little too quickly onto the ground. My eyelids were sweating, and Ana was standing over me now, studying my body. What was she looking for? Was I doing it right? Water dripped from her suit. She tapped her lips with her pointer finger.

"See how close your arms are to your body, and how your legs are pressed together so tightly?"

I raised my chin to look at my body. Good, I looked thin from this angle.

"Just the way you've organized yourself says so much. Your tightness, how compact you've made yourself, how little room you're taking up in the world. Really, how little room you might be settling for. I hope that doesn't offend you. All I'm saying is that it seems like you might be feeling tense."

I moved my arms farther away from me.

"Do you feel tense?"

I hoisted myself to a sitting position. "I . . ." I started, and then I followed her back into the Jacuzzi and waited until we were both sitting again to answer. The funny thing was that I changed my answer on the way. I was going to say, "No, not really," but what I ended up saying once I sat back down on the ledge and caught my breath was "I have to tell you, I *am* tense."

The way Ana looked at me told me she understood. "What are you tense about?" she asked. Her voice was frank and kind of toneless and not judgmental at all.

"I don't know." I forced a smile. "Life?" I didn't like how sad I sounded.

"Why did you move here, Nancy? I haven't asked you that yet."

I looked at the expanse of ocean. There were so many possible answers to give her. I thought of San Diego, of the water polo moms, of what I had told them. "It's a great opportunity for Chuck," I had said, smiling like a machine. That's how we smiled at each other: like machines. Maybe we smiled at everyone like that. We were so fake, so cloaked in bullshit, so hidden from one another. We wore visors to hide our worry lines. We made bake sale cookies to support the team and binged on them in the shadows of our cars. I thought of how we would never think to sit in a Jacuzzi like this. Of how our version of a fun afternoon was water aerobics at the Y followed by lunch at the Cheesecake Factory while we complained about our husbands, but only fake complaints that would make each other laugh because no one trusted anyone, not really. I never told any of them about Chuck's affair, not even Sheila, whose husband had cheated on her, too.

Ana—I wanted to tell her the truth. She was so easy to talk to, and maybe her being a near-stranger made it easier somehow. "To save our marriage," I said. "Chuck cheated on me."

I braced myself for her reaction, but there wasn't one, not really. "Ah," she said, her face totally calm. She was completely unaffected, completely unsurprised, and she said none of the I'm-so-sorry things I expected her to say. And then she winked at me. "Well," she said, "I would say we should punish him, but I'm being good now so that's not an option."

"Yeah," I said, and then I went on. I needed so badly to talk about it. "He's taking me on dates," I told her. "He's trying to undo his mistake." It felt great to share this with another human being, especially one who was actually listening.

"Oh, honey, that sounds exhausting," Ana said. "You must be ex*haus*ted."

That made me laugh. Because it was exhausting, but more because she had said this out loud. It wasn't part of the script. Most people would have said, "Well, that's nice he's taking you on dates." And then they would have tried to fix it. With Ana, there was no concerned babying tone, no trying to make me feel better with platitudes. ("Marriage is hard." "It's a phase.") She was just honest. And clear. Clarity, like she had said. I wondered in what other ways surviving breast cancer could make a person into a better version of themselves.

After I had told her all about Shelly—"Of *course* her name would be Shelly," she said—there was a long moment with me looking at Ana and then Ana looking up at the clouds and then me looking up at the clouds, trying to see if I could find any obvious symbols up there (besides that piece of Swiss cheese?), and then finally I asked her. "What are the bigger things you're planning on doing?"

The look on her face told me she was happy I wanted to know. "My good deeds, you mean?"

I shrugged, maybe to show her I was still a little skeptical of her plan to manipulate destiny. "I'm curious," I said.

"Are you?" She beamed. "That delights me." Her perfect white veneers. "Because yours is the first feedback I'm getting."

And after hearing that—I was the first?—I was more enthusiastic. "Really, I'm very curious. What are you going to do?"

"Well," she began, and then she blew some cool air up into her bangs, which is when I realized it must have been hot in there under her wig. I felt terrible for not having thought of this earlier. "I was going to do this thing tomorrow . . ."

A wave crashed. Another wave crashed. Why had she stopped talking? Was she worried about her plan? Did she think it was stupid? Or that it wouldn't work?

I wanted to make her feel better. If we were going to be friends, I should be supportive. I made sure to sound extra interested when I asked, "*What* thing?"

Ana looked at me and smiled. And then she waited. And waited. And the pause grew into a pause that was just too long. I couldn't take it. Tick-tock, another wave crashed, and it was enough time to make up a whole story in my head about how Ana was embarrassed to tell me and how the best way to change that was to involve myself directly by offering something, and offering something seemed right because I'd been so selfish before, going on about myself and not noticing how hot she was under that wig, and that's when I heard myself say, "Do you need help? Do you want me to come with you?"

8

I made quinoa with cranberries and roasted a chicken for dinner that night, and Chuck said, "You're in a good mood."

"Am I?" I delicately added a few sprigs of parsley to the quinoa. My new favorite health food blogger had written that color was important. We eat with our eyes first.

"It sounds like a good mood." Chuck took off his red Costco hat. His hair was all matted. "You're humming."

He was right, I was humming. I hadn't even noticed. And I didn't know what I was humming either. Probably the last song I'd heard on the radio.

Chuck took a step closer to me. He wanted to kiss me on the cheek again because he had done this yesterday and I had let him. With so much hesitation, he leaned in. An inch from my face, he left a full second-long pause—my exit door if I wanted it. I didn't want it. I wanted to say: If you're going to kiss me, then kiss me, you idiot.

Finally, he did. The smell of his aftershave, the scratch of his stubble. Oh, Chuck.

I hadn't noticed the boys standing there at the end of the table. Behind them on the wall was the nail I had abandoned.

"I'm glad you guys made up," Cam said. His childlike face and his strong body—it was a man's body now.

"Thank God," Jed said, and rolled his eyes, which was so very Jed. He liked to pretend he didn't care about things.

We sat down, passed the food around. Cam complimented my

use of cranberries and Chuck noted how moist the chicken was and I gave myself a pat on the back for taking it out of the oven at just the right time.

Jed was stoked because he and Cam were obviously the best ones on the new team, and Cam, too modest to agree, said he liked their new coach, who was super chill.

"How are your classes?" I asked.

"Fine."

"Fine."

This was always a dead-end conversation.

"Any love interests?" Chuck asked. "Either of you have a girl-friend yet?"

I looked at Chuck: Are you serious? He didn't notice. We had talked about this. I had told him that no, I wasn't sure, of course I wasn't sure. Who knew what kids did these days. But if Cam was gay, we should make room for that. We should let him know it was okay. Chuck and I had had a whole conversation about how we would keep our questions general—we had specifically agreed to avoid using the words *girlfriend* and *boyfriend*.

"Not yet, Dad!" Jed said. "School just started. Jeez, give us a sec-ond."

Cam took a big bite of quinoa, looked at the nail in the wall.

"Or any kind of love interest," I said. "It doesn't have to be a girl." I glared at Chuck. His face changed when he understood what had just happened. He grimaced, tightened his worried eyes. I could see exactly what he would say to me later: I'm sorry, *girlfriend* just slipped out!

"Mom, why do you always say that? We're not gay!" Jed laughed, looked at Cam. Cam kept his eyes on his food.

"Well, I just want you to know you can be whatever you want," I said, and then, for Cam, I moved on to a new topic. "I have a new friend," I said. I was a little embarrassed by how excited I sounded.

"Marcy?" Chuck said. "Brad mentioned she came over."

"She did. Unannounced. She brought a pie."

"Sweet," Jed said.

I could see Cam taking a deep breath. I could see him saying to himself: You're okay, you're okay. He looked up at me finally. I smiled and gave him a little nod. You're okay, baby.

Chuck was talking about mulberry trees now. "They are native to the island, surprisingly."

"So Marcy's your new friend, Mom?" Cam asked.

"No. Well, yes, sure. Okay, I have two new friends. Marcy and Ana."

"Ana," Chuck said.

"It's *On-a,* actually," I said.

"What's Ana like?" Cam asked.

"She's nice," I said. "Kind of a free spirit." I almost told them more. I almost said, "And tomorrow we're meeting up to do good deeds because Ana had breast cancer and—" but it would have been too much to explain. And when the moment passed and I still hadn't told them, I felt good. You're allowed to have your own life, Nancy. Chuck has Costco and the boys have school and this—Ana and yoga—this can just be for you.

After dinner, I gave Cam a long hug and then I gave Jed a hug for the same amount of time to make it equal. Doing everything twice was second nature to me.

When it was time for bed, Chuck pulled back the new hibiscus bedspread like it was something fragile. He whispered, "I'm sorry! *Girlfriend* just slipped out!"

"I know, Chuck," I said, "I know." I know everything about you. There are no surprises.

9

We'd agreed on 3:00 p.m. I pulled into her driveway at 3:05 because I wanted to show her I was more relaxed than she thought. I parked next to her purple Jeep. The fabric of my baby-blue tunic was sticking to my stomach in the heat. I tugged it away. Flow, don't stick. Flow, don't be tense.

I noted the vines again—crazy, but beautiful—and walked toward the door.

"Naaaaancy," she called. Her voice was creepy but joking, and it was behind me. I turned. Saw just her feet on the ledge of the driver's-side window. She sat up. I almost thought it was someone else, but no, it was Ana, with long orange hair. She looked like Wynonna Judd.

"What do you think?"

"You look like Wynonna Judd!"

"Wynonna? I don't want to be Wynonna. I want to be Ashley!" She looked at herself in the little side mirror, tousled her bangs. "Fine, I'll be Wynonna. Ashley's boring."

The top of the Jeep was off. I'd never seen it on. In the backseat was a cardboard box full of sandwiches in Ziploc bags. "Who are those for?" I asked.

"The homeless. Or half homeless, a lot of them are only half homeless. But it doesn't matter how homeless they are. It still counts as a good deed. I was going to do something more complicated, but then I thought, No, keep it simple. Giving hungry people food. Obvious!"

"It's perfect," I said. And I was relieved. Handing out sandwiches? I could do that. Easy.

"And Nancy," Ana said, pressing both hands into her heart, "I have to tell you, I don't know if I'd be doing this without you. I mean, just in terms of the mechanics, it would be hard. Driving and passing out sandwiches at the same time. Although I guess I could walk. But what I really mean is that with you as my partner, I feel like this thing has expanded. The two of us—it's so much better than just me. And your presence—it's giving me courage. Really. I feel validated." She made prayer hands and bowed her head. "Thank you, partner."

"Of course," I chirped. "I'm happy to help." And when I said that, I thought: Pattern! Of course you'd be doing this, Nancy. Helping people who need help—I was always doing that. It was my thing. The PTA at Clairemont had named me "Most Involved Parent" two semesters in a row, which apparently was a record, and which pissed off a lot of the other mothers.

"Get in, partner," Ana said, reaching to open the door for me.

"Okay, partner." I felt exhilarated. I pulled my tunic off my stomach with a buzzy hand and leaped into the car.

Ana flipped her orange hair back over her shoulders, getting ready.

I thought this would be a good time to review: "We're handing out sandwiches today."

"To create space for better destinies," she finished. She took her hands off the wheel. We still hadn't left the driveway. "I would like to avoid disaster if possible. Death. Cancer. And I would hate it if Eunice sold this house." She frowned. "And you, Nancy! Things for you!" She grabbed my knee. "I would hate it if Chuck cheated on you again."

Flash to Shelly's cascading blond hair. "I would hate it, too," I said.

I still thought it was dangerous to want such specific things from the world. If it really were that easy to create destiny, wouldn't everyone be doing it?

And yet something about it seemed very right. Of course good created good. Wasn't that what the Dalai Lama thought? And even if doing this good thing wouldn't create the good we wanted, it definitely wouldn't create any bad either.

"I think it's great we're doing this good thing," I said. "But we shouldn't"—oh, it was so hard to say this looking at her hopeful face— "we shouldn't expect anything though, you know? Because what if it doesn't work?"

"Oh, it's going to work." She covered her eyes with her sunglasses. "It has to."

•

Our first target was a skinny guy weaving green fronds into baskets on the rock wall by Huggo's. "Target!" Ana yelled. She pulled over. "Hey!" she called to him. "C'mere!"

She grabbed one of the sandwiches from the backseat. They were very simple sandwiches—white bread with peanut butter. When the guy got to the car, she said, "Here, man, eat something."

The guy said, "Sweet," and took the bag. His fingers were long and elegant and dirty. In my imagination, he'd been a piano player once. "Mahalos," he said.

"Aloha." Ana flashed a smile. With her smile and the sunglasses and the sun glinting off her wig, making it even more orange, she looked younger, I thought, and kind of like a movie star.

We made our way slowly down Ali'i, giving sandwiches to anyone who looked even a little bit homeless. The big Hawaiian guy with the tiny mustache sitting at the bus stop drinking beer out of a brown paper bag yelled, "Toss it ova!" So I did. It was a bad throw and I was impressed when he caught it. "Mana thanks you!" he bellowed.

The girl in shredded clothes lying on the sidewalk next to her cardboard sign—it simply said HELP—probably didn't want to get up either, so I tossed a sandwich by her feet.

We gave sandwiches to the group of teenagers under the banyan tree who were very friendly and obviously up to no good. None of them wore shirts but they all wore backpacks. "They're selling pot," Ana told me. I instinctively looked for Cam and Jed around the tree and was glad when I didn't find them.

After Ali'i, we did the parking lots behind Ali'i, where there were even more half-homeless people. "The tweakers like the shade back here," Ana told me. We found two gaunt girls in a boxy patch of shade behind the Lava Java dumpster who introduced themselves as Marigold and Petunia in low, just-woke-up voices. Their matching eyes were huge and black and their faces were like skulls. I gave them two sandwiches each and then—I couldn't help it; I was such a mom—I said, "You girls are too skinny!" Which they took as a compliment. "Thank you," they said, looking at each other like they were looking into a mirror, their ghost bodies floating like jellyfish.

Hitting our hungry targets with sandwiches became surprisingly normal surprisingly fast. It felt like we'd been doing this for much longer than only thirty minutes of our lives. And it was fun. I liked being in a car with no top. I liked seeing people be grateful for our food. I liked that we were eating Red Vines from the Costco tub Ana kept in her car. I had wanted change, and here change was and it was palpable. Maybe there was a greater force. Or maybe there wasn't. Either way, I liked how I felt in this car, doing these good deeds. In the moment a hungry person would take a sandwich from my hands, I could forget about the questionable things I had done in my life. All the reasons to hate myself seemed further away, and I felt almost free.

As we drove on, looking for more targets, the sun dipping lower in the sky and our sandwich stockpile dwindling, Ana told me more about her past. Well, because I asked her to. Her mysterious youth when she hadn't been an upstanding (or "outstanding," as she had said) citizen. I wanted to know what she'd meant by that. I couldn't ask directly, of course, so I kept it vague. "Tell me more about yoooou," I said.

Ana bit her Red Vine. "Do you want my whole life story or just the highlights?"

"Whatever you want to tell me." I took a Red Vine for myself because hers looked good.

She took a deep breath. "Welllllllll . . ."

And this was what she told me:

Ana was born in the "armpit of the world," also known as Trenton, New Jersey. Her parents never married. Her dad worked in a factory assembling guns? She wasn't sure. Her mother may have said that once, but her mother said a lot of things. She was insane. "She was the kind of mother they arrest on *Cops*." They moved around a lot. Couch-surfing. Welfare. Poor as shit. In photos of Ana as a kid, she wears Goodwill scraps and looks tenement-dirty. When her mother's in the photos, she's drinking a canned lite beer she probably begged off some horny guy in a trailer park. Some of those guys she married. "Long trail of abusive stepfathers," she said. "They all knew to hit below the face so no one would see my bruises at school."

Her mom died when she was seventeen. "Cirrhosis. It was better that she left this world. Her time here was done." And after that, Ana got her GED. "For both of us," she said. "My mom only made it to seventh grade." She went to community college. Still in New Jersey at this point. But then she had a thing with her biology teacher. She was pretty; he was thirty-six. She was failing the class. She didn't understand biology, but she did understand men. Yes, she'd used her charm to get the things she wanted in life more than once. And sometimes—but rarely—she'd used her body. Growing up the way she did, it only made sense for her to be this way. "And if you're judging me for that, Nancy, well . . . that's okay. I spent a lot of time judging myself. Years and years of self-loathing."

Anyway, fast-forward. Biology teacher gets fired, Ana drops out, gets a job at a bank. ("I cannot believe they let me work there.") It was a new chapter. JCPenney skirts to the knee, alarm clock set at six. New boyfriend with a job who also shopped at JCPenney. They move in together, he proposes, she says yes but means no. The second after she says yes, she looks at his dumb young face and thinks, Shit, what did I just do?

Meanwhile at the bank job, Ana had been skimming money. It wasn't worth explaining how. "I'm a natural-born hustler," she said. "I saw an opportunity and I took it." By the time her boyfriend became her fiancé, she had fifteen grand in cash hidden in the AC vent, which she would open and close with the screwdriver she kept in her nightstand. ("The vent thing—I saw it on TV. But I didn't know if real people did that. I was always worried. What if the AC broke and my cash got wet? Or blew deeper into the vent?")

After the proposal, she started to feel itchy. The fiancé—he was just so *nice*. Translation: not interesting. Not interesting at all. And their little prefab house and the cheap polyester suits, and then at the bank some stuff happened. It wasn't good. Basically, they were figuring out it was an inside job.

"So one day—one regular, boring Wednesday in Trenton—I went home early with stomach cramps. Jerry was at work. And I remember sitting on my pleather couch, thinking, Holy shit, I can't do this anymore. I just can*not*."

Ana pulled the Jeep into a parking spot outside Longs and said, "So I opened the AC vent, took the cash, loaded the car, and drove."

She drove to Vegas, and that's where things got really bad. She formed new addictions and spent all her money on them. Gambling, yes, but mostly cocaine. Met a guy who thought she'd make a good dancer. "I told myself it was art." She shrugged. "Which it was, in a way."

It was a nice club. Very nice. Fancy. And the men liked her. She got popular quickly. A good group of regulars. The money started rolling in. Fast, really fast. She moved to a swanky apartment, got a swanky new car. Hired a tailor to make her striptease outfits. All custom-made to fit her body perfectly. And there were themes. Not the usual nurse and schoolteacher clichés, but interesting, artful themes. Her favorite was the peacock. It started off unassuming, in a cocoon of thick black velvet, and then, bit by bit—and this was to Tom Petty, by the way—she expanded into feathers. It was hard to work the pole with all those feathers, but it was fun. And, if she had to be honest, she liked the attention. Being onstage like that. Their hungry faces. It felt powerful. Because she could control them. She could control their emotions.

But then most of the money went up her nose, and she started unraveling. She tried to keep it together. She'd go to the gym. Well, at 5:00 a.m. after snorting a few lines, she'd go to the gym.

It all ended when she got pulled over one night. A hundred and two on the freeway and she was blazed. They sent her to NA. Which stood for Narcotics Anonymous, in case I didn't know. She thought it was a waste of time. And she knew it wouldn't work either.

And then something happened. Hard to explain. Suffice to say that this was when she decided on Mother Nature as her higher power and found Celia in the sky. Somehow—and she still couldn't believe this, by the way—she never did a line of coke again.

After that, Ana's life was better, obviously, because she wasn't fucked up all the time, but it also became harder in new ways. Without drugs, she had all this extra time on her hands. All this extra time to ask, What am I doing with my life?

She used to drive deep into the desert and look up at the stars and ask, What do you *want* from me?

And then she met Berta. "Berta was a badass. She'd been sober for three hundred years." Berta was also a Buddhist. They had long, long coffee dates, talking about Buddhism. The non-cruelty aspect appealed to Ana most. She wanted to tame her mean streak.

From Buddhism, Ana found yoga. Then astrology. Then she found a whole world waiting to be healed and decided to become a healer. In Hawaii, because being surrounded by water would offset her fiery nature. In Kona, because the volcano, full of fire, would remind her of who she was.

"And here we are now," she said, motioning to the red sign. "At Longs." She chuckled, and then she let out a big sigh. "I hope you don't hate me now, Nancy. I know that was a lot of information."

"No." I was adamant. "I don't hate you at all." And then I sighed, just like her, and I was aware of our matching sighs, and why did that happen? Had I copied her? Or was it contagious, like hiccups?

"I think it's hard not to feel a little judgment when one hears a story like that."

"I feel no judgment," I lied. Because of course I was judgmental. Robbing a bank? That was crazy. But, like she'd said, it only made sense, coming from where she came from. And she wasn't a thief any-more. Or a stripper. She had changed. She was a healer now.

When I looked at her, suffering under the heat of that big orange wig, I thought that she deserved mercy. We all deserve mercy, don't we? And so mercy was what I would give her.

"I don't mean this in a victim, poor-me way," Ana told me, "but sometimes I think if I had had better parents I would have been a better person." She blew cool air up into her bangs. "But I guess they did their best. With what they had, they did their best."

This was a familiar refrain, and one that all parents repeated to themselves frequently, I assumed. I did my best. We had to believe that to get through the day. But often, and usually at night, we questioned our definition of "best." Had I done my best when Jed and Cam at five years old vanished in a supermarket and I continued to shop for ten more minutes before going to look for them? And what about those years I took care of my younger brother? Was it the best I could do to sew up the gash in his leg with fishing line instead of taking him to a doctor? Or what about when he was fifteen with no driver's license and I handed him the keys to my boyfriend's car so he could take himself to the SATs? Was that the best? In a way, I think it was. And maybe in every way it was. We had so little then. Just as we had had so little always. My mother's version of "best" was bleak, hauntingly bleak, and even now, in certain moments, I still felt cast in its shadow.

"What about your parents?" Ana yawned. "What were they like?"

I don't know why I hesitated. This was the part where I usually delivered my line in a smooth, uplifting voice: "My parents were just your average Jack and Jane."

I looked at her tribal bracelet tattoo. It was a parade of triangles and elephants bordered by two rows of dots. The dots were imperfectly spaced and they were also imperfect themselves—some bigger, some smaller. I wondered if this was intentional—some kind of message about the imperfections of life.

And this, somehow—this perceived understanding about the meaning of her tattoo—was all I needed. If it hadn't been the tattoo, it would have been something else. I was looking for a reason. I'd spent the last million years with people who didn't understand me, and now here was someone who did. It felt right to tell her more. I felt like she could hold it. I knew she wouldn't be shocked.

I started small. I told her some pieces. About how my stepdad used to beat me as a kid, and about how when I'd told Chuck, he had protectively said, "What an asshole," but I knew he didn't really get it. Which—he had no reason to get it. His parents really were just your average Jack and Jane.

I was already crying at this point. Ana had the ability to melt me like that. Or I was willing to melt myself in her presence, which still pointed back to her ability to make me feel like melting was okay. I wiped my eyes and said, "I don't want to be crying. It's such a beautiful sunny day!"

Ana said, "Oh, who gives a shit. Every day is sunny here." I thought that was hilarious.

I went on. I told her my dad had left when I was young—I'd never met him, didn't even know his name—and I told her how my mom—I swallowed hard—was gone now, too. "She ended up"—oh, how it still made me tremble to say the words out loud—"killing herself."

"Come here, Nancy." Ana pressed me in close. Her coconut oil smell, how tightly she held me. How safe I felt.

And then I told her more. I told her more and more and more. I told her everything. Well, almost everything. About how I had raised my brother. How I'd found an older boyfriend to take us in. How I'd kept my grades up so I could get into USD, how fixated I was on that the whole time because I knew it would get me out. Because the older boyfriend turned out to be abusive—of course he did, that's how the cycle went. How all I wanted to do was stop the cycle and re-create myself and how now, a million years later, I was trying to figure out who the hell I was under this June Cleaver costume I wore like a straitjacket.

When I said that, Ana said, "We all wear costumes, Nancy," and the bangs of her wig were covering half her eyes, and I had to laugh.

The sun had lowered behind the palm trees at Longs, and the fronds were casting moving shadows on us. I looked at the clock. "Speaking of costumes," I said, "I should get home and put my Mom costume on."

We had four sandwiches left so we ate one apiece and left the others on the curb and drove back to her place.

The last thing Ana said to me that afternoon—she said it in her usual soft and confident voice, but it had turned into a long, emotional day and maybe her guard was down, because just underneath her confidence I could hear her regret.

"It's interesting, you and me . . ." Her whole body was completely still. She looked at me. She didn't blink. "I wonder why you turned out the way you did and I turned out the way I did."

I didn't know what to say, so I hugged her. That was my answer. Our bodies, I thought, fit together in a way that seemed just right. We hugged for a long time. We stood there in the driveway under the neon-pink sky, holding on to each other's shapes.

•

The boys came home with wet hair and chlorine-red eyes and picked at the plate of mangoes I'd set out for them. I told them their dad was taking me out tonight, which meant they'd get a Costco pizza for dinner, which somehow still had the power to excite them.

"I'm going to call Dad and ask him to get Hawaiian," Jed said. " 'Kay, Cam?"

"Yeah," Cam said, and opened his binder.

Jed put his phone to his ear and walked out to the lanai.

It was when I reached for a mango slice that I noticed the burn mark on Cam's arm. It looked like a small bursting comet. "Is that from the fireworks?"

He covered the spot with his hand. "I don't know," he mumbled.

I hadn't thought about that night in a while. Two policemen at 1:00 a.m. and the boys looking at their shoes. "We found them lighting fireworks down at the Shores, with about a gram of marijuana in their possession. Can't have that." Chuck, who'd followed me to the door, had repeated this line: "Can't have that, Officer, absolutely not." The boys swore the pot wasn't theirs—"I swear!" they each had said, too passionately; I didn't believe them—and then they swore never to light a firework again. The cops let them off with a warning. Chuck wanted to ground them for a month. I voted for two weeks. We settled on three.

The boys had done nothing illegal since, but I was always worried.

"You boys didn't bring any fireworks here, did you?" I put my arms around Cam's shoulders, looked down at the equations he'd written out. "I don't want you to hurt yourselves."

"No, Mom," he said. "I swear."

I didn't want to ask, but I thought it was my job to ask. "And you're not smoking pot, are you?"

"No," Cam said, annoyed.

Jed reappeared. "Mom, Dad will be home in twenty minutes," he said. "He's getting Hawaiian. Boo yeah!"

"Crap, I have to get ready," I said.

"Craaaaap," Jed said. When he thought I was out of earshot, he said to Cam, "Can I copy that, dude?"

"Boys!" I called, "No copying!"

"Okay, Mom!" they called back.

But I knew they would do it anyway. It was impossible to separate twins.

•

"Hi, honey, I'm home!" Chuck said in his Ricky Ricardo voice. Which was so stupid, but which made me smile every time. Chuck's Ricky Ricardo was funny because he really committed to character. He'd always been good at accents.

I continued washing the sticky mango juice off the plates at the sink as Chuck took off his shoes by the door. I felt good. I didn't feel annoyed by him this evening. I wondered why. Maybe because I felt like my life was expanding.

I'd thrown on a purple dress I hadn't worn in a long time. It was a dress I used to wear when I felt confident, and it was a little constricting, but only slightly uncomfortable.

I set the dish on the rack, started washing the next one. The smell of pizza wafted toward me. Ham. Pineapple. Cheese. I was hungry.

I dried my hands, turned around. There was Chuck, groomed and handsome, with a gorgeous purple Costco orchid in his hands. His blue eyes in the dusky light. That crazy, unreal dish detergent blue. He'd chosen his "really good shirt" for our date, the gray one from when Costco had had that Tommy Bahama sale. He held the flower in outstretched hands. An offering. "It's better than the San Diego ones, isn't it?" he asked.

I touched his arm. "Much better," I said.

And then Chuck kissed me on the cheek without hesitation, which was the first time he had done that since the affair. Finally, he was taking control.

·

We went to a restaurant at the harbor called Bite Me because Brad had said their poke was the best. On the walls were big plastic fish and pictures of men holding up dead versions of these same kinds of fish. This place didn't seem fancy enough to me. Not that I was a restaurant snob—it just wasn't what I'd been expecting. I knew Chuck was thinking the same thing because he said, "Is this okay? Do you want to go somewhere else?"

"No," I said, touching his arm for the second time that evening. "This place is funny. It kind of reminds me of that place we went to . . ."

"In Mexico?"

"Exactly."

"That was a good trip."

"It was," I said, remembering our green stucco hotel on the beach and the well-made straw hat I'd bought for a dollar.

All the tables at Bite Me were made of wood that looked sticky. We chose one by the window. Chuck scooted my chair in for me, which was a hilariously too-formal thing to do at this restaurant. The waitresses wore cutoff shorts that looked more like underwear, and tight red shirts that said BITE ME, and when I set my hand on the table, it was even stickier than I'd thought.

We ordered the poke, which arrived two minutes later on a cheap dish with no garnish. But Brad was right. It was the best poke we'd ever had.

Chuck told me he was liking this Costco, maybe even better than the old one. There was a real fraternal spirit, he said. Some of the guys had even started a pool team. They played a few nights a week at a bar in town and they were called the Tide Poolers.

"That's fun," I said. "Why don't you join?"

"I want to spend my free time with you, Nance," he said, as though offended I had asked.

But I knew Chuck better than that. He didn't want to hang out in a bar because he didn't trust himself not to drink. Chuck wasn't ready to call himself an alcoholic yet, but alcohol scared him in the way it scared alcoholics. I knew he thought about it more than normal people did.

"So," he said, "tell me about your day."

"I spent time with Ana," I said. "Turns out we have a lot in common." I was about to tell him about the sandwiches—I really was—but then Chuck said, "What do you have in common?" and the way he said that—almost like he was a little jealous?—made me want to keep more to myself.

So I gave him a surface-level answer—"We both love yoga"—and then continued that train of thought by saying the class was really fun and inspiring and I was getting better at the poses already.

Chuck's smile. "I'd love to see you do yoga."

I raised my eyebrows. "I bet you would."

He took my hand. The sticky table. How life was always imperfect. Even in the best moments, it was still sticky tables and sweaty thighs.

Chuck's wedding band pressed into my fingers. The metal was hard, warm. "Nancy." He looked right at me. "You don't have to say it back, but I just want you to know . . ."

I kissed my fingers and pressed them to his lips. "I love you, Chuck."

A pause, and then Chuck let his whole body sink back into the chair. "I'm so relieved to hear you say that."

•

We made love that night on the hibiscus bedspread. We had to be extra quiet because the boys' rooms were just across the hall in this house, which kind of made it more fun. I felt sexy and spontaneous and like I owned my body again. I didn't know when my body had become an imposition—just this thing I was forced to lug around—but now it was back and it was mine. It had been at least six months—we'd stopped making love long before Shelly—so Chuck's old moves felt almost new to me. New but also pleasantly familiar. Something I could trust. We messed up the sheets. Pillows got lost on the floor. My purple dress landed somewhere near the window. Normally, I would have gotten up to fix the sheets and pick up the pillows and find the dress, but I told myself to stay. Stay in this moment, warm and tangled in your husband's legs. We didn't put on our pajamas. We didn't brush our teeth. We fell asleep naked with nothing between us.

10

"Here we are at the beach. The waves are crashing. The birds are chirping. Cars are going by." Ana inhaled and exhaled deeply. She was back in the black wig today with the pink streak that hooked just below her chin. "Here we are, breathing like we mean it. Here we are, shifting our perspective. Shifting our train onto a new rail. Shoulders back. Relax your neck. Relax your tongue. The tongue is the strongest muscle in the body. It works hard for you all day. It needs a vacation. Relax that tongue."

A pause.

"You have chosen to come here this morning. You chose to get up early. You chose the clothes you're wearing. You chose to drive to this beach. After you leave here, you'll make more choices, and every one of them will matter. It all matters. It all counts. Every breath counts. Make it good. You are alive. Breathe like you mean it."

My eyes were closed, but I could see Ana reaching for her book, see her opening to the page.

"A quote I want to share with you: 'Be a lamp to yourself. Be your own confidence. Hold the truth within yourself as the only truth.'" She repeated it. "'Be a lamp to yourself. Be your own confidence. Hold the truth within yourself as the only truth.'" She inhaled, exhaled. "What is your truth and how is it manifesting? How will your choices today affect the rest of your life? Come back. Back back back. What do you want? What do you think you deserve?"

The sound of waves crashing, of birds chirping, of cars going by. The annoying sound of a fly buzzing near my ear and I wanted to flinch, but didn't.

"Taste the salt air. Feel the weight of your seat. Ground. Groundedness. Your mind is a wandering child. When your mind wanders, invite it back. Shush the child. Quiet your mind. Your mind is a quiet place. Your mind is the deserted stacks in a library. Your mind is the wild desert, where there are no footprints in the sand. Your mind is as quiet as a planet we've never been to. Inhale deeply, and then three oms."

•

That morning Ana helped me do a jump back for the first time. I didn't do it perfectly, but still I did it. I, Nancy Murphy, did a jump back. I felt strong and pretty and powerful and in a flush of sweaty optimism, I unzipped my jacket all the way and let it fall in a heap on the grass.

Afterwards I made sure I was last in line so we would have a chance to talk. Patty's cat was still alive, but doing worse. "I know we're born alone and we die alone, Ana, but—well," Patty tugged at her earring, "I just don't *like* that." While Patty was talking, Ana accidentally dropped her Red Vine in the grass. "Don't want that to go to waste," Patty said, and picked it up and ate the rest.

Sara Beth's nails were blue this week, and she thought she was potentially maybe possibly falling in love, but she was scared that if it didn't work out she'd fall on her face instead. Ana told her to embrace the uncertainty and grab life by the balls, which riled Sara Beth up. Her whole demeanor changed after that.

Kurt told Ana his knee was aching, and she suggested Tiger Balming it three times a day. He admitted he was a little embarrassed he hadn't thought of this himself, to which Ana said, "Embarrassment is a worthless emotion. Don't waste your brain cells."

As I watched them all and listened to their conversations, I felt proud to call Ana a friend. She was so loving and inspiring. I think we all wanted a piece of her. When Patty ate Ana's Red Vine from the grass, I thought: Any piece at all, even if only a small one.

After Kurt had left, Ana said, "Hey, partner," and gave me a huge hug. Coconut oil and her wig against my face.

"I loved your quote today," I said. "About how your truth is the only truth. That is so . . . true."

"Right?"

"Who said it?"

She cocked her head. "Ana Gersh." Her eyes sparkled. She bit her Red Vine.

"Another Ana, just like you. How funny." Was I supposed to know who Ana Gersh was? Was she famous like Pema? I decided to be bold and ask. "Who's Ana Gersh?"

"She's a philosopher." Ana tugged the hem of my shirt. She seemed to be inspecting the way it was sewn, maybe. "Here, I'll write it down for you." She grabbed her little notebook off the rock wall, wrote the quote, and ripped out the page for me when she was done. "You can put it on your fridge."

I imagined my family seeing this quote on the fridge. "I'll probably keep it in my wallet."

"Even better," Ana said. "What are you up to today? Do you want to Jacuzzi?"

The truth was that I had wanted her to ask, and I had brought my suit in case she did. "That would be lovely," I said, and we walked to the parking lot, where Ana said, "Follow me?" and I replied, "In my van." I may have stuck out my tongue when I said "van."

Instead of continuing on to her car, Ana paused right there. She looked at the van. She looked at me. She clasped her hands in front of her. "Sounds like you despise your van. Do you despise your van, Nancy?"

I forced a laugh. "I completely despise my van. I'm hoping it will die soon, but Hondas never die."

"Why don't you trade it in today?"

"Today?" I laughed.

"Yeah, today. Right now. I'll go with you."

My first thought? Chuck would be pissed. Which I couldn't say out loud. It sounded codependent. And then I started waffling. How pissed could Chuck possibly be? It was only a *car*.

"Let me ask you a question." She blew air up into her bangs. The sun was shining brighter now and poor Ana was probably so hot under there. "When you think about this van, okay, when you *really* think about it, do you see a long future or do you know you're going to say good-bye to it soon and you're just holding on until you get the okay from your husband?"

"Oh," I said, "I hate that you just said that."

"Because it's true?"

I sighed. "Yes."

"So you and this van are going to part ways soon?"

"I hope so."

"Then why not part ways with it today? Let it go. Set that giant car free. You're probably spending way too much on gas in that whale anyway. You need a little shark car. It'll save you a ton of money in the long run."

I looked at my van. The EAT, SLEEP, PLAY WATER POLO sticker had faded badly on the bumper. And the bumper itself had faded. Did it used to be black? Because it definitely wasn't anymore.

"We'll go to the Honda place," Ana said. "I'm a great negotiator."

My heart started beating fast. I was buzzing like I might explode. Was this how it felt to truly be living?

•

In the Jacuzzi, I said it again. "I got a new car."

Ana sank deeper into the water and then popped back up. "You got a new car."

"I got a BMW."

"You got a beamer."

"I got a white convertible beamer."

"No more hood to hide under. Exposed to the world."

"No more hiding."

"Ex-posed."

I checked to make sure my breasts were still in my swimsuit. They were.

"You should name it," Ana said, dipping again so the water was at her chin.

"My little shark car."

"Sharkeeeeeeee." Ana kept going until she ran out of breath.

"Sharkie," I repeated. I rested my head on the Jacuzzi's plastic side. "Chuck says we got a good price," I said. I'd called Chuck right afterwards. "And it will save us a ton of gas money in the long run," I'd told him. Chuck was a little disappointed he hadn't been there with me to pick it out, but he'd quickly regrouped. "I'm happy for you, Nance," he said, and I was relieved.

"I told you I'm a great negotiator," Ana said.

"You were amazing. I can't believe how you talked to that guy. How do you know so much about cars?"

"I've lived many lives." Ana tilted her head back so all I could see was her creamy white neck. Then she looked at me. "You're indebted to me now," she said, and I couldn't tell if she was serious or not. I had already planned on making her the healthy blueberry buckwheat muffins my blogger said were "to die for times twelve" (or, as she literally expressed this equation, "2 die 4 x 12") as a thank-you, but now I was thinking: Oh, should my thank-you be bigger than that? Maybe muffins *and* flowers. And a card, obviously a card.

Ana stood up in the water, walked the length of the small plastic bench, which was only two steps, and then walked back the other way. "I do have a favor to ask," she said.

"What is it?"

"Will you hand out sandwiches with me again?"

"Ana," I said, "I would be honored."

•

We stood at Ana's kitchen counter making sandwiches. I was on one side and she was on the other. Our fingers were prunes from sitting for so long in the Jacuzzi. Incense was burning from a tiny hole on top of one of the Buddha's heads. The sound of the waves crashing outside was a little louder than Ana's relaxing yoga music. There was no rhythm to that music, but we were working rhythmically anyway. Our own little factory of two. We were quiet for a little while, spreading the peanut butter and adding the top piece of bread and opening the Ziploc, which was the hardest part, and putting the sandwich in and zipping the Ziploc, and I could feel Ana across from me, her movements like a mirror. We tossed our sandwiches into the pile at the exact same time.

I started a new sandwich, but Ana had stopped.

I noted the obvious. "You stopped."

"I just realized something." She looked outside, at the clouds maybe, and then back at me. We were the same height so our eyes were level. "I felt this before, but I wasn't absolutely sure until just now."

"What?"

Her glimmering eyes. "We are kindred spirits."

I hid my joy with a little skepticism. "We are?"

She cocked her head. "How old are you?"

"Forty-eight."

"What!" A look of disbelief. "I just got the chills." She held up her forearm to show me. "*I* am forty-eight."

"So?"

"Don't you see? We are twins, like your boys. We're both forty-eight. Everyone thinks we look alike. And we even have the same freckle on our wrist."

I may have liked that she had noticed this. I had noticed, too, but I never would have told her.

"I'm going to call you Nan from now on. No more Nancy. And don't you see why? Don't you see how the letters of our names match up perfectly? Nan and Ana! Yin and yang!"

She took my sticky hands and drew herself toward me until our foreheads were touching. On the counter: my two pieces of bread, waiting to come together.

Her forehead was hot and maybe pulsing, and she said, "We were meant to find each other for a reason, Nan, and I have a feeling it's a big reason."

At the time, I was sure this reason was as simple as sisterhood. With our foreheads touching like that, I felt so close to her. I felt warm and fuzzy—the same feeling I got sitting in her Jacuzzi. Weeks later, she would say, "If you put a frog in a pot of boiling water, it will jump out. If you turn the water up slowly, it will boil." And even then, I didn't think: Jump. I thought the same thing I thought whenever she spoke, which was: Oh, how interesting.

Water

11

My boys in the pool. There was nothing like watching them. Their young bodies, full of life, never got tired of swimming. When either of them got the ball, I stopped breathing. My heart swelled. A mother's pride.

The ref blew the whistle. The teams sprinted toward each other. A Waverider won the ball. Number 11. Cam stayed back. Defense. Jed sprinted up the side. Number 11 threw the ball to Jed. Yes! Jed caught it. He took a few fast strokes toward the goal. I stood. Chuck stood with me. Jed's arm arced back. He threw the ball hard. It went, went, went—I stopped breathing—and the goalie jumped up—no!—and then—gasp!—it grazed the goalie's fingertips and went in. The ref blew the whistle. Goal! Chuck and I shrieked cheers and bounced with excitement. Together, we held the sign I had laminated last year. GO MURPHY BOYS! In this moment we were a family again.

When the commotion was over, we took our seats in the bleachers with the other Waverider fans. The entire high school had been rebuilt recently, so the bleachers were new and the pool was new and the goals were fresh and white. The blue awning with the WR logo repeating itself along the edges was taut and clean, and the numbers on the scoreboard were crisply visible, even in the glaring sun.

As Brad had said, "Everything is better here." I had clung to this line because I wanted it to be true, and because I wanted it to be true, I was constantly finding evidence to support it, which wasn't hard to do at this pool. It was so much nicer than Clairemont's.

I thought of the water polo moms in San Diego—of how we had a whole system for watching games. It would be four or five of us in the fifth row with three or four of our husbands—Sheila had gotten divorced after her husband cheated—right in front of us in the fourth row. Someone (Dorothy or B) would get there early to stake our claim. Dorothy did it with beach blankets, B did it with cones. Someone else (usually me) brought a cooler full of bottled water and soda and parked it between the husbands and the wives as a centerpiece. I usually brought orange slices, too, which I had a special system for preparing. I would carve the meat of the orange from the rind halfway up each slice so it would be easier for people to eat. This was very time-consuming and, I thought now, such a waste of time.

Today I was perfectly happy sitting in row seven with Chuck. We'd brought one bottled water apiece—this was all we needed. It was also nice to be anonymous. I knew nothing about these parents, and they knew nothing about me. There was so much freedom in that. I could choose to be any type of person, and they would think I had been this type of person all along. So no, I didn't miss my old friends. I was content just observing the barefoot family two rows down eating their KFC from the bucket, and I was content every time I remembered I wouldn't have to strain my back emptying the ice from my huge cooler after this.

"I wish my mom could have been here to see this," Chuck said, touching the brim of his hat.

Chuck's mother, Martha, had come to every one of his games in college. I used to get there late on purpose so I didn't have to sit with her. I liked Martha, but she talked the whole time and asked me too many questions, some of which really weren't appropriate. She always wanted to know if I was experiencing side effects from my birth control, for example.

"What about your mom?" Chuck put his arm around me, kissed my cheek. "Did she watch sports?"

It was a question he may have never asked before, which was rare this far into a marriage. I thought of my mother in her smelly chair. Of how *The Young and the Restless* had been on when she died. If she'd lived long enough to see my boys get to high school, would she have come to a game? She would have wanted to, maybe, but coming to a game would have meant leaving the house, which was very hard for my mother to do, especially near the end. She left only to go to the liquor store or to get her prescriptions refilled. And even those things—near the end, I was doing those things.

"No," I told Chuck, "my mom didn't watch sports. It was always soap operas."

•

After the game we waited for the boys in the parking lot. We leaned on the trunk of their blue Honda and talked about Cam's stellar assists and Jed's powerful arm. He had scored the last goal for a win of 3–2. Jed always scored more than Cam. He was the bold one. He was the star. But Cam had more stamina. He made all the assists. Or not all of them, but many of them. Cam saw the game as a whole, and Jed had a winner's tunnel vision: all he cared about was the goal. That's what Chuck liked to say. He said both ways were good, just different. Now in the parking lot, arms crossed over his chest, looking very pleased, he said it again, with the same enthusiasm as all the other times: "Cam is more analytical than Jed. And Jed is more aggressive than Cam. Both ways are good, just different."

We watched the other Waverider fans filter out to their cars. The KFC family had put their flip-flops on. Coach Iona yelled across the lot, "Hey, Murphy parents! We love your boys!" We waved and yelled, "Thank you! So do we!"

The boys appeared. Their lanky bodies, their loping strides. They walked like such teenagers. Two other boys walked with them. Next to Jed: a smaller Hawaiian boy. I recognized him as number 5. Next to Cam: number 10—he was easy to pick out because he had the palest skin on the team.

"Amazing game," I told them.

"Phenomenal," Chuck said, and gave them high fives.

Number 5 extended a hand to Chuck. "What's up. I'm Liko." He gave a firm shake. "Hi, Mrs. Murphy," he said to me, in an almost provocative tone, as though he may have found me attractive. But no one else seemed to notice, so maybe I was imagining things. Liko smiled—a huge joker smile that took up half his face. His eyes turned into little slits.

"Nice to meet you, Liko," I said pleasantly.

Our eyes turned to number 10. "Hi, I'm Tom," Tom said. His voice was deep and he looked older than a high school kid. He was very attractive and sort of Swedish looking, with fine yellow-white hair and blue-white eyes like glaciers. He shook our hands. His grip was loose and clammy.

"Jed rocked it. He's the king!" Liko jokingly bowed unto Jed.

"Dude, shut up," Jed said bashfully, though I could tell he was loving the attention.

"And Cam, you did a wonderful job," I said. I heard myself and thought: You sound like such a middle-aged mom talking about sports. But fine. Because what else was I supposed to be?

Cam was authentically bashful and looked at his feet. Tom patted the back of his neck. For such a strapping guy, he was kind of gentle. And quiet, because he didn't say anything.

"Wonderful, both of you." Chuck tore off his hat, smacked it against his thigh. "Jed, two goals! Damn. And Cam. Oh man, Cam. So many assists! And what solid defense. You fended those guys off you."

"Fen-ded," Liko repeated, like it was a sexual word. What was wrong with this kid?

"Dude, Liko, shut up," Jed said, and I thought: Yes, please do.

"Can we take you boys out to lunch?" Chuck said. "Anywhere you want." Chuck was trying to be Cool Dad, which was slightly sad and very sweet.

Liko was swinging his arms back and forth and rocking his head a little. Was he dancing?

"Nah, Dad, we're going out with the team," Cam said.

"We normally go to Denny's," Tom offered.

"Okay." Chuck sounded a little deflated, so he tried again. "Have a great time."

Chuck and I bought chicken wraps at Safeway and took them to the park at the Old Airport. Picnicking was something we had done a lot in the beginning of our relationship. We sat at a green picnic table under a tree. I faced the ocean. Chuck faced the mountain. "I can't tell if those are clouds or if it's vog," he said, and took a bite.

"Do you remember how we used to have picnics?" I asked him.

"Of course." Chuck smiled. The lines on his face. The age spots forming at his hairline. He looked so much older now. We both looked so much older now.

Chuck's keychain was on the table. He pulled out the blade of his Swiss army knife.

"What are you doing?"

"Remember when we carved our names into the rocks in Point Loma?" With one stroke he scratched half a heart into the table.

"I remember," I said.

Then he scratched the other half. Inside the heart, he wrote it simply: N + C. The C was the hardest part. It came out looking jagged. "There," he said.

After lunch we looped around the walking path, which was surrounded by a community garden. Sections were divided according to the community groups that had planted them, and were marked with placards. There were succulents and plumeria trees and a tree with strange green orbs floating from its branches. Mongeese dashed across the path in front of us as we walked, always right in front of us like that, as if they'd been waiting to create a brush with disaster— adrenaline junkies. A few roosters had somehow made it up to the limbs of a high tree. Beneath them, feral cats rolled over in the shade. A group of old Japanese men sat in a circle, eating tangerines. Runners ran by. Women in sports bras and sweaty shirtless men. Two ladies power-walking reminded me that I should call Marcy.

One plot—not marked with a placard—had a sculpture on the ground of a dog swimming in a pool. Even with its glossy sheen of paint, meant to invoke life, the dog looked helpless, like it was drowning in cement. Its one big black eye was screaming out for help. But maybe—yes, okay, its paw was very close to the edge of the pool. It was poised for escape. This dog was definitely going to make it.

•

We got back into Sharkie and just sat there for a little while with the seats reclined. This was another thing we used to do in the beginning—just sit in cars for hours like time wasn't a real thing. I thought of Ana, of sitting in her Jeep in the parking lot, of everything I had told her. I still couldn't believe how much I had revealed.

"I'm glad you got this car," Chuck said. He sounded relaxed, sleepy. He took off his hat and put it over his face. He reached for my hand without looking and found it. "And the name Sharkie is funny. Did Ana make that up or did you?"

"*On-a*," I corrected.

"Right, *On-a*."

"We both made it up," I said. Was that true? I couldn't remember now who had said *Sharkie* first.

Palm fronds rocking back and forth in the wind. The sound of waves, of birds.

Chuck yawned. "Jed's game has improved at least ten percent."

I tapped his hand. "I don't like that Liko kid."

"Oh? I thought he was nice."

I almost told Chuck he was a terrible judge of character, but whenever I said this, he reminded me that I was his wife so how bad could his judgment be?

"What did you think of Tom?" I asked.

Chuck contemplated. "He's very tall?"

The thought of asking him felt more comfortable in this position—with us lying back, not looking at each other, the center console between us. Maybe this was why I had revealed so much to Ana. There was something about the solidly front-facing nature of sitting in a car that made honesty easier.

"Chuck?"

"Nancy?"

"Do you think Cam is gay?"

Chuck sighed heavily, which bothered me. "I don't know," he said, "but no, not really. He's sensitive, that's all. But that doesn't mean he is." I could tell Chuck had gone over this in his head just like I had. "Do you think he is?"

"Gay?" I said. "Are you uncomfortable saying that word?"

"No."

"Seems like you might be." I tapped his hand again, coaxing him.

"Well," Chuck shifted in the seat, "okay, maybe a little."

"Would you be upset if your son turned out to be gay?" I was still annoyed by his sigh, but I managed to say this lovingly, with curiosity. Come at your life with curiosity instead of anger. Pema Chödrön had written something like that.

"Honestly?" he asked. "Maybe a tiny bit."

"That's . . ." I wanted to say: That's horrible. But, no, curiosity, not anger. Curiosity, not anger. I settled for: "That's a little upsetting."

"I'll still love him. I just worry it's an obstacle." Chuck un-reclined his chair so he was sitting up again. "Don't you think it might make his life harder?"

I un-reclined my chair. Would it make his life harder? I hated that I thought it might. "Maybe," I said. "But we could never tell him that."

Chuck nodded slowly. "Okay."

"Okay," I said firmly.

He looked at me sideways. "Are we fighting?" His face was adorably worried.

I shook my head in a way that said: Oh, Chuck, I love you. "No," I said, "we're not fighting."

"Good." He put his hand on my knee. "Because I don't want to fight. It's . . ." Chuck squinted at the sky. "It's almost too nice to fight here, isn't it? It's so sunny."

Without thinking, I said exactly what Ana had said to me. I used her intonation and her slightly deeper voice. And for the brief moment it took to say the words, I felt like I was Ana, or like I was becoming Ana, or like Ana had already become an essential part of me.

"Every day is sunny here, Chuck."

12

"Target!"

It was an old man at the intersection. Short white beard, long heavy jacket, bright white shoes. His sign said VETERAN HUNRGY BROKE.

"I've never seen this one before," Ana said, and pulled over.

The car behind us honked. "Sor-ry." Ana waved and hit the emergency lights.

I held out the sandwich for the veteran. "Here you go, sir."

His eyes were bloodshot. Trembling hands. He took the sandwich tentatively. Asked in a shaky voice, "What's in it?"

"Skippy!" Ana exclaimed, leaning over me so her Wynonna hair spilled onto my arm.

"Darnit," he said. The sandwich was shaking in his hand. I thought he might drop it. "I'm allergic to peanuts."

"Oh no." I held out my hand in case he wanted to give it back.

"I'll eat the bread around," he said, looking at the sandwich from a new angle, planning his surgery.

Ana had opened the tub of Red Vines. Sensing what she wanted, I took a few and held them out for him.

The veteran took the Red Vines and smiled. Barely any teeth. A greenish film in his mouth. "I like these."

I was relieved. "Oh good."

"Enjoy!" Ana said, and we drove on.

The basket weaver with the long fingers of a possible former piano player told us his name was Daniel. "And if you don't see me sitting on the wall, I'm probably taking a nap right behind. You can throw it over, yeah?"

"Yeah," I said, "no problem."

Mana at the bus stop, who apparently never took the bus, greeted us before we greeted him. "Sandwich Sistahs!" He raised his brown paper bag in cheers. My throw was better this time. "Mana thanks you!"

At the banyan tree, the boy wearing the backpack glanced both ways like he was about to buy drugs. "Can I get five?" He pointed behind him. "For my friends."

"Absolutely." I counted them out.

"You know who we are?" Ana asked him.

"Some chicks in a Jeep?"

Ana laughed. "Yeah, that, too. But no."

"We're the Sandwich Sisters," I said.

"Sandwich Sistahs, actually," Ana corrected.

"Chill," he said, and zipped up his backpack.

The girl who'd been lying on the sidewalk before—with the sign that simply said HELP—was gone today. Maybe she'd gotten some help.

Marigold and Petunia were fast asleep in the dumpster's shade, their arms looped through the straps of the backpack between them, which they were also using as a pillow. "They crashed," Ana said. I got out of the car and quietly left four sandwiches at their feet.

The parking lots were bustling with targets. Some we recognized, some we didn't. Ana said, "From the Sandwich Sistahs!" to every person. When we ran out of sandwiches, I asked, "What should we do now?"

Ana's answer was to pull into a parking space at Longs. "Let's take pause. We need to sit and be present for a minute." She turned off the engine, looked up at the sky, put her feet on the window ledge. I looked at myself in the little side mirror. Remembered I'd put a plumeria flower behind my ear. Thought: Nancy, you look happy today. And your shoulders look defined.

After our pause, which was brief, we just sat there and talked. Our conversation was endless and flowing and random and marked by long stretches of silence, and the silence was marked by the revving of cars in the parking lot and the country music station playing low on the radio.

.

"It's really nice," I said, "getting to know these people. The locals."

"I just adore our new name." Ana stretched her arms up, which moved her shirt and exposed her stomach. Then she put her head on the center console so her face was looking up at me. Half her legs were dangling out of the car. She affectionately pinched my chin. "Nan," she said.

"Ana," I replied. I took a Red Vine, handed her one. "You know Red Vines are fat-free," I told her, pointing to the FAT FREE on the label.

Ana contemplated her Red Vine. "Whoever invented Red Vines is a genius." She took a bite. "Did you like my quote in class this morning?"

"I did. The Helen Keller one. What was it?"

"Walking with a friend in the dark is better than walking alone in the light," she said, annunciating each word like she had in class. "Honestly, it made me think of you. I don't know what I'd be doing without you, Nan."

"I know," I said, because what would I be doing without Ana? Power-walking with Marcy? Power-walking on my hamster wheel. "I'm so glad we met."

"You're like the stable married mommy version of me," Ana said.

"And you're like the free spirit version of me," I said.

"I want to be more like you." Ana sighed. "Stable." She chuckled. "A homeowner."

"I want to be more like *you*," I said. "You can go anywhere. You can do anything you want without running it by your husband first. You're not tied to anything."

"What's that poem? Two roads diverged at a yellow tree?"

"I think it was a yellow wood," I said.

"Nan, you scholar." Ana kissed her Red Vine and tapped my leg—"Boop!"—like it was a wand.

•

Ana moved to an upright position. She'd made her Red Vine into a flute. A motorcycle roared through the parking lot. When it was gone, I asked, "What was your stripper name?"

"Malificent."

"Wow."

"Does it bother you that I was a stripper?"

"No."

"It does a little though."

"No, it really doesn't," I said. "Because now I know you and like you, so . . ."

"So I could tell you anything and you'd be fine with it?"

"Probably."

•

I slipped off my flip-flops and rested my feet on the dash. Ana braided her hair. Two French braids. It took a while. Then she put her head on the console again. I crossed and uncrossed my legs. We kept changing positions as the sun blazed down. Every thirty minutes Ana reapplied her sunscreen and handed me the bottle when she was done. "You don't want to get haole rot," she said.

"What's that?"

"A skin fungus white people get because they can't handle the sun here."

"Ew." I squeezed more sunscreen into my palm. I would do two layers from now on.

•

We watched people go in and out of Longs. Sometimes we guessed things about them. "I bet that lady has a French bulldog at home," Ana said about a woman who looked exactly like a French bulldog. "I bet he's a mechanic," I said about a scruffy guy with black-oiled hands. Ana said, "I have meaner things to say, but I won't say them.

Because the degree to which we judge others is the degree to which we judge ourselves."

"Wow," I said. I hated that I thought of Marcy then.

•

Ana rolled out the muscles in her neck and when her gaze fell on my feet, she said, "Your second toe is longer than your first. That means you're intelligent." She lifted her foot. Her purple sparkly polish was chipping. "So am I."

•

"I wish I had my cards in here," Ana said in a lazy voice.

"Cards?"

"Tarot. Have you never had your cards read?"

"No."

"What? Why? Don't you want to know what your future holds?"

"No. What if I learn something awful?"

"Well exactly," she said. "You'd want to be ready for it."

•

"Have you ever been married?" I asked her.

"Only four times." She laughed. "So you can see why I have trust issues."

"Do you ever get lonely?"

"I learned a long time ago to own my solitude. If you can own your solitude, it makes you stronger."

Like so many other things Ana said, this just sounded right.

"How's your husband doing?" she asked me.

"He's better. Things are better. I planted a garden."

"Did the garden make things better?"

"Yes," I said, "or no, it was before that. I had—well, it was an epiphany, I guess."

"Tell me. I love epiphanies."

"Oh, I don't know. It will probably sound stupid."

"Tell me, Nan. You know you want to."

That was true. I did want to. So I told her. "And, okay, maybe you had to be there, but I just felt like: Get back on this hamster wheel or change, you know?"

"Oh, girl, I have been there."

"You have?"

"Please. We're all fighting hamster-hood."

•

Ana went into Longs to get us Vitamin Waters. When she came back, I said, "Can I tell you something else?"

"What?"

"I think my son might be gay."

"Cool." She chugged her Dragonfruit. "My first husband was gay."

"He was?"

She went on to tell me that yes, she'd married gay Dave in a blackout at a twenty-four-hour chapel in Vegas. It wasn't love. They were drug buddies. She broke out into hysterical laughter when she explained how they'd tried to sleep together that night—well, later that night, it was technically dawn—and he couldn't get it up. "But," she said, "that experience was what showed him the truth about himself. He was finally able to work through his internalized homophobic Mormon bullshit and face his true self." She touched my arm. "But, Nan, it's easier to be gay these days. What's your son's name?"

"Cam."

"Cam will be fine."

I was almost moved to tears by this obvious and simple reaction: he will be fine. I squeezed her shoulder. "Thank you for saying that. Really."

•

When the volcano update came on the radio, she turned it up.

"This is a civil defense message. This morning's assessment continues to show no advancement of any of the downslope flow areas. All current activity does not pose an immediate threat to area communities."

"Oh good," I said, "maybe that town will be okay."

"Pahoa?" Ana said. "I don't think so. Pele will get it eventually."

"Pele?"

"The goddess of the volcano." Ana turned to me. Seriously, she said, "This is her island, you know. She made this rock. And she can destroy it whenever she wants." She chuckled. "Epic, right?"

I chuckled because she had. But I wasn't sure I agreed with Ana. Because of course the lava could stop flowing. Or it could take a less destructive path. Pahoa might be fine.

·

"If I showed you a picture," Ana said, "just a picture of a landscape with light in the sky, do you think you'd be able to tell whether it was dawn or dusk?"

I thought about that. "Yes," I said. "The light is different."

"Is it?"

"And the feeling is different."

"But it's a picture, so you couldn't feel the feeling."

"But you can. I think you can." Our elbows touched on the center console. "Why are you asking me this?"

"I don't know." She stroked my hand. Then she rested her head there. Her hair was like doll hair. "I'm scared, Nan."

That surprised me. Because Ana seemed so strong. Of the two of us, I had assumed that she was the strong one and I was the one who was trying to be strong like her. "You seem pretty fearless to me."

"I'm not ready to die." She rolled the end of her braid between her fingers. "Even though, honestly, a part of me thinks I deserve to be dead already."

"No one deserves to be dead already." I placed my hand on hers.

She sighed. "If you knew everything about me . . ." She stroked my fingers one by one, and then enough time passed that I realized she wasn't going to finish this sentence.

"What?"

"You wouldn't like me."

I planned to say, No no, I would like you, but I only managed to get out one *no* before Ana bolted back to her upright position and turned the key. "We need to do more good stuff today," she said. "It's urgent."

"But we're out of sandwiches."

"I know." She drove fast out of the parking lot and started up the street.

I tried to stay curious. "Where are we going?"

And then a hitchhiker. She pulled over. This was what she'd been hoping to find. "We'll give him a ride," she whispered.

"I don't know," I whispered back. The guy looked like a friendly hippie—dreadlocks, a thick hemp necklace, a hat that said I LOVE YOU. But still, you never knew with people.

"Two against one," she murmured out the side of her mouth, and then the guy was throwing his sack into the backseat and hoisting himself in, saying, "Up to Magics?" and Ana was saying, "No problem," and I locked my eyes on the little mirror so I could watch his every move. For now he seemed to be enjoying the wind on his face.

"What's your story, man?" Ana asked, glancing in the rearview and pulling the end of her braid.

The guy's story was that he was Brian from Portland and he was here to sell hats. Like the one he was wearing. He took it off and held it between us so we could see. The I LOVE YOU had obviously been handstitched.

"That's an incredible idea!" Ana was fervent. She grabbed my arm. "Yes!"

At Magic Sands we said good-bye and good luck to Brian, and watched him greet the hippie girl—also wearing an I LOVE YOU hat—who was twirling in slow circles in the sand for no apparent reason.

Ana smacked the wheel. "That's what we're going to do."

"What? Make hats?"

"No, we don't have the money for hats. But the idea is good. Saying 'I love you' to people. I mean, right? That's a great idea for a good deed."

"I think 'I love you' might send the wrong message though."

"I see what you mean. We have to change it a little. 'You are great.' No, that's not powerful enough. You are . . . you are . . .'"

"You are loved," I said.

"Genius." Ana rolled her eyes and sighed, pleased. "Nan," she said, "we should win the Nobel Peace Prize. I mean, come on."

We were driving back down Ali'i now, toward Ana's house, where my car was parked. It was four o'clock already. Time to get home and make dinner.

When she pulled into her driveway, I was all ready to say the good-bye things I had prepared a little: Thanks for the wonderful day; I really enjoyed it. And give her a hug and say, "See you soon," and maybe stop at Safeway for milk on the way home because we needed some, but then Ana said, "Come in for a sec?" to which I replied, "Okay, but I can't stay long."

•

We sat on the edge of the Jacuzzi, our feet in the water. We were both still wearing the same outfits we had worn to yoga that morning. It was unlike me to stay in my workout gear all day, but there was something about being slightly dirty that I liked. And I thought: when I was younger, younger and freer, I would often spend full days in a swimsuit, or in my pajamas, or in whatever because it didn't matter that much. I was just going with the flow then.

But I was also thinking about Chuck—he'd be getting off work soon—and the boys—they were probably already home smelling of chlorine and looking for the snacks I hadn't prepared. The orange sun was getting closer to the ocean, and it was probably four fifteen now. "I should leave in about five minutes," I told her.

"Well, that's perfect because I think I just figured out what we should do." She took off her sunglasses. Her eyes, glimmering orange, two little suns. "Okay, just let this sink in before you judge it, okay?"

"Okay."

"I think we should go get some white chalk from Walmart. Fat chalk, not skinny. And then we should write YOU ARE LOVED on the sidewalks in town." Ana squealed, delighted with this plan.

I imagined actually carrying it out. "But people will be walking all over us."

She tapped her finger on her lip. "I know. Obvious! We'll go at night."

Then—the noise of a gong reverberating. It was Ana's phone. She looked at the screen. "Fuck, it's Eunice," she said. And then she picked up and said, "Hey, Eunice!" in the cheeriest voice I'd ever heard.

The sun was dipping lower in the sky. Chuck would be on his way home now. I hoped that he'd stop and get the milk because I might not have time. But he wouldn't think to do that unless I had specifically asked him to, which I had not. When Ana got off the phone, I would tell her I had to leave.

"Uh-huh, uh-huh," she was saying, her voice still chipper. This was followed by a disappointed "Oh," and then she put her whole hand over her neck and pretended to strangle herself. "I understand," she said coolly. "Okay, thank you, Eunice. Good-bye."

She hung up. "Fuck. She's fucking selling the fucking house." Ana slumped out of her straight-backed yoga posture and let her head fall forward. "She's putting the ad up tomorrow."

I cringed for her. "I'm sorry, Ana."

She tugged her braids. She was distraught. "This is bad." And then—woosh!—she whipped her braids over her shoulders, which changed the tone. "But you know what? I sensed some hesitation in her voice." She looked up at the clouds, but only for the briefest second because she already knew what she wanted to find. "If she's putting the ad up tomorrow, that means we need to do the sidewalk thing tonight. It has to be tonight. Maybe that will stop her."

Carefully, I said, "That seems"—I paused, looking for a gentler word than *nonsensical*—"well, it seems a little nonsensical."

"It seems insane, I know. But I'm floundering, Nan. What am I going to do? I feel I need to take some action here."

"I understand," I said, though I didn't, not exactly.

"I'm just—fuck! I just—it just feels like a real *need,* you know? I *need* to do some good right now. At least *try* to change the course of things. Damn. I wish I had thought of this earlier." She touched her heart and tears welled in her orange eyes. "Like in my twenties."

It was a little awkward getting to her. I had to take small steps along the Jacuzzi bench so the water wouldn't splash up on me too much. I sat beside her, put my arm around her shoulders, and that's when she began to cry. At first it was a slow pulsing sob, and then she cried harder and harder and then it seemed like the act of crying was making her cry and then she was crying so hard I thought this couldn't possibly be all about the house. It was about everything now, just everything in general.

"Sshh sssh," I comforted. It took me a second to realize I was rocking her. I was such a mom, even when I wasn't trying to be.

When she was all cried out, she wiped her wet face on my shoulder. She looked like the saddest woman in the world. In a small voice, with her eyes so expectant, she asked, "Will you please do this with me tonight, Nan?"

•

"The boys aren't coming home either," Chuck said over the phone. "Team dinner. I'll just"—I could see him in the living room, putting his hand on his waist—"stay here. Do we have"—I could see him walking into the kitchen, opening the fridge, noting the vegetables I'd planned to cook for a Thai-inspired stir-fry—"hmmm."

I was sitting on Ana's low couch, picking at my toenail polish and watching her do a headstand. "You could cook those veggies," I said.

"That seems like a lot of work." I heard the fridge door close. "I don't think I'm in the mood to cook."

I am often not in the mood to cook, Chuck, but I do it anyway. "Maybe you could order something."

"Let's order in," Ana whispered.

I nodded.

"Or maybe," Chuck said, "it *is* pool night. Maybe I'll go down there and say a quick hello to the team. I can eat there."

"You can eat there," I repeated, not really paying attention. Ana's face was red now. Upside down, she looked like a different person—still pretty, but her cheeks were in the wrong place. I had chipped a good-sized red piece of polish off my toenail. I told myself to stop chipping. I couldn't just leave the chip on her couch, so I put it in my pocket.

"I'll just eat there then," Chuck said. I could see him walking toward the closet now with plans to change his clothes. "See you later?"

"Yes," I said, "have a nice time."

"Love you, Nance."

"Love you, Chuck."

Ana lowered her legs slowly to the floor in one piece, which was impressive. "You're so fortunate, Nan," she said, adjusting her wig. "You have a husband who loves you and children who adore you and a house with a garden up on the cool mountain. You are constant and dependable and your life is beautifully ordered."

"You," I said, "have no attachments and total freedom and you don't have to cook for anyone."

"I never cook," Ana said absolutely.

"Never?"

"No," she said, setting her chin on her knee. "Cooking gives me zero joy."

I laughed.

"Here's a question: do you *like* cooking?"

"I mean, sometimes. But I always cook. It's part of my job. I have to."

"You *have* to?"

"Well, I don't *have* to have to, but, yeah, I kind of have to."

"I don't do anything I don't want to do," Ana said. "I follow my instincts." She squinted her eyes and nodded. "It's like that Ana Gersh quote. 'I am a lamp to myself. I am my own confidence. I hold the truth within myself as the only truth.'"

13

Chuck poured the coffee. I took the milk out of the fridge. The single-sized plastic bottle of milk that definitely wasn't organic—it was all they'd had at the gas station.

We had a rule. No talking until the first sip of coffee. I added my milk, and while he added his, I ran my hand over his poufy bed hair. Then we sipped.

"How was your night?" I asked him.

He kissed me on the forehead, wrapped his hand around my waist. "It was fun," he said. "Dylan is *good* at pool. So is Brad. Oh, and Brad said Marcy's waiting for you to call her, by the way."

"I know. I've been meaning to." I stretched my arms up. My back felt sore. I had known it would. Bent over the sidewalk, writing YOU ARE LOVED for the thirtieth or fortieth time—I lost count—I had thought: Nancy, your back is going to be sore tomorrow. "Did you win?"

"We lost." He joke-frowned. "I forgot how bad I am at pool."

This was true. Chuck was terrible at pool. I didn't respond.

"I want to get better. You should see these guys. I mean, really complicated shots."

I stretched my neck while Chuck peeled a banana.

"What did you eat?" I asked.

"Mozzarella sticks and chicken wings."

I would hold myself back. I would not scold him. At least he was eating a banana now.

"What about you? I didn't even hear you come in. How was your night with Ana?"

"On-a."

"Right, *On-a*."

"It was fun."

"Yeah? What did you do?"

Writing on sidewalks sounded like lunacy without a long explanation, and I was too achy for that right now, so I kept it simple. "We ordered Thai food and talked. I held her snake."

"She has a snake?"

"I mean lizard. Shit. Lizard."

Chuck didn't seem to care about the difference, which meant he hadn't come across the no-snakes law in his Hawaii research. "Lizard, huh?" He took a bite of his banana. "What did you two talk about?"

Our plans for writing on sidewalks while Ana played with my hair because she still missed hers so much. "Yoga," I said, "and just, you know, how to be better people in the world." I felt a little bad for lying to Chuck, so I reminded myself it wasn't really lying. A small omission. It barely counted. Later, when I felt less sore and more awake, I would explain the whole thing.

"Better people in the world," Chuck repeated. "That's big. Do you have any tips for me?" He winked. "About how to be a better person in the world?"

"Well," I put my hands around my mug—we needed new mugs, maybe smaller ones like Ana's, because why were ours so huge?— "yes. My tip is: Don't do anything you'll regret later."

Right after the words had left my mouth, I realized the problem. The problem was that this implicated Shelly. Chuck seemed to pick up on it, too. He shifted his weight and said, "I won't do anything I'll regret ever again, Nance."

"I won't either, I hope," I said quickly. And then to make light of it: "I'll never buy this shitty milk again."

That made him smile.

"Come here," I said, and he leaned over the counter and I kissed his banana lips.

•

After he left, I spent a relaxed morning stretching on the lanai and eating oatmeal and watering the garden. One slim green sprout had sprung from the earth, but I couldn't remember which vegetable it belonged to. That was fine. It would be a surprise. My blog was all about watercress today. "Watercress Peanut Stir-Fry = 2 Die 4 x 8!" I would make that for dinner. Cooking would be fun if I reinvented what I was cooking.

When I had nothing left to do, I called Marcy back. "Oh, I'm so glad you called me today!" She sounded thrilled. "The lei-making class starts in a few hours. Will you come? Say yes."

I had no plans for the rest of the day. And the empty house, which I'd been happy to have to myself since Chuck had left for work, seemed dangerously empty when I imagined the hours ahead. "Okay," I said, "I'll meet you there."

•

The loud-shirted women and their screaming flowers were a manic outburst in the sterile, air-conditioned room. They sat at a long plastic table in the high-ceilinged Activity Den of the community center. They were all old, and their floral shirts were all different but all the same. The table was covered in mounds of flowers separated by color. Every color of the rainbow was represented. Oranges and purples and yellows and pinks and something fuzzy and green.

Marcy had an outburst when she saw me come in. "Nanceeeee!"

A few women looked up, looked me over. Black spandex crops, black top. I had decided not to change because I had decided I felt more active when I stayed in my active clothes all day.

"I saved you a seat." Marcy gave me a one-second hug—she smelled like Aqua Net—and pulled the chair out for me.

"Nancy, this is"—and then she said all of their seven or eight names, and the only two I retained were Auntie Moleka (because she was the teacher) and Holly (because she was the woman Ana and I had seen at Longs—the one who probably owned a French bulldog).

"How have you been? It's so great you came." Marcy smiled with her whole face. Her teeth were yellow and boxy and very small, and her pink floral shirt brought out the pink in her cheeks.

"Thanks for inviting me," I said, scooting in closer. I had arrived a relaxed seven minutes late, and the women were already working. Marcy must have arrived early, because she was halfway done with her first lei.

"Here," she said, "I knotted one off for you." She placed a threaded needle in front of me with care. "So that's it. Just add flowers."

"Thanks." I sat there for a second, contemplating my choices. Was this something I was going to spend a lot of time and attention making, or was I just going to put some flowers on a string? The red flowers at the far end of the table near Auntie Moleka looked nice, but no, it was too much effort to get up. I would just put some flowers on a string. I picked a plumeria from the heap in front of me.

"Good choice," Marcy said, tugging her yellow flower down her string in little jolts. "And hey, I like your nails. Purple *and* sparkles? How fun. Did you go back to the salon?"

Flashback to Ana painting them last night, flashback to Portico wrapping herself around the nail polish bottle and Ana saying, "Portico, you always want what's mine."

I settled on a half-lie. "I did them at home."

"An ancient tradition!" Auntie Moleka boomed in a raspy voice. She had a thick Hawaiian accent—not full pidgin, but almost there, not that I fully understood what qualified as pidgin—and at least four double chins. "There is no replacement for a real Hawaiian lei! Artificial flowers? Nah." She held up her lei for us to see. "You see this, lei makers? Tight flowers. You gotta make it tight. Pull your flowers all the way down. No loosey-goosey. And color! You see these colors?" Red flowers and white flowers and some of the green fuzzy things. She laughed to herself—until that made her cough, and then she was batting her chest and fumbling for her Sprite. When she had recuperated, she pushed her small wire-framed glasses up her big nose. "It looks like a Christmas lei, yeah?"

Holly the French bulldog owner said, "Festive," and the woman in purple groaned, "The stems are so annoying," and the slight woman across from me encouraged herself: "Okay, I can do this."

"She's a third-generation lei maker," Marcy whispered to me. "Fan-tas-tic woman."

Wow, I mouthed, and looked at Auntie Moleka, who was popping open a plastic container of either potato or macaroni salad—I was too far away to tell the difference.

Marcy worked diligently, sitting forward in her chair. I worked in a relaxed fashion, sitting back. Every once in a while, Auntie Moleka offered more gems of third-generation lei-making wisdom. "Stab in the centah!"

Marcy, unprompted, went ahead and told me everything that was on her mind. She raved about Brad's pool skills—"He's *fab*ulous at geometry; that's why he's so good"—and said Brad was just *thrilled* that Chuck had decided to join the team. And wasn't the name Tide Poolers so clever? In other news, she'd found the perfect hat at Hilo Hattie's—with a floral pattern, of course, "to get into the spirit of aloha." And she'd discovered a shortcut from the main road to the beach that didn't even exist on Google Maps. As far as mulberry pie, she planned to bake her own from now on because going down south—it was just too much to ask. On the subject of food, Marcy missed her California burritos and had heard of a Mexican place in town called Pancho & Lefty's that was supposed to be just "fantastic" and we should go there after this. I was starving and said, "Sure."

I listened to her and passively agreed with everything she said— "Mmm-hmm, mmm-hmm"—while stabbing my needle through the centah of my plumerias. I'd added a few orange flowers because they were within reach. I liked that Marcy kept talking because it meant I didn't have to. Her voice was like a distant whir. I could tune in and out as I pleased. The things she was saying and her animated way of saying them—the true delight with which she delivered, "And then I found the *per*fect hat!" for example—reminded me of Sheila and Donna and the rest of the water polo moms in San Diego, who also found inexplicable pleasure in the minute details of their uneventful lives.

Marcy started a new lei while I continued to work on this one slowly. Getting to the knot-it-off part would include asking how to knot it off, and I wasn't ready for that yet, so I just kept adding flowers, making them as tight as possible.

While Marcy told me about the astounding difference in price between the beef at Island Naturals and the beef at KTA, I eyed the other women and thought they were homely. And very serious about their leis—almost sadly serious, because this was obviously the highlight of their day. I may have felt a little superior knowing it would not be the highlight of mine. I may have noted that my laid-back position in the chair and my who-cares workout attire suggested I had a life beyond stringing flowers. I may have also noted that everyone at the table had covered their flabby middle-aged arms with distracting floral fabrics while my shoulders were proudly exposed.

"And then I found a centipede!" Marcy widened her small eyes. She had moved on from the beef monologue.

"Oh," I said, feigning a little concern. "What did you do with it?"

"I killed it," she said. "I sprayed it with Febreze until it died."

Flashback to last night: Ana capturing a roach in a tissue and setting it free outside. I had said, "You didn't kill it?" And she had said, "Hello. Karma?" She'd then told me that according to Buddhism, every life is worth the same amount. All her little Buddha figurines were looking at me from their perches, and I had thought: Is that true?

"I try to put my centipedes outside," I informed Marcy politely. This wasn't true. I'd never even seen a centipede, but I had heard they could be the length of your forearm here. "You know, because it might be bad karma to kill them."

Marcy pulled her lips back. "Oh."

"Anyway," I cleared my throat, "that's what Buddhists think."

"Are you a Buddhist?"

"No." I laughed. A few months ago, no one would have asked me this. "I'm not anything."

"I used to be Catholic," Marcy recalled, maybe a little sourly, "but now I'm not anything either."

•

From the terrace at Pancho & Lefty's, I could see the work Ana and I had done from a more expansive view. YOU ARE LOVED, YOU ARE LOVED, YOU ARE LOVED. The ones I had written were all caps.

Ana's were cursive and sometimes embellished with a smiley face or a star. They were disappearing already under everyone's footsteps, which was a shame. I wondered if enough people would notice before they disappeared completely. And then a tourist took a picture—of one of mine—and I rubbed my lips together to stop myself from smiling because I didn't want Marcy to ask me what I was smiling about. I stretched my arms up. My back still hurt, but it was a satisfying kind of pain.

Marcy ordered her California burrito, and I ordered a mahi-mahi burrito. I couldn't help myself. After she had said, "I hope they put lots of French fries in," I said, "Look. Someone wrote YOU ARE LOVED all over the sidewalks."

Marcy peered over the railing. "Oh yeah."

I rubbed my lips together again, enjoying the present moment with the sun on my arms.

Marcy's burrito turned out to be mostly French fries—"Be careful what you wish for!"—and my burrito was maybe the worst burrito I had ever had in my entire life. I ate part of it anyway because I was so hungry. Marcy resorted to just eating the fries, dipped in guacamole.

I pretended to care about the view of the ocean, but really I was looking at the people down on the sidewalk, waiting for someone else to take another picture so I could tell Ana I'd seen at least two people doing that. I turned Marcy's whir to a low volume—she was talking about her oven now—and leaned my head farther over the railing because I thought a man in a fisherman's hat might be fishing a camera out of his bag. And then there was a change in the atmosphere. It took me a second to realize that Marcy had stopped talking. And she was looking at me. And I was looking at her. And she still wasn't saying anything, which was unlike her.

Casually, I said, "Ovens are frustrating when they don't work."

"Is yours not working?"

"No. It is."

"So is mine. It's brand-new. It's given me no trouble at all."

"Oh." I grabbed my water glass. "I must have misunderstood you."

Marcy moved her sunglasses up so they became a headband. I may have heard the crackling sound of her Aqua Net hair. She rubbed her small eyes. "I know I talk a lot," she said, and set her hands on her pink cheeks. "I'm sorry if it's too much."

I was stunned at this reveal of Marcy's self-awareness. "No, no, it's—"

"You don't have to do that, Nancy. You don't have to make me feel better. It's fine. I talk a lot when I'm feeling insecure, that's all."

Again, stunned. "I understand," I said, paying real attention now because inside Marcy's Stepford Wife chest a real heart was beating. "I do that sometimes, too."

"Really?" she said, not believing me. "You don't seem like the type who does that."

"Okay fine, maybe I don't. I'm pretty quiet. But I still understand."

"Honestly?" she said. "I hate getting to know people. It's so hard, isn't it?"

I laughed. "It can be, yes."

"I left a lot of good friends in San Diego." Her eyes went distant, thinking of them. "I was comfortable in San Diego."

I nodded.

"Here, ugh." She put her sunglasses back on. "All the street signs look the same, don't they? Because the Hawaiian alphabet only has twelve letters. I can't pronounce anything. Thank God for GPS or I would be lost all the time. And I spend so much time alone here. I'm not used to it."

I remembered how Marcy had described her journey down the Pig Trail. "And you're all alone in the forest," she had said. I may have brought it up so she would know that I did, in fact, pay attention to her sometimes. "Like when you went on the Pig Trail," I said.

She shivered at the mention, braced herself like she was really cold. "I still haven't been back there."

"Well," I said, "it must be an adjustment, too, with your daughter at college now. And Brad working so much. This is a big transition, being here. It's scary. But you'll be okay." When I said that, I realized I was speaking to both of us. This is a big transition, Nancy, but you'll be okay. Nancy, Nance, Nan, you will be okay.

"I don't even know who I am here. I think I'm having a midlife crisis."

"I know how you feel," I told her. "But really, you will be okay."

When the waiter brought the check, Marcy pulled up the calculator on her phone to figure out who owed what. Two months ago, this is exactly what I would have done. "Let's just split it down the middle," I suggested, and slapped my credit card on the black booklet with ease.

Marcy spent a few beats considering this new approach. Then she shrugged and said, "Okay, I guess that's easier."

And then, feeling high—I was showing someone a better way to live, even if it was only in this small way—I added, in my least condescending tone, "You know, Marcy, if you can own your solitude, you might start to feel stronger."

Marcy frowned. And then I frowned. Because again, I knew I was speaking to both of us. The thought that I was not above Marcy killed my high and sank me fast. I couldn't even look at her.

So I looked down instead.

The black booklet, the white check. The two identical blue Amex cards, and I couldn't tell which one was mine.

14

I don't feel lonely here, I thought, as I marched deeper into the forest. I don't feel scared here, I thought, when I heard something living brush through the leaves and quickened my pace. They're just shoes, I thought, when the path turned to mud. It's just silence, I thought, when I stopped to tie my muddy shoe and heard no cars and no dogs and no people and no sound in the world beyond the ringing of crickets. When I got to the end, there was a gate. I touched the metal—a tangible "you made it." And then I hurried back down the path—the way back is always faster, the way back is always faster. When I reached the opening—finally, the opening out of the dense leaves—I looked past the white car and thought, Where's the van? And then I laughed. I had to laugh at myself. A silly mistake, it meant nothing. Nancy! The van is gone. This is your white car. Your white convertible Sharkie. When I got in—ah, it felt so good to sit down and ah, these leather seats—I breathed in deeply and felt proud. I had done it. I had walked the Pig Trail alone. As I drove home, I reminded myself to fully enjoy the recently unwrapped mango scent that permeated my brand-new used car. It was intoxicatingly fresh.

15

I abandoned the watercress stir-fry. I didn't feel like dealing with a recipe. I cooked the easiest, fastest thing, which was a box of five-minute rosemary quinoa and some broccoli steamed in the microwave. I knew Chuck and the boys would want more than that, so I also zapped some Poppers.

"Boys, please set the table!" I called. They were watching TV with their long legs all over the place. When they didn't answer, I said it again—"Bo-oys!"—and walked over to them, annoyed that they were forcing me to be so annoying. They heard me coming and put their feet on the floor. "Hello! TV? Don't you have homework?"

"We did it already," Cam said. He was blinking a lot. So was Jed. Bloodshot eyes. Was that the chlorine or—they did look a little dumb. Their limbs were heavy on the couch. Heavier than usual? Were they stoned? I wasn't in the mood to ask. Terrible that sometimes, as a parent, the easiest thing to do is to ignore the problem. I would make up for this later by searching their rooms.

"Mom, you're blocking the TV," Jed said, straining his neck.

"Please come set the table." I pushed the Off button on the imaginary remote in my hand.

Cam obligingly pushed the real Off button, and Jed said, "Oh man! He was about to do a triple flip!"

"Well," I said, "if he can do it once, he can do it again." God, I sounded like such a mother. Or a grandmother. Suddenly my back hurt again.

Chuck had called to say he'd be late. Paperwork. I let the boys eat while I took a quick shower. I still had mud all over my legs. Washing it off reminded me of my accomplishment. I had walked the Pig Trail alone.

I lathered myself with double the usual amount of soap. Paperwork, he had said. And yes, my mind had gone immediately to Shelly. But not the real Shelly—a new version of Shelly here in Hawaii who loved to help the boss with paperwork. Maybe she was even Hawaiian. No, more likely that she'd be blond again. Chuck had a thing for blondes—he was always pointing out the "perfectly symmetrical bone structure" of Sharon Stone or Charlize Theron or some other blond actress. Five years ago, when we'd begun to drift, I got blond highlights, which made me look like a teenybopper, and which didn't fix things. I scrubbed my legs harder with the loofah and reminded myself to get a grip. Be present, Nance. And get a grip. Things are going well with Chuck. He's not going to cheat on you again. At least tonight, he's not. It's too soon.

By the time Chuck got home—"Honey, I'm home!" he Ricky Ricardo'd—the boys had finished everything but the broccoli (I'd overcooked it), and I was eating the overcooked broccoli anyway at the computer, reading my blog. ("Maple-Adobo Tostadas = 2 Die 4 x 15!")

I got up to kiss him, and really to hunt for traces of perfume on his person. I detected none. "How was paperwork?"

"Good," he said in a believable tone, and then he went on to explain the glitch with the payroll system at Costco and how he planned to remedy it, which sounded real. And anyway, I could tell when Chuck was lying, and he wasn't lying now.

The boys were back at the TV, rapt by a snowboarder cutting through a half tube of ice.

Chuck plucked a limp piece of broccoli from Cam's plate. He looked at my plate by the computer. "Looks like everyone's doing their own thing tonight."

"No, no." I stood up. "We'll sit at the table with you." When the boys didn't move, I said, "Now," and they got up and shuffled to the table with hanging heads, and crawled into the chairs on either side of their father. I microwaved Chuck's plate for a minute and brought it to him, and sat down with what was left of my meal.

Jed took out his phone, and Chuck said, "Please, no phones at dinner." Then he winked at me—go, Team Parents!—and took a bite of Popper. He had trouble chewing. The Popper was tough from the microwave. But he didn't complain. He did the work and chewed and asked the boys about practice, and right as Cam began a story about the goalie—"He's really good, but he got suspended, so we don't—" my phone rang.

I got up. Jed, mocking his father's order, said in an ogre voice, "No phones at dinner."

"I'm just going to see who it is." On the screen: ANA. "I'll just be a sec," I said, and made my way out to the lanai.

I barely had time to finish my "Hello?" before Ana said, "Nan. You are not going to believe this."

"What."

"Eunice didn't post the ad. She postponed it!"

"Really?" I was so happy for her. A wave of relief washed through my body, as if I were the one who'd been granted more time in the house. "That's wonderful."

"It means our plan is working." I could hear her clapping. "What are you doing right now? Want to come over?"

"Oh, I wish I could, but I can't."

She chuckled. "The chains of domestic life."

I complied with a little "ha," though I didn't find it very funny. "I'll call you soon," I said.

"Bye, soul sister."

"Bye."

"Bye. I always like to be the last one to say good-bye. So bye." She hung up.

When I walked back into the house, my family was silent and staring at me. "What's going on?" I asked in a way that suggested my answering *one* phone call during dinner was not a big deal.

"We paused the conversation and waited for you," Chuck said sincerely.

"Oh, thanks, hon," I said. I only ever called him "hon" when he irritated me.

"Anyway," Cam said quickly, "the goalie got suspended, so he probably won't be able to play in the next two games."

"Shame," Chuck said, drinking more water to get the Poppers down.

Then we went around the table and said what we had done that day. This was a Murphy family tradition. Everyone but Chuck kept it brief. Cam: "I went to school." Jed: "I went to school and practice and watched a bomb snowboarder rip it up until the TV got turned off." (Chuck and I exchanged a look of parental frustration.) I said, "I went to a lei-making class with Marcy, and then I walked on a trail." Chuck thought that was "marvelous" and then explained the parts of his day like it was a slideshow: this is where I parked, this is where I ate my lunch, this is how we plan to stock product more efficiently, and this is why that's important. He maintained his upbeat attitude the whole time, speaking with such energy about the ins and outs of his job, happily unaware that he had lost his audience back at "I found a great new parking spot around the side, much closer to the employee entrance." Jed and Cam kept yawning—were they stoned or just tired?—while I diligently encouraged Chuck with, "Wow," and "That's great," and his just used "Marvelous."

The boys didn't want dessert—did this mean they were not stoned?—and so yes, they could be excused after they cleared the dishes. While Chuck showered, I cleaned up everything else and thought about how the night before—Thai takeout, yoga poses on Ana's floor, touching a snake for the first time, writing on sidewalks—had been so very different from tonight's domestic chains. But, this—me hovered over the sink, my hands plastered inside my yellow dishwashing gloves—was only part of me now. I had another life. A secret life. A life just for Nancy. And knowing this made scrubbing the Popper barnacles off the plate much more bearable.

•

We made love with Chuck on top because my back hurt. Chuck thrust energetically. I closed my eyes and concentrated on matching his energy. I could do that. I could meet him halfway. And I did, and it got better. When we were done, we whispered "I love you"s. Then Chuck had to use the bathroom. So I got up and brushed my teeth. I straightened the sheets. I grabbed from the floor the one pillow that had fallen. We put on our pajamas. At 3:00 a.m. I woke up in a puddle of Chuck's drool and moved to the far side of the bed.

16

By the eleventh week in Hawaii, I had lost thirteen pounds. I'd taken to wearing my active gear all the time—I just knew that had something to do with it. Ana had given me some of her old yoga clothes—really nice stuff—and Chuck had bought me a three-pack of Costco camisoles. ("Look"—he pointed to the words written across the model's stomach—"Ideal for stretching.") It was a very nice gesture, although size small was still too small for me, and probably always would be.

I had switched my hair products to Aveda—Ana's suggestion; that was the brand she used to use when she had hair—and now my brittle hair was supple, just as she had promised. I hadn't become a vegetarian, but I was eating a lot less meat. Mostly I ate vegetables. Not from the garden, because the garden was still just a rectangle of soil (my lone sprig had gone missing), but from the farmers' market in town. The very nice vendors didn't know my name quite yet, but the way they said "You!" or "Lady!" or "Mango green bean lady!" meant that they knew who I was.

Chuck and I agreed the boys were still adjusting normally, although they had ditched school one day to go surfing, and I was now positive they were smoking pot because I'd found a baggie in Cam's underwear drawer. But we agreed that ditching a little school—only three periods—and smoking a little pot—the baggie had been tiny—were normal things for teenage boys to do. It could have been a lot worse.

After their ditch day, we had a sit-down family meeting. Gently, so as not to push them away, we reminded them that school was important and marijuana was illegal. Yes, we did understand the pressures of high school, but these were just the facts. I lost some Cool Parent points when I blurted out, "I bet Liko smokes pot." Cam glanced at Jed—he's *your* friend—and Jed rolled his eyes at me. Then Chuck, in an effort to win back the points I had lost us, added in his buddy-buddy way, "The thing is, boys, pot lowers your sperm count," to which Jed confidently said, "Well, so does Mountain Dew," and Cam echoed, "It's true," and then Chuck, despite himself, asked, "Really?"

We thought that loosening the leash might have the reverse-psychology effect of making them want to be at home more, so we told them that yes, if their homework was all done, they could skip family dinner and go out with their friends a few nights a week. So far, this plan wasn't working, and they went out as often as they could get away with it, which was often.

Chuck was working late regularly now, and he was also spending two nights a week shooting pool with the Tide Poolers. The team was getting more competitive. Marcy had even gotten them some shirts. White on red—same coloring as Costco, since most of the guys on the team worked there. I hadn't returned Marcy's calls since the day of the lei-making class, but I had, because I was a nice person, texted her an excuse: *I'm SO busy. Hope you're well.*

It wasn't that I hated cooking like Ana did, but I resented that it felt forced upon me. I needed a break. Plus the boys didn't enjoy my new healthy food, so if Chuck wasn't going to be home, I gave them dinner money and let them go out. This won me tons of Cool Parent points.

I spent a few evenings alone, enjoying the hum of the crickets and the kissing noise of geckos, and trying not to turn on the TV. It wasn't that I felt lonely on those nights. No, not at all. It was more that I felt that if everyone else in my family is out, having fun, I should go out and have fun.

So Ana and I started a new tradition. On Chuck's busy nights, I would leave dinner money on the counter for the boys and we would meet around five for Evening Activities. That's what we called them.

Sometimes she would take me somewhere new: the saltwater pool at Kona by the Sea, the blowhole at NELHA, the hidden beach past the mangroves at the end of the harbor. Most of the time, we did "Books and Natch," which meant going to the used bookstore and then to Island Naturals, the Hawaiian Whole Foods equivalent, sort of, but smaller. We'd plate up our dinners at the healthy buffet and eat at the outside tables as the sun set.

If it was a new moon or a full moon, we would find somewhere to lie down and enjoy that. Either we'd go to one of the beaches or we'd just sprawl out on the still-warm hood of her Jeep, eating Red Vines and talking about how the sky in Hawaii had so many more stars than the sky on the mainland. Ana preferred the full moon—she said it gave her power—and I liked the new moon better. The blankness of those all-dark skies was full of possibility.

At yoga—and, I hoped, in life—I was becoming much more flexible. I could reach my toes in a forward bend now. I could also do an unassisted jump back, which was just exhilarating.

The week Patty's cat Marbles finally lost the battle and died, Ana dedicated the class to him, and Patty cried and used her MARBLES shirt as a tissue. The sight of his whiskery face may have made her cry harder. No one made the joke that Patty had lost her Marbles, even behind her back, because we were good people who did yoga and believed in the strength of kindness and compassion above all things. That was how Ana phrased it, in her soothing yoga teacher voice: "We are yogis. We believe in the strength of kindness and compassion above all things."

Sara Beth had officially fallen for this new guy she was dating, and we were all so happy for her, and Kurt was his usual warm and wonderfully shirtless self. I felt a little bad for wishing sometimes that Chuck were more like Kurt—a man with perfect teeth who cared about the state of his aging body. But this, I knew, was completely normal. A person was allowed to have her fantasies as long as she didn't act on them.

After class, Ana and I melted our hard-worked bodies into the Jacuzzi and talked and talked. Ana would rest her head on the plastic edge and look up at the pink house and be constantly amazed that

Eunice still, somehow, had not posted the ad. "We are outsmarting the universe, Nan," she said one overcast morning, and blew a kiss into the wind.

We had our sandwich deed down to a science. Thirty sandwiches was the perfect number. We started getting the ingredients—a two-pack of Love's bread, a two-pack of Skippy, and a three-pack of Ziplocs—at Costco with my discount. The amount of money was a small price to pay for how great we felt to be the Sandwich Sistahs. People were really counting on us now. We went Monday through Friday at the same time—noon—while blasting what Ana called "our soundtrack," which was "Lean on Me," played on repeat. Our targets loved that. "We all need somebody to le-ean on." Their heads danced instinctively to the catchy rhythm, and the ones who were more awake sang along.

After sandwiches, if we were up for it, we picked up a few hitchhikers and took them to their destinations, or closer to their destinations if their destinations were very far. Our hitchhikers were mostly young nomadic guys. Some of them—the cleaner ones—reminded me of the boys. One—Teddy, who worked in construction—had the same striking dish-detergent-blue eyes the boys had inherited from Chuck. When he got out of the car at Matsuyama's, Ana said, "He was a stud. I should have slept with him. That would be a good deed, right?" I was appalled. "No," I said, and she slapped my knee and said, "Nan! I'm kidding!"

One day Ana went into Longs to get us Vitamin Waters and came out with those and something else she had tucked under her shirt. "Nan," she said, hovering her hand over the mysterious package pressed between her tank top and her stomach, "I have found an object." She took off her buggy sunglasses and then she took off my boxier sunglasses with one cool sweep of her hand. "This object officially binds us forever," she said, removing the package slowly from under her shirt. Then she stopped. "Wait." She pressed Play. The familiar beat of "Lean on Me." And then she whipped out the package—said "ooh" because maybe it had scratched her stomach on the way—and held it up for me to see. "Yin and yang friendship necklaces." Yes, that's what they were. One black, one white, their apostrophe shapes dangling from thin silver chains. "Now for the important part." She opened the package and held the necklaces, one in each hand. "Who do you want to be?" she asked. "The black one or the white one?"

White was the obvious choice. I was the pure housewife. Ana was the rebel.

"Black," I said.

"A surprise," Ana said, tilting her face to the sun. "I love surprises."

She put the black one around my neck. "Connected." She clasped it.

Without words, I followed her in this little ceremony. "Connected," I said, clasping the white one around all her orange hair.

·

Chuck and I met at the green picnic table for date night. When I pulled up in Sharkie, I saw that he had covered our N + C engraving with a patterned plastic tablecloth And, as I walked toward the table—where was Chuck?—I saw he'd set a bouquet of peach-colored roses between our Costco meals. Oh, Chuck. He'd chosen a chicken bake for himself (of course) and a Caesar salad for me (of course), and he'd neatly arranged the plastic cutlery on napkins I recognized as being the ones from the dispensers in the Costco food court. The tablecloth was patterned in schools of orange fish swimming in a navy blue sea, and Chuck had smartly added beach rocks to the corners so it wouldn't blow away. Its hanging edges made crumpling sounds in the breeze.

"Nance!" Chuck called, emerging from the bathroom. He did a funny little twirl, which at first I thought was part of a grand hello until I saw his elbow jerk and realized that no, he had turned away from me to zip his fly.

We sat the same way we had sat last time, with Chuck facing the mountain and me facing the sea. I had trouble prying the plastic casing off my salad.

"Here," Chuck said, "let me get that for you," and yanked it apart.

I speared my romaine leaves. The salad was good, same as it always was. I wondered how many Costco Caesar salads I had eaten in my life.

"How many chicken bakes do you think you've eaten in your life?" I asked Chuck.

"In total?" He wiped his mouth. "Well, I usually have one a week. We'll say two, though, because in the beginning, I had three or four a week. So two times a week for fifteen years. Fifty-two weeks in a year times two is one-oh-four times fifteen is about fifteen hundred." A look of disbelief. "Wow."

"Wow." I changed the subject. "How was pool? You played late last night."

"I'm getting better." He raised his eyebrows. "A lot better."

"Well"—I speared—"you should invite me to one of your games so I can see you play."

After a moment of hesitation, and a quick glance at the nearest palm tree, Chuck cautiously said, "Yeah."

"You don't sound very excited about me coming, hon."

"No, I'm sorry, I just didn't think you'd want to come. But you should come, you should come." He took a sharp inhale, as if resetting himself. "So," he said, "what did you do today?"

I passed out sandwiches to people on the street and brought three hitchhikers to their destinations and Ana gave me this necklace you haven't noticed.

I still planned to tell Chuck all of this later, but for now I was enjoying my secret life, and I thought I deserved it, too. Especially since he was being so weird about me coming to his pool games.

"Not much," I said. "I took it easy."

"A relaxing day," he said. "I like your necklace, is it new?"

And then I was annoyed he had noticed. What was wrong with me? "It is," I said. "Ana gave it to me. It's a friendship necklace." I held out the black apostrophe. "She has the other half."

He squinted at it. "So Ana was part of your relaxing day?"

"On-a."

"You two are spending a lot of time together. She must be a great person." Chuck peeled more tinfoil off his chicken bake. "I'd love to meet her sometime."

I glanced at the palm tree. "Yeah," I said. And then, noticing the hesitation in my voice, I really committed to the next part. "I would love for you to meet her, Chuck."

17

But Chuck did not invite me to watch him play pool, and I did not invite him to meet Ana. It rained for a week straight. Ana canceled class. Our targets were nowhere to be found because they'd gone inside to find shelter. Ana said, "It's time to switch it up anyway. That's probably why it's raining. Celia is telling us it's time to switch it up. So tell me what you think of this plan, Nan. Ha. I just rhymed. Okay, on Sunday, we'll set up a stand at the farmers' market. Free tarot! You can be my first client."

"What if it's still raining?"

Ana shrugged. "I'll bring a tarp."

On Sunday it was still raining, but less. I told Chuck I was going to the farmers' market with Ana and that I might be a while. I left the house before the boys woke up. Their game was canceled because of the rain, and we had no family plans today. The last thing I said to Chuck on my way out was "This can be father-son bonding time." "Mmm-hmm," he had said, his mouth full of Rice Krispies.

I walked up and down the aisles of the farmers' market looking for her. "Green bean lady!" my familiar vendor exclaimed. "Hello!" I waved. I realized then that I didn't know her name either. Where was Ana? I decided to call her, and that's when I realized I'd left my phone at home. "Damn," I said, searching my purse again anyway, my open umbrella awkwardly propped on top of my head.

And then I heard her voice. "Nan!" It took a second "Nan!" for me to register that she was the blond woman I'd walked by several times. She was under the massage tent spreading one of her afghans over a foldable table, and she was wearing a short red dress with large billowing sleeves.

"You like it? This is my Marilyn." She broke out into Marilyn's signature wind-blowing-up-the-dress pose and puckered her lips. I saw that she'd adhered some little jewels to her face. Silver studs above her eyebrows, echoing their arches, and a larger red jewel in the center, right above her nose. She was stunning.

"Ana!" I shook out my umbrella and joined her under the tent. "You need to tell me when you change characters."

"No way, the surprise is the fun part," she said, and puckered again, looking down at her lips. "Man, I need to get my lips done again. They need to be refilled. So. Badly."

Ana's lips didn't look "done" to me. "Refilled with what?"

"Restylane." She winked. "It's the best, but I can't afford it right now." She straightened out the afghan, her billowing sleeves trailing her movements. Just behind the table were three massage chairs, all still empty because the market hadn't officially opened yet. One masseur stood among them. He was Japanese, maybe, and rubbing oil into his hands.

"The massage people are letting us squat. Great, right? Because I brought a tarp but nothing to hang it on."

"That's good luck," I said, and smiled at the masseur, who didn't notice. He was using the oil to coif his short hair now and yawning at the rain.

"Good luck?" Ana scoffed. "Try good karma, Nan." She unfolded the chairs she had brought. One for the client, one for her, and one for me, which she put in the corner and adjusted so it was facing the massage chairs. "This way you can pretend like you're not listening, but you will be."

I put my bag and umbrella by my chair. Ana put her deck of cards on the table. "Look." She held a few up. "They have my face on them."

Yes, there was Ana's face in an antique-looking oval, wearing the penetrating expression of a fortune-teller from an infomercial. Portico was coiled between the fingers of one hand, which she held up close to her neck, and her hair was long and dark, same as mine.

"Is this your real hair?"

"Yes." She frowned. Then quickly, as if she had no choice, Ana's hand went to her stomach. "No." Her hand clutched. Her face tightened in pain.

"Are you okay?" I said, tightening my face, too.

She closed her eyes, inhaled and exhaled deeply three full times, and then the pain seemed to subside and she said, "I'm fine."

"Are you sure?"

"I'm sure." She pressed the big red jewel into her forehead.

We made a sign on a piece of cardboard because that was all we could find. FREE TAROT! We couldn't write more because the piece of cardboard was small. "It looks like one of our target's signs," I said.

"It does look shitty," she said, "but we're not charging so what do they expect?"

"Good point."

"Okay, Nan, you're my first client. Come come."

"Great, let me just take off my"—and right as I said *jacket*, a young girl with braces took a seat across from Ana. She bounced in the chair and set her twiggy elbows on the table.

"Oh my God," she said. "I am so excited. Are you going to tarot me?"

Ana was professional. She chose the client over me. "Yes, yes I am," she said, in a deeper and more prophetic-sounding version of her yoga teacher voice.

The girl couldn't seem to stop bouncing. And she couldn't seem to stop rubbing her face or checking her leopard print phone while Ana shuffled the cards. I was surprised when, between her bouncing and rubbing and checking, the girl noticed me staring at her and said, "Hi."

I promptly returned my gaze to the massage chairs. One person was getting a massage now—a large man. All I could see was the back of his Dallas Cowboys shirt. The maybe Japanese masseur kneaded his shoulders, swaying with his eyes closed like he was playing a piano.

"What's your name?" Ana asked the girl.

Breathlessly she said, "Mandy."

"Mandy," Ana repeated ceremoniously, as though blessing the name. "Here's how this works. You're going to ask a question, and then you will choose three cards. So," Ana shuffled the deck, "what is it you would like to know?"

Mandy bit her nail. She looked suspiciously left and right and then behind her. She scooted her chair closer to the table—so close that it pressed into her ribs—and whispered, "Are Trevor and I going to get back together?"

"Are Trevor and Mandy going to get back together?" Ana asked softly, sensing Mandy's need for privacy around this issue. After a healthy pause, she said, "Pick your three cards and lay them facedown on the table."

I pretended to look out at the drizzle while Mandy, who had become completely still, discerningly chose her cards. "They have your picture on them," Mandy said seriously, as though this were an important piece of evidence she had collected.

"They do," Ana confirmed, her voice maintaining its new baritone. She flipped the cards over.

"What do they mean?" Mandy was bouncing again. She tried to scoot closer, which was futile and probably bruising her ribs.

"This is your past, this is your present, and this is your future," Ana said, tapping each card.

Mandy's nail returned to her mouth.

"Your past is the ten of swords reversed. Did your relationship with Trevor end suddenly?"

Mandy rolled her eyes. "So suddenly," she said. "It was seriously so sudden."

"This card also suggests it was recent. Was it recent?"

"Twenty-two days ago," Mandy said. And then more casually, "Like three weeks."

"Your present card is the six of cups, which suggests you might still be thinking about Trevor, possibly a lot. A lot of your attention is focused on Trevor right now, and you are feeling lonely."

"*So* lonely." Mandy scrunched her face. "I feel like a hermit crab."

"And your future," Ana went on. "Ah, the emperor. This is good. This means you will overcome your feeling of loneliness. The past card mirrors the time frame of the future card, so if you broke up twenty-two days ago, you can expect to feel less lonely in about twenty-two days."

Mandy sighed. "So does that mean we're going to get back together in about twenty-two days?"

Ana chuckled. "Why don't you tell me a little more about Trevor, and then I can tell you how it might unfold."

"Cool," Mandy said, bruising her ribs again, "because my friends are so sick of hearing about it. So Trevor and I are in history together, and one day he asked me out. As, like, a group thing." Mandy went on to explain that she and Trevor had spent a few weeks exchanging super-sweet texts and making out. Then, they had sex—her first time—and the next day he told her he couldn't be "tied down" right now—Mandy said this with angry air quotes—because he was only fifteen and he had his whole life ahead of him.

Ana, like a good therapist, became completely invested in Mandy's long story. Then, like a good businesswoman, when she saw the line of people growing behind Mandy and knew it should be someone else's turn now—Mandy had been there for twenty minutes—she took Mandy's hands to calm her and said, "Mandy, don't settle for the crumbs when you can have the cookie."

At this, Mandy's face went slack. "Oh my God," she said, "Trevor is the crumbs."

"Trevor is the crumbs," Ana repeated knowingly.

"Whoa." Mandy was still dumbfounded. "Thank you so much. Can I give you a hug?"

"Sure," Ana said, but before she could get up, Mandy had darted around the table to squeeze the life out of Ana's blond head.

"You totally changed my life today," Mandy said, squeezing harder.

Ana patted Mandy's back. "Mandy, your future is so, so bright."

Mandy smiled and checked her phone with a satisfied sigh. Then she fearlessly walked into the rain without an umbrella.

"This was such a good idea, Nan," Ana whispered, looking toward me but not at me because we were pretending I wasn't a part of this.

"I agree," I whispered back. I was moved. Ana may have just saved a girl from years of eating crumbs.

"Next," Ana said, her voice cutting through the rain.

It was amazing the things people divulged. Sandra, the muscular bulimic woman, wanted to know if she would ever stop bingeing and purging. A very old and barely mobile woman named Dee opened her purse and said, "I just stole this," glancing furtively at the fruit stand a few stalls over. Her sticky fingers were so impulsive! But they were ruining her conscience. Would she become more honest anytime soon?

The next man's crime was much worse. Peter looked unassuming at first—a small farmer in a broken straw hat and a flannel shirt with the arms scissored off. But as he began to talk, I realized my first impression was wrong. He wasn't meek. He was kind of scary, and definitely disturbed. "Sometimes, when I feel the jitters, I take a stick to my horse's behind and beat on her a little." I could tell Ana was trying hard not to break character when she said, "Does it need to be the horse you take a stick to, Peter? Can it not be something else? Like a chair, perhaps?" she asked. "After the horse, I take the stick to myself," Peter said, his leg jittering under the table. Ana asked Peter about his mother, who he described as "a fine lady," and then she suggested that maybe Peter could name the horse after someone he loved. Maybe he could even name it Mom. At that, Peter's lip curled up and his mouth began to twitch and he got up and left before Ana could tell him his future was so, so bright.

Many people were confused about love. The Dallas Cowboys guy sat in the chair after his massage and said he thought his wife was cheating on him. A Latino man asked in broken English if his *corazón* would ever be fulled back up again or if he should no longer think about his *reina* and only think about work instead. A soft-spoken woman in her thirties admitted she had never been in love, not really. In a monotone voice, she recited it like something she had learned but didn't want to know. "I worry the common denominator in all my failed relationships is me."

Ana was uplifting and moving and decisive. Everyone left feeling inspired. She was at her best doing this. She knew just what to say, and she also knew when to say nothing. Later she would tell me it was easy because it was mostly listening. "People just want to be heard. And then they want a line to walk away with. Something that's easy to remember and never too harsh."

Ana always seemed to have the perfect line, and after she delivered it, she reminded each person that their future was so, so bright.

The people didn't stop. Sometimes the line dwindled and I thought we'd take a lunch break, but then it would grow again. At some point I went and bought us bananas and water from my vendor, who told me her name was Coco. "I'm Nan," I said, surprised I had called myself that.

Ana ate her banana in three bites and said, "Next!" As the next person walked up, Ana half turned toward me and whispered out of the side of her mouth, "I feel high on this."

At one the sun came out, blazing and full. People put their umbrellas away. I began to feel hot under the tent. A massage flyer had blown onto the ground in front of me. I picked it up and fanned myself and kept changing the position of my legs. I'd been sitting for a very long time. But my discomfort was apparent to me only in small bursts, which were easy to ignore because I was so thoroughly engaged in the conversations at the tarot table. The way these people were so willing to confess their sins to Ana. It was fascinating.

I stopped fanning and stilled my body, straining to hear the low voice of Jan, a sixty-something woman who was asking Ana where she should throw her husband's ashes. He had never told her. In their forty years together, how had he never told her that?

And then, like a car crash: "Nanceeeee!"

Several people, including Jan and Ana, looked up at Marcy, who was Tasmanian-deviling her way toward me through the maze of massage tables. "I didn't know you came down here on Sundays!" she said, closer now, and just as loud. I stood, mouthed "Sorry" to Ana, who didn't notice—she and Jan had resumed their conversation—and Marcy threw her arms around me with the drama of a soldier who'd just returned from war. Her crunchy hair stabbed my face and I said, "Sshhh."

She pulled away. In her normal voice, which was still too loud, she said, "I'm so happy to see you. I was worried. After that lunch," she tucked her hair behind her ear, "I was worried you might not like me."

"No," I whispered, flapping my hand. "No no no."

Marcy adjusted her visor. "Why are you whispering?" she whispered.

I pointed to the tarot table.

"Oh," Marcy mouthed.

I motioned for Marcy to follow me, and stepped out into the sun, far enough away from the tarot table so that her voice wouldn't ruin any more important moments.

Marcy had made some assessments on the way. "Are you part of the"—she looked at the sign—"free tarot?"

"I aaam," I said hesitantly. And then, with overcompensating confidence, "Yes, I am. I'm here helping my friend."

Marcy looked at Ana with judgment. It was hard to tell because she was wearing sunglasses, but I assumed it was judgment. "Oh." Marcy studied Ana. "She has rhinestones on her face. I wonder where she got those."

"The store," I said quickly, and it came out sounding rude.

But Marcy was unfazed. "Maybe Michael's?" she asked. "Anyway, Brad and I are just going to lunch. Do you want to come with us? It would be great to catch up."

I was starving. I'd been diligently ignoring the noises from my stomach for the last ten minutes. But lunch with Marcy and Brad? I preferred to suffer a little longer.

"No, I just ate," I said, recalling the small banana. "Plus I should stay here and help my friend."

"Oh." Marcy was disappointed, and she didn't seem to understand either. "Are you reading tarot cards, too?"

"No," I laughed. I had no idea how to read a tarot card.

"So you're sitting behind your friend while your friend reads tarot cards?"

"Yes," I said, now resenting Marcy for making me feel self-conscious about this. Was it strange that I was sitting behind Ana eavesdropping as people exposed their inner lives? Yes. But no, because it was more than that. It was us, me and Ana, and we were on a mission, Marcy! But even if I explained this to Marcy, I knew she wouldn't get it. I was looking at the ground now, preparing what I would say next, when my eyes latched on to Marcy's Tevas. Which looked very familiar. Because I had Tevas at home, in the same style with the same blue straps. I was about to tell her, but instead I decided to throw my Tevas away the second I got home, and then I said, "Guess what?"

"What?"

I paused for emphasis. "I walked the Pig Trail alone."

"You did?" Marcy was impressed. "Wow."

In my most laid-back voice, I said, "Yep."

"Did you enjoy it?"

"Very much."

"It was a little scary though, right?" Marcy said, trying to bond.

"No," I said, not condescendingly at all, "I didn't think so."

"Maybe we can go together sometime then. You can lead the way!"

I lied. What else was I supposed to do? "That would be nice."

"Okay, well, see you later, Nancy. Have fun"—she looked at my chair in the corner with judgment—"enjoying the shade."

My stomach lurched. I hoped she hadn't heard. "I will, Marcy. You have fun at lunch."

I watched Marcy walk away in her floral tunic and her khakis and her Tevas, and then I watched her find Brad, and then I watched them hug each other, their silly doughy middle-aged bodies wrapped in a cartoon embrace. Brad saw me and waved, his ridiculous gold watch catching the light and reflecting it sharply right into my eye.

•

At five I told Ana I know and I'm sorry and I really, really want to go to Natch with you tonight, but I have to get home to the boys.

She did not use the term "domestic chains" again, which I appreciated. Instead she said, "Good for you, Nan, that's a good thing to be doing. I feel so good after all the good I did today. Holy. Shit. That was groundbreaking. Those people. Right?"

"I can't believe how much they told you."

"People love to tell me their secrets," Ana said. "I don't know what it is about me, but it always happens."

"It's a gift," I said, and hugged her good-bye. "I'll call you later."

"Peace out, partner."

When I drove past her out of the lot, Ana was stretching. Foot on the wheel of the Jeep and her billowing sleeves reaching for her toes and a Red Vine stuck between her lips like a cigarette. I thought she looked like a queen.

•

On the way home, I stopped for sloppy joe ingredients. That was everyone's favorite. I would make my family sloppy joes and they would forgive me for being gone all day.

"Hello-o!" I sang, slipping off my sneakers on the lanai. No one answered. The TV was on. I opened the door, saw the boys' blond heads. "Hey, I'm makin' sloppy joes tonight," I said in a funny Southern accent.

Cam turned. Bloodshot eyes, definitely stoned.

Jed did not turn, but said, "You missed our game, Mom."

Panic. I felt my face flush. I had been very aware of how heavy these groceries were in my hands a second ago and now they felt like nothing. "I thought it was canceled because of the rain."

"Yeah, but then it stopped raining," Cam said helpfully.

"We called you like a million times," Jed said, his eyes fixed on the TV.

"Oh, babies, I am so sorry." I felt terrible. And maybe they weren't stoned. Maybe their eyes were red from the pool. "Did you win?"

"Yeah." Cam grinned. "And I scored a goal."

"Sweetie!" I set the groceries on the counter and hugged him.

"Hey, I scored one, too," Jed said.

"Sweetie number two!" I hugged Jed, who patted my arm.

"Are you really making sloppy joes?" he asked.

"Yes sir, and I'll make 'em quick," I said in my Southern accent, and went to unbag the fixins. "Where's your daddy?"

"Playing pool," Cam said.

"On a Sunday?"

"There's a tournament or something," Jed said.

"Huh," I said. Had Chuck told me that and I'd forgotten? Or had he not told me?

•

I made green beans and the best sloppy joes I had ever made, according to Jed. "Can you please start making these once a week again like you used to?" he asked, and, still feeling guilty about missing their game, I said, "Sure, I can do that."

After dinner Cam made popcorn and we watched a movie together, which we hadn't done in a very long time. Still feeling guilty, I let the boys choose. They chose *Charlie and the Chocolate Factory,* which was a sweet and childish choice and also, I thought as we watched the magical colors morph around Johnny Depp, kind of a stoner choice. I checked my phone at some point. Chuck had called me fourteen times that day. I pressed Play on one of his messages. "It's me again," he said, sounding overly disappointed. Delete, delete, delete. I deleted all the messages because clearly, he had overreacted. Then I called him—just once—because I knew he would appreciate me checking in. He didn't answer.

By ten, the boys and I had made one movie into a movie night. We were watching a thriller starring Liam Neeson when Chuck walked in. I turned when I heard the door clap shut. His Tide Poolers shirt had a violent streak of sauce down the front like the blood in the movie. Chicken wings, I thought. He put his hands on his waist. Something fell. His keys. He bent to pick them up. Why wasn't he speaking? I rubbed my arms. Goose bumps. Because my body knew before I did. A low ringing in my ears, just for a second, and then it went away.

"Chuck?"

And I knew it. I knew it already. But the way he said "Nance"—

the rise and fall of just that one word, the phlegmy rumble in the back of his throat—confirmed it. Chuck was drunk. This was why he hadn't wanted me to come to his games. This was what he had been hiding.

The boys were too engrossed in the movie to notice. "Hey, Dad," Cam said.

"Hey, Dad," Jed said.

"Hey." Chuck dropped his keys on the table. "Nice to see you," he said, trying to stare me down but his eyes couldn't focus. "We missed you today, Nance."

Cam turned to look at his father. One second later I watched his face fall. He looked at me. I made a look that said: I'm sorry, son. Cam hit Jed's arm. Jed looked at Chuck and rolled his eyes.

"Boys," I said, "why don't you go to bed."

"Hell no, we're finishing the movie." Jed crossed his arms over his chest.

Cam was poised to get off the couch but didn't move.

"We won the game," Chuck said. "We won the game. Woo." And then he was doing a little dance. A geriatric version of the washing machine. Then his torso bobbed forward. He was touching his toes now, or trying to. He couldn't reach them. He popped back up.

Slowly I reached for his arm. "Chuck."

"I love you guys," Chuck said. "I love you all so much." And then he threw his arms around me and pressed me in close, and I leaned my face back to keep it from touching the barbecue sauce on his shirt.

"Love you guys soooo much," he was saying.

I had already decided what to do. "Chuck, please sit down, okay?" I helped him into the chair and handed him the glass of water I'd been drinking. "I'm going to get you some pajamas and the futon," I annunciated, "and then we're going to the ohana."

He stopped drinking the water. "Hana?"

"Yes, just a second." I jogged to the bedroom, picked whatever pajamas were on top, pulled the futon out of the closet, and dragged it into the living room. "Ready?" I said, flipping the lights on outside. I didn't wait for him to answer. "Let's go."

As I guided drunk-bodied Chuck through the dark with one arm while trying to keep the futon high enough off the muddy ground with the other arm, I imagined all the rich apologies he would have for me tomorrow, and knew none of them would make up for this.

I turned on the light, unfolded the futon right underneath it. The ohana was completely bare—just off-white tiles and off-white walls. "Put these on." I didn't let go until I was sure he had the pajamas.

"Why why why," he mumbled, and collapsed onto the futon face-down. I leaned in to take his hat off because the brim was pressing into his skull.

I sighed, touched his hair. Softly, I said, "Chuck, why did you drink tonight?"

And then, quickly, he rolled over onto his back, hitting my leg with his arm.

"Ow," I said, even though it didn't hurt.

I stood up. I put my finger on the light switch. There was no point in talking to him when he was like this, so I don't know what possessed me to ask again. "Why, Chuck? Why did you drink tonight? God-damnit. Everything was going so well."

Chuck mumbled something unintelligible.

Leave, Nancy, this is pointless. Leave. Don't say anything else. "What, Chuck?"

Chuck faceup on the floor. Me above him looking down. He managed to focus his drunk eyes for just as long as it took to say it. "I miss you."

"What do you mean, you miss me? I'm right here."

"I miss you, Nancy."

I was losing patience. "Chuck. I am right here."

"But you're not." Chuck's blue eyes filled with tears, and I remembered that this was the most annoying thing about drunk Chuck. He got so emotional over nothing.

He started muttering again. He was speaking in fragments. "Yoga teacher," he said. "Jacuzzi," he said. "All the time," he said. "Don't even make shepherd's pie anymore," he said.

"What?"

Chuck's head rolled back and forth on the futon. His eyes were closed now. "All the time."

Nancy, don't. There's no point. "Well, you're at work all the time, Chuck."

"All the time," he said again, with the effort of his whole body this time. His arms and legs contorted into a very uncomfortable-looking shape. "All the tiiiime."

Other things I was remembering about drunk Chuck: he told you things he didn't have the courage to say when he was sober, and he made you feel like a single mother of three.

Chuck had rolled onto his side, so he probably wouldn't die from choking on his own vomit.

"Go to sleep, Chuck." I flicked the light.

18

Chuck crept into the bedroom before dawn to get his work clothes. I pretended to sleep. He changed quickly. He made coffee quietly. His car engine started just as the sun peered over the horizon and the black leaves turned green in the light.

I got up right after he left. I made the boys lunch, which I hadn't done for at least a year. Maybe two years. Fat turkey sandwiches and Sun Chips for Cam and Doritos for Jed. Not that this would make up for last night, I thought, as I folded the tops of the brown paper bags. Not that it was my job to make up for anything, I thought, as Cam entered the kitchen. Because it wasn't my fault, I thought, as I guiltily said, "Good morning."

"Hey." Cam frowned. Then he looked down the hall, so I knew Jed was there.

"Jed?"

No answer.

And then Jed appeared. His face was puffy. He'd been crying. He put his sunglasses on. "We're leaving."

"Okay," I said. "I'm sorry about your dad. He's—I don't know, but we're going to figure it out, okay?"

Jed wasn't listening. He was checking his phone.

Cam sighed.

"I made you lunch," I said, pushing the lunch bags across the counter.

Cam reached for his. He knew it was his because I'd written their names on the front like they were still in preschool.

"Don't take it, dude," Jed said.

Cam's shoulders slumped. He left the lunch and walked to the door. Jed followed him. They slipped on their flip-flops and kept walking.

"Love you!" I called after them.

They didn't answer. I went out and stood on the lanai, waving good-bye as they drove away. I didn't expect them to wave back, but I still hoped they would.

∙

My morning routine wasn't working. I tried to push through, but I just couldn't do it. I kept looking at the driveway like I was waiting for someone to appear. Who? Chuck? My imaginary conversation with Chuck was on repeat in my head: "I am not with my yoga teacher all the time." / "And who cares if I am." / "And you need to grow up, Chuck." / "And make your own shepherd's pie!" I was spinning. I had to leave the house.

I found myself at the Old Airport walking path, walking in circles. Circles and circles and circles. When I needed water, I kept going. When my legs hurt, I kept going. When it started to rain, I kept going.

Far away across the runway of the old airport was our picnic table. Our initials, pounded by the rain. This was the start of their decay.

Then my phone rang. I expected it to be Chuck with his first of many apologies. I was surprised he hadn't left a note already.

But it wasn't Chuck. It was Ana.

"Ana," I said.

"Nan." She didn't sound happy. "Remember how my stomach hurt yesterday?"

I said yes, of course, and she said it had been hurting like that for a little while. Why hadn't she told me?

Two weeks ago she'd gone to the doctor and taken some tests.

"And the results came back today," she said. "The cancer's back. Pancreatic."

I gasped.

"I'm going to die soon. I'm cornered."

"No."

"I guess our karma game was bullshit. You can't bargain with God."

"But—"

"But you can sure as hell fight her!"

"What do you need? Do you want me to come over?"

"I need a few days to process this alone. But thanks, Nan, you're a good egg."

"So are you."

"No I'm not. That's why I'm going to die."

"Please don't say that."

"In case anything happens, I want you to know you are loved, Nan. Because I love you."

"I love *you*."

"I'll call you soon, friend. Good-bye." She hung up.

I looked up. Where was I? I was standing in front of the drowning dog statue, watching rain pound down on its frantic face.

Fire

19

Two days later the police called. The boys had been arrested for arson. They'd burned down an abandoned shed in the middle of the afternoon. When the battery of their getaway car wouldn't start, they had called AAA. When the police arrived, they were still waiting. "Just on the street there, watching the smoke," the police officer said.

I turned off the stove. My healthy snack of mushrooms sizzled in the pan. "Please tell me this is a joke."

"No ma'am," the officer said, "this is real."

•

The police station was a plain, cream-colored building down in the lava fields. It was the only building for miles. Random, I thought, as though fallen from space. Or not random at all, I rethought. If criminals tried to escape, there was nowhere to escape to.

I sat in the car with the AC on high while I waited for Chuck. I turned on the radio.

"This is a civil defense message. This morning's assessment shows minor advancement of the downslope flow area. Residents and businesses downslope will be informed of any progression in flow activity and advancement, but there is no need for evacuation as of this afternoon."

I turned off the radio. I felt lonely. I told myself to own my solitude. But I still felt lonely.

Chuck and I had barely spoken since his night at the bar. He had apologized, but his apology was watered down by the fact that he didn't think he had done anything wrong. "I'm sorry, but it was only *one* night," he'd said. Chuck didn't seem to understand the gravity of the problem. I'd asked him to sleep in the ohana until I could forgive him for breaking yet another promise, and he had complied. But he had not complied in the submissive and guilt-ridden way I wanted him to. He had complied with bravado, as if I were overreacting. I was not looking forward to the moment when he would drive into this parking lot and burst out of the car with his whole body pulsing, ready to scream. Every time the boys got into trouble, Chuck lost his temper. And he'd sounded very stressed on the phone. "I don't have *time* for this today."

I wanted to call Ana, but Ana had said she needed time. Also she'd turned her phone off. I knew because I'd called several times already. But it was probably better this way. I didn't need to burden her right now. She was dying. In certain moments—like this one, now, in the car—it would hit me again. Ana is going to die. And the air would get trapped in my throat for a second, and I wouldn't know if I had too much air or not enough, and there would be a soreness in my chest, like now, and I would touch my heart, like now in the car with the AC on, and no more bad news because the radio was off and please please please, and I didn't even know who I was saying please to, and then there was Chuck pulling his beat-up Honda fast into a spot and braking with a squeak and bursting out of the car with his whole body pulsing, ready to scream.

My initial reaction had also been anger. Well, first surprise, and then anger. But now, seeing Chuck angry enough for the both of us, I would take the role of the calmer parent. I would make up for what he lacked today. Even though he was drinking again. I would do this because it was my job.

I told myself to breathe in and out with intention—focus, focus, you can do this, you can do this. I sighed. I got out of the car.

Chuck was already right there, saying, "What the fuuuuuuck were they thinking?"

"I don't know," I said quietly.

He was shaking his head and picking at his skinny black belt and tugging the fabric of his polyester slacks off his legs. His face was like a flaming red balloon. Behind him were miles and miles of dead lava. "We are grounding them," he said, teeth clenched.

"You know," I said, and waited until I had his attention.

"What!"

My shoulders slumped forward. "Please don't yell, Chuck. This is already hard enough."

"Okay, I'm sorry!" He hit his leg. "I'm sorry, I'm sorry"—he smeared his hands down his face. "I just can't believe them. Why would they do this? They're good boys!"

This is what the anger was always really about. Chuck wanted his boys to be good boys.

"I mean, really," he went on, a little more calmly, "what were they thinking?"

"I think they're trying to get our attention, Chuck. The way they just stayed by the car? They didn't even try to run away."

"Well, if that's true, that makes it worse," he groaned, smearing his face again. It was so hot and he was so stressed and his pants were so tight, and I couldn't help but comfort him.

I said, "Come here, Chuck"—he looked confused—"just come here and let me hold you for a second." I put my arms around him. His body was burning up. His heart was beating so fast. I was doing this for the boys. I was doing this to calm their father down. I didn't plan on hugging him again for a while after this.

Chuck managed to be semi-decent to the people who worked at the police station. ("Yes, I brought my fuuuuu—. I brought my check-book, yes.") But when we got back out to the lot with the boys in tow, the first thing he did was whip around and say, "What the fuuuuuck were you thinking?"

Chuck was being way too intense, but it was a good question. What the fuck *were* they thinking?

"I know what you're going to do to fix this." Chuck shot his pointer finger in the air. "You are going to build us a shed. At home, on our property. So you can understand what you destroyed. *That* is the answer."

"Okay, we'll talk about that later," I said. "Boys, come with me."

"And you are grounded, by the way," Chuck added, and fought his way through the heat toward his sad, dented car.

I took the boys' hands. "Let's go."

•

Why did I take them out for ice cream after that? Was it to soothe my babies or was it because I needed to feel less alone? I couldn't bear the thought of more fighting. I needed to be getting along with the boys right now. Was this selfish? Was I exploiting the opening Chuck had created for me to be the Better Parent? Or was it none of these things, Nancy? Or was it just ice cream?

We did McDonald's like the old days and drive-thru because it was too hot to get out of the car. In the bushes below the speakers was a homeless man—he looked really homeless, not half homeless—sleeping in a sleeping bag.

When I ordered a Big Mac, the boys didn't ask me if I was off my diet. I passed them their soft serves and looped the car around. "One second," I said, and got out of the car and set the Big Mac by the homeless man's sunburned face. And then I lingered over him for a second, lingered in the feeling of this. Of being good when I didn't have to be. Tears welled. I missed this feeling. I missed the sandwiches. I missed Ana.

I composed myself on the walk back to the car.

Cam said, "Did you just—"

"—give that guy a Big Mac?" Jed finished.

"Yes," I said, "I did."

"Wha?" Jed asked, his mouth full of soft serve.

The silence told me they were exchanging a look. "Doing good creates good," I told them, backing the car out. "And doing bad—like burning a shed, for example—creates bad."

More silence. And the feeling that no one really knew me, no one but Ana. I started toward home.

After a minute, I said, too severely, "Please tell me why you lit this fire."

"I don't know, Mom," Cam whined. "We're sorry, okay?"

"Yeah, Mom, we're sorry," Jed echoed, not very convincingly.

"Did you *mean* to light the shed on fire?" I made a right onto the winding road that led up the mountain. "Or was it an accident?"

"It's not like we killed anyone," Jed said, annoyed. "It's not even that big of a deal."

"It's arson!" I slapped the wheel. "Arson! Hello! Arson? You're going to have to go to court. And you skipped school. To light something on fire. In the middle of the afternoon." Just the thought of them doing that—it was so ridiculous. It was so ridiculous that I laughed, and when I thought of how ridiculously bad everything else was right now, I kept laughing.

"You're laughing, Mom," Cam said.

My eyes watered. I had to wipe them to see the road. "Because you two are such morons! Who lights a shed on fire in broad daylight?"

Jed grunted. "We're so stupid, dude," he said to Cam.

"Yes! You are so stupid! Thank you!"

"Are you really going to ground us?" Cam wanted to know.

"Of course we're going to ground you," I said, regaining motherly control for a second.

"How long this time?" Jed asked like a seasoned veteran.

"I don't know yet. Check with me later."

As I pulled into the driveway, Cam asked, "But do we really have to build a shed?"

That started me laughing again. I couldn't stop.

"You're acting weird, Mom," Cam said.

"Ah," I said, "ah," and I didn't know what to say to that—I was laughing too hard to speak—but when I saw the house and felt the laughter change, I forced myself to say, "Meet you inside," and the boys slammed the doors. Once they were gone I heaved and heaved—I couldn't control it—and then I was sobbing, deeply and quietly, there alone in the car, right in front of my house.

20

I showed up to yoga with flowers and a whole pan of vegan carrot cake wrapped in tinfoil and a bow, but Ana wasn't there.

"She asked me to fill in," Kurt said. When he smiled, his veneers reminded me of her veneers.

Patty, who was still wearing her Marbles shirt and busy excavating something out of her molar, took her finger out of her mouth to say, "Maybe she has a new boyfriend."

"Well," Sara Beth stretched her skinny arms above her head, "if she does, I understand. It's harder to come here so early when you're leaving someone you love in bed, isn't it?" She looked at me for assurance.

"Uh-huh," I managed to say, and dropped my mat in the grass. I wasn't sure I wanted to stay without Ana here, but I couldn't just leave now either.

"Marbles used to sleep right on the pillow with me." Patty stroked Marbles's face on her shirt. "He kept it nice and warm."

"I don't think Ana has a new boyfriend," I said, doing the same hands-up stretch as Sara Beth. It took me a second to notice I was copying her.

"That's what happened last time she left us," Patty said. "She fell in love and moved to Hawi for two years."

"Right," Kurt said, recalling the time with pursed lips.

"What?" Ana had never told me that. "She moved to Hawi?"

"We didn't even know she was up there until Kurt ran into her at the mini-mart," Patty confirmed.

"It's true," Sara Beth said. "She disappears sometimes."

"Well, that's not what's happening this time," I said. "Trust me."

•

Kurt didn't even have a gong bowl. He took us through the poses in a mechanical way, saying none of the inspirational things Ana would have said if she were here. He had looked up one quote on his phone, and he read it to us emphatically like we were in kindergarten. "This is from the Buddha," he said. "'Believe nothing. No matter where you read it, or who said it. No matter if I have said it. Unless it agrees with your *own* reason and your *own* common sense.'" He set his phone in the grass. He didn't repeat it, and he didn't expound. He didn't tell us what kinds of things we might not believe or where we might read these things. He did not give us one example of how he had used his *own* common sense, or how we might apply this advice to our lives today. Kurt was a nice guy, but he was not a relatable yoga teacher. And he forgot so many things, even the simplest things, like "breathe." He did not remind us that coming to our mats this morning had been a strong choice, or that we were here to cultivate compassion, or that even if nothing was okay, things were still okay because we were here in Hawaii in the morning light with the palm trees and the beach and the birds that never stopped singing.

Kurt's adjustments were just what you'd expect from a dentist who was not really a yoga teacher. Clinical and tentative. My spine didn't crack when he pulled my hips back in downward dog. When I hurt my elbow doing a jump back, I wanted to leave. Maybe this injury meant I could leave now. But it would be too much work to explain in the middle of class and it would be embarrassing, so I stayed until the bitter end, when we om'd a hollow om that wasn't even strong enough to carry over the short rock wall.

•

I hadn't been to the pink house in over a week. I felt a misty wave of longing as I pulled into the driveway, nostalgic for the past and then nostalgic for the future, when Ana wouldn't be here anymore. My elbow hurt when I lifted the carrot cake off the seat, and the morning sun cast me in a long shadow when I got out of the car.

I knocked softly in case she was sleeping. I reminded myself to stay present, to stand on both feet equally. The crazy vines had made their way closer to the door, like they were trying to get inside. A green gecko, stilled by my presence, waited on a green leaf, pretending he wasn't there.

I could leave the cake and flowers by the door; I could do that. But her car was here and she was here, only a wall away, or two walls if she was in the bedroom, and it seemed silly to just leave. I knocked harder, first with my knuckles and then with the back of my fist.

Footsteps. I told myself to remember their sound so that later, when she was gone, I could call upon the memory of their rhythm and compare it to the rhythms of other footsteps and other beats when I talked about Ana to the new friends I would eventually have to make.

As the doorknob turned, I told myself to wipe the lament off my face and replace it with good cheer. But all of this turned straight to shock when she opened the door. Ana was bald. Completely and totally bald.

"Oh my God," I accidentally said out loud.

Ana was not surprised to see me. "I knew you'd come," she said, her eyes flat and no longer glimmering, and this meant that she was gone a little already.

"Your hair."

"Chemo," she said. "From the breast cancer. It's still trying to grow back."

Well, it's not trying hard enough! I wanted to scream. I was angry for her.

"See?" She touched her neck. "I wasn't meant to live. My hair has known that all along."

I swallowed the uncried tears in my throat as Ana took the flowers from my hand and simply said, "Flowers," and took one passive sniff. "And what's this?" She pulled at the orange bow on the cake.

"Carrot cake," I said, the words echoing in my head. It seemed so stupid to be saying *carrot cake* at a time like this.

"I haven't been hungry, but thank you." She took the pan from me and set it on the low table by the door and plopped the flowers on top. On the table was a piece of paper, which she handed to me. "They gave me three to six months."

The piece of paper was filled with writing—in a decorative font because everything in Hawaii was more beautiful, I thought. The important facts were in bold. PANCREATIC. 3–6 MONTHS.

"I bet I can make it nine," she said, and there was a tiny glimmer in her eyes again, and I was very glad for that.

I comforted her. "I'm sure you can make it nine," I said, although I didn't know if I believed her over her doctors. I wrapped my arms around her, squeezed her tight. "Oh, Ana." I felt her fake breasts press into mine, and thought of everything she had already lost.

"I'm so sorry, I'm so sorry," I was saying, rocking us gently from side to side, remembering her coconut smell, which was faint today. The hug felt more intimate now that she didn't have hair. Like she was a baby. Like she really needed me now. But I needed her just as much. What was I going to do without her?

I let her go. I took her hands. "What am I going to do without you?"

"Nan," she said sweetly, petting my hair, which I felt guilty for having. "You're going to do whatever you want."

I nodded, maybe a little too eagerly, like this was a direct order.

"You look good," she said, her eyes going up and down me. "How much weight have you lost?"

"Fourteen pounds, maybe." I didn't know why I'd said the *maybe* because it was definitely fourteen.

"Good for you." She put her hands on her waist, looked down at her body. "I'm probably going to lose a lot more than that."

Movement behind her on the floor. Black and white and it was Portico, slithering under the couch. I was frantic. "Portico's out!"

"I know," she said. She seemed a little annoyed with me. I would calm down.

I was still waiting for her to invite me in and she still hadn't. "Do you want to sit in the Jacuzzi? Would that make you feel better?"

"No," she said, the sides of her mouth curling up. "Let's go for a ride."

•

We drove south. When I asked where we were going, she said, "Life is a journey, Nan, not a destination," which was true, but also not an answer. I let it go. I wondered if I would have let it go if she weren't dying.

I reveled in the feeling of being back in the Jeep. The purple hood, the air rushing all around us, the way the seat really cupped you. I wasn't hungry but ate a Red Vine anyway, for old time's sake.

I wanted to tell her about Chuck and the boys, but that seemed selfish now. She was dying. We should talk about that. "Ana," I said, when we were going slow enough to hear each other over the wind, "are you scared?"

"No," she said, "it's interesting. I don't feel scared anymore."

I touched her bare shoulder. It was so bare without her wig hair on it.

"Last time I got cancer, there was bargaining. But now—now that I know this is really it, there is no more bargaining. Now I'm just pissed." Without thinking, Ana made the gesture of tucking her hair behind her ear, which was the saddest thing I had ever seen. She seemed to notice this, too, because she shook her hand out as if to tell it to stop doing stupid things. "I am so angry, Nan. I could fucking kill someone!"

"I know," I said, clutching my seat belt to make sure it was on because Ana was driving a little too fast now. A road to the left and we almost passed it and she said, "Wooooo!" and made a way-too-last-minute turn and my body pressed into the door and we might have only been on two wheels for a second. "Sorry about that," she said when we'd made it onto the road.

It was a skinny dirt road with tropical brush growing at the edges and it was deserted. On both sides, coffee trees were all I could see. And then there was something in the distance. A little hut. Oh, it was a fruit stand, just a lone fruit stand with no person behind it, and Ana pulled over. HONOR SYSTEM, CAMERA ENFORCED, the sign said. Below was a list of prices. The avocados only cost a dollar. "I want everything," she said.

I hesitated. "Okay," I said, wondering why she wanted all this food if she had no appetite.

But I was helpful anyway. I didn't question her. I was learning it was hard to question someone who was dying. I carefully placed all the bananas and the mangoes on the floor in the back. Ana was faster and more chaotic. She tossed the avocados in from afar, making a little game of it. "Bummer," she said when one missed and hit the wheel then rolled under the car. I got on the ground to find it. There it was, but I couldn't reach. So close—my fingers touched it—but still too far.

"Let's go," she said, and she sounded so sure that I abandoned the avocado immediately and got back in the car. I expected to find her counting out money to put in the box, but her wallet was right there and she wasn't even looking at it.

"Oh, I think I have some cash," I said, which was a lie. I hadn't brought my wallet.

"We're good," she said.

I stammered, "Wait. No. What? Not good."

Even as she peeled away, driving farther and farther from the fruit stand, I was still imagining us parked in front of it, fishing out bills. I kept expecting her to turn around. But she kept not turning around.

"Ana?"

"Yes, Nan."

"They had a camera."

"No, they had a sign that said they had a camera. There was no camera."

"Why did you do that?"

"Oh, Nan." She touched my hair. "I used to have this hair."

Part of me wanted to pull away, but a bigger part of me didn't. "Why?"

"Because, Nan," she said sadly, or maybe she was just resigned. "Justice is the foundation of the Karma Factory."

I had to laugh. "The Karma Factory? Is that what we're calling it now?"

"Obviously," Ana said, "and if I weren't about to die, I'd make it into a 501(c)(3)." She sighed. "If I'm being punished for my sins, then other people should be punished for theirs. The man who owns that fruit stand?" She took her hand off my hair and put it back on the wheel. "Has owed me fifty dollars for the last three years. So I feel like the least he can do is give me this bullshit fruit." She glanced behind her. "It doesn't even look that quality."

"What does he owe you for?"

"A back massage, but that's not the point. The point is I am being punished and other people are not. It's not fair. It's not fair and it makes no sense." Ana slapped the dashboard. "Now is the time for justice. We must give these people what they deserve. Since fucking Celia is apparently sleeping up there!" She stuck her middle finger up toward the sky. Then she repeated the line she had said on the phone, and this time I understood it. "You can't bargain with God, but you can sure as hell fight her."

What I thought: Ana is angry right now. Anger is part of dealing with death—did that come before or after bargaining?—and at some point the anger will pass and it will become acceptance, which I knew was one of them.

Now was absolutely not the time to ask, but I had to. "Does this mean we're not going to hand out sandwiches anymore?"

"I'm dying, Nan," Ana said, angrily scratching the top of her head.

"I know, I know, I'm sorry I asked. I'm just—I'm sorry, it was selfish to ask that."

"But Nan, punishing people who've behaved badly is a good deed. It's for the"—her hand made a sweeping arc—"*great*er good."

"I don't know," I said carefully.

"I understand how you might feel confused," she said. "But things change when one knows death is imminent. You just have to trust me. When you're near the end of your life, this will make sense to you."

I couldn't imagine devoting my last energies to anything beyond relaxing, but I didn't tell her that. Because maybe I was wrong. Maybe I wouldn't feel that relaxed if I learned I had three to six months to live. Maybe I was more selfish than she was, and maybe I only understood cancer from movies. All of which meant that I knew nothing.

So I didn't ask: Don't you want to spend this time doing your favorite things with the people who love you? First because it sounded trite, and second because when I really thought about that, I wasn't sure who loved Ana. Everyone loved her, of course, but they loved her from afar. I was her closest friend. Wasn't I? Yes, she told me that all the time. I was her soul sister. I was the other half of the necklace. I was her somebody to lean on, and now she needed to lean on me, which meant I had to support her.

"Don't you trust me, Nan?"

"I want to trust you, Ana," I said, which wasn't a lie.

•

When we got back in her house, I said, "I really think we should sit in the Jacuzzi for a little while. Just to take pause, you know?"

"You're right, Nan," she said. "A pause is the answer. I've taught you well."

I hadn't brought a suit, so Ana let me borrow her red one. I thought it might be too big in the bust area, but it fit perfectly.

"That looks great on you," she said when I emerged into the living room, wearing just the suit with no towel around my waist to cover me up because who cared about anything now? She was dying.

The living room was a little messier than usual—the afghans weren't folded like they usually were, but strewn haphazardly instead, and one was on the floor. Ana was lying on the low couch in her black silk kimono, threading Portico through her fingers and studying me. "You can have that suit when I'm gone," she said in a businesslike way.

I looked at her sadly. "Thank you."

She held Portico's tiny face in front of her nose. Portico's two-pronged black tongue glided in and out of her tiny mouth, and Ana kissed her.

"Do you want me to put those flowers in water?" I asked. The flowers and the carrot cake were still near the door.

Ana gazed in the direction of the door, her eyes coming unfocused. "If you want to."

I did want to. I wanted to be useful. I took the flowers and the cake into the kitchen. The counter was piled with the fruit from the fruit stand. The mangoes looked good. I opened the drawers, looking for scissors to cut the flowers. I couldn't find any. "Do you have scissors?"

"No, you can use a knife though," she said.

There were only two knives. A small paring knife and a huge butcher's knife. I chose the butcher's knife. The hacking sent stems onto the floor. Using this tool was a little more violent than I would have liked. I put the flowers in the clear plastic vase I found on top of the fridge, and then I tied the orange bow from the carrot cake around it.

Ana was humming. At first I thought it was "Lean on Me," but it wasn't. It was a song I didn't know. She stared straight out the window at the ocean, her arms splayed on the cushions. Beside her on the couch, Portico was as still as a hose. Before, I thought, before the diagnosis, Ana would have been stretching right now. Or doing something more lively. Maybe she would have been eating some of this cake.

"Do you want some cake?"

"Possibly," she answered.

"Good," I said, "because I want you to eat."

I chose her prettiest plate. A maybe homemade ceramic oval in a happy yellow color. I cut the cake into cute little squares, and then I added some of the fruit, because if it was here, we should eat it. Banana and papaya and mango, sliced delicately with the paring knife. I took two forks out of the drawer and poured two cups of ice water and ripped two paper towels off the roll.

I brought her one of the waters, looking for Portico, who wasn't on the couch anymore. "Let's go outside," I said in my most uplifting voice.

She took the water and sipped and said, "Okay, Nan," and I followed her out with the pretty yellow plate of food, which reminded me of something. The way I had lovingly set the food on the plate—this was what I did for the boys when they were sick.

Ana sat on the edge of the Jacuzzi with her feet in the water. The breeze pushed her kimono into her body so every contour was visible. Her firm, perfectly round breasts and the small mound of flesh low on her stomach. She stabbed a banana slice first, chewed it like chewing was a hard thing to do. But then I knew the food started to taste good to her because she kept eating. "This cake is good, Nan," she said.

"Oh, I'm so glad," I said, stabbing a mango slice for myself.

Ana seemed calmer now. Maybe the anger was passing. After a while she said, "I'm full," and put her fork down. She stretched her neck and fingered her half of our necklace, looking out at the horizon. The water was calm today. No waves sprayed us.

I felt the sudden urge to say it. Say it now, just in case. "Ana," I said, "I just want you to know that I'm going to be here for you through all of this. And I want you to know that I love you."

She blinked. She looked straight at me. Her eyes were wide open and blank. "I don't know what love is."

"What do you mean?"

"I might know what love isn't, but I don't know what it is."

I touched my heart. This was heartbreaking. I didn't know what to say.

In a distant voice, not looking at me, she said, "Tell me more about your childhood."

"What do you want to know?" I brought one foot out of the water. Still the purple sparkly polish Ana had painted on.

"Tell me more about your mother."

I laughed. "My mother?"

"It makes you uncomfortable."

"No." I stopped laughing. "It's fine."

"Tell me how she killed herself."

I sighed the requisite sigh. "Pills. She overdosed."

A pause. "Who found her?"

I said it quietly. "I did." I looked away from her. She was staring too hard. I looked at the ocean, and it was so vast and so clean and this was comforting.

"You did," she said. I knew she wanted more, so I gave it to her.

"I found her in her smelly chair. The one she sat in all the time. Toward the end, she never moved from that chair except to go to the bathroom and to refill her drinks. By the very end, she'd switched to boxed wine, the kind that comes with a tap so she didn't have to move to get a refill. Next to her, she always had a drink, a bottle of pills, and the remote. On the day she died, she was drinking white wine. I remember that because she didn't finish her glass. It was still almost full." My neck burned. My shoulders clenched. "Anyway, I thought she was sleeping. I didn't realize she was dead until I tried to wake her up later."

I had said the last part too fast and I was out of breath. My ears prickled, waiting for her response. I could feel her staring at me. I didn't look up.

"I'm sorry," she said finally.

"Me, too," I said, relieved the story was over. Before she could ask me anything else, I turned the conversation back to her. "Why are you asking me this stuff now?"

"I'm not sure," she said. She seemed tentative, which was rare for her. "I guess I'm trying to figure out where I went wrong. Why did you go to college and find a husband and have two kids and I became a stripper who doesn't know what love is? You're healthy and I'm dying. You made it out and I didn't."

"Ana, you've had a wonderful life. I mean *are having*. You *are having* a wonderful, interesting life. My life is boring compared to yours. And you're not a stripper anymore, you're a healer. You changed." I was defiant. "You. Changed."

Ana shook her head. "It seems like I changed, but I didn't. I was never healed. I became a healer to heal myself, but it didn't work. You—you healed. I think you know what love is."

I could see her holding back tears now. She closed her eyes to stop herself. The breeze blew my hair into my face, which made me feel guilty again for having it.

"It's not fair," she said, so softly I could barely hear. And then louder, "It's not fair." And then she dropped her head back and screamed, "It's not faaaair!" When she looked at me, the sadness was gone from her face. The sun flashed in her eyes like two fireballs. She was back to being angry.

"Maybe," I began helpfully, "we can think of some of your favorite things, and we can spend the next few months doing those things."

"Like a bucket list? I don't think that's going to help," she said. "This is a time for action, Nan. For justice. I will not resign myself to victimhood. I will deliver justice to this island with all the energy I have left until my flame peters out. And I'm going to do a great fucking job."

Ana stood. She stripped off the kimono and all she was wearing was underwear, and for some reason her fake breasts seemed so depressing to me, even more depressing than her bald head. She jumped into the shallow Jacuzzi with a splash and stayed underwater for a long time, almost long enough to make me worried, but then she popped back up again. She stayed very still, not rubbing her eyes and not blinking, and her skin was so pale and so new and so oddly unblemished, and other than her worried, angry face, Ana looked like an innocent baby in a bathtub.

•

While I cleaned the cake dish and then the other dishes piled in the sink and then the rest of the kitchen, Ana sat back down on the couch with a yellow legal pad. She seemed peppier now, humming as she wrote. She'd even lit a stick of incense. Smoke rose in one thin, unperturbed line. When the ashes crumbled onto the Buddha's head, I usefully went to wipe him down.

"You don't have to do that."

"But you like things tidy," I said, sponging the rest.

"I don't care anymore."

"Well, I care for you." One more wipe of the sponge and I looked at her. She was back in the black kimono, writing with a huge pencil, the kind children buy at Disneyland that's almost too fat for them to grip. It said I ♥ HAWAII in the pattern of a circular staircase.

"What are you writing?"

"My bucket list."

"Oh, Ana, that's wonderful," I said, picking one of her afghans up off the floor. "I'm happy to go with you wherever you want to go. Maybe not skydiving, but I'll do anything else."

"Good," she said, "because I might need you when I get weaker."

"Good," I said, "because I'm good at being needed."

And then the overwhelming feeling of wanting to be near her. Near her now, just in case, and I went and put my arms around her. "No peeking," she said, and covered the legal pad with her hand. But I had already seen a little. *BUCKET* at the top, and *#1: Gregory.*

I didn't want to invade her privacy but I also did so badly. "Who's Gregory?"

"Peeker!" Ana hit my hand with her pencil.

"Sorry."

"Gregory's an old lover."

"You want to see him before you die?"

"Yes," she said, writing something else.

"You're not going to do anything bad to him, are you?"

"Nothing he doesn't deserve."

This was not what I wanted to hear. "Ana."

"Nan," she said, "I already explained this to you. It's for the greater good. If you're going to judge me, I will go on without you."

The thought of her going on without me was unbearable. "I'm trying not to judge you, Ana. I'm just—this is very hard for me to understand."

Ana sighed. She was annoyed with me. "Nothing has changed, Nan. This is like the sandwiches. And the tarot stand. And the 'You are loved.' It's good. It's all good. It's all part of the same Karma Factory, don't you see?"

I added the afghan to the ordered stack I was now making, and asked the question I really didn't want to know the answer to. "What are you planning to do to Gregory?"

Ana groaned. "Nan, what you should be asking is what Gregory did to me."

"What did he do to you?"

"He cheated on me."

"Ugh," I said, thinking of Chuck. Chuck at Costco right now in his polyester work slacks. I wondered if he was back to drinking at lunch already.

And then it hit me. How had it taken this long?

"What?" Ana asked, sensing I had had an important thought.

"If Chuck is drinking again, he's going to cheat on me again. It's inevitable." I must have looked horrified, because that's how I felt.

"Totally inevitable." Ana yawned. "It's a trip when you can see the future, isn't it?"

Did Chuck work with any blondes at this new Costco? How did I not know the answer to that? I was so naïve.

"Men are disappointing," I said.

"All people, sooner or later, will disappoint you," Ana said, looking at the space above my head.

I hoped Ana didn't think I was one of those people. For good measure, I reassured her. "I won't disappoint you, Ana."

Her sly smile, her black eyes on me, and then the slow knowing blink that marked her understanding. Every time it felt like being laid bare.

"Who else has disappointed you, Nan? And what would you do to them if you had the balls to do it?"

I forced a laugh. "Everyone's disappointing me lately. Chuck, the boys. The boys," I rolled my eyes, "lit a shed on fire." It was a relief to tell her this, and it was even more of a relief when she said, "Oh, Nan, you've been experiencing pain."

"Yes," I said, as though just realizing it myself, "I have been in pain."

Ana put her legal pad facedown on the table and nestled her head in my lap and petted my knee, and I put my hand on her shoulder because touching her head felt too intrusive and it also scared me a little. "I've been in pain, too," she whispered. And then, "Do you think it's fair?"

Right as I said, "Life isn't fair," I realized this was something my mother used to tell me all the time.

"Exactly." Ana sighed. Her breath hot on my knee. "And why should we accept that? Doesn't it seem kind of passive and wrong?"

Did it seem passive and wrong? "Maybe."

She turned her head so she was looking up at me. She touched my necklace with one hand and her necklace with the other hand, and I felt so close to her and it was closer than I felt to my family or any friend I'd ever had, and when she said, "I need you," my first thought was, I need you more. Slowly I placed my hand on Ana's scary bald head. And when I did that, it wasn't scary anymore. It was warm.

"We have to make things right," Ana whispered. "We are the Karma Factory."

Flashback to us making sandwiches. "The factory of two."

"Goddesses." She smiled. Her inviting eyes. "We are goddesses."

I'm not sure why, but it felt necessary to repeat her. "We are goddesses."

21

I woke up in a perfect nest of white sheets. Rays of yellow sun spilled through Ana's window. The smell of the ocean came before the sound. The waves were big today. They crashed and crashed against the rock wall, crashing sometimes with a slap, and they were so close that it could have been frightening, but it wasn't. The waves would not rise over the wall. The birds would never stop singing. The peace in this nest of sheets was real. We were safe and we were calm.

•

We ate mangoes for breakfast and got in the car. The sun, the sky, the ocean. Snow-capped Mauna Kea and tourists spelling out their names with white coral in the lava. I looked for our MURPHY, but it was gone. Our letters had been taken by new families to make new letters. The wind was loud and rushing. We sipped our Vitamin Waters and didn't listen to music.

Gregory lived in Hawi. Yes, he was the guy Ana had lived with for two years. The two longest years of her life, she said, and they'd even adopted a Siamese fighting fish together and named it Paco. "Because he said if we were going to adopt a real kid, we should prepare with a pet."

"You wanted children?" I asked. "I didn't know that."

And she said, "Oh yeah, of course I did," as if it were the most obvious thing in the world.

Like all men, Gregory was great until he wasn't. He owned an Italian restaurant, which was fun in the beginning—free wine, really good pesto—but then he started to work more, and more and more and more and then he was at this restaurant twenty hours a day. He was neurotic and very type A, which was what had attracted Ana to him at first—she thought he had his shit together. So she assumed he was at the restaurant obsessing over details, like the size of the rame- kins and the little tear in one of the chair cushions and the salmon— should it come out with two almond slivers or three almond slivers? Those were the types of things that Gregory cared about. Their home together was spotless. Anyway, fast-forward, it turned out his real obsession was with the anorexic chef. Whom he impregnated. And during the breakup, when Ana had called the chef anorexic, Gregory had called Ana "fatty."

"If yoga hadn't reformed me," she said, "I would have chopped his balls off right there."

Ana was wearing the black wig with the pink streak that framed her face. "This is my least conspicuous one," she'd said when she put it on that morning, "even though it's still pretty conspicuous."

I felt bad for thinking I preferred her in a wig. Seeing her bald was uncomfortable. It made her look so weak.

I checked my phone again. The night before, I'd called Chuck to let him know I wasn't coming home. He hadn't responded. This was unlike him. It meant things were bad in a new way now, worse than they'd been before. The boys were fine. I'd texted each of them to explain. *Not coming home tonight. My friend needs me.* Cam had responded with emojis I'd never seen before, and Jed had responded, *Whatever.*

•

The restaurant was called, simply, Pasta, and the letters on the sign were written in a loopy font that looked like linguine. "I don't see his car," Ana said, pulling into a spot behind the bank like she had done this many times before. She turned the engine off. The prickling sensation in my armpits told me I was nervous.

"Has the plan come to you yet?"

"No," she said, not worried. She tugged at her bangs, puckered her lips in the rearview mirror. "Ugh, these lips are like flat tires," she said. "I want to look hot in case he's in there." She pushed her breasts closer together for more cleavage. "Isn't that sad?"

"You look great," I assured her.

"Thanks, Nan. You're the most supportive person I know. You are my cement-poured foundation."

Before I could tell Ana that she was my attic, or my chimney, or my roof deck (I was still working it out), she set her hand on mine. "Let's take pause, okay?"

We sat there for two minutes. Or five minutes; it was hard to tell. The sound of cars. Of footsteps walking up the stairs to the bank, of the ATM beeping, of footsteps going back down the stairs. There was the constant chirping of birds, birds, birds, and Hawaii really was the most magical place on earth, and I should be grateful, grateful, grateful but Chuck was such an asshole and I was angry, angry, angry and I would focus my angry energy on Gregory now, who was the same type of asshole, or worse.

Ana marked the end of our pause with an om and I joined her. Then she said, "Okay, let's go. I still don't have a solid plan. We'll eat lunch at the restaurant and figure it out from there."

It was three in the afternoon and the restaurant was nearly empty. Only two tables were occupied. A pretty waitress with unfortunate cystic acne on her neck scurried past us in a frenzied state, and then a hostess popped up from behind her podium to say, "Ciao."

Ana elbowed me. "G makes them say that," she whispered.

Okay, so we were calling him G now.

"Two?" The hostess took two menus off the stand.

"Yes," we said at the same time.

"Follow me."

Everything was spotless, but it wasn't the sleek, modern look I had expected. It was a lot tackier than that. On the walls was a random mix of pasta art. A highly detailed pencil drawing of a single piece of penne (some cursive words underneath—maybe its Latin name?) hung next to an almost indistinguishable face made from actual pieces of dry penne. The furniture looked old and it didn't match. Even two chairs at the same table weren't the same chairs. But it was set up in an orderly way, with the silverware very straight on each napkin and a vase of flowers perfectly centered on each table.

The hostess was taking us to the window when Ana gasped. "No," she said, her hand going to her throat. Her eyes were on the fish tank, where a red fish with fins like tattered rags was completely still in the water. "We want to sit there." Ana pointed to the table under the tank.

"No problem," said the hostess, who tilted herself comically in the new direction like she was steering an imaginary car.

Ana chose the chair that looked like a throne, which left me with the little wicker chair.

"Your waitress will be right with you," the hostess said.

"Is Gregory here?" Ana asked.

"No." The hostess seemed relieved. "It's his son's birthday today."

Ana's face darkened. Before she could say anything she might regret, I said, "Thank you!" and the hostess walked away.

Then Ana held her chin up with one pointer finger and looked around the room. She shook her head. "I can't believe he had a son."

I scrunched my face for her. "I'm sorry, Ana."

"And Paco's basically dead. Look at him."

I looked at Paco. He did look basically dead.

"And this table." She ran her hand over the wood. "I remember when he bought this. Three hundred bucks. I told him, 'It looks like it costs *five* bucks!' All these tables are antiques." When she looked at me then, I knew before she spoke that the plan had come to her. "Stay here. I'm going across the street." She draped her napkin on the back of her throne. "And G is comping us lunch. So order tons of food while I'm gone. Seriously, order everything, okay?"

"Oh—"

And then she was gone.

By the time Ana reappeared with two small paper bags, I had ordered two appetizers and two entrees. "I didn't know if you wanted pasta or fish, so I—"

"I'm not hungry. I don't care what you got," she said, dropping one of the paper bags into my lap and then sitting back down. "But we should order more than that."

I opened the bag. Gorilla Glue. Ana unscrewed the cap on hers. She took the salt off our table, squirted a dollop of glue on the bottom, and then returned the salt back to its spot. Then she did the same to the salt on the table beside us. She sensed the waitress approaching before I did and returned the glue to her lap. I was amazed by her swift movements and her still hands. She was crafty, intuitive. How she'd harnessed that intuition for good rather than evil—besides this silly prank of gluing salt and pepper shakers to the tables at her ex's restaurant, which was too silly to qualify as evil—was inspiring, and something to be proud of. Because in this moment, I could see what Ana had meant when she'd told me that she was a natural-born hustler.

"Beets and minestrone," the waitress said, placing the dishes in front of us.

"We'd also like the lamb and the scampi and the penne with pesto, please," Ana said.

The waitress blinked twice before taking her pen and paper out of her apron to write it down. "Your friend already ordered the scampi. Do you want another one?"

Ana flashed a smile. "We're very hungry."

It was obvious the waitress hated her job. She sounded like she'd just been run over when she said, "Another scampi, coming up."

The second she turned her back, Ana got up to do two salts on nearby tables. When the woman sitting by the window looked over, Ana calmly returned to her throne.

"Nan, are you going to glue any?"

"Yes," I said, but I didn't move. The minestrone smelled good, and even though I was too anxious to be hungry, I was thinking about the other type of lunch this could be: the one where we just sat and ate the food we had ordered.

Ana chuckled. "Don't do it if it makes you uncomfortable."

And right when she said that I stood up and tiptoed to the table by the wall. My shaky hands fumbled inarticulately with the salt shaker and then I pressed too hard, releasing too much glue. One gooey dollop hit the floor. I returned the salt shaker to its place on the table. The yellow glue bubbled out around the bottom when I pressed it down.

And then the waitress was coming! I tried to look innocent as I tiptoed back to my seat.

Ana was laughing. "Oh, Nan," she said. "You're a wreck."

"I am not," I said, which was what a child would say.

"I'm going to have to do most of this," she said. "You're going to get us caught."

"No, I want to help."

Ana put her hands up as if to say: Fine, you win. "Okay, Nan, whatever you want."

I did four more tables and Ana did the rest. She became more daring along the way, and started gluing the flower vases, too. I moved the food around on each dish to make it look like we had sort of eaten it, and the waitress kept bringing out more food. At one point, she said, "Is something wrong with your meal? Meals?"

And Ana said, "Nope. And we'll also take five slices of cheese-cake, three raspberry tarts, and a crème brûlée."

When the desserts arrived, I moved them around on the plates while watching Ana move stealthily around the restaurant, becoming even more daring still when she glued two legs of a heavy chair to the floor. Watching her was exhilarating. My heart was beating out of my chest the whole time.

When she returned again, she said, "This was the perfect time to come. No one's here. Our waitress is outside smoking."

Before I could respond, our waitress was walking toward us. "How was everything, ladies?" she asked, massaging a mint in her mouth.

Ana cocked her head. "It was divine."

"Good," the waitress said, and began stacking the plates. "I'll be back with the check."

"Don't bother," Ana said, and stood up. "Gregory is comping this meal. You can tell him Ana says hi."

"Okay," the waitress said, her arms full of plates. She didn't seem to care that much about who was paying for the meal.

And then in slow motion a plate with a piece of mashed-up cheese-cake on it fell to the floor and crashed in a sticky mess of mosaic pieces.

Instinctively, I bent to clean it up.

Ana said, "Let's go. Nan, don't do that," and I put the single piece of broken plate I had salvaged on the table.

Ana took my hand and led me out of the restaurant, swinging our one locked hand back and forth like we were small children in a field in a movie. On the way out, she said, "Gregory is an asshole!" but the way it happened—with the first part of the sentence in a lower voice and the "asshole" much louder—the hostess thought she'd been called an asshole, and promptly yelled "Fuck you!"

I turned back with an apologetic look on my face and said, "No, no," but before I could explain further, the hostess was flicking me off, and then I, somehow, was flicking her off right back.

Out on the street, I said, "I can't believe I just flicked off that hostess!"

"How do you feel?" Ana swung our one locked fist higher up in the sky and then swung it all the way back.

"I don't know!"

"Why are we screaming?!?" Ana screamed.

"I don't know!"

Ana laughed hard. She was folded over herself, howling in the street. This was the happiest she'd been since the diagnosis, and I was glad for that. When she finally caught her breath, she said, "That was fun."

"That *was* fun," I said. And then I felt guilty. "But do you think they hate us? We broke a plate."

"What? No. We didn't break it. She broke it."

Right, that was true. Why was I assuming guilt for something I didn't even do?

"And it's okay, Nan," Ana said, her face alive and pink from laughing so hard. "Everyone who works in a restaurant hates people anyway. The point is that we made the world a little more right today. We just shifted the molecules on this earth one degree toward justice."

She held up her hand for a high five and I slapped it. "Let's get some cookies!" she yelled, loving how it felt to yell.

"Cookies!" I yelled, loving it, too.

People on the street were looking at us like they were jealous of our fun. It was such a relief not to be nervous anymore, and I understood something new about the Karma Factory in that moment. Delivering the karma could be hard sometimes, but afterwards you really did feel like a goddess.

We ordered our cookies hot and sat on the curb in the shade eating them with our sticky glue fingers. Warm white chocolate mac nut cookies and they were delicious. As we watched the people amble by—the tourists with their pasty calves and the locals with their dirty feet and everyone else—I didn't think: I want to be you. I don't want to be you. I want to be you. Which was what I normally would have been thinking at a time like this. Not today. Today with Ana on this curb, I didn't want to be anyone but us.

22

I got there first. I sat in the fifth row. I placed my bottled water next to me on the bleachers, a halfhearted seat saver for Chuck. But when he arrived, sullen and disheveled, with his Walmart Hawaiian shirt buttoned one button off and asymmetrically hanging, I grabbed the water bottle and pretended not to see him. He pretended not to see me too, although I knew he had because he sat in the first row to be as far away from me as possible. Chuck hated the first row.

I concentrated on the pool. There was pale Tom and there was—ugh—Liko and there was coach Iona bent over the water with his hands on his knees, explaining a play. And then there he was clapping his hands, shaking his fist in the air, riling his players up.

A man next to me said to his wife, "We're missing church for this. Why would they have the game on a Sunday?" The wife said, "I don't know, but it's Sundays all month," to which the husband responded, "I don't like it." The wife put her hand on the nape of her husband's neck, massaging it. "God is everywhere, honey. Plus, we can start going Saturday nights." The husband laughed. "To the Spanish service?" The wife shrugged. "Sí." She kissed his cheek. "You won't even notice the difference."

The ref blew the whistle and the teams sprinted toward each other. Jed just missed getting the ball first. I looked at Chuck's sweaty neck and realized something was missing. I had forgotten to bring the GO MURPHY BOYS! sign. Which wasn't surprising. It had been a tense morning.

Chuck had slept in the ohana again. He'd gotten home at 1:00 a.m. Or 1:04, but who was counting. The sound of his car woke me up. Then at 11:00 a.m., he'd strolled into the kitchen like a hungover college student to make coffee, strolled right by me stretching on the lanai. We looked at each other for a second—he looked paunchy and irritable; I looked healthy and radiant—and neither of us said anything. I heard Cam say, "Hi, Dad," but Chuck didn't answer. He hadn't had his coffee yet.

Part of me wanted to run after him and throttle him and say: You need help and we can find help and let me help you. But I had done this before and it hadn't worked. Chuck needed to come to his own conclusions. And my main focus right now wasn't Chuck. It was Ana. For the next three to six to maybe nine months, helping Ana was my main focus. If Chuck thought I was spending all my time with her, then he was right. I still hadn't told him she was dying.

Cam made an amazing pass and I clapped and said, "Woo!" I looked at Chuck, and, good, he had noticed and he was clapping, too. I watched him scratch his sweaty neck. The front row was in the sun and he was boiling. I could pass him my water bottle. But I would not. Chuck could come to his own conclusions. If he was thirsty, he could get his own water.

What happened next: I saw it happen before it did. The KFC family was sitting next to Chuck today, passing the humongous bucket of chicken parts between them, and Chuck kept glancing over. Kept glancing and kept glancing and then he said something to the barefoot mother, probably, "Hey, that smells good." And then she patted her barefoot toddler on the back and pointed to the sweaty man, and the toddler made his way on wobbly legs to Chuck with the tub, and then it got even more embarrassing.

Instead of just picking whichever piece was on top, Chuck spent real time fishing in the tub for a thigh. Of course he had to have his thigh. After some digging, he found it and held it up with a smile and said something else, probably "Hope you don't mind I took a thigh!" and the wobbly toddler, who'd been waiting, somehow made it back to home base without falling into the bleachers.

I watched the back of his neck working as he gnawed. When he was done, he got up to throw the bone in the trash can. He made his way there slowly, his eyes on the game, not aware that he was blocking people, who were shifting to see around him. Then he wiped the grease from his hands onto his bare legs and rubbed it in like it was sunscreen. No one told him to move because these people were too nice, but I knew everyone was happy when he sat back down. Oh, Chuck. I almost felt sorry for him.

In the third quarter, Jed dunked an opponent—really dunked him, pressed his shoulders down into the water full force, not even trying to hide it from the ref—and he was given a red card and taken out of the game. No one booed because we all agreed with the ref's call, except for Chuck, who stood up and shuffled around like a mad ape.

On the side of the pool, Coach Iona with his hands on his knees said something to Jed, and Jed untied his cap and smacked it on the concrete. Great, anger is inherited. Or learned. Either way, it was Chuck's fault.

Meanwhile, on the other side of the pool, Cam and Tom were having what appeared to be a lighthearted conversation—both of them smiling—so at least one son had been spared from the anger complex.

Then Liko—ugh—gave Jed a high five, and Jed got out of the pool and paced around the players' bench with his hands on his waist, stopping to kick the gear on the ground. Eventually he sat down to watch the rest of the game with his torso hanging over his legs in a defeated posture.

All of Cam's throws were bad after that. He wasn't paying attention. Or his brother being kicked out of the game had drained the energy from both of them. It was like that with twins. One felt what the other was feeling. Sometimes this made them more powerful, and other times, like now, it sucked them both dry.

I sent Ana a text: *How are you feeling?*

•

Chuck and I stood on the farthest sides of the blue Honda in the parking lot. The Waveriders had lost the game, and the boys were taking longer than usual. Coach Iona waved at us, and we waved back. He didn't tell us that he loved our boys today.

Chuck kept looking over at me, and I kept looking at the gate, waiting for the boys to appear. Then Chuck let out a long sigh, fluttering his lips at the end of it. "Nance?" He sounded exhausted. And then he looked at my water bottle longingly, so I took a nice long sip before responding.

"Chuck?"

"Never mind." He took off his hat, smoothed his thinning hair back, returned the hat to his head, and leaned back on the trunk of the Honda.

I tried to compose myself. "Chuck, I'm upset you're drinking again."

"It's under control," he said, defiant.

I wanted to scream: You've said this before! We've done this before! Hello! So I said nothing instead.

Chuck let his arms fall by his sides. "I feel like you're pushing me away."

Pushing him away? He was pushing—"I feel like you're pushing *me* away, Chuck. You're the one who's down at the bar shooting pool every night!" Nancy, don't yell. People can hear you.

In a cool, measured voice, which pissed me off because it made him the calmer one, Chuck asked, "Aren't you the one who told me I should join the Tide Poolers?"

And then I decided to tell him. We needed to remember what was important. "Ana is dying, Chuck. She has terminal cancer."

"Oh," Chuck said. I couldn't see his face under his hat, but I hoped he looked sorry. "Has she had terminal cancer this whole time?"

"Chuck. That is *so* the wrong question to be asking. How about 'How is she feeling, Nance?' or 'I'm so sorry you're about to lose your best friend in the world, Nance.'"

"See? But that's what I mean, Nance. I thought *I* was your best friend in the world."

I rolled my eyes, but all I said was "Chuck," because he did have a point.

And then there were the boys walking toward us. Tom with Cam and Jed with—ugh—Liko, just like the last time.

"Boys!" Chuck called. He sounded so excited. Even in his worst moments, he really was a good dad.

Before anyone could say hi, Cam made a whiny request to go to Denny's. "Pleeease."

Chuck scrunched his face. "Aren't you still grounded, young man?"

"Aw, come on, Mr. Murphy." Liko hit Chuck's arm in a manly way. "Everybody gotta eat!" Then he looked at me, and said, "Hey, Mrs. Murphy," in that lascivious tone, and this time I knew I hadn't imagined it.

Chuck, unable to resist being Cool Dad, caved immediately. "Fine, but I want you home by four o'clock. You have a shed to build."

Tom looked at Cam as if to say: A shed? And Cam looked back at him like: I'll explain later.

"Fi-ya," Liko said in a spooky voice, and twinkled his fingers.

Chuck looked at his feet, thinking of what to say next. "I know! Tom and Liko, you boys should come over for dinner some night. I'll show you the ball Tony Azevedo signed for me."

I hadn't seen that ball in years and I knew Chuck hadn't either. Had we even brought it to Hawaii?

"You got a *Tony* ball?" Liko put his hands on his hips. "Naaah," he said, pulling his head back.

"Oh yes," Chuck said, "I do. How about you all come see it next week? You pick the day."

"Hump daaaaay," Liko said. Of course he would say that.

Chuck tried to understand.

"He means Wednesday, Dad," Cam said.

"Wednesday, hump day," Chuck said. And then, "Oh, I get it!"

So passive-aggressively and also like the lamest housewife on earth—why?—I put my hand on my hip and asked, "Am *I* cooking?"

"Sloppy joes," Jed confirmed.

"Sloppay," Liko said.

"Pleeease, Mom?" Cam whined.

"Fine," I said, "fine." And then because I was such a good person—how much good karma would I receive for this?—I added, "We would love to have you for dinner."

After we'd waved the boys good-bye—"No fires!" I yelled; "See you at *four* o'clock!" Chuck reminded them—I turned to Chuck and said, "Alcoholism is a disease, Chuck. Until you get help, I can't help you."

Chuck's face. He looked so stressed-out. "I'm not asking for help," he said quietly.

"You think it's under control, but it's not, Chuck. It never is."

"This time it is," he said. The way he seemed to really believe this was astounding.

"I have to go."

"Do you want to go to lunch and at least talk about it?"

"I don't know," I said. I worried that if I said yes, he'd convince me it really was under control, and I couldn't go through all that again.

"We can go back to Bite Me, if you want. And have some poke. And just talk."

I sighed. Without even realizing it, I'd taken my phone out of my purse and was checking the screen for new red bubbles.

Ana had written back. *Come over?*

"Chuck," I said, "I don't think lunch is a good idea right now. Plus I have to go see Ana. She needs me."

Chuck took his keys out of his pocket. "She needs you," he repeated.

"She does," I said, trying to sound sure.

"Well," Chuck said, "I guess I'll go play some pool then."

He turned and walked away before I could say anything. Maybe that was better right now. It felt like there was nothing else to say.

·

The door was open.

"Ana?"

Half-empty glasses on the low tables in the living room and Portico on the low chair, still as a hose and possibly asleep. The flowers I'd brought her were on the counter next to the fruit. The mangoes were rotting.

"Ana?"

The sliding glass doors to the lanai were open all the way, which they never were. The thick salt smell and the breeze ruffling the pages of her yellow legal pad.

I poked my head outside. "Ana?"

There she was, on the far side of the lanai, splayed on a rainbow afghan. No wig and wearing her black silk kimono. She was on the phone, speaking in a British accent. "Yes, three o'clock would be grand." She winked at me. "Thank you, kind sir." She hung up.

"Nan!"

"Ana!"

"Come come." She patted the afghan and scooted over to make room for me.

"All your doors are open," I said, lying down next to her and looking up at the sky. It was blue and blue and blue and completely clear.

"I want the birds to go inside."

I smiled. "Why?"

"I don't know." She touched my hair. "Haven't you always wanted a house full of wild birds?"

This was the type of thing only Ana would say. I would miss her saying things like this. I tried to look at her, but the sun was too bright. "I guess I've never thought about it."

"Well," she said, and then, "Ow," and she jerked her body suddenly and her knees pressed into my legs.

I sat up. "What's wrong?"

Her hand to her stomach. "No," she whispered, "I'm fine." She closed her eyes, breathed with intention. I breathed with her, louder than her, leading by example like she did for us in class.

"Do you want me to call your doctor?" I reached halfway for her phone.

"No," she said louder. She winced. "No doctors."

"But they can prescribe you something for the pain," I said. Flash-back to the orange bottles that filled the shelves behind my mother's mirror. Why was I remembering that now?

She shook her head. She was in too much pain to speak.

I made myself touch her bald head. We were best friends, and she was dying, and if there was a time for intimacy, it was now. "I don't think anyone deserves to be in pain, Ana."

"I do," she whispered. After one more deep breath she rolled over. She pressed a button on her phone and then—just like that—she seemed fine again. "Guess what I'm doing?" Her lips curled into a smile.

"What?"

"Making fake appointments with my ex-hairdresser, Laurel. Because she told everyone I was a witch."

"A witch?" I felt defensive. "That wasn't very nice of her."

"I know! And I tipped her so well." She picked up the phone. "I'm calling again." And then it was ringing and then she was saying in broken English (maybe pretending to be Indian this time?), "Yes, Laurel, is the Friday at five p.m., yes yes. Devandra. My phone num-ber is"—she said some random numbers. "Thank you." She hung up and started laughing hysterically. "Oh, Nan, you do one, you do one. I'm running out of voices."

I don't know why I said "Okay" so easily. Maybe to please her. "I'll do my Southern accent."

"Yes!" Ana pressed the button and put the phone to my ear. It was ringing.

A man picked up. "Hair Would Go, how can I help you?"

I laid it on thick. "Yes, I'd like an appointment with that there Laurel tomorrow at noon." Same feeling as at the restaurant: anxiety and excitement and my armpits prickling and my ears burning off my head, and this was exhilarating.

I imagined the man flipping the pages of his calendar. Maybe I heard them. Hard to tell over the noise of the crashing waves. "The earliest I have is next Friday at eleven thirty."

"That would be dandy," I drawled.

"Name and phone number please?"

I looked at Ana for an answer, but she was laughing too hard to give me one. "Oh, um, Dolores Greeeeeel," I said. And then I made up some numbers. I almost thought the man would say, It sounds like that's a fake name, but he said, "Thank you, see you soon," instead, and hung up.

"Dolores what?" Ana managed to say through her laughter.

"Greel?"

"This is fun!" Ana exclaimed. "Let's do it again."

"Okay."

"But wait!" She rolled onto her back. She blinked at the sky. "It should be bigger."

For a second, I thought she was talking about the sky. "I know," she said. "We should order soil. And get it sent to someone's house. And dumped in their front yard. So they'll just have all this soil in their front yard."

"But then won't they have to pay for it? Soil is expensive." I had learned that at Lowe's.

"We'll get the cheapest kind," she said. "I think you should do it in your Southern accent again. I love listening to that."

I was flattered.

"Pleeease, Nan," she begged.

I needed more information. "Whose house would you want to send it to?"

"You know who I keep thinking about?"

"Who?"

"That guy who beats his horse."

"Peter," I said. I remembered him exactly. His scrawny arms hanging out the sides of the flannel shirt with the arms scissored off, his jittery leg. How he'd left before Ana could tell him his future was so, so bright.

"Peter," Ana said. "Peter deserves justice for sure." She puckered her lips, thinking. "But I don't have his address." She tapped her chin. "I'm sure I can get it though."

"How?"

But Ana had already moved on. "Ooh, I know who we're send-ing this soil to. My old boss Stan. He was the worst. He offered to let me live in his garage, and when I said I wanted to, he said, 'You are a grifter and an opportunist!'" Ana sliced her finger back and forth in the air, making a face like a snarling dog. "Waving his finger at me just like that."

"No!"

"Yes!"

I was already looking up the number for Lowe's. And then I was calling. And then the phone was ringing and then I was placed on hold with music that reminded me of music the water polo moms would listen to—soft old hits—and I thought—why?—of my mother walking in on me and a friend making prank calls when I was fourteen and her saying, "You're not fooling anyone, Nancy."

When the Lowe's person said, "Lowe's," I snapped back into the plan, which was somehow now removed from what we were actually doing. All I could concentrate on was my beating heart and the need to be totally believable.

"Heya there, sir," I said. "I'd like to order some soil." I was first impressed by how quickly I had gotten good at this, and then I was a little scared by how quickly I'd gotten good at this. The man said the minimum for soil delivery was thirty-five pounds, and I heard myself say, "Exactly what I'm lookin' for." My ears burned hot, and when he told me the total was three hundred something dollars, they burned hotter and went numb. A voice inside me said, Say never mind, that's too much money, but then there was Ana's expectant face and my heart pounding for a decision and you only live once but people only tell themselves that when they want to be reckless but it's still true that you only live once, and fuck you, Mom, and fuck you, Chuck, and fuck it all, and then I heard myself say, "Perfecto!"

When I hung up, I noticed my trembling hands weren't actually trembling at all.

"Wow," Ana said, rolling around on the afghan like a happy puppy, "Nan, that was so good. You're good at being bad." She was belly laughing. She couldn't catch her breath. Waves crashed. And then she said, "How do you feel right now?"

My heart still pounding. I was wide awake. I felt good and I felt bad and I felt caught between the mother at the water polo game and this woman lying on the ground ordering soil to a stranger's house because he deserved it. And then there was also the woman who was just trying to eat a little better and get her shoulders more defined. Nance and Nan and I was obviously Nancy and I was all these people and none of them, and I didn't know anything except for exactly what I said, which was "I feel powerful."

•

We dragged the couch outside and watched the sun lower in the sky. My head on Ana's shoulder and Ana playing with my hair because she still missed hers so much. "I wish I were going to die with hair," she said. We watched a mother whale teach her baby to breach in near silence.

"Do you think those are Sylvia's whales?" I asked her.

Ana chuckled. "All the whales on this island are Sylvia's."

It made me sad to think that Chuck didn't know who Sylvia was. It made me sad to think he was at the bar right now, making things worse. His confusion was exhausting. As was his jealousy. In a stripped and grainy voice, I told her, "My husband is jealous of you."

"Me? Li'l old me?" she asked in my Southern accent.

"He can't stand not being the center of my world."

Ana's hand paused in my hair. "The way the Beloved can fit in my heart, two thousand lives could fit in this body of mine. One kernel could contain a thousand bushels, and a hundred worlds pass through the eye of the needle." She began stroking my hair again. "That's Rumi," she said.

I repeated the only part I'd really heard. "Two thousand lives could fit in this body of mine." That made complete sense to me right now. Well, or it didn't. Okay, it either made complete sense or it didn't make sense at all.

"Who's at the center of your world, Nan?"

Again, only a question Ana would ask. And it was the question lurking in my head. How had she heard it before I had?

"Who's at the center of my world?" I repeated, buying myself time. The obvious answer was the boys.

"I'll tell you the answer," Ana said. "Who's at the center of your world is you. You are the center of your world."

"But isn't that kind of self-centered?"

Ana shook her head. "No, my darling, that is reality."

I watched the swelling waves without really watching them. They rose and fell and rose and fell. The ocean looked like it was breathing. And then there were our small chests expanding with air and emptying out. When I sighed, I wondered if a wave could sigh. Like that one. The way it flopped too early. The way it didn't fully crest.

•

We ate peanut butter sandwiches as the sun got bigger and more orange in the sky, and Ana said, "Will you stay here tonight?"

I didn't even think about it. "Of course."

As the horizon line swallowed the last piece of orange, I held my eyes open for the green flash. "Did you see it?" I asked her.

"What?"

"The green flash."

"Oh," she said, "I don't believe in the green flash. I think somebody just made that up and everyone else believed them."

•

She gave me her red silk pajamas to wear and we got in bed early. She said, "Normally, this is when I would thank Celia for her guidance today."

I took her toothbrush out of my mouth and through the foam, I asked, "What do you see when you look at the sky now?"

"A void."

I was glad my mouth was full of toothpaste because I didn't know what to say to that. I went into the bathroom to spit.

Then my phone rang.

I wiped my mouth and walked into the living room, hurrying but not hurrying toward the phone, and then there was Portico on the ground, and I howled like a maniac—"Aaah!"—as I watched my foot step just barely past her slithering body.

"I almost killed Portico!" My heart was beating in my temples.

Ana chuckled. "You can't kill her. She's too smart."

I grabbed my phone off the couch. I'd missed the call. Cam. Why would he be calling? But it was probably nothing. I walked back over Portico and into the bedroom, where Ana was lying halfway off the bed with her head touching the floor.

"Why isn't Portico in her cage?" I asked, still flustered.

"I want to see what she does with freedom," Ana said. "Who called?"

"Cam."

"Are you going to call him back?" Something was happening to Ana's windpipe in that position. She sounded like a robot. She laughed, but only a little. It was too much strain to really laugh with her windpipe like that. She was in her funny, giddy mood and I loved her like this. But then—it happened so fast—her hand on her stomach and her face cringed in pain and she rolled over.

I rushed to her, put my hand on her back. "Are you okay?"

She made a little squeaking sound.

"Are you *sure* I shouldn't call a doctor?"

She shook her head just barely. And then like the other times, the pain seemed to pass but maybe only sort of, and she curled her legs into her body and asked me softly, "Can you make me peppermint tea, please?"

"Of course," I said, and kissed her bald head, which surprised me. I knew I wouldn't have done that if she weren't dying. I did it because after she died, I would think back to this moment and wish I had kissed her bald head. But the reality of it was nothing like the misty picture I'd imagined. My lips touching her scalp—we were just fumbling body parts colliding in space and it was awkward. Both the intimacy of it—I had kissed the side, not the top of her head—and the position of my body, pretzeled between the bed and the floor with my foot strangled beneath me.

I went to the kitchen. Peppermint, peppermint. I couldn't find it anywhere. I went back to the bedroom. She was still curled in a ball. "You don't have peppermint tea. Do you want something else?"

"No," she groaned. "It has to be peppermint."

"I'll run to the store then," I decided. "I'll be right back, okay?"

•

I drove fast. I was still wearing the red silk pajamas. Before I got out of the car, I threw Chuck's sweatshirt on. He'd left it in the backseat. LIFE IS GOOD, it said. I remembered the day he'd bought it. It was right after Shelly. When he came home wearing it, I had rolled my eyes at how delusional he was and walked out of the room.

When I turned into the tea aisle, who was there? Mana. Mana who spent his days at the bus stop never taking the bus. Mana who had made up the name Sandwich Sistahs. I was so happy to see him. "Hey!" I said. He was holding a box of Smooth Move. He looked at me like he didn't know me. Because he didn't, not really. He only knew me in the context of being one half of the Sandwich Sistahs. I wasn't recognizable without Ana. Still, he was very polite. He had understood that my effusive "Hey!" meant that he should know me, and he said, "Nice to see you again, ma fren." And then he read Chuck's sweatshirt. "Life is good, yeah? Yeah, life is good." He smiled. He had maybe four teeth. "Well," he patted my arm, "see ya, sistah," he said, and walked toward the registers. I stood there thinking, Wait. Does Mana call everyone *sistah*? That makes it less special.

I grabbed three kinds of peppermint tea and paid. In the car on the way back, Cam called again. "Honey?" I answered.

"Mom! Where are you?"

I'm in the red silk pajamas of a woman you haven't met. She's like a sister to me and she's dying. "With a friend. What's wrong?"

"Dad is being insane. He made us work on the shed for five hours. And it got dark so he parked his car in front for lights. He just sat in there and blasted Journey and got wasted."

To a stranger, this would have sounded like borderline child abuse, but I knew the boys were being dramatic. They were teenagers who didn't want to build a shed. Or I was raised on dysfunction and had no conception of "normal." But in this moment, I needed to believe it was no big deal.

"Did you guys sing together?" I asked. I was trying to look for evidence that it had been fun in some way.

"At first, but then Dad got wasted." Cam sighed. "I hate this."

"Is that Mom?" Jed said in the background.

One second passed and then Jed was on the phone, saying, "Dad's passed out in the car and all the doors are locked. Are you coming home?"

"No," I said sternly, in a voice that reminded me of my mother's. "Your father has done this many times before. Just leave him there and go to bed. In the morning you will go to school."

"Seriously?" Jed said. "Where *are* you?"

I'm almost back to Ana's, and when I get there I will rip off this stupid sweatshirt and I will make us tea and I will try to forget that you called me, and aren't you almost eighteen years old? You're not a baby anymore and you can deal with this, and your childhood has been so much easier than mine. Maybe it's been too easy. This is not a big deal. Compared to my life at your age, it's nothing. Compared to cancer, it's nothing. It's an eye drop in the ocean.

After I get back to Ana's, I will make the tea. I will tell Ana everything is okay even though it's not. And when she falls asleep, I will wonder what I'll be doing after she's gone. I will still be trying to forget this phone call. I will still be trying to forget you and your brother and your father and that house and the way I feel when I walk inside it.

When Ana falls asleep, I will look at her face and tell myself to remember it well. Since we look the same, this won't be hard. In the bathroom mirror, I will see the necklace first. It will glint in the low light. I will dab coconut oil on my wrists. I will look at my reflection in the mirror and then there will be a flash, and in this flash it won't be my face. It will be Ana's face, and I will try not to blink.

23

But at 7:00 a.m. I felt guilty, and by 7:30, when the block of morning sun had crept to the edge of the floor, I was silently folding the red silk pajamas and fixing my eyes on the rise and fall of sheets to make sure again that yes, she was breathing. And then I was in the car on the way to Denny's, where I would buy to-go breakfasts for Jed and Cam and not Chuck.

School started at 8:15. The boys usually left at 8:00, which really meant 8:05. I put on Chuck's stupid sweatshirt again while I waited for the food. I was cold. It was the only thing I had.

By 7:55 I was speeding up the mountain, imagining that I would just catch them on their way out. I would hand them this food and they would happily eat in the car on the way to school, and with every bite of French toast, they would forgive me a little bit more.

But the blue Honda wasn't in the driveway. They had left already. Only Chuck's car was there, parked at the end of the drive in front of what would be the shed. So far it was exactly half a shed—two walls waiting for two more. The boys had done a lot of work.

I grabbed the Denny's bag, walked to Chuck's car. The driver's seat was reclined and empty. Sometimes on his car nights, he liked to spread out in the backseat, but he wasn't there.

I found him in the kitchen popping Advil in his mouth—probably four pills; he always took too many—and swallowing them with coffee. How many times had I told him you weren't supposed to do that?

I knew that he'd heard me come in, but he took the time to wash his cup in the sink (which he normally didn't do—he was proving something by doing that) before he spoke.

"You're back," he said, and turned toward me. His bloodshot eyes fell on the Denny's bag. "Is that for me?"

"Sure," I said, and set the bag on the counter. "Take it."

"Thank you," Chuck said. "I'll take it to work."

I sighed as loudly as possible. "What happened last night?"

"If you were here, you would know." He looked straight at me, his bright blue eyes and all the red veins around them.

I tried and failed to say it nicely. "Do you remember that you passed out in your car?"

The look on his face: he did not remember. He scratched his neck just for something to do. He looked below me, at my chest. I saw him reading the words. *Life is good.* "Is that my sweatshirt?"

I didn't answer his question. "You're ruining everything, Chuck."

"No," he said. "We're both ruining everything." He took the Denny's bag, and I listened to his familiar footsteps walk away. The car door slammed, the engine turned on, and after Chuck drove away, all the birds were quiet except for the laughing bird, and it was laughing hard.

•

I opened the fridge. We needed eggs. I didn't feel like getting eggs. I didn't feel like cleaning the pizza debris from the living room. Greasy plates on the arms of the couch and the box on the table, and when I opened it, there were still three slices inside that no one had bothered to refrigerate.

I told myself to relax as I yanked my spandex up my legs. I would do some stretching and feel better. I laid out my purple mat. I inhaled the foggy morning air. And then I just stood there like a stranger, looking at this life. Through the windows of the ohana I could see piles of Chuck's clothes. And a lamp—he'd put a lamp in there. Where had he gotten a lamp?

There was my car, my I-am-not-having-a-midlife-crisis white convertible car, parked askew in the wet dirt. There was the half-built shed, badly placed between the house and the ohana on what I could see now was uneven ground. It seemed to be leaning. There was the lush jungle that surrounded the property and the green grass rolling softly up the hill, and there in the grass was my garden where nothing grew.

I made myself stretch anyway. Because this was who I was now. I was a woman who did yoga in the morning on her porch in Hawaii, and I was a woman who cooked oatmeal the old-fashioned way in a pot on the stove and who ate it while really savoring the taste, or really trying to. I was a woman who owned her solitude in this empty house that smelled like pizza while googling inspirational quotes as though frantically searching for something she had lost.

When the bird started laughing again, I went outside and picked up a rock. But no, Nancy, Nan, whatever your name is, you are not a woman who hurls rocks at living things.

So I got into the car and drove instead. Down the mountain, out of the fog. To the ocean where life was clear and sunny and at least I had a purpose.

•

I didn't knock. I just opened the door. "Ana?" I said quietly, in case she was still sleeping.

"Nan." She was standing in the kitchen squashing a ripe banana in her fist. The peel broke and the yellow meat spurted out, and then she threw it in the sink behind her. "Guess what?" she asked, picking up a new banana.

"What?" I said, walking closer.

The pocket of her black kimono was moving, and then Portico's head slithered out. Ana pushed Portico back inside her pocket without looking. She squeezed the banana. More yellow meat spurting out. It looked like baby food all over her hands. "Guess who called me?"

Gregory telling you you owe him around two hundred dollars for all that Italian food?

"Who?"

She threw the banana into the sink, picked up another. She was almost out of bananas, but the rest of the fruit from the fruit stand was still on the counter. I wondered if she planned to squeeze the mangoes next.

"I have a favor to ask of you."

"Anything," I said.

She squeezed the banana and threw it into the sink but didn't reach for another this time. Instead she walked around the counter and spread her arms out wide.

"Oh, Ana." I hugged her. I breathed in her coconut smell. Or maybe it was my coconut smell, I didn't know. Portico writhed against my stomach.

Ana pulled back and held my arms and sighed. "Eunice called. She officially listed the house." A beat. "Can I move in with you?"

"Of course," I told her. I was elated, and then I was already imagining the conversation with Chuck—she's *dying*, Chuck—and telling myself why this would be good for the boys. To meet someone who was dying—it would make them understand how fortunate they were.

"Oh, Nan," Ana said, her bald head catching the light. Her eyes looked like they'd already sunk deeper into her head. "You are my truest bluest friend."

"It's no problem. We'd be happy to have you."

"Thank you," she mouthed. She looked at the fruit. "I guess I can stop squishing these bananas now." She chuckled, but barely, and put a tired hand on her forehead. "Sorry, sometimes I just get so angry."

I was soothing. "It's okay. Squishing bananas is probably a healthy way to express anger."

We both chuckled at that, and then Ana hugged me again. It felt good to hold her. It felt good to be needed. In a sick way, a secret part of me might have been glad for the weight of her catastrophe. Her imminent death and all the details surrounding it made my problems seem stupid, which was a relief. Instead of feeling sad about Chuck, my mind filled up with her logistics. Would she need movers? Was this furniture hers? Where would we put Portico's tank? Portico would have to stay inside the tank; we would have to have that conversation. And when? When was this happening?

"When would you like to move in?" I asked her.

Ana inhaled and exhaled deeply. "Eunice gave me two weeks," she said. "But honestly, I don't want to be here anymore."

"Let's leave now," I said.

My spontaneity surprised her. "Now?"

"Now."

"Now."

"Now!" I yelled, and then I don't know why—to make her feel better, probably—I picked a mango off the counter and hurled it at the sink. "And we can be angry if we want to!"

"Angry and vengeful!" Ana yelled, like this was now a therapeutic exercise we were doing. She picked up a mango and hurled it the other way.

If there had been enough time to form a sentence in this moment, I would have said, I hope that sliding glass door is open.

But it happened so fast.

The mango whipped across the living room.

After the initial whop, it sounded like ice cubes crackling in a drink as the fracture spread fast throughout the pane. The sliding glass door was now in pieces but the pieces were still in the frame. They were holding on to nothing but each other's shapes. I waited for them to fall. I waited longer. They didn't fall. The new prisms cast light in all directions, and it was kind of beautiful.

•

It only took us thirty minutes to pack Ana's stuff. She put on her relaxing yoga music and turned it up so loud that it became energizing rather than relaxing.

"There is a difference between needs and wants!" she boomed, tossing another Buddha figurine into her camo duffel. "I want everything, but I need almost nothing!"

I didn't tell her this, but I thought that Ana's needs and wants were kind of reversed. The things she needed were the things I would have left behind. She chose the pretty things over the essentials. In the bedroom, she held up a pair of black lace panties and said, "You know what? I'm not going to wear underwear anymore," and let them fall to the floor. Her cheeks were flushed and her eyes were spinning in the light.

I put the bananas in the trash while Ana finished packing. There was nothing to do about the broken door. After the ice cube sound had stopped, Ana had said, "Shit, Eunice is going to charge me for that."

Adrenaline rushed through me like a drug. The loud chanting in another language reverberated throughout the house, and I kept thinking the blast of gongs would make the glass fall, but it kept not falling, and I kept putting the bananas in the trash, and what would Chuck say and how would the boys react, and would I get a divorce? But none of this mattered because right now my hands were just moving to the beat of the music that had no rhythm, and the snake was free and writhing on the floor, and in the middle of this chaos I watched my focused hands wipe banana meat from the sink, and I was impressed they were doing that because I could barely feel them.

Ana marched to the stereo and jabbed the power button. The silence was alarming.

"Let's go," she said, her voice echoing in my head like the gongs that were no longer there. She was out of breath and sweaty and her face was the color of a wild strawberry, and I knew for sure that this was the most alive she'd been since the diagnosis.

She grabbed Portico off the floor and put her in the tank and picked up the tank with surprising force. "I'll carry this," she said. "You carry the duffels."

The duffels were in the doorway of the bathroom. They weren't very big. "Are you sure this is it?" I asked her.

"Oh yeah," she said, bouncing the tank up to get a better grip. "I'll meet you at the car." She started to walk away, and then she turned around. "Oh, and I left Eunice a present in the toilet." She raised her eyebrows. "Don't flush it." As she walked away again she called, "Nan, do not flush it! I will know if you did!"

I lifted the toilet seat for the same reason I drove slower past a car accident: just to see how bad it was. And then I stopped breathing because it was bad.

I picked up the duffels. They were heavy. I had to get to the car. And then—I don't know—my hand was reaching for the flusher.

"Naaa-aaaan," Ana called, and before I knew it, my hand had retreated.

"Coming!" I said, and hauled the duffels across the living room.

At the front door, I paused. Good-bye, house. Good-bye, Jacuzzi. Good-bye, couch. Good-bye, rainbow afghans and all the crap in life we acquire but don't really need. I felt particularly enlightened about this last one, as if I'd reached a new understanding about the art of letting go, even though it wasn't actually my stuff we were letting go of. Good-bye, baggage, I added with attitude, even as my body buckled under the weight of her duffels.

Before I left I took one last look at the site of the crash. The fractured glass was still hanging on. I shut the door quietly so I wouldn't disturb it.

24

The boys came home right after practice because they were still grounded. And because I had texted them: *Please come home right after practice.* I thought it would be easier if they had a little time to get to know Ana before Chuck threw a fit. I'd been very nice and a little manipulative about it on the phone—"It would really mean a lot to me to have her here, Chuck, and she's *dying*"—but my sweetness had not charmed him.

"How long?" he wanted to know.

Ana and I were sitting on the couch with Portico and talking about Peter—"I bet he and his horse live up on this mountain," she was saying—when Jed and Cam walked in.

"Hi, boys," I said, suddenly needing to be the perfect mother.

"Hi," Ana said. She'd put on the black wig with the neon pink streak because she thought they'd like her best in that one.

Jed put his hands on his waist, which reminded me of his father. Cam just looked sad, which upset me.

"I know, babies, I'm sorry. I rushed home this morning with breakfast, but you were gone."

"Yeah right," Cam muttered.

"I promise I did," I said.

"She did," Ana confirmed, although she couldn't have possibly known because I hadn't told her. Still, I liked that she had come to my defense. Chuck probably wouldn't have done that.

"Please be polite and say hello to our guest. This," I said, presenting her with an open palm, "is Ana."

"Your mother didn't tell me you were so handsome," Ana said. "Are you fraternal or identical?"

Cam sighed. They hated this question.

"Oh, time out," Ana said. "You hate that question."

That made Jed smile.

"Sit down," Ana said. She moved Portico to the other hand and scooted over on the couch.

"Ana's going to be staying with us for a while," I said.

"Where?" Cam wanted to know.

"In my room."

Jed rubbed his eyes. "Is Dad living in the ohana now for real?"

"Just for a little while," I said in my most comforting tone.

They exchanged a look. They seemed to be saying: We knew this would happen. And then Jed rolled his eyes. "Whatever. Dad sucks right now."

Cam, still looking at his brother, agreed. "Yeah, I'd probably kick him out, too."

"Sit down with us," I said, pleading a little.

They exchanged another look, and then they sat. Jed took the recliner, and Cam sat between Ana and me on the couch. "Mom, can you make us dinner? I'm hungry," Jed said, not looking at me because he was transfixed by Portico, who was wrapping herself around Ana's wrist.

I looked at the fridge and knew it was empty. "I guess I could run to the store."

"We should make pasta all'Amatriciana," Ana declared, pronouncing it with a thick Italian accent.

"What," Jed said with a counterfeit sneer. "You're Italian?"

"Me?" Ana motioned to herself. "No. Are you Italian?"

"Maybe I am." Jed's head danced like Liko's, which was unsettling.

"We're not Italian, are we, Mom?" Cam asked.

"No, honey," I said, "we're not." Since I didn't know who my father was, I could have been lying. It was always easier to pretend he wasn't an actual person with a heritage.

Jed shifted forward. "I think we should eat your snake."

Ana held Portico up. "Do you think she would taste good?"

"Sick!" Jed laughed.

"I'm down with pasta," Cam said.

"Pasta all'Amatriciana is pasta with bacon," Ana told us. I wondered if she actually wanted this or if she just knew bacon was a thing that would appeal to teenagers.

"I could do bacon," Jed said, too casually. I could tell he was trying to impress her.

"I'll run to the store," I said, getting up. "Ana, are you okay if—"

"We're great." She raised her eyebrows.

"Okay." I snatched my purse off the counter. Phone, phone, where was my—

"Phone," Ana said, holding it out for me.

"Thanks," I said. We were such a good team. I slipped on my flip-flops at the door. "I'll be right back."

"Bye, Mom," Cam said.

"Bye, Mom," Jed said, reaching out to touch Portico's head.

"Bye, Mom," Ana said. As I walked away, I heard her say to Jed, "Do you want to hold her?"

●

I stood in line at Safeway with my teeming cart. This was the biggest shop I'd done in a long time. Bacon and four different types of pasta and the good kind of Parmesan and three packs of Red Vines for Ana and Ranch Corn Nuts for Jed (his favorite) and fruity Mentos for Cam (his favorite), plus all the essentials we'd run out of—milk, eggs, ketchup, lettuce, bananas. The bananas weren't ripe enough to squash, but we could wait and squash them later if we felt like it.

Sting's "Fields of Gold" fuzzed through the speakers. The AC was almost too cold. My eyes floated to the magazine racks. Oprah in a decadent gown holding two small, clean dogs and the words: *A Brand*

New You! I was about to pick it up, but then the line moved forward and I moved with it and no, Nan, you don't *need* that magazine, and the answers probably aren't in there anyway, and then the word *Fan-tas-tic* spilled out over everything.

That familiar voice and, oh no, oh yes, it was Marcy, two people ahead of me, talking to the cashier about bags. "I love that you still provide bags here," she said. "You're the only ones who still do that."

I crouched down, maybe pretending to tie my shoe even though I was wearing flip-flops. I could see Marcy's Tevas and her perfectly applied bland pink nail polish and the haole rot on her calves. Khakis and a tunic—that's what she was wearing.

"I'm cooking mahi-mahi for my husband tonight," Marcy informed the cashier, who hadn't asked about her dinner.

I wanted the cashier to ignore her or grunt or say, "Who cares," but, like every cashier in Hawaii, this one was also too nice.

"You know what's good? A little seaweed flakes on top," she said, to which Marcy replied, "That is a fan-tas-tic idea, thank you."

As I watched her Tevas walk away, I noticed her heels weren't cracked at all. I didn't look at my heels to compare because I already knew how badly cracked they'd gotten. They had split into canyons.

As I hoisted myself up in the most dignified way possible and shook out my leg because it had started to fall asleep, I imagined Brad and Marcy's mahi-mahi dinner and knew it would be boring. Or I hoped it would be boring. After their boring dinner they would probably take a boring stroll down Ali'i and have boring sex, and maybe I could cultivate some compassion for Marcy, who didn't even know how boring she was. And yes, I was able to cultivate some compassion, and the great thing about that was that it was not only inarguably nice; it also made me a better person.

•

When I got back, the twins had switched positions. Jed was next to Ana now and Cam was lying back on the recliner with Portico stretched straight down the center of his chest like a zipper on a jacket.

"That was fast, Nan," Ana said, impressed.

"You call Mom Nan?" Cam asked.

Ana smiled at me. "I do," she said. "Is that okay?"

Cam shrugged.

"You're weird," Jed told Ana.

"*You're* weird." Ana kicked his leg.

"Boys, can you get the rest of the stuff out of the car, please?"

It surprised me that I didn't have to ask twice. They just got up. Maybe we were all being our best selves for Ana. Cam lowered Portico into the tank, which was on the coffee table for now, and followed his brother out the door.

I set the grocery bags on the counter. "How are you feeling?" I asked her.

"I'm okay," she said, touching her stomach.

"No pain?"

She traced her collarbones all the way across, from one shoulder to the other. "Life is pain, Nan," she said.

"That's what my mother used to say," I told her.

"What? Life is pain?"

I scolded myself. Why are you talking about your mother, Nancy? You don't want to be talking about her. So I didn't tell Ana the rest of my mother's refrain, which was "Don't marry losers like I did." Because every time my mother talked about the pain of life, she was referring to one of her failed relationships.

I changed the subject. "I got you some Red Vines."

Ana got up off the couch—in a lively way; good—and wrapped one arm around my waist and said, "I love you, Nan."

Flashback to her telling me she didn't know what love was. Obviously she'd been wrong about that. Because here she was, saying "I love you" to me, and I knew she meant it.

•

The four of us cooked together. Since Ana knew the recipe best, she became the head chef and told us what to do. Jed chopped the ingredients, Cam sautéed them, I cooked the pasta, and Ana set the table. She dug two candles and two Buddhas out of one of her duffel bags and set them between the plates, and then she put on some nice jazz music.

Jed said, "Ambiance," and I was proud of him for using a more complex word than *cool*, or *dude*, or *yeah*.

Ana went outside and came back with a dead branch. "Found art!" she exclaimed, and hung it on the nail above the table that I'd abandoned all those months ago. The four of us agreed that we had been skeptical when she'd walked in with the branch but now we could see how it was very clever.

Jed, Cam, and I sat in our usual places, and Ana sat in Chuck's chair. The steaming pasta looked delicious.

Before we ate, Ana said, "Wait, let's hold hands for a second."

Jed shrugged. Cam shrugged. We took each other's hands.

"Close your eyes." Ana inhaled and exhaled deeply. "Breathe."

"What are we doing?" Jed asked.

"Just go along with it for a second," Ana said gently.

I opened my eyes for just long enough to see Jed close his again.

"What *are* we doing?" Ana chuckled. "That's a great question."

"Yep," Jed said.

"What we are doing is sitting here," Ana said, "at the dinner table. The piano music is playing. There are crickets. We smell pasta. We see the candles flickering through our eyelids."

A long pause. The crescendo of the piano. "In a moment, we will eat this pasta. In this moment, we are grateful for its enticing smell and its beautiful presentation in that decorative bowl. We are grateful to Mom for going to the store. We are grateful we had the energy to cook tonight. We are grateful we feel hungry; an appetite is a sign of health." Inhale, exhale. Low, calm notes from the piano. "This is it. The moments before this and after this—those are gone. This is it, this is it. *This* is it. Enjoy this. Be grateful. Eat like you mean it." Pause. I half expected her to om. She didn't. "Buon appetito."

We opened our eyes.

I looked at Ana first. Her eyes were black and glimmering. She was staring straight at me. One candle-lit tear rolled down her cheek.

"Are you *cry*ing?" Jed chided, but underneath that he seemed alarmed.

Ana looked at him. "Yes." She didn't wipe her tear. "Is that okay with you?"

Before Jed could say more stupid things, I flooded them with information. "Ana has cancer, Jed. Cam. Ana has cancer. Okay? So she's allowed to cry whenever she wants. She's dying."

The boys looked scared.

"Plus," Ana chuckled, "crying makes you pee less."

"You're dying?" Cam's concerned face.

Ana nodded.

"Shit," Jed said.

"Shit is right," Ana said. "But this will not be our dinner topic. No more cancer talk. Agreed?"

She looked at each of us and we nodded.

"Let's enjoy this food." She scooped a heap of steaming pasta onto Cam's plate. She was so selfless. Then she scooped for Jed, and then me and then finally herself.

"Bacon pasta," Jed said, his mouth full and his eyes bulging. "Dude."

"It's divine," I said because I knew she liked that word.

"Oh, Nan," Ana said sweetly. Then she pulled a long steaming bunch of spaghetti from the pile with her fingers and lowered it into her mouth.

I laughed. "No fork tonight?"

A line of red sauce ran down her chin. She smiled. "It tastes better with your hands."

Jed laughed. "I want to try." He pulled the spaghetti up and waited for it to stop steaming—he was more sensible than she was—before lowering it into his mouth.

We waited for his verdict.

"You're right, it's totally better," he said, going in for more.

Cam and I tried with our hands and decided that no, we preferred our forks.

"You are the fork people," Ana said, "and we are the animals."

"Where are you from, Ana?" Cam asked her.

Ana stuck out her tongue, which was red from the sauce. "The armpit of the world."

"El Cajon?" Jed asked.

Ana sipped her apple juice. "What's that?"

"It's a part of San Diego," I told her.

"Oh, well, I'm sure it's nicer than New Jersey. That's where I'm from. When I was nineteen, I moved to Vegas, and then I moved here." Ana made dots in the air to show us.

Cam twirled his pasta. "Did you go to college in Vegas?"

"No," Ana said. "I dropped out of college and became a stripper."

I looked at the boys. They looked at each other as if to say: Whoa. And I felt proud to have this eccentric friend who could teach them something new about the world. Which, clearly, they needed. I couldn't believe Jed thought that El Cajon was the armpit of the world.

"You weren't really though, right?" Cam's wide, earnest eyes.

"Why not?" Ana said. "It's a real job."

"What's the most money you made in a night?" Jed asked, maybe not believing her either.

"Six grand," Ana said. "An Arabian prince and his entourage."

"No way," Jed said.

"Way," Ana said.

"Mom"—Jed slapped the table—"I'm going to be a stripper."

"Whatever makes you happy, honey," I said, which I knew got me some Cool Mom points. Although, of course, I hoped something other than stripping would make him happy.

"College is a better choice," Ana said. "If I had to do it over again, I would go to college."

The boys seemed to really get this when Ana said it, and instead of rolling their eyes or rolling their whole heads around in the latent beginnings of a tantrum, they nodded like knowing adults.

"How's high school going?" Ana asked them.

"Sucks," Cam said.

"It's okay," Jed said.

"I'm with Cam," Ana said, patting his hand. "High school blows."

"Yeah, okay," Jed said. "I think it blows, too."

"I hated high school," I said, remembering what a shell of a person I'd been.

"Let's cheers," Ana said.

They reached for their apple juices. I grabbed my water. We held our glasses high above the flames.

Ana made the toast. "Fuck you, high school!"

Mid-sip, I paused. Movement to my right, and there was Chuck in the doorway looking either confused or angry or both. It was hard to tell with all the lights off.

I cleared my throat. "Chuck."

"Fuck high school?"

Okay, he was definitely angry. Which—I might have been too if I were him.

"Come here, Chuck," I said. "I want you to meet Ana."

Ana stood up, which was very polite. Chuck walked toward her carefully and they shook hands, and she said, "It's a pleasure to meet you, Chuck. And we were kidding about fucking high school."

Chuck took his hand back. "Why is there a tree branch on the wall?"

Ana raised her eyebrows. We all tried not to laugh.

"It's moving." Chuck leaned closer. "There are ants crawling all over it."

"It's alive!" Jed made a scary face.

Chuck looked at me: Are you serious?

I may have winced for him. I'm sorry?

"Anyway, Chuck," Ana said, "thank you for letting me stay here."

"You're welcome," Chuck managed. I could tell he was really trying.

"Are you eating with us?" Ana asked.

"I just came to get my shirt," he said. "I have a game tonight."

"Nan tells me you play pool," Ana said.

"I do," Chuck confirmed. And then to the boys, "Boys, did you work on the shed this afternoon?"

"No, Dad," "No, Dad," they echoed.

Chuck nodded. He didn't look pissed. He just looked sad, which was worse. "Well"—he pointed to the hall—"I'm just going to . . ."

"Get your shirt," Ana finished.

We were quiet while Chuck got his shirt. It took two seconds. When he came back out, I said, "Please be careful tonight, Chuck."

"Don't worry." He walked toward the door. When he stopped, I knew exactly why. "What is this?" he said, pointing at the tank and then crouching to see more.

"A lizard," Ana said. Candlelight flickered on her face.

In a flattened voice Chuck said, "It doesn't look like a lizard," and then he walked out the door.

We were completely silent, listening to Chuck's footsteps recede down the stairs. Ana closed her eyes. She said, "The energy in this room has changed."

•

In bed, I said, "We were like a happy family tonight."

She grabbed my hand. "I love your boys."

"They love you," I told her. "Jed called you a baller."

"He did? When?"

"After dinner." I held her eyes. Remember her now, remember her like this. "I'm so happy you're here, Ana."

"There's nowhere else I'd rather die."

"I can't believe you're going to die."

"I wonder what it's going to feel like."

"Me, too."

"I hope it feels like nothing." A beat. "You didn't flush that turd I left for Eunice, did you?"

"No."

Her smile. "I knew you wouldn't."

"I thought you would know if I flushed it."

"How would I know?"

"I don't know. You know things."

"I don't know jack shit, Nan, I just talk."

"No," I said, because she was wrong. "You know things. You pay attention. That's why I like you."

"Okay," she said, "I know things." She hit my leg with the pillow.

"Hey!" I hit her back.

She got up on her knees and started batting me with a new pillow. I got up and fought back. We laughed, laughed harder, laughed until we could barely breathe. We kept going until Ana said, "Wait, wait, I'm sweating. This is going to ruin my night cream," and fell onto the bed. I hit her once more and fell onto the bed next to her. We landed on opposite ends, with her feet at my face and my face at her feet.

"Good night, Nan." She put her hand on my foot and left it there, so I put my hand on her foot.

"Good night, Ana."

"Good night, Nan," she whispered. "Don't say anything else. I like to be the last one to say good-bye."

Wind

25

"Your shoulder blades are wings made of ice," she said. "Melt them. Melt them onto your back. Feel them drip. Stand up tall. Taller. Taller. You are an ivory tower. You are a telephone pole. You are attached by a string to a cloud. The cloud floats up. You lift. Lifting. You are lifted onto a higher plane. Good. Now extend your hands up, up, up and look up at that cloud. Yes, Nan, that's beautiful, yes."

Remember this, I told myself. Everything Ana is saying about these postures and the neon-green gecko with two hot-pink spots and one orange one making kissing noises on the overhang and how Ana strokes her cheek with the eraser of that huge I ♥ HAWAII pencil when she is concentrating.

When Ana put me into savasana, I splayed my arms and legs expansively off the mat to show her that I was a person who was willing to take up space in this world. She pressed my shoulders down with her warm hands and traced my eyebrows with her warm fingers. I heard her walk back to the chair and take a sip of the peppermint tea I'd poured her. The pencil made a soft scratching sound on the yellow legal pad as she wrote. The birds and the geckos and the water heater and how there were so few people in the world you could really be silent with like this.

After one or five or ten minutes, she said, "Now come back. Back, back, back. Wiggle your fingers, your toes. Roll to your right side. This is important for your kidneys. When you're ready, sit up. Head comes up last. Press your palms into one another equally. The right into the left and the left into the right. Good. Now touch your thumbs to your third eye. This is your intuition. This is the voice you should never ignore." A pause. "Ooooommmmmmmm." Just the two of us and we were so loud. The power of our voices together reverberated up the mountain, down the mountain. Its echo might have carried for miles.

"Peace to all beings, no exceptions." We bowed. "And that means no exceptions."

I opened my eyes. Ana had put a blanket over her head like someone in the wilderness preparing for a natural disaster. She smiled at me, a huge smile. All those glistening white veneers and how they dulled the brightness of everything else.

She whispered, "You are reborn."

"I am reborn," I whispered back.

She tapped the eraser against her lips. "I wonder what they're doing down at the beach without us."

"I miss that class," I said, thinking of Patty and Kurt and Sara Beth. I wondered if Patty had bought a new cat yet.

"I don't," Ana said certainly.

"You don't?"

"No," she said. "I'm dying, Nan. I don't have time for longing."

I told myself to remember that: I don't have time for longing. I watched her write something down and thought, I should start writing some of this stuff down.

"So," I said, "who's next on the list?"

Ana looked at me as though this were very interesting, what I had just said. "Your loyalty astounds me, Nan."

"I want to help," I said. "I like doing this stuff with you."

"You enjoy the Karma Factory," she said.

"I do."

"It's kind of like a secret club, right?"

"Especially when you wear that blanket over your head. You look like . . ."

"Jesus?"

I laughed. "Maybe."

"Or the Unabomber."

"No." I shook my head. "I don't like that one. Too violent."

Ana chuckled. "Unabomber." She tapped the eraser on the pad. "You know who I can't stop thinking about?"

"Who?"

"Peter with the horse. It's just *tugging* at me." She pulled an imaginary string out of her heart. "And I know he lives somewhere up here. I swear I can feel it." She looked out at the grass, at the jungle surrounding us.

In the silence my stomach whined like a whimpering dog.

"Are you hungry, Nan?"

"I am," I said, getting up. "I'm going to make some oatmeal. Do you want some?"

Ana smiled. "You are such a mom, Nan."

I don't know why I said, "No I'm not."

"Yes you are. It's a good thing, it's cute. And yes, I would love some oatmeal."

"Great," I said, rolling up my mat. "I make it on the stove, the old-fashioned way."

"Then what do you do?"

"I usually look at my blog."

"Your blog? You've never told me about your blog before, Nan. What other things aren't you telling me?"

Of course she didn't know. She couldn't.

Keep it light, Nancy. "No other things."

"I want to see your blog. Will you show me?"

"Of course."

Just then the gecko from the overhang—or another one; there were so many—fell to the armrest of Ana's chair. Quickly she covered it with her hand. "I caught you," she said in a joke menacing way. Then she said, "Watch this, Nan." She lifted her hand partway off the gecko. Then a little more and a little more so its head was poking out, and then its middle with the pink and orange spots, and then she took her hand off and quickly pressed just the end of the gecko's tail into the armrest. The gecko raced away soundlessly. Under Ana's finger was just the tip of the gecko's tail, which was still alive and wriggling. She picked it up and pressed it between her palms. Then she lifted her thumbs to her third eye. The blanket was still on her head. When she smiled her glistening teeth were all I could see. "I can feel its heartbeat," she said. And then she held her cupped palms open for me. The tail was still moving, but less. "Take it, Nan."

I didn't move.

"Hurry before it fades!"

I wrapped my right hand around the wrist of my left hand. The braver right hand made the unwilling left hand move toward her. She dropped the tail into my hand. The second I felt it move I shrieked and the tail fell through the wooden beams on the lanai.

Ana laughed, and then I was laughing, and she said, "You're scared of death, man!"

Still laughing, I said, "Don't call me man! My name is Nan!"

Then Ana stopped laughing. When she looked up at me, her eyes were blank and her skin was pale, too pale. "It's okay," she said, her voice hollow, "we're all scared of death."

•

Ana drank her oatmeal out of a mug—"This is the path of least resistance"—while I showed her my blog.

"See? And then she has all of these amazing recipes you can make in under twenty-three minutes," I said, scrolling.

Ana read aloud. "To die for times ten."

"That's her rating system," I said, hoping Ana would find this smart.

"Whole-wheat flautas with cranberry sauce. To die for times twelve," she read on. She sounded unconvinced.

"So that one must be really good," I said, too enthusiastically.

"Have you made a lot of these?"

"Not yet, but I plan to."

Ana pointed to my blogger's face on the screen. "Who is this person?"

"Here, let's go to the 'About Me' section." I clicked.

Ana read: "Hi, I'm Sandita, a health-food nut/lover of life/vegetarian activist living in San Antonio. Blah blah blah." Ana took the mouse and scrolled down to the bottom, where there was a picture of muscular Sandita about to eat a tortilla chip with a radiant hunk of red salsa on it. "I am so relaxed when I eat this food," her talk bubble said.

Ana leaned back in her chair. "Nan, I'm sorry, but no one with a body like that is relaxed. Look at her biceps. She's not a lover of life. She's at the gym all day lifting heavy metal objects off the ground."

I sprang to Sandita's defense. Because by this point, I felt like I knew her. "Actually," I said, "Sandita enjoys Pilates once a week, but other than that, her only form of exercise is the brisk walks she takes with her dog, Jacobo."

We both did a double take of Sandita's biceps then, which did look oddly pronounced for an easygoing pedestrian.

"I'm sorry, honey, but Sandita might be a fraud. And by 'might be,' I mean she is one. I'm good at spotting frauds." She stretched her arms up. "Because I used to be one."

•

In the shower, Ana was singing. Again, I thought it was "Lean on Me," but again it was something else. When the water stopped, she called, "Can I wear your clothes?"

"Sure!" I called back. I was in the kitchen doing dishes and think-ing about Sandita in San Antonio and wondering if, right now, she was cooking chicken adobo with organic ingredients only or at the gym flexing her biceps in the mirror.

Ana appeared in my purple dress, the one I'd worn to Bite Me with Chuck on our date when things were going well. It made me a little sad to remember that night.

"What do you think?" She twirled. The dress was way too small for Ana, and so tight I was surprised she was forming sentences while wearing it.

"Is it comfortable?" I asked nicely.

"Like a glove." She leaned her head back and ran her hands down her sides.

"Well, whatever makes you feel good is good right now."

"Oh, I need shoes." She scampered down the hall.

"Where are you going?" I called.

"To the doctor!"

The doctor? I thought Ana was done with doctors. And why did she seem so happy if she was going to the doctor? "I thought you said no more doctors!" I called. It was fun calling to each other across the house. It felt so marital.

She came down the hall clacking in a high pair of heels. Hers, not mine. I'd never seen them before. She pouted her lips and stuck her butt out. "So?"

"Mmm-hmm," I said, toweling off a pot. "How are you feeling? It seems like you have a lot of energy today."

"I do." She looked out the window as though she'd just thought of something. "And I know it's not going to last," she said somberly. "So"—she sighed—"I'm going to take advantage of it now, you know what I mean?"

"Yes, Ana, that's great." I kept toweling the dry pot. "Do you want me to come to the doctor with you?"

"That is so sweet of you, Nan, thank you, but I need to do this one on my own." She looked around. "Have you seen my keys?"

I put the pot down. Because the pot was dry. It didn't need me to keep drying it. "They're on the key rack by the door."

"A key rack. You *would* have a key rack, Nan." She went over and took them off what I had mentally designated as her hook. "Okay, I'll be back later. Don't get too lonely without me." She blew me a kiss and then she was gone.

•

I spent the day waiting for her to come back. Hours passed. Should I be worried? But no, Ana was an adult and Ana could take care of herself, and I would not be worried and I would not call her and I would stop checking my phone to see if she had called me. She would come back. She would have to. She lived here now.

I googled "pancreatic cancer symptoms" and they were brutal, and I felt helpless. Suddenly cleaning the house seemed very urgent.

I put on the same jazz music we had listened to at dinner, and swept and scrubbed and it felt good. Her words echoed in my head: "Neat people fear death more than messy people. It's about control." And when I had dropped the gecko tail: "You're scared of death, man!" I knew she had meant to say *Nan*.

I organized the bedroom for a person who would be convalescing here. Or I tried. I stood at the end of the bed and imagined her dying in it. I imagined her withered to skin and bone by anorexia-cachexia, which affected 80 percent of PC victims. She would probably want to sleep most of the time. So I fluffed the pillows. I put a box of tissues on the nightstand. I sprayed some Febreze. And then I ran off to mop the floors before the feeling of helplessness immobilized me.

At 3:32 she called. I picked up on the first ring. "OhmyGod I'vebeensoworried. Are you okay?"

"Nan." The way she said my name told me this was serious.

"What?" Was she in the hospital? Could I hear the drip of her IV in the background? But no, a car honked in the background.

"You need to come down here right now. Patricio's. I'm parked in front. Do not go inside. Meet me at the car."

"What's wrong?"

"You're going to want to see for yourself. Trust me. And hurry. Seriously. Chop chop!"

·

The sight of the purple Jeep in a parking lot made me sad for the old days. I pulled in next to her and got out of my car and into hers quickly because whatever we were doing had a time limit.

"Ana, what is going ooooh—"

What was wrong with Ana's lips? She'd either gotten them stuck in a pool drain or she'd been stung by eight hundred bees. They were puffy and white-pink and filmed in a shiny layer of Vaseline.

She pressed her buggy sunglasses up her nose. When she spoke, her voice was there, but her lips didn't move. "I know," her voice said, "I got my lips done. They look bad today, but tomorrow they'll look fabulous."

"So that was your doctor's appointment today," I said slowly, figuring it out on the way.

"Nan, whatever makes me happy right now is a good thing, right? Restylane makes me happy right now. Don't judge." Some words were obviously harder for her to pronounce. Like "Restylane." She grabbed my wrist. "But that's not why we're here. Look inside Patricio's."

I squinted. We were pretty far away. All I could see was the Patricio's decal, and behind that the shadowy shapes of tables and bodies.

"Here," she said, handing me a pair of binoculars from her lap. I hadn't noticed them there because I hadn't noticed anything after her lips. Since when did Ana keep binoculars in her car?

I laughed, taking them. "Why do you have these?"

"Bird-watching. Whatever. Will you look inside freaking Patricio's please?"

I pressed the binoculars to my eyes. It was hard to hold them steady. There were people's feet, and people eating, and a salsa bar with lots of bins that looked empty except for the orange one piled high with pickled carrots because those were gross and no one liked them.

"What am I looking for?"

"To the left. Look to the left."

To the left, there was a family and a policeman and someone I recognized from somewhere, but I couldn't place it right now, and there was a blond woman at a table sipping a fountain soda and—

"No."

"You see him?"

"This can't be happening."

"It's happening."

"No."

"Chuck," Ana said, like his name was something dirty.

I couldn't believe it. Chuck with a woman, and of course she was a fucking blonde. Chuck at a bad Mexican restaurant with a fucking blond woman at 4:00 p.m.? I kept looking, trying to make it go away. But no, there he was. My Chuck, nodding along as the blond woman spoke. She was animated. She used her hands to accentuate her point. And Chuck was smiling that particular smile he used when he wanted to impress people, the one where he stuck his chin forward extra far. He was making that extra effort for her. And his body language, how attentive he was. His whole being was trying to impress her. And he was wearing his Hawaiian Walmart shirt, not his work shirt. Which meant that he had changed his clothes for this date. I felt dizzy and frozen and hot in the sun, and I wanted it to stop but I couldn't look away. Things were bad between us, but now they were irreparably bad. Cheating on me again? This could not be repaired. This was the last straw, this was the avalanche, this was divorce court.

The chips at the center of the table. Chuck and the blond woman reached for them at the same time. Did their hands touch? It was too fast to see. Chuck ate his chip with his mouth closed, which was so deferential. And then they were standing up and walking to the door. Chuck opened the door for her. How rarely he did that for me. Smiling as he held it open, gesturing for her to go. Smiling so incessantly that it must have been hurting his face. They emerged and took a few steps down the corridor of the strip mall and—no! They disappeared behind a big white van.

"Fuck. I can't see."

"Fuck that van," Ana said.

They were probably kissing good-bye behind that van. I had to go see for myself. I reached for the door handle.

"Don't do it, Nan," Ana said. "Think about this."

"I'm going to fucking kill him." I opened the door.

"Nan, no." Ana grabbed my wrist.

I shook her off me. I was ready to break something.

"Nan," Ana said. "Screaming at Chuck in a parking lot isn't going to accomplish anything."

My eyes were still fixed on the spot where they'd gone missing.

"Don't get out of this car, Nan. There is a better way to go here. Screaming in parking lots is not the Karma Factory way." And then in a lower voice, she added, "We are women of grace and fucking dignity."

I thought I saw Chuck's leg and flinched. "Oh!" And then yes, there he was, walking to his car, and that stupid grin was still on his face. I put the binoculars down and I could still see that grin.

He opened the door and took a paranoid look around him. It was then that I decided to leave it up to the universe. If Chuck saw me, I would jump out of the car and run at him and throw these heavy binoculars at his head. If he didn't see me, I would trust that Ana was right to wait and I would stay in the car. I had one foot in the car and one foot on the pavement. It was so ridiculous how I never knew what to do.

Chuck set his keys on top of his car and then he stood there in the sun, unbuttoning the top two buttons of his shirt. He really needed to start working out. That paunch. And that skeezy car. And that ridiculous tropical shirt. He looked like a retired mobster who'd moved to Florida to avoid indictment.

I waited for him to see me, or, if not me, then at least my conspicuous car, which would count too, or if not my conspicuous car then Ana's even more conspicuous car. That would also count as his having seen me. But—what an idiot. He saw nothing. He was off in his dream world, dreaming about what the blond woman looked like naked. Fucking asshole. And then the blond woman was driving by, driving slower past him. A red Mazda. Shelly Two—I was already calling her that. Shelly Two waved and Chuck waved back. Then Chuck got into his decrepit car and drove away. Where, I didn't know. Because I didn't know what Chuck did anymore.

"Nan honey, breathe," Ana said.

I tried to breathe. I closed my eyes so I wouldn't have to look at her lips. It was too disturbing to see yet another person I loved looking like a stranger.

I brought my foot back into the car.

With Shelly, it had just been that one time, that one drunk night. "It's like someone else did this, not me," he'd said. I'd imagined a dark dark room and their drunk clashing bodies and it happening so fast that neither of them could really remember the details. But this. This was so much worse. It was daylight, it was conversations, it was fucking Mexican food. It was a real connection. And Shelly Two looked like a real person. Possibly with substance. She was clean. She wore stylish shorts. She had no humpback or the limp I'd been hoping to discover when they'd walked to the door together. Shelly Two had nothing I could easily make fun of. And her calves were more toned than mine. And she was blonder than me. Obviously, because I wasn't blond at all. Shelly Two was really blond. Charlize Theron blond. Or blonder. And she had made him smile like that.

"Nan?" Ana touched my shoulder. "Come here, my darling," she said, and pressed my still-shocked body into hers. She smelled like me because she was wearing my dress. I was too shocked to cry. I felt the angry energy wearing off and I knew that when it did, I would be very tired.

"I was just going into the coffee shop to get some iced tea," Ana said, "and I looked in the window of Patricio's and I was like: Is that Chuck? He didn't see me, don't worry." She patted my back. "Kind of crazy, right? Since I only met Chuck last night. If this had happened yesterday, I wouldn't have even known who he was."

I wasn't really listening to her because a new daunting thought had taken over. "I'm getting a divorce," I said. I didn't say this angrily, but with the wonder of a person who has been walking on a road for a very long time and then suddenly the road ends. And the person says, Oh. Oh? Oh, the road has ended. So suddenly? There must have been a sign on this road. Or many signs. Didn't you see them? Why didn't you see them?

"If it makes you feel any better," Ana said, "my divorces have all been pretty positive experiences. It might not feel that way to you now, but you'll get through it. The only way out is through, Nan. It just takes time."

Time. Over time, I would get used to the idea of a divorce.

But what about the meantime? What about the rest of today? And tonight, at home? What would I say to him? Would he continue to live in the ohana until he found his own place? A divorce could drag on forever. What about right now?

I said all of this to Ana. "I mean like tonight, what am I going to do?" Instinctively, I had looked at her, the person I was talking to. Those lips. I would have to get used to them. But for now, I looked away, looked back at the parking space where Chuck's shit Honda had been and a new car was parked there already, a shockingly yellow car, and the world was moving on too fast without me.

Ana reached behind my seat and pulled out the Costco tub of Red Vines. "You want one?"

"No thanks."

She was inspecting the tub from the bottom now. "Good, because it looks like they melted."

"*I'm* melting."

"May I make a suggestion?"

"Yes." Again I accidentally looked at her and again, I looked away and again my eyes fell on the yellow car. Circles. I was spinning. I closed my eyes. That was the only thing to do. Go through your life blind, Nancy. Go through your life like a blind fool.

"Okay, here's what we're going to do."

The *we* made me like this plan already.

"We're going to go home. You're going to take a nice long bath. I brought some bath crystals you can use. They will invigorate you. I will make dinner for the boys. We will lock all the doors. I will explain to the boys what is going on."

"No," I said, "We can't tell them about this."

"Fine. I will tell the boys the *PG* version of what is going on. I'll just say something happened and we have to lock Dad out tonight. Okay? This will give you time to think about what you want to do. You will go to bed early and you will sleep—I have some pills that will help you sleep—and you will feel better in the morning. And as far as karma, I think it's clear that Chuck deserves some right now. Be-*yond* deserves. I don't have a plan yet, but do I have your permission to carry out my plan when it comes to me?"

This might have been a place to take pause, but I didn't. Not a split second of dead air passed before I said, "Yes."

•

LAVENDER DEAD SEA SALT, RELAXING THE WORLD ONE BATH AT A TIME. What a dumb slogan. But it did smell good. And I wanted to believe it was relaxing me.

Ana had drawn my bath. She'd sat on the edge of the tub, feeling the water with one hand and her lips with the other—"I can't stop touching them"—and then she'd lit candles and turned the lights off. I'd looked at the filled bathtub and said in a drained voice, "No one takes care of me but you."

"I'm here for you," she'd said. She told me she loved me and that she would make pasta for dinner again and bring me some when it was ready. She'd also left me with an orange bottle of hydrocodone for the pain. "Take two. They'll knock you into heaven."

I committed to stillness and tried to relax. It didn't work. I tried to feel invigorated instead, which didn't work either. This was too much to expect right now. I was in pain. Pain pain pain, and there were the orange pills on the sink that would make it go away.

But, Nan, you will not take those. You will not take a medication that has not been prescribed for you. Because you are not your mother. You will go through the pain. The only way out is through.

I heard the boys get home. The slamming of their car doors— one, two—and then their long-legged steps into the house and then Ana greeting them with energy, so much more energy than I had right now. I felt tired just listening to the ups and downs of her voice. I couldn't hear the words, but I knew they were kind and loving and wise, and I knew the boys were hanging on to every one of them. How she was here tonight, filling in for me, picking up the pieces when I couldn't, and especially now, now at a time when most people would have checked into a hospital and waited passively to die, Ana was here, being the most selfless woman I had ever met.

When the water had gone tepid, she cracked the door open and whispered, "I brought you pasta. Can I come in?"

She would see me naked but who cared right now. "Sure," I said. My voice sounded weird to me.

The first thing she did was look at my body. "You have a great bod, Nan. You should really own it more."

I imagined covering myself with my hands, but I didn't move. It felt good not to care about her seeing me naked. When disaster hit, you stopped caring about everything that didn't matter. It pared you down. Clarity. This must have been how Ana felt all the time.

"I put the pasta by the bed, okay?" Her puffy lips seemed to be moving more now when she talked. She was wearing one of my tank tops and sweatpants that might have been Chuck's, and good for her for making herself comfortable.

She held up my phone. "Chuck called. He left a message. Do you want to listen to it together?"

I gave her a look that meant yes. She pressed the button.

"Hello, Nancy, I'm just calling to let you know I have a work event tonight, so I won't be home until late. Don't wait up. Okay, thanks, bye."

"Sounds like a business call," Ana said, touching her lips again. "But right in this moment, you are okay. When you get out of this bath, you're going to have some dinner if you want it and then you're going to take some pills and say good-bye to this day, okay?"

I loved her for telling me what to do. "Okay."

"I love you, good night."

"I love you, good night."

"I love you, good night," she said last, and closed the door.

•

In bed, I twirled the pasta and listened to the muffled sound of things exploding on the TV and thought about how Chuck had always been such a Chuck and never a Charles. I couldn't believe I'd ever dyed my hair blonder for him. I'd done that after Shelly, and then dyed it back. I couldn't believe I had believed he would never cheat on me again. It was so infuriatingly textbook.

The pasta smelled good, but when I took a bite it wasn't. Very undercooked. Which made sense. Ana hated cooking. I spat it into a Kleenex and turned off the lights and went to sleep.

But twenty minutes later I was still going to sleep and I hadn't gotten there yet. I had too many thoughts in my head. An event, he had said. What event? With whom?

I rolled into a new position. Again. And again.

I counted sheep up to three.

One: Why?

Two: Work event, my ass.

Three: Counting sheep has never worked for you.

And then I was thirsty.

I rolled off the bed, dragged my feet down the hall. I noticed the smell only one split second before I saw her.

"Nan." When she said my name, smoke poured out of her mouth.

Cam and Jed were on either side of her, eyes bloodshot and looking paranoid.

Ana blew the rest of the smoke into her armpit and smiled at me, but only a little because her lips were still paralyzed. "Hey," she said, "how are you doing?"

I stood there, trying to comprehend. My arms hung limp at my sides. I felt like a ghost, but a heavy one. "Are you smoking pot with my sons?"

Ana looked at the boys, who looked at their laps. "Is that bad?" she asked me.

I was too tired to sugarcoat it. "Yes."

She passed Jed the pipe, but then she realized she shouldn't do that in front of me so she put it on the table instead and got off the couch. Her hands on my arms and her innocent face and those lips, those lips. "Sorry, Nan, they just had some and pot's really good for cancer, you know?"

Suddenly my head hurt. "Let's talk about it later."

"Whatever you need, Nan."

"I need water."

"Oh, here, let me get it." Ana rushed to the sink. Every time she seemed energetic like this, I reminded myself of what I'd read online: *PC victims have good days and bad days.* Her energy meant it was a good day, and we should be grateful for that.

The boys. Jed was texting and Cam was looking at me. "Hi, Mom," he said.

Jed turned. "Hi." He waved, then looked at his hand like it was a foreign object.

"Here." Ana handed me the water. She kissed my cheek. "Sleep well, okay?" To the boys, she said, "Say good night to your Mom, kids."

"Night, Mom," Cam said.

Then Jed lost it. He opened his mouth and the laughter erupted.

And that's when I thought, Fuck it.

I walked straight to the bathroom and swallowed two pills before I could change my mind. As I put the orange bottle down, I glanced at the label. But then I picked it up again because who was Alan Jeffries?

I looked at myself in the mirror, as though expecting that person to answer my question.

But who was that person?

I splashed water on my face, asking it to heal me, but it was just water.

26

I woke up feeling like I was encased in cement. A familiar tune. I knew this tune. Where was this tune from? Oh, my phone. My phone was ringing. I opened one eye and reached for it. My groggy finger pressed the button. "Hello?"

"Nancy," he said.

In my head I said, "Chuck," but what came out was "Mmm."

"I almost died of a heart attack this morning, Nancy." Chuck sounded upset. "Do you know why?"

"Mmm."

"Because there was a snake in my car. A snake that looked a hell of a lot like Ana's lizard!"

This was too loud. I held the phone farther from my face.

"Nancy! The woman put a snake in my car!"

It was taking me a second to piece this together. "Where are you?"

"Costco!"

The bathroom door opened and there was Ana. Those lips. But they did look better today. "Who is it?" she mouthed.

"Chuck," I told her.

"What?" Chuck said.

"At Costco," I told her.

"I know I'm at Costco," Chuck said, annoyed.

Ana smiled. "Is he bringing Portico home?"

"Are you bringing Portico home?" I asked Chuck.

"The snake? Am I bringing the snake home? Are you kidding? And no. It escaped the second I opened the door."

I shook my head for Ana. She scrunched her face, but she didn't seem that sad about it.

"Nancy," Chuck said. "This woman is destroying our lives."

Right then Ana leaned over to kiss me on the head. I wondered if she'd heard Chuck through the phone.

"Chuck?" I asked the dead air. "Chuck?"

I looked at the phone. Call Ended.

"Ana, I can't believe you did that!" I called to her in the bathroom.

She popped her head out of the doorway. She was wearing my hoop earrings. "So biblical, right?"

"But Portico's gone."

"A sacrifice," Ana said. "I was happy to make it for you. Plus Portico's smart. She'll figure it out."

I imagined Portico getting run over, becoming a flat S in the Costco parking lot, or turning into a crisp pile of just scales somewhere in the lava fields. "Right," I lied. "She'll figure it out." And then I touched my head, which felt like it was full of cotton balls. Those pills.

"Ana?" I called. She was back in the bathroom. "Who's Alan Jeffries?"

A pause. "Nobody important."

"You smoked pot with my kids last night."

"I know," she said. "Are you mad?"

Before I could answer, my phone beeped. Text from Cam: *Don't forget dinner tonight. Dad promised to show them the ball.*

"Damnit, Chuck."

"What, honey?" Ana reappeared again, her whole body this time. She was wearing my green dress now, which looked a lot more comfortable than the purple one. She stated the obvious. "I'm wearing your dress. And your makeup. Is that okay?"

I sighed. "Sure."

"What's wrong, Nan? You look concerned."

I told her about the dinner. She told me there was a simple solution. "Just tell Chuck to behave himself."

I sent a text: *Dinner with Tom and Liko tonight so you please FIND BALL and BEHAVE yourself. 6 p.m.!* Right as I hit Send, I said, "This is going to be a disaster."

•

Ana made the executive decision that we would have pasta all'Amatriciana again instead of sloppy joes, and the boys happily agreed. I was relieved not to be in charge of the meal. Like last time, we became her sous chefs. Jed chopped the garlic, Cam stirred the sauce. I cooked the pasta while Ana lit the candles and put on music. Not jazz tonight, but reggae. Jed, slicing the fat off the bacon, said, "Sweet, Liko loves reggae."

Ana, floating by in a flutter of green fabric, said, "Jedi loves reggae more," and set two Buddhas on the far end of the table. "We'll put these near Chuck so they can bless him with good energy."

"Great," I said. And then to Jed, "Is your new name Jedi?"

Jed smiled like he was flattered to have received this nickname. "I guess."

Ana winked at me first. Then to the boys, she said, "Do you guys know how cool your mom and I are?"

"So cool." Jed stuck out his tongue.

"Oh, Jedi, don't be a little dick. Your mom and I *are* so cool. And here's why. Remember when it said 'You are loved' all over the sidewalks in town?" Ana put her hand on her hip and waited, looking at the boys, who were standing beside each other at the stove. They looked almost exactly the same in this moment.

"Wait," Cam said. "Did you guys do that?"

Ana raised her eyebrows twice. "And we handed out sandwiches to homeless people. Well, needy people. Ugh, I should have been saying that the whole time, Nan. *Needy* not *homeless*. Boys," she said, "your mother and I are basically Mother Teresa."

"Mom," Jed said, turning toward me with the knife.

In my Mom voice, I said, "Careful with that, please."

He lowered it. "Is that why you gave that homeless guy a Big Mac?"

"Naaaaan," Ana cooed, "you gave a needy person a Big Mac?" She fluttered over and wrapped her arms around me from behind. She set her chin on my shoulder. The boys stood across from us, still looking almost exactly the same—same height, same eyes, same freckles on their noses. The only difference was that Jed was holding a knife and Cam wasn't.

•

Tom arrived first, a pack of Maui Caramacs in his hand. Fully dry, his hair was even blonder, almost albino blond, and, again, it seemed like a mistake that Tom lived in Hawaii because he looked like he'd just stepped off a snow-ridden field in Norway. He wore a nice sand-colored polo shirt and gray shorts, and I thought he'd probably dressed up a little for the occasion, which was adorable.

"Sorry I'm kinda early," he said, slipping off his cotton shoes.

Cam went to open the door for him. "No problem, dude," he said. "Come oooon in." I could tell he was a little nervous.

"Hey, Tom! Want some bacon fat?" Jed held up a strip.

Tom looked at it as though actually considering. Then he seemed to understand this was a joke and his face relaxed. "Sure!" he said, with overcompensating irony so that it wasn't ironic anymore.

"Thank you for the Caramacs, Tom," I said, trying to rescue him. I covered the pasta, wiped my hands on my apron, or my Mom apron, as Ana had called it. I shouldn't have resented this because it literally said MOM on the front, but I still felt resentful—how many things of mine had she called Mom things? Point made. But then, I was being silly. And I couldn't resent her. She was dying.

"Can I get you something to drink, Tom?"

"No, let me get it." Ana rushed toward him. Was she skipping? "Hi, Tom, I'm Ana." She stuck out her hand and gave him a firm shake. "I live here now. This family has adopted me."

Tom seemed unsure if this was a joke or not.

"Do you want some apple juice, Tom?" I asked.

Cam gave me a look: No, Mom, apple juice equals not cool.

"I love apple juice. Isn't it the best drink?" Ana rolled her eyes in delight. Before Tom could weigh in, she said, "I'll get you some, Tom."

And then Cam said, "Can I have some, too?"

"Everyone can have some!" Ana bellowed, skipping toward the fridge.

Tom stood by Cam, watching him stir the sauce.

"I just have to . . . do this," he said to Tom. "But you can sit or whatever."

"Okay, yeah," Tom said, moving toward the couch. Portico's tank was still on the coffee table, and it was now filled with offerings. Ana had been performing "a new kind of burial" all day by dropping things into the tank. So far they included twigs and clumps of grass and a bird's nest she'd found in the driveway and the core of a pear she'd eaten earlier and most of the huge tub of Costco salt we had in the pantry.

Ana fluttered to Tom with his glass of juice. "Here you go, Tom," she said. "Cheers."

"Cheers," Tom said, and they clinked.

"And a little for my dead homies," Ana said, pouring some of her juice into the tank.

Tom didn't ask. He sipped his juice. The song switched to Bob Marley, which reminded me of Chuck in his college days.

I poured the pasta into the sieve. Jed finished chopping and went to join Ana and Tom on the couch. Cam stirred the sauce, but he wasn't looking at it. He was looking at Tom.

And then footsteps, and Liko appeared at the door. In a black shirt with some graffiti words on the front that were illegible. No, he hadn't brought chocolate or flowers.

"Yo," he said.

"Yo," Ana said back, copying his voice exactly.

"Dude," Jed said, springing off the couch.

"Come in," I said in my nicest voice.

In the silly voice of a gatekeeper, Ana said, "Name yourself." She chuckled. "Who are you?"

"Who are *you*?" Liko said, kicking his last flip-flop into the pile.

"I am Ana," she said regally.

"Yeah, dude, this is Ana, we adopted her. She's chill," Jed said, too nonchalantly.

"Well, I am Liko," Liko said, and pointed to himself with both hands.

"Can I get you something, Liko?" I was determined to be kind. "Apple juice?"

"It's good," Jed said, as though apple juice was a rare drink Liko had never heard of.

"Coo," Liko said.

Coo? I tried not to judge. Kindness. I poured him some apple juice. The microwave clock said 6:13. Cam had plated the pasta. It would get cold. "Let's eat," I said, "Chuck will be here soon."

"He's going to show us that ball, yeah?" Liko asked.

"Yeah, man," Jed assured him.

I looked at the door. If Chuck found that ball, it would be a miracle.

•

Ana dimmed the lights. Liko said, "Like a freakin' séance in here," bobbing his head to the syllables. The way he spoke had a particular rhythm to it—everything came out in the same up and down beat.

"Yeah, it's badass right?" Jed said, to which Liko replied, "Like a voodoo den."

Cam and Tom sat on one side, Jed and Liko on the other. Ana sat next to me at the head of the table. When Chuck got here, he would sit across from us.

"Yum," Tom said, looking at the pasta.

"I hope I cooked the sauce right," Cam said.

"I'm sure you did," Tom said, and smiled at Cam, who blushed.

"I'm sure you did, sweetie poo." Liko kissed the air, and then he smiled that joker smile of his.

Before I could form a response to that, Ana said, "Let's hold hands."

The twins glanced at each other, a glance that said: What will our friends think of this? But Liko and Tom held out their hands like it was normal. Maybe they said grace at home.

Ana, her face glowing in the candlelight, said, "Breathe." She inhaled and exhaled deeply. "You are here."

A pause.

"Some of us will rise and some of us will fall. Some of us have small black hearts. Small blackened black hearts. Some of us will have time to change that. To grow and grow and find love, and our hearts will become big and joyous and they will pump blood through our bodies joyously."

"Sick," Liko said.

Ana continued. "We are on a journey. All of us together. We are all surviving. We are all hanging on . . . to this moment. With our big and tiny and joyous and blackened black hearts, we are all right here, learning to breathe."

"Ay-men," Liko said, and Ana repeated it, but she pronounced it like her name. "Ah-men."

"That was rrrrreal," Liko said, stuffing his napkin into his lap. "Way more real than how my auntie says it."

The door clapped shut. "Hey!" Chuck said. I could tell just from that "hey" that he was in full-on Cool Dad mode. He would play his role up tonight and make these boys swoon. He walked through the dark living room and appeared in the flickering candlelight wearing his work clothes—had he really been at work all day?—and he was holding a ball.

"Sorry I'm a little late." He looked at me almost like he thought he should touch me—how far to take this charade?—but he didn't touch me. He looked at Ana and his face didn't fall. He was really trying. Trying to win us over with the same grin he had used on Shelly Two at Patricio's, and I wanted to kill him just as much as I wanted him to apologize and explain.

"Hey, Liko, hey, Tom," Chuck said.

"Hey, Mr. Murphy," they symphonied.

Proudly he held up the ball. "Look what I found."

Liko grabbed the ball. "No way," he said, and turned it over to find the inscription. "Dayum, he even wrote your name. 'Chuck, play hard.' This is money. Dayum!"

Jed took the ball, looked, repeated, "Dayum!"

I told myself not to ask, but I had to. "Where did you find it, Chuck?"

Chuck took his place at the far end of the table. He scooted in and picked up one of the Buddhas and made a face like: Huh?

When he still hadn't answered me, I asked again. "Chuck, where did you find the ball?"

He scratched his neck. "The closet."

"Really? Which closet, hon?" I set my chin on my fist.

Chuck's clenching smile. I could see him flailing under that smile. I knew the ball was a decoy. Even from here, it looked too new. It also looked like he had done something to it to make it look weathered. Rubbed it on the pavement, maybe. Also, on the real ball, Tony had written, "Play better," not "Play hard," which meant that Chuck's memory was failing, which meant that we were old.

I asked again. "Which closet, hon?"

"Who cares, Mom," Jed said, passing the ball to Cam. The boys wouldn't have remembered the original ball. The last time they'd seen it was when they were about ten.

"What kind of pasta is this?" Chuck asked.

I knew Ana would sing it in Italian, and she did. "Pasta all'Amatriciana."

"Your recipe?" Chuck was grinding his poor teeth to dust in his mouth. He'd been a grinder since I met him. He carried stress in his jaw. And he had a special mouth guard for sleeping, which I knew he wasn't wearing alone in the ohana without me to remind him.

"Yes," Ana said. "I hope you like it."

Chuck picked up the fat Buddha in front of him. "And this is your doll?"

"Those are Buddhas, Chucky," Ana said, sounding very light and bright.

"Please don't call me Chucky," Chuck said, and smiled harder.

"All right, sir." She saluted him.

Chuck scooted his chair out. "I forgot something in the car," he said. "Be right back."

We watched him disappear into the dark.

Tom and Cam were still inspecting the decoy.

"Dude, plate me up some more pasta," Liko said to Jed, who quickly complied.

"So, boys," I said, not knowing what I would say next. And then— why?—"How's school?"

"Fine," "Fine," "Fine," they echoed.

Liko said, "Stupid."

Ana hovered her fingers above the candle flame. "Liko?"

He grunted. His mouth was full.

"What's your deeeeal?" she asked him slowly. But then he was still chewing so she went on. "Do you plan on going to college?"

"Ana wishes she went to college," Jed explained. "That's why she's asking."

Liko swallowed. "I'm going to college, hell yeah," he said. "That's where all the hot chicks are. Col-lege." Joker smile, and his teeth were smeared with red sauce.

"Word," Jed said.

God, I hated peer pressure so much.

Then footsteps. The door clapped. Chuck was back.

Half an hour, I thought. This dinner will be over in half an hour.

When Chuck walked past me, I looked over at the exact right time to see the bulge in his pocket. I waited for that sinking feeling. Chuck was putting fifths of vodka in his pockets again and he was so dumb to think I wouldn't notice, just like he was so dumb to think I wouldn't know the ball was a fake.

"You want more pasta, Dad?" Cam asked.

"Thanks, son," Chuck said in his Ward Cleaver way.

"So Chucky. I mean Chuck, sorry," Ana said. "How was your day today, Chuck?"

Obviously, she wanted him to tell the story of finding a snake in his car.

But Chuck was unwilling to go there. "Great pasta," he said. I had to give him kudos for that, even if he did have vodka in his pocket.

"I'm glad you're enjoying it," Ana said. "We made it with a lot of love." She picked a noodle from the heap with her fingers and slurped it up and smiled. "So you had a good day, Chuck?"

Twenty-five minutes. No, twenty. In twenty minutes, this dinner will be over.

Quickly—he was losing patience—Chuck said, "It was fine, thanks."

"We were just talking about college," Ana informed him. "I was telling all four of these boys they need to go to college." She pounded the table once and laughed.

"Absolutely," Chuck agreed.

Jed whispered something to Liko.

"No whispering at the dinner table," I said.

Liko's eyes got big. His mouth turned into an O. "Dude," he said to Ana, "you were a stripper?"

Chuck furrowed his brow. He couldn't tell if this was true or not.

"Does that intimidate you, Liko?" Ana asked him. Her eyes were dark and spinning, and she was sweeping her pointer finger through the candle flame now, back and forth and back and forth.

"Hell no, it doesn't intimidate me," Liko said, sitting up straighter.

"She made six grand in one night," Jed blurted out.

"Daaaaayum," Liko said.

Tom nodded like this information was very interesting. Cam shifted in his chair. Jed's face flushed.

Chuck said, "I'm going to the bathroom," not very cheerily, and left the table again.

When I realized I'd been twirling the same bite of pasta for way too long—I'd only taken one bite this whole time—I gave up and put the fork down.

Ana said, "I used to dance for guys like you, Liko. I know guys like you like I know the back of my hand." She trailed the back of her hand through the flame.

"What do you mean, *guys* like me?" Liko's joker smile. He was acting like he didn't care what she thought of him but of course he did. He wanted to know what kind of guy she thought he was.

"Small guys," Ana said, "with big trucks."

"That's right I got a big truck," Liko said, and held his hand up for a high five from Jed, who slapped it. "Got the big-ass wheels."

The toilet flushing, Chuck coming down the hall, and then there he was, looking like he'd been smacked. The bottle was gone from his pocket. He must have stowed it behind the toilet. Or drunk the whole thing.

"What kind of car do *you* drive?" Liko asked Ana, proud that he had finally come up with a retort.

"Jeep Wrangler," she said. "Purple. It's in the driveway."

"Oh yeah, I saw that thaaaang," Liko said.

"Nice car," Tom said, maybe because he hadn't spoken in a while and felt that when invited to dinner, you should say things every so often.

"Thank you, Tom," Ana said effusively, and Tom smiled, which wiped the worry off Cam's face.

"Hondas are the best car," Chuck said to no one or everyone. "They last forever."

Ana grabbed a candle and held it to her face. "The eternal Honda," she said in a spooky voice.

Liko looked at her. "You're kinda batshit, yeah?"

"Meeee?" Ana said, placing a hand on her heart.

"Yeah girl, you," Liko said. That joker smile and the tomato fragment lodged between his two front teeth.

"Moi?" Ana dramatized a look of disbelief. "A girl?"

"Yeah, girl, you girl." Liko pointed at her with both hands.

"Boys," Chuck said, "should we talk about H-two-oh polo?"

Oh, Chuck. He was trying to do things right, and he was doing them so wrong.

"No, Dad, let's not," Jed said, rolling his eyes for Liko.

"No? Come on, boys!" Chuck put his hands on Liko and Tom's shoulders and shook them a little. Tom took it because he was polite and Liko put his hand on Chuck's shoulder and shook back hard enough for Chuck to say, "Whoa there, Nelly."

The song ended, and in the silence, we all heard Cam whisper to Tom, "Are you okay?"

Fine, Tom mouthed, embarrassed because we were all looking at him.

"Are you okaaaaay, sweetie pooooo?" Liko said in a baby voice.

"Shut up, dude," Cam said, and rubbed the sweat from his temples.

Liko's head danced in a zigzag don't-mess-with-me pattern. "Why should I shut up?" With every word, his body moved into a slightly different position.

Tom looked at his lap. Ana leaned forward and touched the tips of her fingers together and glared at Liko. My neck was prickling. I set my water glass down. No one spoke.

Until Liko said, "You guys are obviously boyfriend boyfriend. You should just tell everyone." And then he was laughing hard and slapping his belly.

The kinder part of me could tell how uncomfortable he was, and the Mom part of me wanted to attack this horrible child, whose obvious destiny was to become a convicted felon.

Cam crossed his arms over his chest to make himself smaller. Tom was still looking at his lap.

"Okay," I said sternly. But I didn't know what else to say. Not my proudest moment.

Chuck was looking at Tom and at Cam and at Tom and at Cam, and when they didn't defend themselves, he brought his hands to his cheeks slowly and then he was muttering something under his breath.

"Chuck," I said, trying to snap him out of it.

"Oh shit, you didn't know that?" Liko widened his eyes.

A bead of sweat rolled from Jed's hairline down to his nose.

Ana pressed her palms together, staring straight at Liko.

My neck was on fire.

Gently, Tom put his hand on Cam's shoulder.

"You," Ana said to Liko, "are going to get what you deserve."

"You're batshit, lady," Liko said and wagged his finger, but he was obviously a little scared.

"Cam, why don't you and Tom go outside?" Ana said, which was exactly the right thing to say, and why hadn't I said it first?

Cam nodded. He stood. Tom stood. They walked toward the door. It was silent except for Bob Marley. The happy beating drums of reggae music—it was just so absolutely wrong right now.

For a few beats, no one moved. And then Chuck squeaked his chair back and followed them out of the house. To tell Cam that he loved him, I hoped.

Liko relaxed into the chair and checked his phone. Ana was still boring a hole into his head with her eyes.

"Liko," I said.

He didn't answer. From his phone, an arcade noise. Like a pinball machine.

"Liko," Ana said.

Liko didn't look up. He flicked us off.

"Dude," Jed said, "that's my mom."

The sound of a car starting in the driveway.

"Where are they going?" Jed asked. And then he sprang up. "I'll go check."

I should go outside, I thought. But something made me stay. Maybe it was the look Ana gave me. A mutual understanding, though I couldn't have articulated it then.

Liko put his phone away. He rolled out of his chair like a stuntman. "I'm gonna pee and then I am outta this mess." He went to the bathroom.

I got up. I looked out the window. The boys' car was gone, and Tom's car was gone. I hoped Chuck wasn't driving.

I started pacing. Back and forth, back and forth along the wooden floor beams I could barely see in the near dark.

The toilet flushed.

I looked up. Ana was standing by the front door. I had no idea why.

The bathroom door opened. Ana flicked the light. The living room lit up. I stopped pacing.

Liko walking down the hall. Right in front of me he stopped. He stood there, his feet inches from mine, and stared at me. The pimples on his nose. His small black eyes, full of hate. I thought I saw his lip quiver. And then his lips, curling back. I expected him to growl. He looked like a pit bull. "What you gonna do?" he said, heavy Hawaiian accent and his whole body seething.

I was going to kill this person.

And then Liko was done staring me down. He pushed past me, bumping my shoulder on the way.

"Hey!" I said. I felt my fingers press into my palms.

Liko kept walking.

"Hey!" I said again.

Ana was blocking the door. She was standing squarely in front of it.

"Move," Liko said.

Ana said nothing. She just blinked at him.

"You're going to apologize to Cam." I was behind him now, right behind him, yelling into his hair.

He turned. "Cam's a little bitch!" he said, right into my face, his nose almost touching my nose, and then he spat on my floor.

And almost before the spit had touched the floor, my fist was smashing into Liko's cheek.

And my initial reaction—what is wrong with you, Nancy?—was yes! Because I hadn't punched anyone in a long, long time, and I'd forgotten how good it could feel. Like such a release. Like the simplest way to solve a problem. So basic. Just use your hands.

Liko was stunned. His mouth was hanging open. Saliva dripping off his lip and there was blood in it.

I couldn't feel my hand. I couldn't feel anything.

If Liko had said anything else in that moment, I know I would have punched him again.

But he didn't say anything else. Maybe he knew I would have punched him again. My fists were still clenched. I had become the pit bull.

Ana stepped away from the door.

Liko took a step. He took another step. He didn't look at us. He walked out of the house.

Why wasn't I shaking? I looked at Ana. Why wasn't she?

We were the same height, so our eyes were level.

We said nothing.

The only sound was the reggae song, and it was a song about love.

27

"Nan?"

Warmth. Comfort. Encased in cement. Outside, the birds.

"Na-aaaan?"

Fingers tucking hair behind my ear. I opened my eyes. Ana. And light, too much. Light all around her face, radiating like a wallet-sized portrait of a saint. Her face in shadow. No wig. Just her plain bare head, as bald and smooth as an apple.

"Honey, it's time to wake up now," she cooed.

"Mmm." The reality of this day was expanding when I wanted it to contract. But it was already there, covering me in light and words. I was thirsty. I didn't want to move. If I moved, if I reached for the water glass, I would be a body again and it would be over.

"Those pills really knocked you out, Nan."

Oh—it all rushed back, the whole night—no. I gasped a sharp breath. I opened my mouth several times like a fish. My tongue was made of sandpaper.

She held out the water glass. It was dirty in the light. "Have some."

I didn't speak. I didn't move. But I was blinking rapidly, trying to find my thoughts.

Ana set the glass back down.

Drunk Chuck. Poor Cam. Tom. Jed. Where had they gone last night? Were they okay? And Liko. Liko. My fist crashing into his cheek. How could I have done that? After all this time?

"Nan?"

My hands on the sheets. Unbruised, unscratched. "I hit a child," I whispered.

"Oh please." And then Ana said exactly what I wanted her to say, exactly what the other voice inside me was saying. "He deserved it."

"What if he tells? Oh God, what if he tells his mother? Or the police?"

"He's a thug," Ana said, her hand firm on my leg. "Thugs don't talk to cops. Trust me."

"Did they come home last night? Where's Cam?" The last thing I remembered was looking out the window, waiting for the blue Honda to reappear. None of them had picked up their phones, and that's when I'd decided to thank Alan Jeffries for his pills and go to sleep.

"Well, that's why I'm waking you up, honey. Someone burned a sign last night at the high school and the boys got dragged in for questioning." She laughed. "The pigs just called. We have to go pick them up."

"What?" I sat up.

"I pretended to be you on the phone. I did a really good job. You would have been proud."

"Oh my God, Ana," I said somewhat disapprovingly, although, really, I was glad she'd taken the call instead of me. The last thing I wanted to do right now was talk to cops.

"No, Nan, not 'Oh my God.' Oh my *free* will." She whipped the covers off me. "Now get up! We are brave mama bears today. Let's fucking own it."

I didn't think. I got up.

"You're going to take a shower. And wash away that guilt!" She took my hand and led me into the bathroom and turned on the water. "We need to leave in ten minutes," she said, pulling my pants down, pants I didn't remember putting on. "When you get out of this shower"—she unbuttoned my pajama top—"you will not feel guilty, Nan." She looked straight into my eyes. "Do you hear me?"

"Yes."

"Good. Now go. Wash your sins away! I'll make coffee." She closed the door.

•

Ana and I, walking hand in hand into the police station. I wore a light scarf. I didn't take my sunglasses off. I spoke in a low voice. When the clerk couldn't hear what I was saying, Ana explained for me. There were uniformed people everywhere, and I was waiting for one of them to slam me against the wall and cuff me. This one or this one or this one. I could only see their feet.

I signed a piece of paper. The boys came out. Their familiar flip-flops. "Free to go," a uniform said.

Ana said, "Thank you, kind sir." And we left. And then we were in the parking lot, and then we were getting into the Jeep, and then we were driving through the fields of lava, and it was more surreal than usual.

"Boys," I began, and before I could say anything else, Ana said, "Did you light this fire or what?"

In the rearview mirror, I saw Cam turn to his brother.

"No," Jed said, "we did not."

Cam put his sunglasses on. "No, we did not," he repeated.

"Are you sure?"

"Yes, Mom," Jed said, keeping his voice steady.

"Yes, Mom," Cam repeated.

I didn't believe them.

"Let's talk alibis." Ana adjusted her sunglasses. "Where did you go last night?"

"In circles, basically," Jed said. "Dad kept asking Cam how he felt about being gay."

"Yeah," Cam said, "and I was like, 'Dad, I don't know. It feels the same as being straight, probably.'"

"And he wanted to know when Cam figured it out," Jed said, "and all this other stuff."

"I know Dad loves me though," Cam said.

"Because he said that like nine hundred times, too," Jed said.

"Freaking Dad." Cam sighed.

"Dad was a hot mess last night," Jed said.

"Oh, and he thought he saw some chick he knew named Brenda, and he was all, 'Brendaaaa!' out the window, and he made me pull over, and—"

"—and the chick was like, 'Um, sir, I'm not Brenda,'" Cam finished.

"That part was actually kind of funny," Jed said.

"Totally," Cam agreed.

"The chick was like, 'My name is *not* Brenda, sir,'" Jed said, and laughed.

I tried to say it with curiosity. "Who's Brenda?"

"Who knows," Jed said.

I tried to breathe. "What did this *not* Brenda woman look like?"

"Um," Jed said, "like a woman?"

"She was wearing a tube top and some shorts," Cam said. "And walking down Ali'i with her friend."

"And she had blue eyes and blond hair," Jed said.

"Oooooooh." Ana hit my arm. "Was she walking toward her *red* car, by chance?"

"I don't know," Cam said.

"Did your father say anything else about this Brenda person?"

"No," Jed said.

"No," Cam repeated.

"Interesting." Ana nodded.

And then Jed, who was so naïve, asked, "Why do you care so much, Mom?"

And Cam, who was just as naïve, said, "Yeah, Mom, who cares?"

So I told myself to drop it for now. It was a good thing the boys didn't see this Brenda person as a threat. It meant that they were still wholesome. We hadn't ruined them completely. And maybe their not getting it wasn't that surprising either, since we'd never told them about Shelly.

I tried to focus on the rushing wind. On the fields of lava. On the salt air. On the sky. And then there was Ana's voice. "Brendaaaaaa." And I felt like I was losing my mind again.

A whole minute might have passed. I was trying to imagine it. The

boys and Chuck in the car and Chuck yelling "Brenda!" at this woman—
ugh—and then them driving in circles and then—and then what?

"How long did you drive in circles?"

"And where did you *go*?" Ana asked. "Were you near the *high
school*?"

"No," Jed said. "We went to Magic's, then to town, then back to
Magic's, then Dad wanted Denny's."

"But he was passed out by the time we got to Denny's," Cam said,
"so we came home."

"You didn't stop to light a li'l old fire on the way home?" Ana
pretended to light a lighter.

"No," Jed said.

Cam didn't answer.

I knew that was exactly what they'd done. And to think of Chuck
passed out in the car while they did it—that was a bold move. In a
way I knew was wrong, I was almost proud of them. At least they were
expressing anger without hurting other people. Except for, I guess, the
taxpayers who would have to pay for the damages.

"Hey," Ana said, "how's *Liko* doing? Did you guys see him this
morning? Is he wearing a Band-Aid on his face?"

"Wait," Cam said.

"Did *you* punch Liko?" Jed asked.

"He told everyone he got jumped by an ice dealer," Cam said.

"Your mother is the one who punched Liko, boys." Ana patted
the top of my head.

"No way," Jed said.

"Way," Ana told him.

"Dude, Mom, you rock!" Jed said.

"Yeah. Whoa. Go, Mom," Cam said.

"But he's doing okay?" I asked.

"He's totally fine," Jed said.

"Yeah, Mom, he's totally fine," Cam said.

"Mom punched Liko!" Jed clapped his hands a few times. "Dude!"

"You're a badass, Mom," Cam said.

I might have been trying not to smile. Ana turned up the road toward the high school. "I want to see where the fire happened. I love ashes."

"Do we *have* to go back to school today?" Jed asked.

"Cam?" I turned to face him. "Are you going to be okay here today?"

Before he could respond, Ana said, "Here, Cam, take this," and opened the center console. "Nan, will you pass him the Swiss army knife?"

There was no Swiss army knife, but there was another knife, a gold one. "You mean this?"

"Yeah, give it to Cam."

"This is a weapon."

Ana took it from me and passed it to Cam. "Cam, if anyone corners you in a bathroom, you cut them up." She laughed. "But I'm serious."

Cam hesitated before taking it. "I'm probably not going to use this."

"No, you are absolutely not going to use that," I said. "Give it back to me right this second."

"Here," Cam said, and gave it back.

"Damn, Mom, you're a boss lately," Jed said.

"Cam," Ana said, "if anyone corners you, you sock them in the trachea, you hear me?"

"No," I said. "If anything happens, you go to the principal. And you call me. Do not sock anyone."

"Yeah, call Mom." Ana slapped the wheel. "She'll show up and sock them for you."

I rubbed my eyes. "No more violence. I'm serious."

And then—"Here!"—Ana was pulling over.

Yes, here were the remnants. A patch of charred earth, ashes in the shape of the wooden slab it used to be.

"This wasn't a fire-fire," Ana said. "This was a little cookout fire. I can't believe they brought you in for questioning over this."

"What did the sign used to say?" I asked.

"Something about excellence," Cam said.

"Ha!" Ana hit my arm. "Come on, Nan, that's funny."

I didn't respond. I wanted to go back to sleep.

We drove up to the main entrance, where Ana turned to face the boys. "Gentlemen, I have something to say." A pause. She was waiting until she had their full attention. "Don't waste your time being upset. If dying has taught me anything—and this is my second time dying, by the way—it's to enjoy the ride. You go into this school and you own it today. Don't let anyone mistreat you. You be you and you be proud. And get good grades. You hear me?"

"Totally," Jed said.

"Yes." Cam was laughing.

"And fuck high school!" Ana shouted, her arms up in the air, her fingers spread far apart. "That's it, boys, kill 'em today."

They jumped out the sides of the car and walked through the entrance, their heads barely hanging.

•

Ana took me to lunch at the Four Seasons because she wanted to die with her bank account at zero or less. We sat outside. The horizon, how it stretched. The sky, so blue and clear. Soft breeze and the water was calm. We ordered poke and shrimp cocktail and strawberry mango smoothies. "Kama'aina discount," Ana told the waitress.

"No problem," the waitress said, relaxing a little now that she knew we were local. "You ladies don't live in Pahoa, do you?"

"No," Ana said.

"Good, cuz they're evacuating. It just came on the radio."

"Oh no," I said, imagining all those people having to leave their homes. I pictured it like a movie because it didn't seem real.

"Hope they make it out in time," the waitress said.

"They will," Ana said certainly. "It's the twenty-first century."

When the smoothies arrived, Ana took a sip and said, "This is so much better than Ensure. You know that's what I should be drinking right now." She touched her wig hair. She was solemn. "I should be drinking Ensure and dying in an institution."

"It's amazing you're having so many good days," I said.

"Right?" She plucked a shrimp off the side of the martini glass. "But let's not talk about it anymore. It's too depressing. I want to enjoy my life while I still have it."

"Are you in pain though? Does your stomach hurt? Or, I mean . . ." I trailed off. I didn't want to say the word *pancreas*.

"I am in pain. I'm just not showing you." She chewed her shrimp with vigor and squinted at the sea. The sun glinted off the water in one straight line, straight from the horizon to us. "My flame is going to start petering soon. I can feel it."

I thought I could feel it, too. It seemed inevitable.

"But I'm not ready yet. I have unfinished business." She set the shrimp tail on the plate. "I can't stop thinking about that horse. I don't know why. I think I had a dream about it last night. That poor horse, being beaten for no reason. Maybe I can relate," she said, her voice thin. "I just have to free that horse, Nan. It feels imperative."

"Ana," I said, pleading a little. "After last night and the boys and the fire and the police station and—it's too much."

"Nan, I know you're upset right now, but I would urge you to ask yourself: Does this stuff really matter? The boys are fine. Liko is fine. Chuck is going to be fine. Yes, you might get a divorce, but you also might not. You don't know yet. My opinion? Is that you should enjoy your life while you still have it. And use your time on this planet to set things right."

As usual, it was hard to argue with her. She was dying. She understood things I couldn't claim to understand.

The sun, the sky, the ocean. The ukulele music playing in the background, and this was the best smoothie I'd ever had. Was I enjoying it enough?

I wasn't sure. Because I also wasn't sure who was drinking this smoothie. Who was this woman at the Four Seasons, talking about freeing a horse? And why was she wearing this blue scarf that was kind of ugly?

"Nan," Ana said, "I think you'll feel better after you free this horse with me. It's a good deed, clean and simple."

The wind blew my scarf into my face. The blue striped pattern covered my view. Yes, I thought, ugly. An ugly pattern. But on the day I'd bought it at Marshall's, I had loved this pattern. Well, Sheila had loved it, really. She was the one who told me to buy it.

Ana plucked the last two shrimps off the martini glass. She put one on my plate and one on hers. "This is the last time I'll ask for your help, Nan."

I looked at the clear, clear sky, and then at the vog in the distance. Was that Pahoa?

"We don't even know where he lives," I said.

Ana smiled. Her lips, her teeth, her pearly skin. She looked like a movie star. She looked like someone you would want to be sitting with at the Four Seasons.

"I got his address."

"You did? How?"

She shrugged. "Small town."

I sipped my smoothie. This is the best smoothie you've ever had.

"Please stop tripping out about Liko, Nan. It's tiring, seriously. What you did last night was good. You were protecting your child." Then she burped, which was not a movie star thing to do. "Good," she said once more.

I stared at the perfect, clear horizon. "My lines are getting blurred."

"Lines," she repeated, like that was an interesting word. "Between good and bad, you mean."

"Exactly."

Ana sat up straighter, pulled her shoulders back. "When you're about to die, you'll see this as clearly as I do." It seemed like she almost felt sorry for me. My poor brain was in a knot about something that was so simple to her.

"I wish I had your clarity," I told her.

Gently she placed her hand over mine. I watched my wedding band be covered by her pale fingers. "You can take part in my clarity," she promised. Her inviting eyes, so full of energy. How lucky she was to be having this many good days, and how soon they would be over. "Please help me. I need you. The horse is the last deed."

We both already knew I would say yes. Because how could I say no to her? I couldn't.

"The last deed?" I wanted her to promise.

Ana covered her heart with her hand. "I swear my life on it."

28

We left before Chuck got home. *If* Chuck was coming home. We took Ana's car. The boys in the back and us in the front. Ana wore a satin periwinkle dress I'd never seen before and she'd put on extra makeup.

"I just want to look pretty right now," she'd called to me from the bathroom while we were getting ready. I was in the closet, looking for more scarves to donate to Salvation Army. Or to Marcy, if I ever saw Marcy again. "There's this documentary you should watch," Ana continued, "about women with cancer who go to this hair salon because they want to look beautiful. It is *so* inspiring, Nan. And kind of a desperate, vain attempt to avoid the deathliness of death, but still. Very moving. People at the end of their lives—they're so raw and real, you know? We should all live like we're about to die."

"Uh-huh." I was only half listening. I was too busy looking for more ugly scarves in my closet.

She emerged in the doorway wearing shimmering green eye shadow, lots of blush, and heavy mascara. "You're beautiful," I told her.

"Good." She struck a pose. "Because I don't want to look like an invalid in front of the boys."

•

I felt better once we were driving away from the house. I always felt better driving away from that house, just like I always felt better when I was in her car. The wind on my cheeks, the lush jungle rushing past. I liked not having to drive. I liked being the passenger. I could just sit here and watch the world pass me by.

This was the point on the mountain where the lush jungle dried out. In one more minute, it would all be lava. It was dusk. The wobbly horizon line reminded me of rush hour on the 5. The air was thick and gray and smelled like sulphur. The vog—and it was unmistakably vog now—had rolled over all of Kona town. It looked sad, almost. If you took out the tropical ocean, it could have been some bleak boondocks place in central California.

"Out of curiosity, where are we going?" Cam asked.

"Books and Natch," Ana told him. "And it's a new moon tonight."

Cam had assured us twenty times that nothing bad had happened at school, but at the red light I felt the need to ask again. "Are you sure no one gave you a hard time?"

"I'm sure," Cam said.

"It's true, Mom," Jed said. "Nothing happened."

"I still want you to have the knife," Ana said, whipping open the center console. She found it quickly, held it up. "A gift. From me to you."

I took it before Cam could. "Thank you, Ana," I said. "I'll hold on to this. Cam, you can have it when you graduate." This was a lie. I planned to throw the knife in the first dumpster I saw.

"Thanks, Ana," Cam said, like a polite young man.

"Hey," Jed said. "What about me? Where's my gift?"

Ana bit her lip. "I have something else in store for you, Jedi."

Jed thought about that. "Is it a knife?"

"Of sorts," Ana told him.

"It's not a gun," I said.

"No, Nan. Of course not." Ana slapped my knee. "Who do you think I am? I would never give your child a gun!"

"I know," I said, "I was kidding." But was I kidding?

•

Ana went to New Age and I went to Fiction. Cam and Jed went to the coffee table books about Hawaii. After a while I went to find them.

"Look, Mom." Cam flipped the book over for me. Two pages, one photo. The volcano spurting lava. "We want to go see it," he said.

"Wipe out that town," Jed finished.

Ana's voice behind us: "You bad, bad boys," she joke-scolded.

Even the short walk to Natch seemed sadder with all this vog in the air. It's like a metaphor for your blurriness, I thought. But ignore it, I rethought. And enjoy your life.

We plated up our dinners at the healthy buffet. Ana chose canta-loupe and brown rice. "I need to eat like a baby now," she said.

The boys piled their plates high with organic macaroni and slices of eggplant pizza. I got what I always got: salad with fish and beets, plus a side of lilikoi dressing. When I looked at my plate, two things occurred to me. One: Chuck had never seen me eat this meal before, and I'd eaten it so many times. Two: I'm not hungry. Oh, and three: Enjoy your life.

Enjoying my life was hard right now, but I was trying.

We went to our old patch of yoga grass to eat as the sun lowered in the hazy sky.

"This is where your mother and I met," Ana said, laying out two yoga mats for us to sit on.

"This is where Ana taught yoga," I said, and noted how I had used the past tense. Soon, after she died, I would be saying, "This is where we used to eat with Ana as the sun set."

The twins sat on one mat. Ana and I sat on the other. I looked at the grass. Maybe I was looking for one of Patty's dropped earrings, or for some other evidence that we had been here. I found nothing. I picked a blade of grass and rolled it between my fingers.

Ana ate slowly, her hand affixed to her stomach the whole time, as if waiting for the sharp pain to come back. I was waiting for it, too. If she needed to be rushed to the hospital, I knew where the hospi-tal was. It was half an hour south with no traffic, maybe twenty-five minutes going fast. I remembered something the real estate agent had said—"Kona is not a good place to be sick"—and how easily we'd cast that advice aside. "No, we're healthy," we'd replied, as if health were a thing you could keep in a box and hold on to forever.

I touched her back. "Are you okay?"

"I'm fine," she whispered. I knew she didn't want the boys to hear.

As the last bit of sun was being swallowed by the horizon, Jed said, "Wait for it, wait for it." And then—I couldn't believe it—there was a flash. A definite green flash. The boys agreed that it had been a definite flash.

Ana rubbed her stomach. "I saw nothing."

"You must have blinked just like one second off," Cam said.

Ana's hands on her cheeks. "Story of my life."

We lay back in the grass as the sky darkened. "The new moon," Ana said, "is about new beginnings. It is a blank page. It is a time to set intentions. First, however, you must know what you want."

The birds, the waves, a guy yelling, "Hey bra!" to his friend.

Ana repeated the last part. "You must know what you want."

"I want a new iPad," Jed said.

"I want courage," Ana said.

"I want courage, too," Cam agreed.

Ana touched my hand. "What do you want, Nan?"

"A lot," I heard myself say.

"Abundance," Ana said. "Good thing you're married to a guy who works at the most abundant place on earth." Ana chuckled. "Cost-co."

She squeezed my hand. I squeezed back. Like so many other times, I thought: Thank God you're here.

A long silence. The birds, the waves. How this sky, even with the vog, had so many more stars than the sky on the mainland.

"I'm gay," Cam said.

Tears welled in my throat. "I'm so proud of you, Cam."

"Thanks, Mom."

"Me, too," Jed said.

"I know everyone knows," Cam said, "but I still wanted to say it."

"You are brave," Ana told him. "My gay husband didn't come out till he was thirty-four."

Jed was shocked. "You had a gay husband?"

"I might have had two gay husbands," Ana said.

"Are you really going to die?" Cam asked her.

"Dude, I was just thinking that," Jed said. "Like, I can't even wrap my head around it. You look . . . I don't know . . . you don't *look* like you're going to die."

She said it with no emotion, but like it was just a fact. "I am going to die."

The waves, the birds. Waiting for Ana to say something else. She blinked. I thought I saw one glistening teardrop roll from the corner of her eye and fall into the grass.

•

We found Chuck passed out in a foldable chair right in the center of the half-built shed, his chin pressed into his chest and a flower in his crotch.

"Should we wake him up?" Jed asked.

"No," I said, "leave him." Leave him, leave him, leave him.

But then everybody left except for me. I said, "I'll be right in," and waited until they'd disappeared through the front door before taking Chuck's cell phone out of his pocket. The whole time I was telling myself, Nancy, you are not a private investigator. Nancy, you should let this run its natural course. Nancy, do you really want to be in a marriage with someone you feel the need to investigate?

But I had to know. Now she had a name and her name was Brenda, so it wouldn't be that hard to check.

Of course Chuck didn't have a password on his phone, although I'd told him to set one three hundred times. He was making this too easy. Maybe he wanted to get caught.

Brenda, Brenda. I looked at his text messages first. And there was Brenda—third one down—right after Jed and Costco.

The exchange had been written the day before and it was short.

Brenda: *Do you think we should tell your wife?*

Chuck: *I can't tell her yet. Sorry.*

I waited for some reaction, but there wasn't one, not really. The space behind my eyes seemed to be throbbing, but other than that I just felt numb. Maybe that was my reaction: numbness. I was beyond emotions at this point. I was exhausted. And maybe I didn't want to believe it either. I still wanted to be wrong somehow.

So I read it again. While rubbing my temples, waiting for my head to hurt.

No, still numb.

I could not deal with this.

And I couldn't talk about it either, because that would make it real. I decided right there that I wouldn't tell Ana. I just wouldn't tell her.

I didn't bother cramming the cell phone back into Chuck's pocket. I dropped it into his crotch instead, right on top of the flower.

•

Before the boys went to bed, Jed asked Ana again what his gift would be. "What did you mean by *sort of* knife?"

"Be patient," she said, looking up at him under her heavy mascara. Despite her hand on her stomach, there were no signs that she wasn't a healthy, thriving person. I didn't think Jed or Cam knew she wore a wig.

I hugged Cam for longer than usual and then I hugged Jed for just as long. "I am so proud of both of you," I told them.

Ana put her arms around the three of us. "I just want to feel what this is like," she said.

We stood there for a long time. Ana started humming something. I thought it was "Lean on Me," but it wasn't. And then she stopped. "Family," she said, her cantaloupe breath hot on my cheek. I knew she would repeat it, and she did. "Family."

•

I washed my face in the bathroom. Wash off that guilt, Nan. I splashed the water on my skin again and again and again and again. The towel felt scratchy but good. The scratchiness of a cheap towel. I rubbed hard and then harder. When I took the towel off my face and looked in the mirror, there was Ana, standing behind me. She set her chin on my shoulder. The plastic smell of her wig. How our faces could be easily confused. But no, no they couldn't be. There were differences. She had higher cheekbones, I had a pointier nose. I had real lips, hers were fake. The line of her hot-pink chunk of hair fell between us. It separated us. Or it confused us further. From this angle, it wasn't clear who the pink hair belonged to. It could have been mine.

"Nan?"

"Ana?"

"It has to be tonight." I saw in her eyes that she meant it. There would be no negotiation. I would try anyway.

"It's been such a long day, I—"

"Nan, you're not listening." She winced. Hand on her stomach. She whispered, "It has to be tonight."

29

By the time we were searching the closet for black hats to match our black spandex outfits, I was giddy, too.

"How about this one?" Ana held up my giant white beach hat with the pink bow around it and buckled over, muffling her laughter in her palm.

"Or"—I was laughing so hard I could barely breathe—"we could just put stockings on our heads!"

"Yes!" She doubled over. "Yes!"

Having to suppress the laughter made it funnier. I laughed so hard my head pounded. I was delirious.

When she caught her breath, she said, "Wait, do you *have* stockings?" And that started the laughter all over again.

"Ssshh," Ana said. "Sshh." She put a finger to her lips. She looked at the door. She whispered, "Should we check again?"

I tiptoed down the hall. Finally, the boys had turned their lights off. When I got back to Ana, I gave her a thumbs-up. She was wearing the giant white hat and shooting fake pistols with her fingers. We held each other's eyes for a second and then buckled over again. Ana crumpled to the floor and I crumpled to the bed. When we couldn't laugh anymore, there was only the silence of crickets, chirping in unison like the string section of an orchestra, and then Ana said, "It's go time."

From that moment on, we were serious. We tiptoed down the hallway. We froze at any sound. Ana had placed our shoes by the staircase so we wouldn't have to search for them in the pile now. She had parked her car near the street so the engine wouldn't wake them. In the driveway, I looked for Chuck in the center of the half-built shed, but he was gone. The ohana lights were off. He must have made it back inside.

•

Peter lived higher up Kaloko, just like Ana had predicted. We drove slowly up the winding road. The steepness at certain parts pushed us firmly back into our seats. I'd never taken the road this far up. Ana had. She had gone to see the place earlier so we wouldn't get lost now.

"Don't worry, Nan," she said, "this isn't going to be a hard one. All we have to do is open the barn door."

She'd taken her wig off. When I looked over, all I could see was the shape of her bald white head and her pale hand on her stomach.

"We will open the door and the horse will be free," she said, slowing down, which meant that we were close.

We will open the door and the horse will be free, I repeated to myself. But wait. "Wait," I said, "where's it going to go?"

"Into the wild," Ana said, like that was very obvious. "To join the wild horses. There are tons of wild horses on this mountain. Or, not tons. But there are a few." She slowed the car even more, and then she stopped. "This is it."

It was a big property. Big and completely stripped of jungle and surrounded by a fence. A high fence that followed the long curving driveway up to two structures. A house and a barn. I could see the outline of the barn, and in the house a light was on. Only one light. Maybe his bedroom.

"Shit, he's awake," Ana said, and sped up. Once we'd passed the house, she turned the car around, parked it behind a tree at the top of the property, and killed the engine. Then she buckled over and I thought she might be laughing again, but no, it was the pain.

I inhaled and exhaled deeply, showing her what she had shown me. My hand on the back of her neck, but only for a second. Ana took my hand and squeezed it.

"Are you sure you want to do this right now?"

"Yes," she said softly. She made herself sit up. "Yes."

We sat there for a full minute, or a full three minutes, holding hands. We didn't need to say out loud that we were taking pause now. The crickets were even louder this high up the mountain. The mountain, the mountain, I kept thinking. The mountain that wasn't a mountain like in other places. In Hawaii, a mountain was a dead volcano.

When Ana squeezed my hand again, I knew the pause was over. I opened my eyes. There was her white face in the dark and there were her dark eyes and they were spinning. "Okay," she said, "I'm ready. You ready?"

"Yes."

Her smile. Her veneers. How the wet saliva caught the red light of the buttons inside the car and shone red. "Here's what we're going to do," she said. "I'm going to run up the driveway, open the barn door, and run back. When you see me at the mailbox, you drive down and get me and we'll leave. Easy-peasy."

"Okay," I said. Then we could go home and shower, or I could take another bath and maybe take some more of those pills and sleep.

She brought her feet up so she was crouching on the seat. She was going to jump out of the car instead of using the door. "I'll be right back," she said. And then her lips were pressed into mine hard for a full thirty seconds, or maybe two very long seconds. When she pulled her face away, she whispered, "Thelma and Louise!" Then she jumped out of the car.

The symphony of crickets pulsed and pulsed, and then I could hear her feet on the gravel. That wasn't good. That meant Peter could hear it, too. But she was going fast. It wouldn't take long. And maybe he was asleep already. Maybe he slept with the lights on. The sound of her sprinting feet receded and receded. Was I supposed to turn the car on now or wait until I saw her at the mailbox? I decided not to turn it on. It would be too noisy.

I crawled into the driver's seat and waited. I realized I had never driven this car. The driver's seat had a different feel to it.

I tried to sit completely still so I could hear everything.

Do you think we should tell your wife?

I can't tell her yet. Sorry.

I fixed my eyes straight ahead and blinked at the dark.

She was taking too long. Why wasn't she running back yet? Maybe a problem with the barn door. Maybe it was taking a while to open. A padlock, maybe. I hoped she wasn't trying to break open a padlock.

And then the gravelly sound. Closer and closer. Good. She was sprinting. I put my hand on the key, ready to turn it, and then there she was! Waving madly, her hands two fast white splotches in the dark. I turned the key. I pressed the accelerator. Too hard. The car jerked forward. Breathe, Nan. I pressed again more lightly. Her hands were telling me to hurry up. I'm coming!

When I got to her, I hit the brakes hard, too hard. She flung the door open and jumped in and before she'd slammed it shut she was already saying, "Go, go! I think he saw me!" She wasn't laughing at all.

I went numb. "Hurry!" she said. I pressed the gas hard, too hard. We flew. And then a light. At the bottom of the huge property, a light. A figure and a light? What was that light? I wanted to slow down, but we had to go fast, we had to hurry. The light was moving into the road so I veered left and I wasn't breathing, and just when I thought, okay, yes, we have enough room to pass, Ana pulled the steering wheel right so hard and so fast I thought we might flip, and I jammed my foot into the brake but not fast enough and then there was a thud, not a smack or a pop but a thud, and it was alarmingly soft. Please oh please please let that be a coyote, please please, but that doesn't make sense—there are no coyotes in Hawaii—and I was paralyzed and then there was the sound of plastic, yes, plastic, and it was rolling, rolling, and it was a flashlight rolling down the hill.

I pressed both hands hard into my chest. My heart was beating fast. A thin layer of sweat all over my body. The still night, the crickets, and then an unexpected gust of wind. "Stay here," Ana said. She opened the door.

My hands shaking. Violently shaking. Ana walked closer, closer, closer to the thing we had hit and then she stopped. Her eyes on the ground. She lifted her hand to cover her mouth. She kept her hand there. She stayed for one, two, three, and then she walked back to the car and got in. She took her hand off her mouth. She said, "We need to leave."

I couldn't move.

"Now," she said. She put us in reverse. My hands trembling. I looked over my shoulder. I backed up fast, too fast again, and I winced. She put us in drive.

What I saw then. Jeans, a sleeveless teal shirt, blood on the back of his head.

My breath losing control and my eyes seeing double, triple, and I blinked and blinked and my hands were on my chest, pressing hard into my heart.

Ana inhaled and exhaled deeply. "Drive."

A second gust of wind.

I drove.

30

I took three pills and stayed on the farthest side of the bed. Ana moved closer. And closer. And closer.

"Do you want to talk?"

"Do you want to talk?"

"Are you sure you don't want to talk about this, Nan?"

I didn't answer. She put her arm around me. It felt heavy. I didn't move. Outside, the sound of rain, drowning the crickets.

"It was an accident," she whispered.

"You swerved the car," I said.

"You were running us off the road," she said.

"But you hit him. Why did you hit him?"

"*I* hit him? *You* were driving."

"But *you* swerved the car, Ana."

"And you didn't stop me, Nan. You could have stopped me and you didn't."

"I couldn't have stopped you. You pulled the wheel so hard."

"I didn't pull it *that* hard."

"This is not my fault," I said.

"We were confused."

"This is your fault."

"We did this together."

"*You* did this."

"*We* did this."

"That poor man."

"He was a bad man."

"You don't know that. How could you know that?"

"He beat his horse, Nan. And probably his wife if he had one. He was a bad man. Trust me. I know bad men."

"What if we get caught?"

"If we get caught," she sighed, "I will take the fall for us." She placed her hand on my hair. "I'm dying anyway. We can say I did it."

"You did do it," I pleaded.

Ana stroked her fingers through my hair. "Oh, sister."

31

In the morning, rain, hard and pounding. The wind shook the windows, shook the house. I watched the trees be whipped by the wind and the windows be drowned by the rain. A planter fell off the lanai and crashed. I turned to face Ana, but she wasn't there.

Sandpaper mouth, groggy. I still hadn't cried. I reached for my water glass. As I drank I thought: I don't deserve this comfort, a man is dead. The car, the swerve. How tightly I had held the wheel. But how tightly had I held the wheel? Could I have pulled us back? Could I have stopped her? Us? It?

The thud, the flashlight rolling, rolling. How Peter's body had landed. Like he was sleeping. The teal shirt, the blood. The memory of him at the tarot stand. "When I feel the jitters, I take a stick to my horse." His jittery leg. His scrawny arms. "After the horse, I take the stick to myself." The bruises he must have had somewhere on his body. What his last name was. If he had a wife, children. A job where people expected him to show up. Other places he went.

There were many things on the nightstand, but all I saw was my phone. You should call the police, Nan. Nancy. Nancy, you should call the police. But what would I say? It didn't make sense. "It was her fault, it was not my fault." But I had been driving. That's what they would say. They would say, "How was it her fault when you were driving?" And how would I respond? "We were sort of both driving. It might be hard to understand." And they would say, "That is correct, we do not understand." And then what? Sirens, handcuffs, rooms with two-way mirrors. Orange jumpsuit, courtrooms, prison. The boys in pieces, Chuck in pieces, all of us in pieces.

Another planter crashed on the lanai. I went to the window. The glass was shaking. Chuck's car was gone. The boys' car was gone. The half-built shed shuddered in the wind. A branch fell to the ground. Another. Time was passing. Too much time had passed. They would say, "If it wasn't your fault, then why did you wait so long to call?"

·

Ana in the fetal position on the living room floor. She was wearing my robe.

"Are you okay?" I asked because I had to.

"Storm," she groaned. She was shivering.

"Do you want a blanket?" I was already taking one off the couch and spreading it over her. A mother's instinct. I couldn't help it. She needed me. She was dying.

"Celia's pissed." The sides of her lips curling up. Her eyelids fluttering closed. She was wearing the black wig with the pink streak again. "This storm is for us."

For *you*, I wanted to say. It's for *you*.

"But what she doesn't realize is that she's washing any evidence away." Ana pulled the blanket tighter around her shoulders. "Stupid bitch."

"They're going to find him, Ana."

"I know," she said.

Portico's shrine tank on the coffee table. With Rice Krispies in it now. Next to the tank the remote. "Don't do it," she said.

But I had to. I turned the TV on. I flipped through the channels. First slow, then fast. I went through all of them. Nothing. I went through again. "Mute, please," she said, and I muted it for her.

"Tea, please. Can you make me tea? And Red Vines. Two standing up in a jar."

"A jar?"

"Pleeease."

I made the tea. I found a jar for her Red Vines. On the counter a note from the boys. *Mom and Ana, Have a GREAT day doing yoga. Can we make dinner tonight?*

They had never left me a note like this before. But now, on this day of all days, a note? I didn't deserve this. How happy they were, how happily unaware—I wanted to cry, but I was too numb to cry. The cold metal feeling of shock, the fuzzy hangover of the pills. How would we make dinner together? How would I possibly get through that? How would I get through anything now? It seemed impossible.

"I don't think I can do this," I told her. My best friend, my soul sister, my support system, curled up on the ground like a baby. I set the tea and the jar of Red Vines on the carpet next to her hands.

"You can," she whispered.

"I can't," I said. "I can't." I scrunched my hair and tugged it. It felt good to feel something. "But there's no way out. I don't see a way out."

"The only way out is death," Ana said, more voice in her now.

"What am I going to do?" I tugged my hair harder. I paced faster. "I can't *kill* myself."

"No," she said. Did she chuckle? "Then you would be your mother."

I stopped. "What did you say?"

Ana rolled her eyes like I was being dramatic. "Didn't your mother kill herself?"

Fuck you! I wanted to kick her. But she was dying. And she was right.

My mother. Dead in her smelly chair. Wine spills on the carpet. They looked like birthmarks. How it reeked. How her hair had frozen around her face. The organization of her table. How she handled the things she loved with such care. Wine cups in a stack. The pack of red straws. Trash can by her feet. Orange bottles in a row.

Ana, propped on her elbow, was studying me. The feeling of being laid bare. What was it that she understood about me? And why the hell did I care? I wanted her to look away.

"Tell me again," she said, "what happened to your mother."

"I told you already," I said.

"Can you tell me again, please?" Her eyes like a doe.

I tried to calm down. "Overdose," I said evenly.

"In her chair," Ana said slowly.

"Yes, in her chair. She died in her chair watching soaps and drinking red wine from a box, and she took too many pills and fucking overdosed and died, okay?" And then I lost it. "Fuck! Why are you asking me about this right now?"

Ana stretched her neck. She was making me wait. She stretched to the right and then she stretched to the left. Then her eyes settled back on me. A flash passed across them. "Last time, you said it was white wine."

My shoulders locked. I wanted to scream. I wanted to run. "White, red, who fucking cares! Fuck, Ana!"

She blinked. "Interesting" was all she said.

My whole body was vibrating. I was going to explode. Calm down, Nancy. Breathe.

Ana stirred her tea with her finger. It was still steaming. "I've never seen you so emotional," she said.

I made my voice toneless, vacant. "Of course I'm emotional," I said.

This hollow version of Nancy no longer interested her. Her eyes wandered to the TV. She took a sip of her tea. And then she said, "Look."

On the screen was Peter's face. Peter smiling on a sunny day with a toothpick in his teeth. Over his chest his name appeared: PETER TACKMAN. I fumbled for the remote. I pressed the mute button right in time for the newscaster to say, "If you have any information, please call this number."

"That means they have nothing," Ana said.

"Oh my God," I said. "Oh my God, Ana. Oh my God!"

"Oh my free will," she corrected.

I was defiant. "Oh my *God.*"

She rolled onto her back like a lazy dog. "The boys want to cook with us tonight. Isn't that adorable?"

"I'm going to say no. They can go out tonight."

She bit her finger. "I already told them yes."

"You already told them yes?"

"You were sleeping," she said. She winked at me. "I like playing Mom. It's fun."

"Oh my *God*," I said, just to piss her off.

"Plus, we should act normal right now. We shouldn't do anything out of the ordinary."

I knew she was right. This was when we put on our costumes. This was when the charade began. This part was even worse than the crime itself, because it would have to go on forever.

"Nan," she cooed. "Are you mad? Don't waste your time being mad. Plus, you can't be mad at me." Her sad puppy eyes. Her overdone frown. Like she was taunting me. "I'm dying."

•

The storm didn't stop. A tree fell straight across the driveway so we couldn't leave. I called the tree service. No one picked up. Ana was fine and then she wasn't fine and then she was fine again. "I'm weakening," she said, "but it's not over yet." She kept asking me to get her things. She was trying to keep me close because she could feel me wanting to get away. Can I have more tea, please? Can I have more Red Vines, please? Nan, can you make me a peanut butter sandwich? You make the best peanut butter sandwiches. Pleeease?

She didn't eat the sandwich. She barely looked at it.

I said, "You're not eating."

She pouted. "Because I can tell you didn't make that sandwich with love."

She was dying so I had to be nice. She was dying so I had to refill her tea again and again and again. So many times I began to wonder if she was just pushing me to see how far I would go. She would take three sips and say, "Can you put in a little more hot water, please?" She finally got off the floor and moved to the couch. Her used tea bags—she tossed them into Portico's tank.

I said, "We should put that outside soon. It's starting to smell."

She said, "That would be disrespectful. This is a memorial, Nan, a mem-o-rial."

The wind, violent. Every planter crashed off the lanai. I went outside to pick up the pieces, and really so I could spend ten minutes away from her. The wind whipped my hair. Mud on my feet. I cut my finger on one of the pieces and felt more awake. The blood on his head. His teal shirt. His family. How Ana had told him to name the horse Mom.

She'd turned the volume up so high that it drowned out the pounding rain. "Look what I found on TV!" she yelled. "It's the cancer documentary! About the women who go to the hair salon to feel beautiful before they die! Come watch with me!"

"I'm cleaning!"

I looked at the screen. The woman being interviewed was crying. She was bald, but not completely bald like Ana. On the top and on the sides of her head were clumps of baby fine hair. Then Ana turned the volume up even more. So loud that the blasting sound of this woman crying erased all the thoughts in my brain.

"Can you turn that down, please!"

Ana pretended not to hear me.

"Ana!"

"Come watch with me, Nan!" She patted the cushion beside her.

I walked around the couch and stood in front of her, the trash bag of broken pieces in my hand. "Turn it down, please!"

Her toes twinkled happily on the coffee table. "Fine, *Mom*," she said.

The woman on the TV behind me said, "I can't believe this is happening to me. You never think it's going to be you."

"Ana," I said, "what happened to the horse?"

Ana laughed. "You look like a swamp monster, Nan."

I waited.

She sighed. "The horse wasn't in the barn."

"Oh my God," I said. "Oh my God!"

"Ugh, stop saying that," she said. "You're killing me!"

I looked at her. She looked at me. There was nothing in her dark eyes. Who was this woman on my couch, and how did she get here? I wanted to go back in time.

"I love you, Nan," she said. She blinked several times. "Don't you love me?"

I couldn't look at her anymore. "I have to take a shower," I said.

I took the trash bag back outside. Why had I brought it in? Because I thought I deserved to carry heavy loads. No, Nancy, you just weren't thinking. You just weren't thinking! I opened the door and tossed the bag out, and as I walked past her on the couch, she repeated what I had just said in a wee voice: "I have to take a shower."

I screamed it. "Oh my *God*!"

•

Jed and Cam were drenched. "A tree fell," Cam said.

"So we couldn't drive up," Jed finished.

"I know," I called from the kitchen, "I called the tree service but they—"

"Hi, booooys," Ana cut me off. She was still on the couch in her robe. My robe. She had recorded that depressing documentary about fighting breast cancer with hairstyling, and now she was watching it again. Over the course of the day, she had put on a pair of Chuck's socks and the big white beach hat with the pink bow.

"Nice hat," Jed said, flicking the brim.

"I know you love it, Jedi," she said.

"Wait right there," I said to the boys, who were dripping water and mud all over my floor. I brought them dish towels to wipe themselves off. As if the floors mattered right now. But I knew it was best to act normal. Nothing out of the ordinary.

"What are we cooking?" Jed asked.

"Frozen Costco pizza, it's already in the oven," I said. "I couldn't go grocery shopping because of the tree, so this is all we got." This was a lie. There were plenty of things we could have cooked together, but I wanted dinner to be over as soon as possible.

Cam shrugged. "Cool."

The boys sat on the couch with Ana while I did everything. Only ten minutes until the pizza would be done. I set the table haphazardly. I ripped paper towels in half instead of looking for the napkins. I didn't light any candles.

I heard Jed boasting to Ana, "Yeah, we put some Rice Krispies in this morning," and Ana said, "I love it, Jedi."

Every time she spoke, I cringed.

I took the pizza out five minutes early. Done enough.

"Dinner!" I shouted.

Back in San Diego, every time I shouted "Dinner!" Chuck would shout "Dinner!" right after me like an echo. Had we ever done that in this house? Why had I forgotten about it until now?

Chuck and Brenda. I couldn't go there right now. Keep it together, Nancy. Keep it together for your children.

The three of them shuffled to the table. Ana held the crook of Jed's arm. They sat. "Wait, we need candles," Ana said, and scooted her chair in, which meant she did not plan on getting up to light these candles herself. She looked at me. I looked away. My eyes fell on the dead branch she had hung on our wall. "Jedi, will you do it?" she requested.

"Totally," he obliged. He whipped a lighter from his pocket—don't say anything, Nancy, don't say anything—and expertly lit the candles. Silently I sighed.

The boys, without being asked, held out their hands. Ana smiled. "We are here," she said, "at the dinner table. This is the biggest storm in the last ten years. I learned that on TV today. Monsoon rains, they said. Let these monsoon rains wash over you and through you. Let them wash away your sins. We have nothing. Nothing, nothing, nothing, except for this moment, right now, right here."

"Thank you, Ana." I gave her a tight smile.

"Wait, I wasn't done yet," she whined.

I tightened my smile while trying to hold Jed and Cam's hands gently.

"We all make decisions," she boomed. "No one decides for us. We are in control. We decide to play water polo, we decide to eat pizza, we decide when to step out in the rain. We decide to be happy. We decide to give up. *We* decide." She inhaled and exhaled with force. "We decide, we decide, we decide. There is no one to blame for your life but you."

A long pause. A very long pause. I rolled my lips together to stop myself from speaking, and then Jed said, "Dayum!" He squeezed my hand. He looked so rejuvenated by her.

I ate half a slice of undercooked pizza and asked the boys how they were doing. Fine, they said, fine. I asked them to please do their homework. They swore it was already done. Then I excused myself. "My stomach hurts, I'm going to lie down."

"*Your* stomach hurts?" Ana said.

"It does," I said, not bothering to feign any symptoms.

She was searing a hole through my head with her eyes. I didn't look at her. I washed my plate. I went to the bedroom. I flopped onto the bed. Ten minutes later, I flushed the pills before I had any more time to think.

I turned off the lights and tried to sleep. The teal shirt, the blood, the flashlight rolling, rolling. How he had landed like that, so peacefully. A bad man, she had said. He deserved it, she had said.

The smell of marijuana wafted in. I didn't get up to scold them. It seemed unimportant now. The windows shook in their frames, the rain would not stop pounding. There were no more planters on the lanai to be broken.

When my mother died, my brother had said the same thing. She deserved it. And then he had said, "This isn't our fault."

Sky

32

It was too beautiful. A clear pink morning sky like the storm had never happened, and it didn't seem honest. If you took a picture of this morning, there would be nothing ugly in it.

She was snoring. She was parked in the middle of the bed, her arms and legs splayed in all directions. Her sleeping face looked different somehow. It was not the serene face she usually wore. Her breath got shorter, and the muscles around her eyes and mouth constricted— she seemed to want to speak—and then she relaxed again, but even relaxed, she looked worried.

Sounds in the driveway. I peeled back the covers quietly, went to the window. Chuck's folding chair had been whipped across the lawn and he was walking toward it. Already in his work clothes. Wet hair, he'd just showered. When he got to the chair, he paused. He took a step back, took his hands out of his pockets. I waited for him to kick the chair. But then he bent to pick it up. He tried to fold it. It wouldn't fold. It was broken. He carried it back with him anyway and set it by the ohana door.

After taking a moment to survey the damage, Chuck made his way down the driveway to his car, which was parked next to the boys' car behind the fallen tree. Hands in his pockets again. His feet were slow and heavy. He stopped to throw fallen branches out of the driveway and into the grass. Where was he going so early? Work? Breakfast somewhere before work? Breakfast with Brenda? He hadn't come in to get coffee. Was he making it in the ohana or going out for it now?

He got into his car but didn't leave. He just sat there, looking at the house.

Footsteps on the lanai, and then the boys walking down to their car in matching strides. Board shorts, flip-flops. Jed's shirt was too big for him. Cam's was the same orange as her Wynonna wig.

Chuck got out of his car.

The boys stopped.

Chuck waved. He said something I couldn't hear. The boys looked at each other, then walked faster to their car. Chuck said something else. He was standing in front of their car now. And then it was the three of them, standing together. Chuck reached for Jed. Jed stepped back. Then—this surprised me—Cam stepped forward and hugged his father. And then—more surprising—Jed put his arms around the both of them. Only for a second, but still.

After that they were talking again. I love you, I'm sorry, I love you. That's what I imagined they were saying.

The boys drove away first. Chuck stood there and watched them, and then he got back into his car. He started the engine. At the end of the driveway, he turned on his blinker. No one saw this but me. The road was empty.

I showered in the boys' bathroom so I wouldn't wake her up. I scrubbed as if I were covered in his blood. My skin was red and raw by the end and I deserved that. When I reached for the towel, I remembered how I'd switched the towels when we first moved in. These were the yellow ones Chuck and I had used in San Diego. It felt like I hadn't seen them in years.

Spandex crops and a tunic I hadn't worn in a while because that was what I found in the laundry room.

And then a car. In the driveway. Doors slamming. The police. The police, the police and blinking lights and questions and I don't know why I ran to the little mirror in the hallway first. To see if I looked like an innocent person, maybe.

The necklace—my black side of the yin and yang—was perfectly framed by the dip in the tunic. I couldn't be wearing this; this tied me to her. She would confess and this would tie me to her. My hands were trembling. I tried to unclasp it, but I couldn't. I tried to yank it off. I couldn't. Breathe, Nancy. I tried again. The clasp opened. The necklace fell to the floor. I left it there.

I ran through the living room. Something rancid—Portico's tank with new colors in it. I didn't stop to see what they had added. I opened the door. Too beautiful again. No spinning lights, no police. It was a giant truck. Big Island Tree Service printed on the side. Had I made this appointment and forgotten? But they hadn't answered the phone. Had they? I was going crazy.

I walked down the driveway. Act normal. Nothing out of the ordinary.

A man in a hard hat revved a chainsaw. They would cut the tree before moving it.

"Hey!" I called, walking closer. "Did I call you?"

"You Chuck?" The man laughed.

"No," I said seriously. I stared at my feet for too long. What if this man had known Peter. What if the other man, who was still in the truck, had known Peter. A small town.

And then I realized the man was waiting for me to speak. "Thank you for coming," I said, and turned—too abruptly, that was awkward, don't be awkward—and walked away. Should I turn back around? No, that's worse. Keep walking. But oh God, that was so awkward. They would tell the police later that I had seemed off. Keep walking. Keep walking. You're fine. You're fine.

•

Yes, Chuck had a coffeemaker in the ohana now. I hated that. And I hated that his clothes were in a laundry bag from Tyke's and I didn't even know where Tyke's was. He'd found an extra pillow somewhere. He had two pillows now. His futon bed looked uncomfortable and depressing, and good because he deserved that, but it also looked like a prison bed, and that's what I deserved.

Standing there in Chuck's new life, I heard her words: We are born alone and we die alone. And I wanted to tell her this. I wanted to tell her everything. "He has a coffeemaker now, and I was thinking about what you said, how we are born alone and die alone." I wanted to go into the house and wake her up and say this to her.

But I couldn't go to Ana now. She had swerved the car and she had done it on purpose. She had known exactly what she was doing when she swerved the car. Hadn't she?

For now, I thought, as I opened the door, be kind. She's dying, Nancy. It's only a little while longer.

•

Things I hadn't noticed in my rush out of the house: Ana's tarot cards spread out over the dining room table. All those antique ovals and all of her faces inside of them. Her cheesy TV psychic expression and Portico threaded through her fingers like rope. Portico's tank had pasta in it now, heaped like hair. On top of the pasta was Ana's blue Buddha. And then, movement. I held my breath and looked in from the side.

"No."

Maggots.

Anger. Adrenaline. The tank was heavy but felt light. I wanted to throw it off the lanai. I set it by the doormat instead.

Sound of the chainsaw. The tree service had removed a good chunk of the tree—just enough room to pass. I could leave now. I could be free.

"Naaaaaaaan?"

The sound of her voice. I froze. A cool tingling up my spine and up my neck and up the sides of my ears. I thought of something she'd told me once: Your body is smarter than you are.

"Naaa-aaaan?"

If she needed something, I would get it. And then I would leave. Errands. That's what I would say.

I paused outside the bedroom door. "I can see your feet," she said. I opened the door. Her face looked calm. The peaceful face she wore when she was awake, the face of a yogi, of a healer, of a wise woman who knew things you might not know. Alabaster skin and her bare shoulders, and she might have been naked under the sheets.

"Hey." She looked me up and down. Slowly she lifted her index finger. Slowly she pointed to the center of her neck. "Where's your necklace?"

"It fell off."

"Interesting," she said, and touched her lips.

I made myself ask. "Can I get you anything?"

She tapped her lips. She didn't take her eyes off me. "Did I ever tell you how my dad used to make me French toast?"

I shifted my weight. "No, you didn't."

"After he beat me, he would make me French toast." She shook her head and smiled. "It was his way of apologizing." Her fake lips, her fake teeth, her wig. The fact that these things still made her beautiful annoyed me. "I think you owe me an apology, Nan."

"Oh?" Be calm. "For what?"

She pointed her finger at me. She drew circles around me with that finger. "Your energy toward me has changed."

I looked at my feet. "I'm happy to make you French toast, Ana."

She touched her heart. "I would love that," she said.

I smiled for her. She said nothing. I smiled harder. She squinted at me. "Okay, Nan," she said finally, "I see what you're doing." She blew me a kiss. "We can play nice."

"I'll be back with your French toast," I said, and closed the door.

"Door open, please!"

I pushed the door back open. "No problem!" I sang.

I went to the kitchen. I cracked the eggs and stirred them fast. Compassion. Kindness. She would know if I made this French toast without love. I watched the butter melt and bubble. I watched my hands pull the bread through the egg. I felt nothing.

The sound of the chainsaw stopping. The sound of the truck driving away. After they had gone, another sound. The police. I ran to the window. No police. I was going crazy.

I arranged the French toast lovingly on a tray and brought it to her with a glass of apple juice and two Red Vines in a jar. This kindness would release me from having to spend the day with her. "Here you go," I said, setting it on the nightstand.

She was reading a book. Chuck's Hawaii book. *Big Island Revealed*. She'd taken it out of his drawer.

"Oh, Nan," she said sweetly. "You *do* love me."

I put my hands in my pockets, but I was wearing spandex that had no pockets.

And then a noise and I flinched. I went to the window. Not the police. Nothing.

"Don't worry," she said. "If they come, I will take the fall. I told you that already."

"Ana," I said, "I have to ask you something."

She raised her eyebrows. She was amused.

"Did you hit him on purpose?"

"No," she said, looking straight at me. Her eyes were steady, focused. "Who do you think I am?"

I looked at her. She looked at me. Steam rose from the French toast.

"Well," I said, "I'm off to run some errands."

"Where?"

"The store."

"Can I come with?"

It took courage to say, "I'd like to be alone right now, if that's okay with you."

"Nan," she laughed. "Come on. You hate being alone."

"That's not true."

"Please," she said, "you know you hate it."

"Okay, I'm going to get going," I chirped. "Do you need anything from the store?"

She held my eyes. And then—hand on her stomach. She winced.

The requisite "Are you okay?"

She shook her head.

I went to her. Her face, still strained. "Nan," she whispered. She was breathing normally again. Good. "Don't leave me."

"I'm just going to the store. I'll be right back."

She blinked several times.

I stood. "I'll see you in a little while."

"Wait. If I die while you're gone, what will you have wished you had said to me? What do you want to say to me before I die?"

I knew what she wanted. "That I love you, Ana."

"I love you, too, Nan."

I blew her a kiss. "Bye."

"Don't be alone for too long." She winked. "You'll get depressed."

I smiled harder. "See you soon."

She winced again. I pretended not to notice, and left the room.

But I felt like a bad person so I went back to check. Through the crack in the door, I expected to find her holding her belly and breathing it out. But no, she was picking at her fingernail, looking bored. Then she picked up a slice of French toast. Syrup dripped onto the sheets. She didn't notice or she didn't care. She lowered the toast into her mouth and took two big bites, one right after the other.

33

I feel lonely, I thought, as I walked deeper into the forest. I feel scared, I thought, when I heard something living brush through the leaves and quickened my pace. My shoes, I thought, when the path turned to mud. When I stopped to tie my muddy shoe and heard no cars and no dogs and no people and no sound in the world beyond the ringing of crickets, there was only the thud of my heart beating, and it was beating fast.

I screamed. I screamed as loud as I could until there was nothing left.

Afterwards, silence.

No one came to save me.

The crickets didn't stop to make room for my noise.

The world was the same as it always was.

Nature didn't care.

34

Safeway was crowded. All these people and I couldn't look into their eyes. Hands on the cart, eyes on the food. I walked like I was underwater. I examined every product. I didn't want to go home.

I'd heard the "Hey you!" but I didn't think "you" was me until someone touched my arm.

It was Marigold. Or Petunia. I didn't know which was which. "Sandwich Sistah," she said. Her hollowed cheeks and barely any blue in her eyes because her pupils were so dilated. And then Petunia or Marigold—the other one—walked up with a loaf of Love's bread. "Fuckin' A, this store is backward," she said, dropping it into their cart, which was full with the big backpack they slept on.

"Look who it is," the first one said, and the second one looked at me, barely any blue in her eyes either. "Sandwich Lady!" She hugged me. She was so thin. "Girl, we been missing you. Look, we even making our sandwiches like yours now." She motioned to the jar of Skippy in the cart.

"When you coming back?" the first one asked.

And then they were both looking at me, their gaunt electric faces and their sweatshirts hanging off their scarecrow bodies, and I don't know why I said, "Soon. I'll be back soon."

•

A police car on the road, so I turned right to get away from it, which was the wrong way. Another police car, so I turned to avoid that one, too. I ended up on the highway driving north. I kept checking the rearview mirror to make sure the SUV behind me didn't have a blue light on top of it. Because that's what police cars looked like in Kona— just regular cars with blue lights on top. This made them harder to spot.

The sun, the sky, the ocean. Snow-capped Mauna Kea and the unfair beauty of it. I drove all the way to Waikoloa before turning back. It was late afternoon. I'd been gone for hours. I still didn't want to go home. But the milk was getting hot. But she was dying.

•

But when I got home, she wasn't there. Her car was gone. She hadn't left a note.

I unpacked the groceries. My phone beeped. A text from Cam: *Ana is taking us to volcano!*

I wrote back: *Great.*

All I felt was relief, and maybe this was the wrong thing to feel. An afternoon relieved from her. But what about tomorrow? And the days after tomorrow? How many days did she have left?

I put her tarot cards away. I swept the floors. I swept my necklace into the dust bin. I was about to throw it away, but I picked it out of the dirt and set it on the windowsill instead.

The teal shirt, the blood, the flashlight rolling, rolling.

I hadn't eaten all day. I didn't feel like eating. I made myself eat anyway. I ate a banana. And then a Red Vine, maybe to see how it would feel. I chewed it partway and spit it out.

How he had landed, like he was sleeping.

I didn't turn on the TV. I cleaned it instead. I took her tray to the kitchen. She'd eaten all the French toast and both of the Red Vines.

How she had said, "Drive." How I had obeyed her. How I had wanted to leave, too.

•

By six the house was immaculate. I had replaced Ana's dead tree branch with our family photo. If a stranger saw this photo, they would think, Those people look wholesome. I tossed the branch outside. The sun, low in the sky behind the trees. My barren garden, just a wet rectangle of soil.

The sound of a car coming closer. I turned. It was Chuck. I didn't move. He got out of the car, walked toward the ohana. He was carrying a bag of takeout food. I couldn't tell from where. He looked tired. And old. Lines on his forehead I hadn't seen before, and this meant I looked older, too. "Hey," he said carefully, like I was a bomb he might set off.

I nodded at his bag. "Dinner?"

"Yeah."

"You going out tonight?" I was speaking evenly, which impressed me. "Are you going to play pool?"

Chuck touched his neck. "I don't think so."

"Chuck." I wanted to make sure he was looking at me when I asked.

"Yeah?" Those bright blue eyes. I hadn't seen them in the light like this for what felt like so long.

"Who is Brenda?"

His face twisted. He was trying to figure out how I knew.

"The boys told me you were looking for her the other night."

"Oh," Chuck said. I could tell he was trying to remember. And then he did remember—I saw it on his face—and he said, "Oh," again.

"Are you having another affair, Chuck, because if you are, I can't—"

"I am not having an affair." He seemed exhausted.

"Are you sure?"

He rubbed his tired face. "I'm sure."

"Okay." I wanted to believe him. "Okay." I crossed my arms. "Who's Brenda?"

"I didn't want to tell you."

"Tell me what?"

"She's a coach."

"What kind of coach?"

His shoulders slumped. "A sobriety coach," he said quietly.

"Why wouldn't you tell me that?" I was hurt.

He moved his bag to the other hand. "I had to do this on my own."

I was still hurt. "I'm proud of you," I said. "Do you want to come in? I can make you some real dinner, if you want." I felt the muscles in my neck tighten, expectant.

Chuck looked down. "I got dinner, but thank you."

It hadn't occurred to me that he might say no.

He glanced at our cars. "Ana's not here," he said.

"She took the boys to the volcano."

"She's alone with the boys?"

"Is that a problem?" I was mad he'd said no to my food.

Chuck said nothing.

I said nothing.

He checked his watch.

I excused him so he wouldn't have to do it himself. "Go eat," I said. "You don't want it to get cold."

•

An hour later he left. I didn't know where he went.

•

The sky darkened. The moon rose. I took another shower. As if I were covered in his blood. I scrubbed harder. This time I bled.

I put a pillow in the center of the bed. But a little off-center so my barrier would look like an accidentally tossed pillow. It would be unwise to upset her. I didn't trust her angry.

•

In the middle of the night, they came home. Outside the bedroom door, they whispered, good night, good night, good night. I listened to Ana take off her clothes. My weight shifted toward her when her body hit the bed. The first thing she did was move the pillow. The second thing she did was string my necklace back around my neck. And then she put her arm around me and five minutes later she was asleep. Locked under her arm, I couldn't twist and turn anymore, and the rise and fall of her body against mine was soothing even when I didn't want it to be. It was comfort, the most basic comfort of two bodies together, and there was nothing to do but sleep.

35

"It hasn't hit Pahoa yet, but it's about to. It's so close." Her glimmering eyes. How chaos excited her. She painted another sloppy stroke.

I was letting her paint my toes one final time. So that if she died today, I would have this purple sparkly polish to remember her by. I'd agreed because it was easier than disagreeing. It was also a strategic move. I thought if I did what she wanted, she might stop punishing me.

That morning Jed had walked into the kitchen bald. "Ana did it. Don't be mad," he'd said, making his arms into an X like I was going to throw stones at him.

I choked on my coffee. Don't be mad? You look like a skinhead!

"I did it for people with cancer," he said, proud.

I couldn't stop coughing. "Where's Cam?"

"Don't worry," Jed said. "He didn't do it. He chickened out."

Ana stopped to inspect her work. I had to get up. Just for a minute. I needed a break from her. "I have to go to the bathroom," I said.

"Okay," she said, "let me just do this last"—another sloppy stroke—"okay, you can go."

I went to the boys' bathroom. Jed's beautiful hair was all over the floor I'd just cleaned. On the sink was the razor. A Japanese brand. Jed must have bought that recently, because I'd never seen it before.

When I got back to the living room, the documentary was playing again. The woman on the screen was sobbing. "And on top of dying, you have to be ugly." She touched one of the patches of hair on her head like it disgusted her.

Ana's toes twinkled happily on the coffee table. "Do you mind if we watch this again? It inspires me."

"Sure."

I put my foot back in her lap. Only a few more toes to go. A new woman appeared on the screen. She had barely any hair, but still, there was some.

"Ana?"

"Nan?"

"Can I try on your wig?"

"Of course, daw-ling." She globbed on more nail polish. "I'll grab it for you in a sec. You wanna be Wynonna or Marilyn?"

I pretended to consider the options. "I want the one you're wearing."

"Oh," she said. "I don't want to take it off. It's keeping my head warm."

A car in the driveway and it was the cops. But I was crazy. It wasn't the cops. Chuck or the boys had forgotten something at home and they'd come back to get it.

The woman on the screen: "It ravages you. It takes everything you have. I hate chemo."

Footsteps up the stairs. Onto the lanai. Two pairs of feet. The boys.

Ana, who was facing the door, looked up. The way she smiled. The way she said, "Welcome."

I turned.

I froze.

"Hello," I said, because it seemed like my turn to speak. Rapid-fire heartbeat in my ears. I took my foot off her lap and went to the door.

One was young, one was old. They stood in the same way, with their hands on their hips. Their navy-blue uniforms seemed out of place in this tropical palette. They wore reflective sunglasses, so I couldn't see their eyes. It was just me, in four oval lenses, reflected back in miniature.

"Please." I swallowed. "Come in."

"With shoes, it's okay?" the young one asked.

"Oh sure, yes. Yes, it's fine, yes." Don't be awkward. Stay calm. Nothing out of the ordinary.

"I'm Bailey," the young one said. He was Hawaiian. Buzz cut. Friendly voice.

"Crowley," the old one said. Angular body. Wild eyebrows. He scared me more.

I put my hands in the pockets I didn't have, rubbed my legs instead. "Nice to meet you both." I shook their hands like a sweet little housewife. My palms were clammy. Theirs were dry.

"We're here because we're looking for someone," the young one said.

"Ana Gersh," the scary one said.

"That's me!" Ana said from the couch. She waved. "Hello! Hi!"

Gersh? I thought her name was Ana Stevenson.

"Hello!" The young one sounded too excited.

"What can I do for you, officers?" she purred.

"We found one of your tarot cards," the scary one said.

The young one held up a plastic bag. Inside was the card, partially covered in dirt.

I saw her eyes spin and then settle. "I looked better with my real hair." She pulled the blanket higher over her shoulders hesitantly, like she was in pain, like every time she moved it hurt. Then she looked at each of them separately. I watched her gain their sympathy, or try. "I'm dying of cancer," she whispered.

"What was that?" the scary one asked, emotionless, which terrified me.

Ana looked at me. Then the cops looked at me. "She's dying of cancer," I repeated for them.

"Sorry to hear that, ma'am," the scary one said.

"How did you find me?" Ana asked. Her puppy dog eyes.

"Guy who made this card for you told us where you were," the young one said.

"Hard lady to track down," the scary one said.

"Me?" Ana's hand on her heart. She was overdoing it.

"Your old landlady told us you were up here on Kaloko," the young one said.

"Saw your car from the road," the scary one said. "Hard to miss."

I watched this exchange with wired eyes. Sweat was collecting on my hairline. I would have to wipe it soon and that would look bad. It would look like guilt.

"What's the relation here?" the scary one asked. "You sisters?"

"No," I said too loud.

The scary one looked at me. He looked at Ana. "You wear the same necklace."

"We're soul mates," Ana said. Her hand on her stomach but she wasn't wincing yet. Like she was getting ready for the pain.

"Either of you ladies know Peter Tackman?" The scary one looked at Ana, and then he looked at me.

I didn't move, didn't speak.

"Oh," Ana said, as if she'd just remembered, "the guy who died, yeah? I think I saw him on the news."

The way she said *yeah* at the end of that sentence. She was speaking their lingo, the lingo of Hawaii. She was trying to appeal to them.

"Any idea why he would have this card in his wallet?" the scary one asked.

Ana shrugged. "He must have come to the tarot stand," she said. "Peter. I don't know if I remember a Peter. Nan, do you remember a Peter?"

Abruptly, like a hiccup, I said, "No."

"Wait," Ana said, "I think I do remember. Did he chew toothpicks?"

"Yes, he did, ma'am," the young one said, too excited again.

"Did you give this card to him?" the scary one asked.

Ana shook her head. She didn't look worried at all. "No," she said. "He must have stolen it. Which card is it, out of curiosity?"

The young one lifted the baggie to inspect.

But the scary one already knew the answer. "Wheel of Fortune," he said. "I looked it up this morning. Means something about turning points. I wouldn't consider that a lead."

"No," Ana said certainly, like she was his partner. "I wouldn't consider that a lead either."

A long pause. I stayed completely still. Ana rubbed her belly. The scary one reached for his belt and this was it, this was the moment. The cuffs and we need to take you in for questioning and it's over now.

"Well," the scary one said, scratching his back. "We probably wouldn't have come to find you if this man had had more in his wallet. But there was only a credit card and this card of yours. Seemed strange." He set his hand on his waist. "But neither of you ladies knew Peter?"

We shook our heads.

He glanced at my necklace, then at Ana's. "Most likely a hit-and-run," he said.

The young one nodded at his mentor. "Happens too much on these winding roads up here."

"We need more signs. We're working on it." The scary one patted his chest. "Well, you two be careful on the road."

"Absolutely, Officer," Ana said, a little seductively.

"And sorry you're sick. You take care of yourself, Ms. Gersh," the young one said.

Her name was Ana Gersh.

"My soul mate's taking care of me." Ana winked at me.

"Mahalos," the young one said.

"Bye now," the scary one said.

We waited in silence until they had driven away. Ana lay back on the couch. She didn't take her eyes off me. Feeling returned to my fingers. I wiped the sweat from my hairline.

"Gersh?"

"It's my old name."

"How many names do you have?"

"Names mean nothing, Nan."

"You broke your promise," I said. "You didn't confess."

She rolled her eyes. "Nan."

"You said you would confess."

"Please. You didn't confess either." Her dark eyes tightening.

"I didn't do anything wrong," I said, my voice hollow.

She set her finger on her cheek. "You sure about that?"

"Yes," I fired back before I had time to think.

Ana tapped her lips. "We tell ourselves stories in order to live."

The keys on the key ring. My purse by the door. I could leave now. I could be free from her.

Ana pulled the blanket off her shoulders. "You know what I just realized?"

I was already at the door. "I'm leaving."

"This secret?" she boomed.

"I'm leaving!" I yelled, searching frantically through the pile of shoes.

"This secret binds you to me!"

I grabbed my keys. But—no—they were her keys. She'd put her keys in my spot. I tried again. Your keys, Nancy, *your* keys.

I crashed through the door, jogged across the lanai. Her voice behind me, following me. She screamed it at the top of her lungs.

"This secret binds you to me forever!"

36

"Chuck's in the staff meeting," the woman at the desk said. "It's over in half an hour."

"Shit." I scratched my head. I tried to think. I felt insane. The woman looked at me like she felt sorry for me, and I felt more insane. "Where's the meeting?"

She pointed down the hall with her pencil. "Third door on the left."

I burst through the door because I had to. Chuck was standing in front of a room full of people in the red Costco shirt he wore to boost morale. He was saying, "And the go-backs at the end of the day"—and then he saw me. I motioned for him to come here now and I backed out of the door so these people would stop looking at me. I heard him say, "Brad, would you mind taking over for a sec?" Low voices in the room, a chair squeaking on the floor, footsteps, and then there he was. He closed the door lightly behind him. He folded his arms across his chest. "What's going on?"

"Chuck, I can't. Ana, I—"

Why had I come here? I couldn't tell him.

"Nancy." His hands on my arms. "What happened?"

"I don't know, I don't know." I felt calmer with him touching me. "I don't know."

"You don't know?"

We killed someone. No, *she* killed someone. There was an accident.

"Will you come home, please?"

"Why? What's wrong?"

"I don't know, I just—Ana, I can't be—I think we should—I don't know what to do. I think we should ask her to leave. But I can't. I need you to do it."

He sighed. He was disappointed in me.

"Please," I begged.

He took his hands off my arms. "Nancy, if you want her to leave, ask her to leave." Voices in the meeting room. He looked at the door. "I really need to get back in there."

"Chuck," I pleaded.

He put his hand on the doorknob. He wasn't even going to hug me good-bye.

"Chuck. Please. Help me."

He said it nicely, which made it worse. "I think you need to help yourself." He turned the knob. In a way that sounded too final, he said, "I'll see you later."

·

Spinning. It was too hot outside. Someone in the parking lot called my name. "Hi, Mrs. Murphy!" I pretended not to hear.

The thud, the flashlight rolling, rolling. Bound to her. Forever. And Gersh? Gersh? What the fuck, I didn't even know her fucking name! And Gersh—there was something about that name. Had I heard it before?

My eyes bugged open. My hand covered my mouth.

I had heard it before.

From her.

That quote she'd written down for me.

I stopped right there in the parking lot. I sat on the curb. I knew it was still in my purse. Where is it, where is it? I said, out loud or in my head, and I was boiling and dizzy, and where was that fucking piece of paper? and then here it was, here it was, and I unfolded it.

Be a lamp to yourself. Be your own confidence. Hold the truth within yourself as the only truth.
–ANA GERSH

I was already typing it into my phone.
Search.
I clicked the first link.

Be a lamp to yourself. Be your own confidence. Hold the truth within
yourself as the only truth.
—BUDDHA

37

Like a good person, or like a person who knew she'd be more likely to leave if she had a place to go, I booked Ana a room at Holiday Inn Express. "Ana Gersh," I told the person behind the desk. "Yes, I will pay in full now."

On the way back to the car, a homeless woman approached me. "Hey, nice lady," she said, her voice hoarse. Leathery skin hung off her bones and she was barely wearing any clothes. "You got a few bucks? I'm hungry."

Relief washed over me like something pure and purifying. "Yes, of course." I pulled a twenty out of my wallet and handed it to her.

Her worn face lit up. She was imagining what she would do with the money. "God bless you," she said, and I thanked her. I needed a blessing. I would take anything.

•

The boys' car in the driveway. Why? It was only one in the afternoon; they should be at school.

"Ana?" I called, slipping my shoes off. "Boys?"

I would say it with kindness.

Ana, I booked you a room, and I would appreciate it if you left. Yes, tonight.

Ana, I would appreciate it if you left tonight. I booked you a room at the Holiday Inn.

"Boys?" I called again. "Ana?"

And then I heard her laughing from down the hall. A burst of laughter, and then it stopped.

"Hello?" I followed her voice. "Hello?"

The bedroom door was closed. Strange because she usually liked it open. I don't know why I stood outside the door instead of just opening it, but that's what I did.

I heard movement. And then she was saying something. I couldn't make out the words. Was she on the phone?

And then—a man's muffled voice. But it couldn't be.

And then something fell. Something light. The box of Kleenex I'd put by the bed.

And then Ana moaned.

No.

Please God no.

Please please please please please as I opened the door.

I stopped breathing.

I covered my mouth.

I gagged.

Jed's naked back. The twisted sheets. My bedspread on the floor.

Ana looked straight at me. Her eyes quivered and gleamed.

Everything blurred. Jed's back, Ana's face, her dark eyes like smudges, the neon-pink streak, the heap of white sheets.

And she didn't stop. And she didn't tell Jed to stop. She moaned again. Louder, she moaned. She craned her neck back and moaned.

He leaned toward her neck.

I screamed his name. "Jed!"

He gasped. He didn't look back at me. He looked around the room, searching for a place to hide. He rolled off of her and buried himself under the sheets so it was just his feet sticking out, and then Ana was waving at me with just her pinkie. In a high-pitched voice to the rhythm of her puppet finger, she said, "Hi, Nan."

I walked down the hall. The hall started breathing, turning black at the edges. In a second I would fall. I grabbed the side of the couch. I slumped over it. I closed my eyes tight, tighter. I tried to breathe.

In the bedroom, Jed yelled at her. "I don't know!"

I made my way to the sink. I drank water with my hands like an animal.

Jed pulling his T-shirt over his head as he walked into the kitchen. He said, "Mom."

"Go back to school," I told his feet. I couldn't look at his face. My voice was cold. "Now."

His toes curled. "It was her dying wish, Mom."

I still couldn't look at him. "Tell me you wore a condom."

His voice cracked when he said, "I did."

"Go back to school."

"It's not his fault, Nan!" Ana sang from the bedroom.

"Go," I hissed, and Jed, startled by this version of me, hurried out the door.

When it clapped shut, Ana screamed, "Bye, Jed!" She was coming toward me down the hall. She was tying her robe. No, my robe. It was *my* robe. She plucked a grape from the fruit basket, popped it in her mouth. "Don't be mad," she said. "We all have needs."

She reached for my arm. I pulled away. I blinked at her. Her fat cheeks. Her duck lips. That bullshit thing she did with her eyebrows when she was pretending to look serene. The pink streak alongside her face hooking her chin like a warning.

"Go ahead," she said. "Tell me you hate me. Tell me why I am the worst person you've ever known." She let her head fall to the side like she was bored. She exhaled like she was fogging up a mirror. She brought her hands to her waist. "This is my favorite part."

Maybe I had known before, but I hadn't wanted to know. I said it like I was sad for her, and I was. "You have no one."

She kept herself looking bored. "We are born alone and we die alone, Nan."

"But you have no one."

"I need no one," she said louder.

"Then why are you here?"

She ate another grape. "I needed a place to crash."

"A place to crash? Who are you?"

"I," she bellowed, "am whoever you want me to be. I am the space you need filled. I am your projection."

"I don't even know what that means."

"Yes you do."

"Ana," I said.

She answered with her puppet pinkie. "Nan?"

"Take off your wig."

Her eyes flickered as usual, but this time I saw fear. "Why?"

"Take it off."

"No."

It happened in slow motion. I reached for her hair, she grabbed my wrist. I pushed her. She tripped. I didn't expect her to fall, but she did. She landed on the carpet. Her breathing got shallow, a shallow wheeze. Hyperventilating. I crouched over her. I tore the wig off her head. I rubbed my palm against her scalp, hard so I could feel the bristles. Which wasn't necessary. The hairs on her head were visible.

Ana hadn't shaved in a while.

I wanted to smack her. I smacked the floor instead. I screamed her name. "Ana!"

She was quiet. And still. Too still.

"Ana?"

I checked her breath.

"Ana!"

I pressed her eyelids back with my thumbs and saw white.

"Anaaaaa!"

38

I'd been in the waiting room for over two hours when the doctor finally came out and said, "Gersh?"

I set the magazine I hadn't been reading on the table. I'd told them I was her sister because I knew they wouldn't tell me anything otherwise. When they'd asked me to sign in, I had written Nancy Gersh.

He was a small Hawaiian man with round glasses and a goatee. "Dr. Maka," he said. "Hello."

"Nancy." I shook his hand.

"Your sister is fine," he said first. "Her blood pressure was very low. It might be the new medication. Common side effect of antidepressants is low blood pressure. Her stomach pain—I imagine it's stress. She told me she's been very stressed recently. We have her on a drip now, but I'd like to keep her overnight, just to be sure."

Antidepressants? I must have looked shocked because he said, too consolingly, "But don't worry. She's in good spirits."

I thought of all the times I'd googled antidepressants, and what Ana would have said if I had told her. Would she have admitted she was taking them herself? Or would she have said, "Breathe it out"? I guess I somehow thought we'd taken a silent oath to breathe it out together. Why had I assumed that?

On the loudspeaker: "Dr. Maka, patient in room 348."

"Is that Ana's room?"

"No," he said. "She's on the second floor."

I imagined Ana in a hospital bed, depressed, with a needle in her hand.

Kindness. Compassion. No, I hoped she was suffering.

"Do you have any questions?" the polite doctor asked.

"I do," I said. "I have a big question."

He perked up. "Yes?"

"What about Ana's cancer?"

He pushed his glasses higher up his nose. "Cancer?"

"Cancer."

He looked confused.

I was impatient. "Does Ana have cancer or not?"

"No," he said. "That would be very serious."

I sighed. "You're telling me that Ana does not have pancreatic cancer."

"Nancy. If that were the case—well, let's just be happy that is not the case."

"Does she have breast cancer?"

He couldn't help but look at me sideways. "No."

Even as I said the words, I somehow still didn't believe them. "Ana has never had cancer."

"That is correct," he said. "Ana is healthy. She had a mammogram recently. It came back clear."

I chuckled. It was her chuckle. "Ana is not dying."

"I hope not anytime soon," the doctor said.

I chuckled again. Like her or like me, I didn't know.

Ana did not have cancer.

Ana had never had cancer.

Ana was not dying.

Flash to her writing her bucket list. Her concentrated face, that ridiculous souvenir pencil.

Flash to her saying, "I'm dying, Nan. I don't have time for longing."

Flash to the piece of paper she'd shown me: PANCREATIC, 3–6 MONTHS. And its decorative font. Had she typed that up herself?

Flash to the night of Peter: "My dying wish, Nan."

To Jed: "Her dying wish, Mom."

Outside the hospital window there was a red bird perched on a palm frond, and it was laughing.

On the loudspeaker: "Dr. Maka, room 348."

The doctor nestled his iPad under his arm. "I should get going," he said. "Would you like to go back and see your sister now, Ms. Gersh?"

I said nothing.

For too long.

He tried to hide his disapproval. "Or if you have somewhere to be now, you can pick her up in the morning, yeah?"

"Yeah," I said. "Right."

On the loudspeaker: "Dr. Maka, room 348."

"You have a good night, Ms. Gersh." He nodded at me and then walked through the door. It swung back and forth in his wake.

Ana seemed far away. The parking lot seemed far away. Both options felt wrong, so I stayed right where I was, my Tevas planted on the mint-green floor, listening to that red bird laugh.

39

Jed opened the door. "Mom?"

I was in Cam's bed because there was nowhere else to go. Jed's bed scared me right now, my bed scared me more, the living room still smelled like Portico's rotting memorial, and I hadn't wanted to lie down on the kitchen floor.

"Mom?"

I opened my eyes. The Harry Potter bedspread I'd bought Cam when he was ten and beyond it, Jed.

God, his head. My poor baby. He was standing there like such a kid, with his backpack slung over one shoulder.

"Hi," he said.

But his deep voice and his broad chest and the way the backpack looked almost like a silly prop. Jed was a man now. It was hard to look at him.

"Mom, I'm sorry," he said. "I didn't mean to . . ." He searched for vague language. We couldn't talk about this directly. He tugged at his shirt. "I didn't mean for that to happen. I know she's your friend. She just, like, talked me into it or something. I know that sounds stupid. It's totally my fault."

"It's not your fault," I said like I was sure, or like I wanted to be.

Jed's hand on the doorframe, sliding up and down. It reminded me of the first night in this house when Chuck kept saying, "Can you believe we're here?"

"But it is kinda my fault," Jed said. "I mean . . . yeah."

"No." I was adamant. "It's not your fault."

There was a spot on the doorframe where the paint had chipped, and he was picking at it. I wouldn't ask him to stop. A fragile white chip of paint fluttered to the floor. "Are you gonna tell Dad?"

"No," I said. "You're an adult. You choose what you want to tell your dad."

"Thanks, Mom," he said, relieved.

"Is Mom in there?" Cam said.

Jed looked at his brother. His nose in profile reminded me of Chuck's.

Cam peered over Jed's shoulder. "Hi, Mom," he said, cautious, which meant that Jed had told him.

"Come in here, babies," I said.

They sat cross-legged on the floor under the blue Waverider flag Cam had tacked to the wall. I didn't move from the bed.

"Are you okay, Mom?" Cam asked.

"I'm fine, honey," I said. "I will be fine." I rolled onto my back, touched my forehead. I blinked at the popcorn ceiling. I waited for a piece of it to fall. "So much has happened in the last few months."

"Dude," Jed sighed, "so much."

I turned to face them. My twins. My innocent little baby men. How Cam used to have this dark freckle by his nose when he was young, and how now you could barely see it.

"Was school okay?" I asked.

Cam looked at Jed. Jed tugged his shirt.

"Liko told everyone on the team Tom and I are gay," Cam said, "so no one wants to change in front of us now. And he told everyone Jed—"

"Don't tell her." Jed slapped his brother's leg.

"Tell me what?"

"It's stupid," Jed said, his shorn head hanging low.

"He told everyone Jed's gay, too," Cam said fast, and held up his hands to shield himself from Jed, but Jed didn't hit him again.

"I hate that guy," Jed said, and hit his fist on the carpet a few times.

"I want to quit the team," Cam said.

"We're not going to get scholarships if we quit though," Jed said. Hand on the back of his head, rubbing against the grain, feeling this new landscape. It reminded me of when he'd gotten braces and he couldn't stop licking his teeth. Cam had done the same thing.

"I assume you didn't tell your coach," I said.

"Nah, Mom, we can't." Jed was pulling at the carpet now. "I miss Clairemont," he mumbled, as though he didn't want it to be true.

"Do you miss it, Cam?" I asked.

"Yes and no," Cam said.

"You have a boyfriend here, dude, that's why you like it," Jed said.

"True," Cam said.

"Whatever, Mom, we can handle it," Jed said. "The season's almost over anyway."

"Only six more weeks till Christmas break," Cam said.

"Five and a half actually," Jed corrected.

"Oh good," Cam said, looking too relieved.

The front door clapped shut. "Boys?" Chuck called.

Their worried faces. They didn't know the details, but knowing their parents were sleeping in separate houses was enough.

"Boys?" Chuck said again, and then he was there in the doorway, rubbing the chipped spot on the frame.

"Hi, Nancy," he said, solemn. He took off his hat, ran a hand through his hair. He looked good.

"Hi," I said. I rubbed the fabric of the pillowcase between my fingers. I curled my legs into what I hoped was a more attractive position. I wanted Chuck to love me again. I wanted him to love me more. "Will you join us?" I sat up to make room for him on the bed.

"No, don't move, it's fine. I'll sit on the floor," he said, and sat next to Cam so it was the three of them, all my family, sitting cross-legged in front of me in a row.

Jed was rubbing his head again, and Chuck asked, "How does it feel?"

"Like I'm exposed," he said, and I wondered if that's what she had told him. You will be exposed to the world now.

Chuck slid his hand across the top of Jed's head and said, "I like it."

"I like it, too," Cam agreed.

"You should shave yours, Cam," Jed said.

"No," Cam said. "I don't think it's my thing."

"Fine," Jed laughed, "it'll be *my* thing."

I could tell this made him uncomfortable—the idea that they would have their own "things."

"So, boys," Chuck patted his knees, "can we discuss the shed?"

"Dad," Cam groaned.

Jed's head slumped forward.

Chuck laughed. "I was actually coming to tell you we should abandon that project."

Jed's head shot back up. "Yes!"

"Yes," Cam echoed.

Jed hit his fist on the floor. "Let's burn it," he said.

Was he kidding?

Chuck let that sink in. And then he hit his fist on the floor. "Good idea," he said, "let's burn it." He never could resist the opportunity to be Cool Dad. "Wait, Nancy, is that okay with you?"

"I don't care," I said.

"Seriously, Mom?" Cam asked.

"Burn it down," I said.

"Mom, you're a *boss,*" Jed said.

All three of them had their eyes on me. This is when, Nancy. This is when you tell them. "I have to tell you all something," I said before I had time to think.

Their expectant faces. All of their eyes that bright unfiltered blue. They waited. And waited. And then Jed couldn't wait anymore. "What is it?"

I was touching something. Something in my hand. The necklace. I pressed the yin or the yang or whatever it was between my fingers. Hard and then harder, until the point of the apostrophe dug into my thumb, until I was in pain.

I am your projection, she had said.

"Nancy?" Chuck asked.

There was an accident.

We—

She—

It was in this moment that I knew I'd never tell them. I'd never tell anyone. It would become one more thing to carry. But I was strong. And everyone thought I was so nice. I knew I could do it.

Finally, I spoke. "Ana's gone," I said.

Chuck tried to sound concerned when he said, "Are you good with that?" Or maybe he really was concerned.

I sighed. "I am."

"Where'd she go?" Cam asked.

"The hospital."

"Is she dead?" Jed's bewildered eyes.

"No," I said, "and she doesn't have cancer."

"What?" the twins said at the same time.

"What?" Chuck echoed.

"She lied about that." I unclasped the necklace. It came off easily. I looked at it in my palm. The cheap fake silver had turned green in blotches.

"What?" Jed's fist on the floor. "Why would she lie about that though? That makes no sense! What a psycho!"

"I thought she was kind of crazy," Cam said. "But I liked her, too."

Then Chuck surprised me by saying the right thing. "I'm sorry, Nancy. I know she meant a lot to you."

I wanted to wrap my arms around him, but we weren't there yet. "Thank you, Chuck."

"Dude, Hawaii is full of crazies," Jed said.

"Word," Cam said.

"The boys are having some issues at school," I told Chuck.

"What issues?" Chuck asked, concerned.

"I'll let them tell you," I said, "if they want to."

Jed winced. "It's bad."

"Especially at practice," Cam said.

"We miss Clairemont," Jed said.

"I do, too," Chuck said. "But things weren't perfect at Clairemont either. Remember number nine? Steve?"

Cam recoiled. "Steve."

"Steve sucked," Jed said, "but this sucks worse."

"And it sucks you guys have been fighting," Cam said, not looking up.

We all let that sink in. It felt like our collective sadness made the whole house sag on its beams.

"Boys," Chuck said, "can you give your mom and me a minute?"

On their way out, Chuck gave them each a hug. "I love you, Jed."

"I love you, Cam."

Chuck closed the door and sat back down on the carpet. Why didn't he sit next to me?

"Hi, Nancy," Chuck said.

"Hi, Chuck."

"Ana's gone," he confirmed.

"Gone," I said, like I was still getting used to it myself.

"She's not coming back?"

"No," I said, "she's not coming back."

"Okay," Chuck said. And that was it. He didn't say, I was right. He didn't remind me of how she'd put a snake in his car. He just left it. Which astonished me. It was so kind.

I looked at my fingers. Green from the necklace. "Chuck," I said, "do you think you'll stay sober this time?"

"I hope so," Chuck said. "It feels different this time."

I couldn't tell if he was lying or not. It was impossible to tell, because I don't think he knew either.

"How do you know when it feels different? Doesn't every time feel different in the beginning?"

"This might sound ridiculous," he said, picking at the carpet like Jed had, "but the other night, I saw you and Ana sneaking off to go somewhere, and I had no idea where you were going. And I just had this feeling that I had lost you, or that I was losing you. That you were about to be gone."

My hand covering my mouth. Tears in my eyes. He had seen us leave that night. If he hadn't been drunk, maybe he would have figured it out.

Chuck stood up. He took my hand. I was still holding the necklace. "Oh," he said, "did it fall off? I can put it back on for you."

"No." I slipped it into his pocket. "You can get rid of it."

"No problemo," he said. Oh, Chuck.

I wrapped my arms around his body like my arms belonged there. He smelled like the soap they used at Tyke's, and I still didn't know where that was. I squeezed him. I squeezed him so hard.

How the elements needed each other, she had said. How the sky needs the earth, how fire needs water, how wind needs stillness. How the two halves of the necklace fit together perfectly to make one whole. How I had always needed that other piece to feel like I was surviving.

What it was like to hug Chuck. He was so much taller than I was. My head didn't reach high enough to settle on his shoulder. His belt pressed into my ribs. But it was fine. Because I knew how to make it work. I knew that if we held on tight enough, we could keep going.

40

In the morning I went back to her.

I followed the nurse to her room. She didn't see me at first. She was talking to the old woman parked in a wheelchair by her bed. She'd somehow rigged the hospital gown to give her more cleavage, and she was saying, "If you don't have a Jacuzzi, deep tissue massage is your new best friend," and the old woman, wide eyes, was tilting her head so her hearing aid could pick up Ana's voice more clearly.

I set her duffel bags on the floor. The Buddhas clanked. Their conversation stopped.

"Nan," she said. The flicker of blue light in her eyes. She smiled. All those sparkling white teeth. Her pink cheeks, her alabaster skin. Even without the wig, she looked healthy. I could see now that she'd looked this healthy the whole time. "I didn't know if you'd come," she said.

"I brought you your things," I said, looking at the old woman.

The woman pointed at me with a shaky finger. "Is this—"

"Yes," Ana told her.

"Oh," the old woman said, "I'm sorry about your house. To lose everything in a fire. It must have been devastating."

"I told Glenda about how your house burned down," Ana said. "And how I have nowhere to live now that you're moving back to San Diego."

"Aaah," I said, amused.

"So we've decided"—Glenda set her trembling hand on Ana's leg—"that Ana will move into my house."

"Glenda's my new best friend," Ana explained.

"Ohhhhh," Glenda said, and blew Ana a wobbly kiss.

"You are!" Ana told her.

"This woman," Glenda said to me, "has been through so much. It's incredible. Isn't it incredible?"

"Incredible, yes," I said. "Beyond credible."

"You're a survivor, Ana," Glenda told her.

Ana smoothed her palm up the side of her head. All those tiny black hairs. Even since yesterday, it seemed they had grown. Soon it would be a buzz cut, and people would think she was edgy. "I am a survivor," Ana said. When she looked at me, her eyes were alive and glimmering and totally empty.

The nurse appeared in the doorway. "Glenda, time for your appointment."

Glenda looked for a clock on the wall but didn't find one. "Already?" she asked.

The nurse, in a rush, took the handles of Glenda's wheelchair and popped the brake. "Nice to meet you, Nan," Glenda said.

"It's Nancy, actually," I said. "My name is Nancy."

Glenda smiled as though she hadn't heard me, and then the nurse wheeled her away.

Ana leaned back into her pillows. "Nan," she cooed.

I folded my arms across my chest. "You look well."

"I feel great here. They have the best food and—"

"You look well because you're not dying of pancreatic cancer."

She stared straight at me, looking bored, and said, "A miracle it went away."

"And you never had breast cancer either."

She said nothing.

"How could you lie about cancer?"

"I didn't want you to leave me."

"I wasn't going to leave you."

"Everyone leaves," she said, and flicked something off the sheets.

"Everyone leaves because you lie to them," I said. "You're a liar."

She chuckled. "So are you."

I sounded like a child when I said, "No I'm not."

She tapped her IV. "I expected you to turn us in." Her eyes flashed. "But you didn't."

"Because I don't deserve to be punished for you."

"Yeah, Nan." That sly smile. "Whatever gets you to sleep at night." She kept tapping the IV. "But don't walk out of here thinking you're better than me. You're not. We are the same."

"We are not the same."

"Oh but we are. You might have a cute mountain house and a sweet, troubled husband and two beautiful—*beautiful*—children. Sorry about Jed, by the way, that was not nice of me. But your little family and your little house on the prairie—none of that means you're better than me. You've just had more luck."

I laughed. "You believe in luck now?"

"Who doesn't believe in luck?" she said.

I looked out the window. The palm trees. The blue morning light. It was a perfect sunny day. I didn't know why it felt necessary to ask. "How long have you been taking antidepressants?"

The way she looked at me, the way her hooded eyelids blinked so slowly. What she had just understood about me. Why I still cared. "Oh, Nan," she said.

I shifted my weight. "What?"

"If I tell you, it will hurt."

I tightened my arms across my chest. "What will hurt, Ana?"

"No," she said, snuggling her shoulder blades back into the pillows. "You don't want to know."

"Tell me," I said.

She shrugged. "Fine. Here it is. Ready?" She left a healthy pause, and then she said, "You are not who you think you are."

"What the hell is that supposed to mean?"

"You are not who you think you are." Her whole body was still. Only her mouth moved. "I might have lied to you, Nan, but I don't lie to myself. I know who I am."

"So do I," I said because it was the only thing to say.

Ana didn't move, didn't blink.

And that's when I realized that this—her silence—was her power. It was Ana's most powerful card, and she played it all the time. Doing absolutely nothing made her seem smart when she didn't know what to say. It made her seem strong when she was lost. It was a way to intimidate with zero effort—if you were scared. If you were in awe, her silence made her wise. These blank spaces were Ana's genius. You filled them in with your favorite obsessions, never noticing you had done all the work. When she said nothing, you assumed there were a million interesting thoughts in her head, and that she was holding them back for a reason, a reason that you were too blind or too dumb to understand, when in reality she was probably thinking about what she'd have for lunch.

We were staring each other down, neither of us moving, neither of us blinking. Looking into her eyes like that, I thought I saw so many emotions pass across her face. She was angry. She was sad. She was deeply depressed. She was hideous. She was beautiful, especially in this light. She was lost. But she was right. She was nothing. She was a mirror. She was me.

I blinked first.

The smile that spread across her face so slowly. All those sparkling fake teeth.

"I know you hate me now, Nan. I get it," she said. She was speaking in her wise yoga teacher voice, the one that made you want to trust her. "And I'm sorry." She sighed. "I'm sorry for the pain I've caused you."

I said nothing. I stayed still.

"Do you forgive me?"

Nothing.

"Can you forgive me?"

Stay still.

"Which brings me to a bigger question." She lifted her finger.

"What?" I blurted out.

She pointed to her heart. She laid her palm across it. "Can we be forgiven?"

"I don't know, Ana, can we be forgiven?" I said this like she was taunting me at the playground. Why I became such a child around her, I'm still not sure.

"I'm asking you," she said.

I went from child at the playground to child in the classroom. I was buying time. "By who? Who are we asking to forgive us?"

"Everyone. For everything. Can we wipe the slate clean? Can we wash our sins away? Can we be forgiven?"

Why did I feel like she was outsmarting me again? And why was I still here? I didn't have to be here. I could leave.

"You wanna know what I think?" she asked.

I wanted to know so badly.

"I think you don't know the answer," she said.

I didn't speak, didn't move, didn't breathe.

Neither did she.

Again, I was the first to blink.

Outside, the palm trees slow-danced in the easy Hawaiian breeze. I looked for the red bird but didn't see it. There were other birds, maybe chirping, but I couldn't hear them over the humming and beeping of hospital machinery outside the room, and the episode of *Wheel of Fortune,* which was broadcasting at low volume on her personal TV. I looked at the door. From the doorknob to the wall, a row of tiny ants. And this was the thing about Hawaii. You couldn't get away from nature if you tried. Not even here, in the hospital, where the goal was to defy the natural hazards of life and living. Seal the doors and anti-bacterialize your hands at every station and still you lose.

I looked at my feet. My Tevas planted on the mint-green floor. A stain one tile away.

The ants moving in a line across the door.

When I looked at her again, I flinched. Maybe because it hurt to say the words.

"I'm leaving you now, Ana."

"Wait," she said. Was there a tear in her eye? "I never read your cards. Don't you want to know how it ends?"

"No one knows how it ends." I swallowed. Salt at the corners of my eyes. "Anything could happen."

"No," she said. "With me, anything could happen. With you, we know not much will happen. We know how it will end. It will be just like it is now, but in the future. Nothing will change." Ana clasped her hands in prayer in front of her chest slowly, very slowly, so she wouldn't disturb the IV. "I want you to know something."

I waited. She was making me wait again. I was letting her do it.

"I want you to know," she said, "that every time I look at my shadow, I will think of you."

I walked to the door. It felt good to move. I turned. I said it in her yoga teacher voice. "Good-bye, Ana."

She refused to cry. She was telling herself to hold on. I knew she would miss me.

I waited.

She placed two loving hands on her heart. She swallowed her tears again. She bowed. "Good-bye, sister."

41

"I already called the San Diego store," Chuck said. "They said they would take me back."

"When did you call?"

"A month ago."

"So you've been wanting to leave."

"It seems wrong, doesn't it?" He motioned at the backdrop. "It's so nice here."

"I know," I said. "But I guess that doesn't matter."

The Hawaiian sunset, neon pink like her hair. How the light here was like butter, the air like a warm hug. Here was the jungle that surrounded us, and the grass we called ours rolling softly up the hill, and the debris from the storm reminding us that nothing was ours, not really.

•

The boys weren't exactly stoked, but they agreed it was better than the alternative. I told Cam that Tom was welcome to visit anytime.

"We'll take him surfing," Jed said.

"Dude, we only went surfing once here. That is so lame."

"Dude," Jed said, "we are the lamest."

The Clairemont coach would let them play in the last few games. "However," I told them, "if you light anything else on fire, you're grounded until college."

Their arson charge was dropped to a fourth-degree misdemeanor. We paid the fine. They would pay us back by doing yard work around the house in San Diego.

Chuck and I realized we were sending a mixed message by letting them burn the shed, but we let them do it anyway.

Together, we stood on the lanai and watched the fire engulf the air. It was mesmerizing.

·

On our last day in Kona, after the boys had gone to school and Chuck had gone to work, I laid out my purple mat and stretched. The birds and the water heater and I heard her voice the whole time. Breathe, she said. Close your eyes. Imagine you are made of feathers. Imagine yourself as a bird above your life. You are untethered but you hover. Pleasantly you hover. You watch, amazed. This life is amazing. You are both weightless and so full.

I made oatmeal on the stove, and while it cooked I went through the cupboards. All this food we were going to throw away. All this bread. All this peanut butter.

Repentance, I thought, as I opened the Ziploc. Repayment, I thought, as I put the sandwich inside. I feel better already, I thought, as I drove down the winding road toward town.

Our old route. From Huggo's to the King Kam and then the parking lots. Top down, I drove slowly. Daniel didn't recognize me until I held up a sandwich. "New car," he said, dragging his elegant piano player fingers over what would have been her headrest. He moved with such grace. "Mahalos," he said, and in the moment he lifted the sandwich from my hands, I felt better.

The girl whose sign simply said HELP was back. I tossed her two sandwiches. She gave me a thumbs-up. This was the most alive I'd ever seen her.

Mana at the bus stop bellowed, "Where's your sistah?"

"Busy!" I yelled.

He caught the sandwich with the free hand—the one that wasn't holding the brown paper bag. "You da best!"

The boys weren't at the banyan tree, and Marigold and Petunia weren't at their usual dumpster. I left sandwiches in those spots anyway, and then I handed out the rest to new hungry people I hadn't met before.

When I had one sandwich left, I went to McDonald's. Maybe the man in the sleeping bag was still there. He wasn't. I set the sandwich under the speakers for when he came back.

I walked back to my car feeling lighter. Maybe it wasn't real. Maybe I didn't deserve to feel lighter. And maybe it was selfish— doing this good thing to make myself feel better, to make myself better. But, even if it was selfish and even if I didn't deserve to feel better, no one could argue that a person who did good deeds wasn't a good person, at least some of the time.

In the shadows of the car next to mine, a woman scarfing a Big Mac. She chewed with her eyes closed. Sandy hair, responsibly combed. I tried not to look, but I couldn't look away. Her doughy hands, her floral hat. Wait. And then she turned her head.

Marcy.

The second she saw me, she put the burger down. She wiped her mouth. She chewed faster.

Hi, I waved.

She rolled the window down. "Oh," she said, covering the ketchup on her chin, "I'm embarrassed."

"Don't be," I said. I noticed she was wearing my San Diego Zoo shirt.

"It's great to see you, Nancy," she said, studying my face. "You look good."

"Oh." This was nice to hear.

"I mean it. You look great."

I wanted to say, "You, too," but I had caught her at such an inopportune moment. I couldn't bring myself to lie. I gave her a hopeful smile instead.

"You're glowing," she went on. "You seem less stressed than the last time I saw you."

"I do?"

She shrugged. She was too polite to tell me I'd been a wreck before.

I laughed. What to say. "We're going back to the mainland."

"You are?" Her face twisted and fell. "I'm jealous. I hate it here."

I shook my head at the sun, the sky. It was the most perfect sunny day.

"Listen," I said, "I'm sorry I never called you. I just—I don't know—I got caught up."

"It's okay," she said. "Maybe I'll see you in San Diego. I'm a better version of myself there, I promise."

My hand covered my heart like a reflex. "I hope to meet you then." I waved good-bye.

"Nice shoes!" she called after me. "I have those exact same ones! Same color even!"

I'd never gotten around to throwing the Tevas away. "Good choice!" I called back.

On the drive home, I enjoyed everything. The wind in my hair, the sun on my face, the smell of my mango air freshener and the smell of the wet jungle and how easily they blended together.

42

We would make it home just in time for Thanksgiving. Chuck would brine a Costco turkey for two days like he did every year. The rusty garage door would moan when it opened and the roof would leak when it rained, and together we would complain about these things. Someday we would fix them.

I would still hear her voice. Sometimes in the mirror, I would catch a glimpse of her. Ana, my twin, my sister, how I had envied her freedom. How it would take me so long to understand her freedom wasn't real. Ana wasn't free. She was her sad past, replaying itself. In a way, she was still a child. She'd chosen the sky as a mother, as a guide. The sky. It was the biggest thing she could have chosen. The biggest empty thing.

While taking out the trash or scraping cheese off a pan, I would think: yes, I am a housewife and yes, my life is small and yes, sometimes boring.

But then maybe my boring life was a miracle.

Because, Nancy. Nan. You survived your past.

You reinvented yourself when you left home. When you left home, you left the past behind. You told no one the truth—of how your older boyfriend was paying you for sex by the end of that relationship, or of how you stole his credit cards and maxed them all out. Or of how, when you found your mother in her smelly chair, you had never really thought she was sleeping.

It had been just the two of you in the house that day. When you

found her, there was no mistaking it for sleep. She was having a sei-
zure. And you let her have it. Because that was what she deserved. You
could have given her the medication and you didn't. You weren't worried about anyone walking in to find you because there was no one.
She had no one. She was alone. And that was her choice—she had
chosen her loneliness. Her last breaths were frantic. Her face was frantic. You still might not be sure how you just stood there and watched
without mercy.

The first thing you did was drink her wine. White wine in a plastic cup on her table. Recently poured and nearly full. You downed it.
You thought that when the police came, if they were coming, the scene
should be found in its authentic state. The charade. It began when you
went to refill the cup, but the white wine was gone. Red wine in the
fridge. You used that instead. This is what had confused your story.

You've never told a soul about how she really died. You buried
the past, and you became someone new. And every time the past has
needed to be buried, you have buried it, and you can do it again. You
do not get stuck. You do not get depressed. You move on. You keep
moving. *This* is freedom.

When you remember her frantic face, you might be sorry. If there
is a God, you might say, God, I am sorry about my mother. I am sorry
about Peter. I am sorry for everything I have ever done wrong. From
now on it will be different. I know that innately I am a good person. I
will show you. I promise.

•

The pilot said, "Good morning, ladies and gentlemen. Clear
skies today. The temperature here in Kona is 82. The temperature
in San Diego is 75. Not much wind today. It shouldn't be a bumpy
flight." The mic turned off, and then back on. "My copilot here just
informed me the volcano has hit Pahoa. Destroyed the new police
station and the section of highway at mile marker 79. No casualties—
everyone was evacuated in time. Just wanted to let you folks know in
case you have family there. That's it for now. Mahalo."

"Phew," Chuck said.

Jed and Cam weren't paying attention. They were making origami with the barf bag.

"They're safe," I said, in awe, like I couldn't quite believe it.

•

When you're in a plane, all you can see is sky. You look out the window. You are above the clouds now. The clear blue sky never ends.

Out this window is everything. Inside is you. This is your bag under the seat, this is your book in your lap, this is the way you sit, this is the way you carry your body when you walk to the little bathroom.

Why do the thoughts come now? They always come when you don't expect them, and every time it feels new. But you've had these thoughts before. You remember and forget them. Sometimes you think this is all life is: a process of learning what you have already learned.

If there is no escape. No better destination.

If the horizon's just a line in space.

If this is all you are.

These are the pants you wore today, but they're not that comfortable. Next time you take a flight you will wear different pants. Next time you will bring more snacks. This Thanksgiving you will make a pie from scratch, maybe mulberry. And next Thanksgiving you will make it again, and then again the following year. Mulberry pie will become a new Murphy family tradition. And you can make extra pies and give them away. Everything counts, even if you're the only one counting.

Your reflection in the little mirror is almost too much. You close your eyes. For a minute, or for ten long seconds that feel like a minute, you breathe.

This is the sound of you breathing. This is the sound of the engine. Inside this small space, the air recirculates. It always feels cold. Outside you are rushing through the air so fast. There is always this rushing.

Stay here. Stay calm. Stay still.

Open your eyes.

Do you see me?

You won't want to see me, but you will.

This is us in the little mirror. This is us inside the runaway plane, trying to stay still.

You splash water on your face, asking it to heal you. All you want is to be healed.

You go back to your seat and you kiss your husband on the cheek. You open your book. You have been meaning to read this book for months. Today is the day.

ACKNOWLEDGMENTS

First, thank you to the town of Kona for being such an easy, warm source of inspiration while I wrote this book. Kona, I love you.

Jenny Jackson, thank you for your wisdom. I'm so happy you're my editor.

Allison Hunter, your enthusiasm is kind of mind-blowing, and I would be lost without you.

Victoria Chow, Lauren Weber, Emma Dries, Nora Reichard, Maria Carella, and all the people at Doubleday who had a hand in making this happen, I appreciate everything and am lucky to have you.

Special thanks to Mark Huntley for letting me take over his space, and to Annie Piper, whose yoga dialogue is the most inventive I've ever heard.

Last, I'm beyond grateful to the kind friends who read early drafts and gave me their feedback. Vauhini Vara, Tasha Tracy, and Jen Silverman, huge mahalos to all of you.

About the Author

Swan Huntley is the author of *We Could Be Beautiful*. She earned her MFA from Columbia University and has received fellowships from the MacDowell Colony and the Ragdale Foundation. She lives in California and Hawaii.